THE CAPTIVE

THERESA WISE

Published by
Shale Rock Publishing
P.O Box 1373
Tonasket, WA 98855

Printed in the United States of America

CONTENTS

PART ONE

PART TWO

THE TAKEN TRILOGY

The Captive featuring Beth
Identity Lost featuring Emily
Trapped featuring Kathrin—planned availability 12-1-2022

CHARACTERS

CHARACTERS LIVING IN AUBURN, WASHINGTON, WEST OF THE CASCADE MOUNTAIN RANGE

Beth Farell—one of three women held hostage
Emily Jacobsen—a hostage
Kathrin Reilley—a hostage
Nick Thoren—kidnapper
Edward J. Farell Esquire—Beth's father
Carla Farell—Beth's mother
Ashley—new friend of Kathrin's

CHARACTERS LIVING IN OKANOGAN COUNTY, WASHINGTON, EAST OF THE CASCADE MOUNTAIN RANGE

Glenn McKlain—a reluctant kidnapper
Luke Lazaro—kidnapper and Glenn's adopted father
John Decker—kidnapper

CHARACTERS LIVING IN MALAWI, AFRICA

Andrew Powell—missionary
Amie—a three-year-old orphan

PART ONE

1. The Bank

Auburn, Washington

"You have no idea what kind of trouble you could get yourself into, up in a big city like Seattle, Beth. Even Auburn isn't safe. Look what happened to your Aunt Laura."

The distress in her dad's voice blared in Beth's ear in spite of the din of traffic a few yards away.

"Yeah, Dad, I get it. But it doesn't mean I'll be raped like your sister was."

"You've kept me from the world my *whole* life. I'm a college freshman now. I want to live, Dad. So I'm going with Emily to that concert tonight."

"Not as long as you're living under my roof, you're not. I forbid you."

Beth sighed inwardly. Not again. Didn't he ever get tired of that same old trick? "You can't stop me, not even with one of your fancy court orders." She gritted her teeth to keep her temper in check. "Don't worry, Dad, I'll be fine. See you tomorrow. Love ya. Bye."

Her dad's ring tone started in before Beth had stuffed the cell into her pocket. She groaned. "How long will he keep this up?"

Harsh voices jerked Beth's attention back to her surroundings, overriding the cell's insistent ring. She ignored it and scanned the bank's parking lot. The noise didn't come from the empty cars. Nor was the source her friend Emily, who was digging around in her Subaru next to Beth.

Her eyes followed the sound to an adjacent alley between the bank and a little coffee shop. The noon-day sun—peeking through gathering clouds—shed light on a struggle between four middle-school boys and a smaller-framed blond kid with a patch on his shirt.

Beth frowned and moved a few steps closer to get within earshot. Before she cleared the lot, one of the boys hooked the terrified-looking teen's arms from behind. Fist curled, another big bully went face to face with the defenseless young man, whom Beth dubbed "Patch."

"Stop … talking … to my girl," the bully shouted.

"I promise I won't talk to her anymore." Patch's voice shook. "Just please, let me go."

The ruffian threw his fist into his captive's stomach. Patch sucked in a sharp breath and doubled over. His knees collapsed.

"Now you'll never forget." Bully rubbed his knuckles. "You're a loser man, and your dad's a loser jail-bird." His voice changed to a high squeak. "Tweet, tweet, jail-bird."

The gang burst out laughing.

Beth's stomach turned over. A mixture of rage and terror raced up her spine. *Brats!* she thought. *Don't be such a coward. Go over and help him. But what if they have a knife?* She cringed, torn with indecision. *Four to one odds aren't good. Besides—*

"Okay, I found my debit card. It must have fallen out of my purse onto the floorboard." Emily's crabby tone broke into Beth's teeter-tottering thoughts.

Beth turned and motioned her friend over. "C'mere! Quick! A couple of punks are beating up on some poor kid."

She ran back, grabbed Emily by the arm, and tugged her along.

"Wha—"

"We've got to help that kid," Beth insisted. "It won't take a minute. You have the ultimate distraction, a perfect model's figure in a skimpy outfit. Ha! I've got nothing."

"Yeah. You've got how pretty your long, brown hair is when the sun brings out the red highlights."

"Thanks, but everything about me is average, right down to my plain, brown eyes ..." Her voice trailed off. Talking had kept Beth's fears at bay, but now they were close to the alley. The bullies were still at it. The underweight teen sagged, held up by one of the boys.

Beth's mind swirled with visions of a knife and blood spewing. Her heart hammered. Her knees weakened. Fear crippling her, she stopped short. Emily bumped into her.

The mean kid pinched Patch's nose and yanked up his head. "Aw, let's go. He's *scared*." He mimicked the voice of a toddler. "Poor baby, he probably messed his pants."

Another round of laughter. The pimple-faced teen let go of his captive.

Patch crumpled to the ground, curled up, and whimpered.

Bully kicked Patch in the shin, then the delinquents strutted away like proud young roosters.

Patch struggled to his feet. He held his stomach and limped down the alley.

"I'm such a chicken." Beth's head dropped, but she kept her eyes on Patch as he hobbled away. "Why didn't I do something? Why do I always freeze up? I should think about the other person and forget myself."

"That middle-school stuff happens all the time. We can't rescue every kid." Emily's tone sounded irritated; her words came fast. "C'mon. Now we have only twenty minutes before class." She started speed walking toward the bank. "Is this the first time you've run into a bully?"

"No, I have a brother. Just kidding. He's a good boy, mostly. Yeah, I believe this is my first time seeing actual bullies."

"Your first? Where have you been? Oh yeah, wait." Emily rolled her eyes. "You were homeschooled, never got to go to a *real* school."

Beth had only known Emily a few weeks, but she'd never criticized homeschooling before. She hoped her other classmates didn't feel the same. If anyone could find fault with her lack of experience, it would be Beth.

"Hey, it's a real school. My mom is a tough teacher." Beth's voice fell. "But yeah, guess I am a real-life Rapunzel."

"How weird is *that* in today's world? Your parents never let you go to a prom or—"

"I went to dance classes, and I worked at Dad's law office. That's worldly exposure big time. I remember once we—"

"*Out of order?*" Frustration crept into Emily's voice.

Beth peeked over her friend's shoulder. Sure enough, the ATM screen was covered with a sign. "Come on, Em. Let's go inside. We've got time."

They stood in line five long minutes. Emily huffed and crossed her arms. The line moved an inch. Her huffing turned into foot-tapping. "We are so going to be late."

Like that'll move the teller along?

A baby squalled two places ahead of them.

"Geesh! Can't that mother keep her kid quiet?"

Whoa, embarrassing! Beth had no idea Emily could get pissed so easily.

A brunette standing in the next row over stopped texting and glanced at Emily. She didn't look judgmental, only curious.

Her slight figure exaggerated her thick mop of pixie-cut, dark-brown hair. Narrow, dark eyes stood out in her fine-boned face, complimented by her light complexion. She looked part East Asian. Very cute in her red blouse.

Right then, the bank doors flew open. From behind her, Beth heard people scuffling and urgent-sounding voices. More latecomers? *Are they in as much of a hurry as Em?* She hid a smile as the thought of "teller wars" came to mind. *Which line will move faster?*

Beth turned … and froze. Her smile vanished.

An average-sized man wearing a ski mask barged through the glass doors and shoved his way past the bystanders. Directly behind him another man stood by the door … fatter than the first, wearing an identical ski mask.

Beth gasped. "A gun! He has a gun." Her eyes widened. Adrenalin surged.

Before Beth could wrap her mind around what was happening, a skinny third man with a cowboy hat burst in. His clothing hung on him. A red bandana hid the lower half of his face.

Another gun! Beth's heart jumped into her throat.

A woman's terrified shriek jolted Beth back to her senses. *Run!* But panic paralyzed her. Screaming and confusion broke out everywhere. Two teller lines collided into each other trying to escape.

The fat man blocked them. "Everyone on the floor!" he rasped. "*Now!*" His gloved hand swept the room, pointing the deadly weapon over everyone's head.

Commotion exploded. The crowd dropped to their knees. Beth joined them, trembling. Emily fell beside her. They sprawled out on the cold, tiled floor.

Whimpers echoed across the room. Beth felt them rise

within her. She closed her eyes and swallowed, willing her sobs to stay inside.

A pistol's earsplitting blast shattered above them. In a fit of hysteria, Beth flinched and clutched at Emily. Others screeched, curled into balls, and covered their heads. The sulfur stench of gun smoke assaulted Beth's nose. She trembled uncontrollably. *Oh, God, help us!*

"Y'all shut your mouth!" The first masked man raised his gun high. "And don't you move, or I'll start spraying bullets." He snorted, teeth filling in the gap in the skier's mask.

Terrorizing people amuses him! Anger rose, masking Beth's fear for a moment. She turned her head toward Emily. "Whoa, he's nasty, but Fatty and Skinny—"

Skinny peered at her.

Beth closed her eyes *and* her mouth. A second later, she cracked her eyes open again.

The man she'd labeled "Nasty" stalked to the counter, jabbed his weapon at a bank teller, and handed her a cloth sack. "Doll Face, give me all the money in the drawers, and you best not piddle around." The gun never wavered.

The pale teller's hands shook.

In a calm, friendly voice, Nasty ordered the teller at the far window, "And you, Hun, give me all the cash in the vault. Y'all got ninety seconds or"—he swung his weapon on a frightened-looking, preteen girl—"Precious gets it. Just so ya know, the countdown has begun."

"No! Please!" the hysterical mother pleaded. Tears gushed. "She's only a child. You—"

"Now didn't I tell you to shut your mouth?" His voice thundered even though it was expressed with an unruffled tone.

Heart racing, Beth studied the thieves again. Skinny began

to cough. His face reddened. Wrinkles and a stooped posture betrayed his age. He looked like an elderly cowboy out of the Old West, except for his coveralls and sunglasses, which she noticed all three robbers were wearing. Fatty still guarded the door.

Beth's mind numbed. It all seemed surreal, like an illusion. Yet, here she was cowering in the midst of a real-life bank robbery. She couldn't believe this was happening. She shuddered.

"Time's up. Gimme the money." Nasty tore the sacks from the tellers' hands and hiked them over his shoulder.

The guard, Fatty, suddenly came to life. "You're coming with me." He reached down, grabbed the Asian brunette's arm, and jerked her to her feet. She cried out in terror. He snatched her phone from her grip, tossed it aside, and pulled her through the doors. Her little body struggled to keep upright.

Fatty stopped and turned toward the clerks, his thick voice still raised. "I figure you alerted the cops already. Tell them if anyone fires at us, tries to follow us, or blocks us in any way, we'll shoot one hostage at a time. Tell 'em, or you'll be responsible for a trail of dead girls."

Women cried out in terror, cringing on the floor.

Beth's heart plummeted when Skinny seized Emily's arm. "C'mon, let's go." He yanked her up and dragged her along with him.

"He's taking Emily!" Beth cried out. "Somebody help her."

Nobody moved except the thieves.

Emily went without a fight.

When light reflected off the weapon jabbing her ribs, Beth understood why. Only one thought screamed at her. She might regret it, but she had to *do something.* She couldn't just lie there and watch him take her friend. She'd let those teen bullies get away with their cruelty, but not this time!

Heart pounding, Beth leaped to her feet and slammed into the old man. She hammered him and tugged at his arm with all her might. "Let go of her! You can't take her."

Obviously caught by surprise, the bony cowboy tried to fight Beth off, but he fell into a coughing fit.

My chance! She grabbed Emily and ripped her free.

Beth's victory was cut short. An iron grip tightened around her forearm. Something cold and hard poked sharply between her ribs. A gun. She slumped, defeated, and let go of Emily.

"Hun, if you're so anxious to go along, then let's go." Nasty ordered in a cordial tone.

"No, please," Beth begged.

Nasty, smelling of musky aftershave, forced Beth to move forward. Skinny regained control of Emily.

"Let go of me. Ow! You're hurting my arm. Let go." Tears stung Beth's eyes.

"Give me your phone."

She pulled it from her pocket. The gunman grasped her cell and smashed it on the floor. Then he crammed his gun deeper into her flesh. "Move it, girl!"

Beth moaned. She had no choice but to do what he said. Her life meant nothing to him. Terror gripped her throat; her body went rigid like a stone statue. She strained to move her stiff legs. Soon, she couldn't breathe or fight or make a sound.

Beth felt the sensation of shrinking deep inside herself—to hide, like a turtle withdrawing into the safety of its shell. The tumult around her slowed and became a blur. A dream. Faintly, she saw them walk out of the brown-brick structure. The buzzing in her head muted the shouts. Close to fainting, she could hear her heartbeat. Now, instead of rigid, her extremities felt weak and helpless.

Got to fight. Breathe.

The buzzing soon ceased, and her mind cleared. It was all horribly real. Fatty propelled the terrified brunette toward a white SUV. She stumbled, slammed against the vehicle, and whimpered.

Nasty threw the sacks into the back of the same vehicle. With his grip clenched around Beth's arm, he opened the back door on the driver's side. Then he signaled with a slight twitch of his head. "Get in."

Beth hesitated. *If I get into this car, I may never see my city, my home, or my family again.* Tears blurred her vision. "No. Please, don't do this."

A gloved hand shoved her into the SUV. Her knees buckled, and she crumpled onto the back seat.

2. Kidnapped

Heading northeast on Washington State highways

Let's get outta here." Fatty thrust the petite brunette onto the front seat. Then he scooted his oversized body around the car's back door and slid onto the back seat beside Beth. He was sweaty and stinky.

Beth recoiled, wrinkling her nose.

Cowboy Skinny pushed Emily onto the seat with Fatty and Beth, then slammed the door. Three of them were now crowded into the back seat. Beth sat behind Nasty, the driver; Fatty in the middle, and Emily squished on his other side.

At that moment the jittery, sweaty man next to Beth leaned forward. He looked around then slapped the seat back. "Come on, Nick, *move it!*"

"Chill, Decker. Luke's not all the way in." Nasty Nick swung his head around and glared at "Fatty" Decker.

Luke—who Beth would always think of as Skinny—crammed himself into the bucket seat up front with the Asian brunette.

The girl cowered and didn't say a word.

With six bodies stuffed in close quarters, the last door slammed shut. Nasty Nick punched the accelerator. The wheels squealed.

Beth clenched her hands together to still their shaking. Where were they going? Fear crept up her neck. The familiar passed by—homes, streets, her city.

"Thanks." Emily poked Fatty Decker's arm.

What could Emily be up to? Beth cringed at her friend's triumphant-sounding voice.

"Thanks for what?" Fatty—aka Decker—snapped.

"Now I know that you're Decker, and he's Luke." Emily reached forward and poked Skinny's shoulder. "And you're Nick." She pointed to the driver.

"And you're *dead* if you think you're gonna tell the authorities, Miss Blondie."

Emily snorted at fat Decker's threat.

Em didn't look a bit scared. Beth shrank deeper into the corner.

Skinny Luke wrapped his fingers around the back of the brunette's head and pushed. "Get yer head down." She bent over. "Don't want the cops t' stop us for overcrowding or speeding, do we?"

The Asian girl's cries turned into pitiful whimpers.

Not Emily. She was the brave one. Cocky too. "My dad's a cop. And I'm telling you—you don't want the wrath of Jacobsen to fall on you. I know, I've had it fall on me. If you let us out right now, you might stand a chance."

Abruptly, Decker hurled the back of his hand across Emily's mouth with an awful smack. Her body jolted. She yelped.

"Shut your smart-aleck trap, or I'll give you more of the same."

Beth tensed, ready to duck. No further sound came from Emily. When the immediate threat passed, Beth tilted her head forward around mean Decker's fat noggin to check on her silent friend. Blood oozed from her lip. It appeared Decker had knocked the fight right out of her.

My poor Em. That miserable brute!

Nasty Nick took them down a narrow alley for one block. Then he turned left and went two blocks.

Meanwhile, the sound of sirens drew closer. Beth sucked in a breath of hope. Even though the cops were heading for the bank, she thought they would catch up to them. Then they'd be rescued, and it would be over. *Please, God, help them find us.*

As one, the robbers yanked off their masks and replaced their sunglasses.

Beth's heart skipped a beat. They let the captives see their faces!

In spite of her fear, Beth looked them over. Skinny Luke's hair lay sparse and white. His nose was long and straight, his skin weathered and creased.

Nasty Nick's sandy hair was cut short, except longer on top. The rearview mirror only revealed sunglasses, nothing of his face.

Decker and Luke were tan. Like most men, Luke sported a five o'clock shadow, but black, curly hair carpeted Decker's head and jaw. Some strands of white peeked through the black.

The getaway car turned right into a residential zone, jerking Beth back to the present. Was the zigzagging to throw off the police? Sirens blared, but none seemed to be coming their way. Yet, Beth clung to her fragile hope of rescue.

Two blocks later, Nick drove the vehicle up onto a metal ramp and into what looked like a large moving van parked alongside the street. Once inside, Nick turned off the engine.

Beth gasped. Tears sprang to her eyes. "What are you doing?" *Oh, don't talk …* She crouched preparing for a blow from Decker.

No fist came, but no answer either. He appeared distracted,

like he didn't even hear her.

Nick turned on the dome light. Then the crooks leaped out. With gun in hand, Luke stood beside the SUV, clearly keeping watch. Seconds later, a sharp noise of metal scraping metal provoked Beth to turn around and peer through the back window. Decker and Nick were shoving the metal ramps inside.

The large steel doors slammed shut, blocking out the sun and plunging the van's interior into blackness, save for the car's dim light. Shortly, the doors to the cab closed, and the engine started with a rumble.

The van, with the girls inside, moved through the city streets.

Beth glanced at the other captives. Emily's snug-fitting shorts and low-cut tank top were going to be trouble with the men. Her bright-pink lipstick accentuated her full lips. Wavy blond hair framed her glamorous face and flawless complexion. Female classmates had confided in Beth how much they envied Em's hour-glass figure.

Not Beth. Not today. She was grateful her blue dress and lace bolero covered her, as did the quiet brunette's blue jeans and blouse. A wedding ring sparkled on the Asian girl's fine-boned finger. Beth touched her shoulder. "What's your name?"

Angling her body toward Beth, the Asian's narrow, black eyes looked out at her from under thick, dark bangs. Her countenance brightened a bit. "I'm Kathrin. How about you?" Her child-like voice was surprisingly calm.

Emily introduced them, then whispered, "You realize those scumbags will probably ki—I mean, most hostages don't survive. Since we have nothing to lose, we should work together to escape."

"Yes, let's plan something. We're gonna be all right, girls." Kathrin used a confident, reassuring tone. "God will help us."

Nervously, Beth glanced up at Luke, whose eyes were fixed on them. "What do you want us to do?"

"I don't know yet. Got any ideas?"

They didn't have a chance to discuss plans. The large van came to a stop. It seemed a mere five-minute trip. The van's back doors opened, and light flooded in. Nick stood waiting, his sunglasses on top of his head.

Luke yanked the SUV's door open. "Move it. Get out."

Shaking, Beth clambered from the vehicle. Emily and Kathrin followed her to the back of the moving van.

"C'mon. Jump down out of the van. Y'all know what'll happen if you make a noise. It would be a crying shame to have to bury those tender bodies." Nick's voice was expressive and dramatic. His eyes were alert and shining, as though it were good news.

With a lengthy distance to the ground, Beth crouched at the edge before making the leap. Nick grabbed Beth around the waist, leering at her as he lifted her to the ground. His gaze lingered even longer on Emily.

He gives me the creeps, Beth decided. A combination of Southern manners and crudeness. His brown, iron-jaw and beady, brown eyes fit him. He seemed to be in his thirties and proud of his muscles packed upon a stocky frame.

After a quick look around, Beth discovered they were in a rural part of town, in the driveway of an abandoned house and garage. The closest neighbor was too far away, and with all the overgrown bushes and huge maples, how would anyone ever see them? A painful lump formed in her throat. Her arms clutched her body as if to hold it together.

Nick lowered Kathrin to the ground.

Luke opened the SUV's tailgate and retrieved the white sacks of stolen money. They still wore gloves, leaving no fingerprints.

Decker hoofed it to the garage. He opened the door, stepped through the threshold, and disappeared into the darkness.

After closing the moving van's steel doors, Nick and Luke escorted the girls inside the web-infested, dusty garage. The only illumination came from the headlights of a parked vehicle and daylight sifting through filthy windows and the doorway.

The next moment, the three bank robbers unzipped their long, striped coveralls and stepped out, revealing dark-green border-patrol uniforms.

"You're not really border-patrol officers, are you?" Kathrin's brows drew together.

Nick grinned; thin lips stretched across a wide mouth.

Beth tried to make sense of it.

Meanwhile, Decker grumbled, "I told you to take only *two* hostages!" He held up two fingers. "But some bonehead can't follow orders. Look for something to tie—"

"There's rope hanging on the wall over there." Luke pointed. "It's dusty, but—"

"It'll work. At least someone's worth their weight."

Nick threw Decker a lewd gesture.

Decker grabbed the white sacks from Luke and hid them underneath the seat of the parked van marked "Border Patrol."

Nick hustled Emily into the new ride, patting her rump.

She bristled, spun around, and whacked his arm. "Don't touch me!" Her tone was sharp with disgust. Her nostrils flared.

The sandy-haired thief snickered.

Beth stepped up into the patrol van's back doors and

became engulfed with terror. Its windowless panels and mesh barrier closed in on her like a mouse trapped in a cage. Benches lined the walls. Beth slid in next to Kathrin. The wooden seats and back rests were hard and unmerciful. Emily plunked down on the bench across from them with Luke following.

Luke cuffed Emily then locked the handcuffs to a chain anchored to the floor. For some reason it wasn't long enough so they could sit upright. They'd have to hunch over and rest their elbows on their knees.

"How can I ride like this?" Emily pulled at the chains. They clinked. "It'll kill my back."

Luke didn't answer, but with another set of cuffs, he moved to Kathrin's side.

Beth's eyes widened. With those on, she'd never be able to get away or protect herself. Those evil men would have total dominance over her. Her head involuntarily shook "no." Panic threw her out-of-control. Her body dove for the exit. Nick blocked her. She pushed at his chest, screeching with hysteria. "Help! Somebody help."

Nick gripped Beth's arm. She thrashed about wildly. His fist came hard at her stomach. The force rammed the air out of her lungs. Her insides screamed in pain. Beth buckled over his fist and collapsed. Lightheaded, she floundered, struggling to breathe.

"Yo, Baby. You freaked." The women-beater—the younger one—yanked her to her feet and with all the social graces of a Neanderthal shoved her back onto the hard bench.

Out of her wits with fear, Beth held her arms tight to her bruised stomach. The old, uniformed man jerked Beth's arms out in front one by one. Then he bound her wrists with harsh, scratchy ropes. With another piece of rope he linked them to the I-bolt in the floor.

Restless energy compelled Beth's knee to bounce. Her hands fought against the rope, but there was nothing she could do.

Decker stepped up into the driver's seat. The van leaned with his weight. Once everyone was aboard, the three criminals donned their official green caps, and the driver backed the van out of the garage. He took the nearby ramp to Highway 18 and merged into traffic. "Is anyone following us?"

Nick raked his fingers through his hair. "Nah. I have it all under control. My idea of the moving van worked slick, didn't it?" There lived a swaggering arrogance in his tone. "Those cops! They're like kindergarteners playing with the major league. Me." He let out a quick laugh and raised a thumbs-up sign. A large tattoo of a half-dressed woman on his forearm revealed what Beth feared was on his mind.

"Stop your bragging and grow up," Decker snapped. He and Nick exchanged a few more verbal blows.

Beth cowered, wishing she could close her ears at their crudeness.

Later on, the van grew quiet, other than road and traffic noises. The silence gave Beth time to think. Where were they taking them? And why? What would happen to them? She found comfort in her friend, Em, and in Kathrin. *How horrifying this would be if I were alone!*

Emily's head dropped. Beth had never seen her friend look so troubled.

Kathrin closed her eyes. "Lord, I'm scared," she prayed ever-so-softly. "Help us. Please, protect…" She went silent, but her lips still moved.

They continued to head northeast, uphill. Trees rushed by. Decker leaned forward and flipped on the radio.

The reporter spoke rapid-fire. "…US Bank of over

$675,000. Police Detective Lankerton announced the three hostages attend Green River Community College. According to eye-witness reports, the girls have been identified as Mrs. Kathrin Reilley, twenty-seven; Miss Emily Jacobsen, twenty; and Miss Elizabeth Farell, nineteen.

"The identity of the three masked men remains unknown. If you see them, do not approach. They are armed and dangerous. Immediately call 911 or your local police department. Every possible effort is being made to capture the suspects. Checkpoints are being set up at all exits to the city."

Decker swore and turned off the radio.

Beth gulped. She knew from experience how dangerous these men were, but hearing it officially increased her anxiety.

Old, skinny Luke cast gray eyes upon Emily. "Are you Kathrin?"

"No, she's Kathrin." Emily raised her bound wrists as far as the chain would allow and pointed a bling-studded finger at the Asian woman.

"Sorry it has t' be like this." Luke stared at his feet. "I'm really not such a bad old cuss." He looked up again. "Decker, why don't we let the gals out here? They're just kids. They'll slow us down."

Decker jerked his eyes from the rearview mirror to the road ahead then back again. "Need I point out that they can identify us now, Uncle Luke? Blindfold them. I don't want them to know where we're going. I think we're beyond the checkpoints, but if we come to one, pull off the blindfolds and keep the women quiet." A chubby hand reached toward Nick. "Man, my mouth is dry. Hand me a beer."

A chill swept through Beth. How did those men plan to keep her and the other girls from identifying them? *Will they kill us? We already know too much. They can't let us go … can they?*

While Luke dug out the blindfolds, Beth studied his ordinary, grandpa-looking face, but it gave no clue to what he was capable of.

Emily released an exasperated sigh. "If you hadn't insisted on going to the bank, Beth, or if that …that ATM had been working, we'd be…" Her voice cracked. "We'd be at the concert tonight instead of…" She turned away.

Beth jerked her head in Emily's direction. Her attack had blindsided Beth. "Why are you blaming *me*? You wanted to go too." Her face burned. "Hey, I tried to save you, remember? If I hadn't, maybe I wouldn't be here right now. Did you think of that?"

Kathrin in her child-like voice sounded composed. "None of us are to blame." Her dark eyes were full of compassion. Clearly, she meant to comfort them.

Meanwhile, old Luke reached forward and tied a bandana around Kathrin's head. He reeked of smoke.

Beth simmered down. Em had to be terrified too. Maybe the blame game was only a cover-up. Em was strong … usually. *To see her like this…* Beth choked. Em's grief and fear infected her. She lowered her head and hid behind her long hair. She wanted to burst into wails, but she fought to hold it back. Hot tears ran down her cheeks.

This is not helping. Think good thoughts. Try at least.

Luke tied the blindfold on Emily. Beth was next.

Even if she was rescued, Beth knew that life would never be the same. Thanks to the media, the whole world knew her name by now. *They will forever associate me with this ugliness. I'm only a teenager, and already my whole life is screwed up. Ruined in one blasted moment.*

She sighed. Wouldn't everyone she met after this horrid ordeal pity her? *I don't want pity. All I ever wanted was approval.*

Anguish poured out in tears. Her hand clutched the necklace her father had given her. *I've just begun to live. And this day … may be my last.*

Beth swallowed hard then drew a ragged breath. She stared at the rope chafing her wrists. Her jaw clenched. Her body wouldn't stop quivering.

When the bandana shut out the world, Beth listened for clues, hoping to figure out where the men were taking her. It gave her something to focus on other than fear. The odors of sweat, smoke and Emily's lavender body spray became more distinct.

"We've got one behind us." Decker sounded alarmed.

"A cop? Where? I can't see him." Nick's seat creaked as he shifted around.

"It's about eight vehicles behind. I'll do the talking. And don't pull your gun unless the cop pulls his first. Got it?"

Nick, clearly irritated, dragged out his words. "Yo, I got it."

Sirens began to blare. Decker cursed.

Hope rushed in and set Beth on edge. She felt the van decelerate and move to the side of the road. Her heart soared. She squealed and clapped her hands. The other prisoners did the same.

"Shut up and sit still!" Decker yelled.

Oh, thank God! They found us. We're going home. Her smile stretched from ear to ear. Such relief. It felt like a boulder had hurtled off her shoulders.

The siren whirled louder as the patrol car barreled toward them. The girls tugged their blindfolds down. Beth held her breath. Her muscles tightened. From the back window, red and blue lights flashed in her eyes as the cruiser zoomed by and raced up the highway ahead of them.

Beth's smile faded from shock. "No, wait! Come back."

"We're over here," Emily shouted.

"Don't leave us," Kathrin pleaded.

Beth stared at the disappearing squad car, willing it to come back. It did not. Her hope nosedived. "No." Her words drew long with a despairing moan. "Please." She wanted to cry. She slumped.

Kathrin strained at her chains, trying to reach out to Beth.

"Woo-wee! What a rush." Nick laughed, loud and long.

3. Blindfolded

Heading northeast on Washington State highways

"You gotta do a better job controlling those women, Uncle Luke."

Decker's old uncle mumbled a tired response.

Beth gazed out at freedom. Like tears, mist had collected and now trailed down the window. Heavy, low clouds had formed. She noted they were still on Highway 18, heading over Tiger Mountain.

A moment later total blackness replaced her view. Rough hands retied her blindfold. Not long afterward, the vehicle took a right turn and sped up. Beth sagged. *I-90. It runs east-west, and we're definitely not headed west to Seattle.*

"They'll search a hundred times harder for us than for those bags of money," Kathrin said in her quiet voice. "Really, it would be to your benefit to release—"

"Shut up!" Decker ordered. "I'm tired of your yapping. Keep your mouth shut or I'll blow your head off."

"And besides, we're not done with you fine young women."

Beth's flesh crawled at Nick's salacious tone. What did he mean "not done with them"? *Maybe they're holding us for ransom?* But her troubled mind painted a grimmer picture: Nick and Decker taking turns with th—*Oh God, please not that.* Bile rose to her throat. She grimaced.

For many miles the straining engine, the incline of the van, and the popping in her ears confirmed what Beth already suspected. They were headed over Snoqualmie Pass to the east side of the state.

During the next several hours, exhaustion overcame Beth. She dozed restlessly. One time she awoke to the sounds of slow-moving traffic. She decided the periodic decelerations meant small towns. The men seemed less tense, more gabby.

"Nick, give me a sandwich," Decker said. "You want one, Uncle Luke?"

"Nah, no appetite since the chemo."

That explains his chronic cough and emaciation. Beth opened her ears wider.

"How can you be so sure Glenn won't rat on us?" Decker asked.

"The last time ya laid eyes on Glenn, he was nine. That was fourteen years ago. Ya don't know him like I do." Luke's voice softened. "There's no way he'd want my last few months alive t' be spent behind bars."

The slow, bumpy ride, the sound of gravel beneath tires, the many turns, and the constant climbing verified that they were headed up an unpaved mountain road.

Decker slammed on the brakes. "You drive, Nick. I want another beer."

Opening doors. Scuffling feet. Doors closing. Then they were on their way again.

The more hours that passed, and the more distance that came between her and home, the more Beth's hope of being rescued felt like grasping onto mist. How could the cops ever find them in the middle of nowhere?

It seemed forever before they arrived at their destination, but it was probably closer to six hours. Luke freed Beth from the I-bolt, but her wrists were still bound. Someone with a strong hand dragged Beth from the vehicle. She bumped her head. Her nose detected an unpleasant, vaguely familiar odor. Birds sang all around her, but the sounds of her city home were painfully absent.

She moaned as she stretched and straightened up from the long drive. The early evening sun felt good on her arms. A horse whinnied in the distance.

"Where are we?" Emily's tone resembled a demand more than a question. "It stinks."

"We're either at a riding stable or a perfume factory," Beth answered.

"This is rubbing my ears raw."

"Stop, Emily. Don't take it off. The blindfolds have t' stay on 'til we get there." Luke's calm voice sounded as though he was within reach.

"We're not there?" Beth slumped from weariness. "How much farther?"

From a distance a new male voice asked, "What's going on?" It sounded like the stranger was approaching. "Why is the border patrol here? And what's with the blindfolds?" His footsteps stopped close by them, his voice more bewildered. "Why are you in that uniform?"

"I'll explain in a second, Son," Luke said. "Glenn, do you remember my nephew, John Decker? And this-here is Nick."

"Just call me Decker."

"Yes, Decker. It's been a long time. Hey, Nick." The new guy's voice was friendly, deeper than the other males.

What did Skinny Luke call him? Beth pondered. *Glenn, Son?*

"Come with me, Son." The crunching noise of their footsteps diminished. Beth caught only parts of Luke's explanation. "Remember how I told ya that little Sophia needs experimental surgery for her brain tumor?" His voice faded.

Beth strained to hear more. *Blast this blindfold and rope!*

Luke's son suddenly blurted, "You *what*? Robbed a *bank*? You gotta be kidding."

"Easy, Glenn," Luke continued in his hushed tone then coughed.

Glenn exploded at the old man's words. "That's why the women are blindfolded because you kidnapped them? No, Dad. You wouldn't. I can't believe that."

More whispers from Luke. More anger from the young man.

"You told me this was a hunting trip with friends. You *lied* to me!" Glenn was hurting. It was in his voice. He sounded betrayed.

"I had t' lie, Son. I didn't want ya involved. I knew ya wouldn't agree t' it, anyway. But we need …" His voice choked and trailed off. More coughing.

Beth wished she could scoot closer, but she could tell that at least one of the kidnappers was close by, guarding her and the others. She didn't dare move.

Glenn's voice rose. "So, you're okay with me going to prison? Living with a prison record for the rest of my life because of what you and your partners did? How could you do this to me?" The anguish in the man's voice was poignant. Obviously, it was tearing him up.

"If ya get caught, it'll only be a three-year sentence. Without the money, Sophia won't even have that long t' live. We had t' do something, Son. We'll let the gals go."

"They're not a couple of baby foxes you found." Glenn let out a long, frustrated breath. "God help us, Dad! You're going to be charged with robbery and kidnapping. And they'll slap me with accessory charges."

Luke didn't respond. Neither did the others.

Beth heard gravel crunching under angry feet. Someone was stalking up to her. Not knowing what this faceless man might do, she shrank back, cringing from the fury and speed of his approach.

"I'll have no part in this." Glenn's deep voice came out forceful and resolute right next to Beth's ear. He grabbed her palm with his warm, rock-hard hand and began cutting the rope.

"Do that and you die," Decker threatened.

The unmistakable sound of a gun cocked close by. The man's grip froze. Then he began to saw at the rope again.

"Fine." Decker thrust the gun barrel against Beth's temple. She cringed. "Okay, if you don't care about your own life … keep sawing and *she* dies."

Beth gasped. Her heart nearly exploded. "No, please!" she whimpered, quivering. "I don't want to die." *God, help me.*

"Don't hurt her." Glenn stopped cutting and dropped Beth's hand. "I'll do as you say."

Decker chuckled and removed the gun from Beth's head. How quickly her life was all but gone and suddenly given back, so vulnerable, at the whim of heartless criminals.

"Hand over your knife, your gun, and your cell," Decker ordered. "Search him, Nick. And *you*, Glenn. You're going to show us the way to your cabin or these b—"

"No need for threats. I told you, I'll do as you ask."

People moved around, but nothing more was said. Someone retied her wrists. While waiting, Beth swatted at flies—or were they bees?—buzzing around her head. Shortly afterward, her ears picked up the *clomp, clomp, clomp* of horses' hooves, the swishing of tails, and the creaking and clinking sounds of saddles and bridles.

"Up in the saddle with ya." Luke grabbed Beth's arm. "Put yer foot up in this-here stirrup." His hand encircled her ankle and lifted it.

She reached out, hampered by the blindfold, and hung onto the man's gaunt shoulder. He guided her hand to the saddle's handle, or whatever it was called.

"Now, pull yerself up." The horse flinched. "Easy, Charlie."

The smell … it seemed like horse sweat and leather. "Will he run away with me? It's scary enough without being tied up and blindfolded."

"No, don't worry, Sugar. I've got the reins."

With Luke's help, Beth's backside landed on a smooth, creaking seat. The horse shifted his weight, causing her to cling to the saddle's handle.

"Can ya turn loose of that so's I can get up there too?" When Luke mounted, the animal caught its balance. The old man's arm touched Beth's. "I need to grab the reins." He leaned forward.

Beth felt the old man's closeness and breath on her ear. The hair on the back of her neck bristled. She stiffened and leaned away, hyper-vigilant to his every move. He had clearly taken his seat behind the saddle. They weren't touching now except for their arms.

Emily's shrill voice split the air. "Get away from me! I'd rather walk."

"If you want," Beth heard Glenn say, "but with that blindfold you'll be tripping over things and running into trees. If you do decide to ride, I won't bother you." His voice sounded different now that he wasn't yelling and angry. It was smooth, gentle even.

With a flick of his wrist, Beth and her captor were off into a sudden lope. The wind blew the horse's mane across Beth's hand like the touch of a feather. Her own hair fluttered back.

Jostled around, racing blindly headlong into the dark unknown, she felt fear squeeze the breath out of her. She strained every muscle to stay on board. The other girls' shrieks and protests reassured Beth of their presence.

A few minutes later, their faithful steed snorted then huffed with each laborious stride. Suddenly, the horse stumbled.

Beth's body jerked forward. "We're going too fast!"

"I got it covered." Evidently, the outlaw finally took pity on the animal. He slowed their mount to a walk.

Since the evening sun heated the left side of her face, Beth presumed they were heading north. Were they being taken to some God-forsaken wilderness? How would anyone ever find them?

My family must be worried sick.

They rode on for what felt like an hour, including up a short steep hill and under branches. Not long after that Beth heard a far-off, gurgling brook. Soon, it heightened to a steady rushing sound. The air felt cooler and moist. The warm rays of the setting sun diminished as the horse splashed his way across the stream.

The smell and feel of the brisk, misty spray from the tumbling water aroused Beth's thirst. Charlie lowered his neck and sucked at the creek, nearly throwing Beth over his head. She scrambled to stay aboard.

Once they were on the other side of the stream, Luke dismounted. "Ya better get down and stretch yer legs a spell. Don't try anything foolish. I'm gonna keep my eye on ya."

Movement tortured Beth's thighs. It felt as though the broad horse remained between her legs. The stream's tumbling and bubbling distorted distant noises and speech.

Someone took her hand and placed a tin cup in it. "Here, take a swaller."

Eagerly drinking the water, Beth marveled how cold and delicious it tasted. She stopped short. *Did he get it from the stream?* "Uh, it's filtered water, right?"

"You *are* a city gal, ain't ya?" Luke sounded amused. "Don't worry, Sugar, ya won't get sick."

"Let's get moving." Decker's rough voice bellowed over mother-nature's bluster.

Beth heard Emily groan from behind her. "Not that torture machine again."

Nick must have walked up to Emily. "This time, Pretty Baby, you're riding with *me*." He used his favorite expletive for emphasis and added, "I love those shorts you're wearing. That shirt is *mighty* nice too." His smutty tone chilled Beth to the core.

"Let … go … of … me!" Emily's voice sounded strained, as though she were struggling.

"Are you out there, Elizabeth?"

"Yes, Kathrin, I'm over here," Beth answered. "It's good to hear your voice." She didn't feel as alone in her dark world.

Luke took Beth by the arm and led her to the sweaty-smelling horse. Like before, he helped her into the saddle.

Her tenderized backside screamed when it hit the hard leather. "Ohhh, that hurts."

The horse caught his footing as Luke jumped up and settled behind Beth. He reached his arm around her to gather the reins and shook his wrist.

Charlie took off. Every jar of the horse sent signals of torment up Beth's spine.

During the next few minutes she came up with a plan. She would bend over enough to pull her blindfold off. Then she'd jab Luke in the ribs and snatch his gun. She would be the heroine. Everyone would think good of her.

Then reality dumped on her. *Dream on, Beth. It's never going to happen.*

A new thought suddenly sent prickles up her spine. *Wait a minute! Is that Luke behind me?* There wasn't a trace of Luke's smoky odor. The rider hadn't coughed once. His breathing was sure and steady.

It's not Luke! Who is it?

Not knowing rattled her. *Nick?* She shivered and shrank away from him. Her heart raced, then slowed. *No, Nick is riding with Emily.* Beth could hear the evil man mocking her.

Then *who*?

Whoever it was, he was sitting awfully close behind her. So close that her back brushed his chest whenever the horse lunged forward. His arm constantly pressed against hers to hold the reins.

Is it Decker?

No, this rider was too silent. No labored breathing, no grunts. His fat stomach wasn't touching her.

Her breath caught. Could it be Luke's son, Glenn?

"Keep your dirty paws off me," Emily snapped from some distance away.

"Nick, leave the women alone until we're at least a safe day's ride." Decker's stern voice sounded close but not right behind her. "Those cops may be hot on our trail, so cool it, would ya?"

It had to be Luke's son riding with her. At least he was behaving himself. Beth hadn't heard Em complain when Glenn rode with her.

Farther up the trail, the darkness behind Beth's blindfold became pitch black. The wind turned gusty and cutting. Beth shivered.

Glenn shifted around. At first, Beth couldn't figure out what he was doing, but she understood when he placed something warm around her shoulders. "Here's a jacket. The wind is blowing down from the snow, and it can get mighty cold at night."

"We're traveling all night? How can you see where you're going?" Beth pulled the sizable jacket snuggly around her arms.

"We've got about a forty-minute ride yet. There's a full moon tonight. It's quite bright."

"Are you Luke's son?"

"Not biologically, but in every other way he's my dad." His voice came across respectful, kind.

"Thank you for trying to set us free," she whispered.

Beth felt him lean toward her. His warm breath brushed her cold ear. "They never should have kidnapped you." Then he sat upright again.

"Will you help us?"

"We'll talk later." He pulled the horse to a stop and dismounted. Then Beth felt the steady gait start up again. Was anybody leading this horse?

Panic exploded. "Hey!" Beth called, helpless and terrified. "Somebody. The horse is wandering off with me."

From the blackness she heard a chuckle. "You're going to be fine. I've got him." Glenn sounded amused.

Beth wanted to believe she would be fine. His words were comforting, but she didn't know what to think of Glenn. He seemed less monstrous than the others.

Beth felt herself wanting to place her hope in this unseen man. She needed some kind of hope. She wasn't sure how much she could trust him, though. It was like walking on thin ice. One wrong step and down she'd go.

What was that scent on his jacket? Sweet but earthy. *Not a bad smell.* It reminded her of dried grass. *Maybe hay.*

She wondered what he looked like. He stood a good chance of being average looking. Because of his large jacket, she pictured him overweight, round-faced with small, close-set brown eyes.

The evening sounds took on an echoing nature. The hooves resonated against a hard surface. Emily's words bounced off what sounded like canyon walls, making them indistinguishable.

It wasn't long before they left the protective walls of the ravine. Icy wind stung Beth's ears, hands, and face. "Ohhh, it's freezing." Her voice shook.

How she longed to be home where it was safe and warm, hanging out with her sister, Heather, and the rest of her family.

The thought of never seeing them again weighed like a millstone around her heart. Tears soaked her blindfold. *I hate these men.* Scared, shivering, and exhausted, Beth wondered how much longer she would have to endure this ordeal.

Five minutes later the horse stopped, threw its head, and nickered.

"I'm going to ride now." Glenn climbed aboard. His weight caused the horse to shy away and catch his balance. "Easy, boy," he soothed.

Glenn's voice continued with gentleness. "The canyon floor has slippery, wet rocks. It would have been risking the horse's legs to carry our combined weight across it, especially mine."

A short pause. "You don't need this anymore." She felt him doing something to her bandana.

The material fell away. Beth's eyes adjusted.

On the distant rolling hills, black silhouettes of tall pines stood at attention like night watchmen. The sight of a magnificent, full moon struck her. It rested atop the pine-studded hill, bigger and brighter than she had ever seen. "The moon's more brilliant here without city lights."

"Mm-hmm," Glenn answered.

Thanks to the luminescent ball, she could see her surroundings fairly well. Even though the night tried to hide them, her spirit rallied when she saw Emily and Kathrin. Beth felt like a *Titanic* survivor clinging to driftwood in a murky, wide-open ocean and then spotting her friends floating on driftwood not too far from her.

By moonlight she saw their blindfolds in place but no jackets. A gray pack horse trailed Luke's.

Beth twisted in the saddle to see the man behind her. Glenn's Stetson shaded his face. She couldn't make out any distinctive features, but from his dark shape she found him broad-shouldered and almost a foot taller than she was.

No wonder the horse had trouble bracing himself.

She turned back. With his body close to hers, his warmth soon radiated over Beth, chasing away the worst of the chill. She reclined back, almost touching him.

"You can lean against me if you want," Glenn offered. "I won't take it as an overture. We're just cold."

"You won't think I like you or something?"

Glenn chuckled. A friendly chuckle.

What a pleasant sound after the other men's curses and roughness.

"After all you've been through today, I'm sure you hate us," Glenn said. "But we can keep each other from freezing. Nothing more."

"Okay." Beth's heart didn't feel quite as heavy as it had felt earlier. "But don't think that just because I'm a pretty, little city girl I won't—"

"Slash my throat if I get frisky?"

"Yes." Slowly she rested her back against his solid chest. His arms wrapped her on both sides. What a strange, interesting sensation. To be frightened of a man, a virtual stranger, yet appreciative of his warmth. She imagined it was like curling up to a wild, free-roaming stallion.

Unpredictable, but strong and safe.

The scent of the pines became more prominent. The air grew colder, causing Beth to value the combined heat of man and horse all the more. Thank God, Glenn kept his word and behaved like a gentleman.

In the distance, a shape took form out of the shadows. Beth recognized a rustic log cabin, dark and silent. "Is that where you're taking us?"—a quick pause—"Of course it is. The outlaws' hideout. I don't want to go inside. It looks creepy."

"That's because it's dark," Glenn said. "It'll be warm and cozy as soon as we get the fire going."

Off to one side of the cabin leaned an old stable, and not far from it stood an outhouse. Beth pointed. "I've seen those on TV, on Grandpa's old westerns."

"Oh, the outhouse." Glenn chuckled.

By now, Beth was ready to try it out. It had been a long, *long* day.

Decker trotted up to the cabin's covered front porch and yanked his horse to a stop. "Okay, ladies, this is it."

4. The Hideout

Somewhere in the Pacific Northwest

Beth's riding partner dismounted. He reached up, waiting with open arms. She tried to get a glimpse of Glenn's face, but the shadows hid his features. To her disappointment, his hat was doing a good job of keeping his appearance a secret.

She gasped inwardly. *What am I thinking? Why do I care what he looks like? He's a criminal!*

"I can get down," she snapped, clambering off the horse. Pain shot through her legs when her feet touched the ground.

A falling mass caught Beth's eye. She whipped around. Decker and Kathrin tumbled together, smashing onto the ground with a thud and a winded grunt. The huge man did a face plant, with little Kathrin landing half on his back. Their mount nickered and pranced to the side.

Luke dropped the lead rope and rushed over. "What happened?"

"He's been drinking." Her head raised, Kathrin pushed herself off the man's back.

Decker lifted his shoulders off the ground, spitting dirt. "I'm not drunk. My foot slipped out of the stirrup." He rose up on his knees and wiped the dirt from his face.

"And you knocked me down with you," Kathrin said sharply. She climbed to her feet and stood waiting in the moonlight—blindfolded, handcuffed, and shivering.

Emily swung her leg over the horse's rump. Gripping her waist, Nick guided her to the ground, but his hand slid under Em's blouse.

Beth couldn't believe her eyes.

"Get your hands off me!" Emily hammered her elbow into his chest. "How *dare* you."

"Don't get your feathers ruffled, Baby. I didn't mean to grab you there."

"You creep." Blindfold still in place, Emily swung at the air, missing her target.

Nick laughed.

Scum bag.

"You women, quit dilly-dallying and get in the cabin. I'm starved." Decker yanked Kathrin's blindfold off and shoved her forward. Nick did the same to Em.

The girls walked as pitifully as Beth felt. It was good to be on solid ground at last, even though her aching thighs would've argued that.

Beth's mouth puckered in a sarcastic quirk. *Mom and Dad will be happy to know that my etiquette training is paying off. I feel so ladylike right now.* Her knees remained a foot apart as though she sported a full diaper. She painfully stepped up the stairs and waddled across the hollow-sounding wooden porch.

Nick snorted. "What's the matter? Aw, bless your heart. Does it hurt?" He whistled eerie notes from a familiar song, but Beth couldn't place the tune.

Battered and humiliated, the girls stepped inside the dark cabin.

Beth took one sniff and made a face. *Eww!* The cold, gloomy cabin reeked of stale smoke and oil.

How evil and unnatural it feels in here.

Luke and Decker brought a dim glow to the room by igniting old-fashion oil lamps. In the fluttering twilight, Emily skittered next to Beth and murmured, "Wonderful, no electricity."

The girls clung to each other, trying to hide themselves in the shadows.

"Are you okay?" Kathrin whispered.

Beth quirked a sideways smile. "Never better."

Kathrin gave her a little squeeze. "Don't lose hope. God's still with us."

Beth drew comfort from Kathrin's words.

But it didn't last long. While she watched the men, a sick panic overcame her as if she were cowering in a bear's cave with the mother bear blocking the exit.

Nick scanned the room and then looked through the doorway of another room hidden behind the fireplace. Apparently satisfied, he plopped the stuffed white bags onto the wooden table and wasted no time unzipping them.

"We'll count that later. Go out and help Glenn with the horses." Decker slipped a duffel bag from his rounded shoulder. "You women sit over there." He jabbed a finger toward a dirty cot in front of the huge stone fireplace that adorned most of the back wall.

The girls did as they were told.

Nick grumbled, dropped the lumpy bag onto the table, and then slammed the door behind him.

The moment the door closed, Decker scattered the rest of their gear across the table and floor.

The men had changed out of their uniforms. It was no surprise to Beth that Luke was wearing western attire. *A hat must be a cowboy's appendage, bank robbery or not*, she mused. The haggard-looking cowpoke piled logs in the fireplace and set them ablaze. A small stove crouched in a corner. Nearby it, a guitar leaned against the wall.

Everything was rough-hewn, probably cut with a chainsaw. Clearly, no woman's touch, and—of course—no phone. A wooden bunkbed lined one wall, and a sink stood against another.

I would think I had been transported through time to the old west if it wasn't for that overstuffed rocker and matching footstool.

Two men stepped in from the murky darkness. Nick made fast tracks to the money bags.

The other—an unfamiliar, tall, dark-haired cowboy—sauntered across the room and headed straight for the coffee pot. *Is that Glenn? The guy I leaned against? It must be. How strange to finally see him. Then he's the one who tried to rescue us.* She studied him closer, which wasn't easy to do. If only he would've taken off that stupid hat.

Glenn was leaner than she imagined. A nice build, actually. About six-foot-two, and he seemed to be in his early twenties. He *appeared* to be good-looking, at least from what Beth could see of him. *Wish I could see more—*

Her thoughts came to a screeching halt. *Beth, what are you doing? He's a crook.*

Decker's gravelly voice jerked her back to the here and now. "Your dad trusts you. Just remember that." He approached Glenn and returned his gun to him.

The young cowboy nodded and slipped his gun into its holster. "So, where's my pocketknife?"

Decker scowled. "Fine." He slapped the knife into Glenn's palm.

The men joined Nick around the table. Nick and Luke, both grinning, leaned over their loot like excited kids on Christmas morning. Nick ran his fingers through the loose pile.

"Look at all this cash. Woo-wee! How much do y'all think there is?"

"We'll divide it up after dinner." Decker's dark eyes gleamed.

The grump almost looks happy, Beth thought.

"I don't want any of it." Glenn grabbed a chair and plopped it down backward next to the table.

"Fine with me," Decker crowed, grinning.

Glenn sat down with his back to the ladies and straddled the turned-around chair like he would a horse. His forearms rested on the chair back, which supported his long, lean frame. He slid his hat back off his forehead.

Beth leaned in. *If only he would turn around so I could see his face.*

Decker stretched. "I suppose I wouldn't be able to buy dinner around here even with a hundred thou' in my pocket."

"That's exactly what it'll cost ya. Just keep yer panties on, and I'll rustle up some chili." Luke grabbed a large can out of the cupboard.

All through dinner, the thieves swapped ideas on how they were going to spend their loot. Decker hogged down his third bowl of chili, slurped a can of beer, and burped unashamedly.

"Untie her." He pointed at Beth. "You, Miss … Miss whoever you are"—his words slurred—"do the dishes." He tossed the keys to Luke. "Uncuff them all so we can get some work out of these prima donnas."

Decker leaned back in his chair. "Ladies, if you try to escape, there's about fifty miles of woods to get lost in. There's plenty of hungry bears, wolves, and mountain lions prowling around looking for a meal." Decker smirked. "On second thought, escape. Then we won't have to decide what to do with you."

Beth rubbed her sore wrists and got to work gathering up the enameled dishes. "Being torn apart and eaten alive by a ferocious grizzly is enough to keep *me* out of the woods," she whispered to Em.

Kathrin picked up a dish towel. Emily folded her arms and scowled at the men.

Beth wanted to shake Emily. Her friend's attitude was going to get her into trouble. *Maybe Kathrin and me too*. Beth turned away and started scrubbing, determined not to let Emily's insolence rub off on her.

The men's voices droned in the background. Decker lifted his arm to his mouth and smeared residue beer and chili on his sleeve. "Say, Uncle Luke. Did my mother tell you the reason—"

"Yeah, yeah, yeah. Sis wanted me t' talk ya out of the heist, but—" Smoke curled up from a slim, dirty joint pinched between Luke's fingers. He held it to his lips and took a long drag.

Decker laughed. "It didn't work out that way, did it?"

"Nope." Luke blew a sickening sweet cloud from his nose. "That was down-right dirty. After all the years ya served the feds faithfully, t' fire ya without a second chance."

Decker cussed. "As of this Monday, the agency said I'm done. I can't imagine not patrolling the border anymore. But"—he sniggered—"robbery is my new employment."

While the men counted the bundles of money, Beth scoured the blackened fireplace pot.

Emily bent in close to Kathrin and Beth. "If one of those creeps goes outside alone, two of us should try to go out and grab his gun," she whispered.

Wide-eyed, Beth turned to Em. "But how? Will they let two of us go out together?"

"Why would they go outside?" Kathrin asked. "It's night, and there's nothing out there but trees."

Emily rolled her eyes. "They gotta pee sometime. That room behind the fireplace is not a bathroom. While one of us distracts him, the other could grab his gun. We've gotta *try*."

"Nick's already punched me once," Beth protested. "I don't want to go out there even if he *is* alone. Do you?" She searched Kathrin's face.

"No, I don't want to go out there with Decker either," Katherine whispered. She briefly closed her eyes. "Please give us wisdom, Lord."

"Just the cowboys then. Their low-slung holsters make it easier to grab their guns." Emily leaned in. "How could we distract him?"

While they considered, Beth sneaked peeks of the criminals.

The thieves were so engrossed in dividing their stolen treasure, they didn't noticed her scrutiny. Decker downed one beer after another. The fizzy brew dripped from his dark, kinky beard.

Cancer had clearly taken its toll on old Luke, but evidently nothing discouraged him from smoking.

Nick's words, personality, and actions seemed impulsive, reckless. His direct, probing eye contact would make a dog whimper and cower. Over-confidence and a rebellious attitude were written all over him.

An argument rose between the thieves over who deserved the last remaining dollars. Glenn left the quarrel and stood by the fireplace. His right hand rested on the log mantel, his foot on the rock hearth. The firelight framed him, creating an appealing silhouette.

Beth turned back to her work. Her fingers being frothed with suds, she pushed back wayward strands of hair with her wrist. "I guess I could try to make a getaway with a horse."

"Good idea. Anything to create a diversion." Kathrin carried the stacked plates and cups toward a shelf. The stack tilted. She overcorrected. Comically, the dishes wobbled all the more—this way and that—almost crashing to the floor.

Wide-eyed, Kathrin gasped, her arms shifting to and fro until everything stabilized. She let out a sigh.

A corner of Beth's mouth lifted.

Emily made one swipe over the small counter. "Okay, Beth. Go out and do the horse thing whenever Glenn or Luke go ou—"

"Yo, what are y'all up to?" Nick, acting all macho, stepped up beside Beth.

She froze mid-motion.

"I heard you," the man persisted. "Sounded like y'all were talking about us *fine* gentlemen."

Emily turned to face her enemy. "We were trying to calm Kathrin down. You lowlifes haven't been easy on us, you know."

"I'm sorry, Kathrin." With a sinister grin, he placed a beefy hand on Kathrin's delicate shoulder. She backed away. "We didn't mean to scare ya. We just want to be *friends*."

"Leave her alone, you pervert?" Emily snapped.

Nick clucked his tongue like a disappointed parent and shook his head. "Didn't your mamas teach you to mind your manners? That ain't no way to talk to a *friend*, being all ugly, calling us lowlifes and perverts."

"If you really want to be a friend, see to it that we get home safe and sound." Beth was surprised to hear those brave words come out of her own mouth.

"Now, Sweet Pea, you know we can't do that without spending our lives behind bars." He playfully nudged Beth's arm with his elbow. "Then you want to be friends?"

Beth kept her head down, her face solemn.

"Why don't we make the best of things?" Nick said. "You beautiful babes need to relax and—"

Emily threw her towel on the counter. "How can we *relax* when you—"

"I haven't hurt you, have I?" It seemed as though Nick believed he'd gone out of his way to be nice, and he deserved a reward.

Did he forget about punching me in the stomach? Beth's thoughts tumbled.

"C'mon, ladies. Let bygones be bygones. Let's shake on it, okay?" He reached out his hand.

The girls didn't move.

After this obvious rejection, Nick's tone changed to impatience. Sparks flew from his stare. "Aw, now see what y'all have done? I'm fit to be tied. I'm done with conversation."

He grabbed Emily's hair from the back of her head and yanked her to him.

Emily screeched, struggled to pull away, and kicked at his legs.

Nick laughed and wrenched her golden locks tighter.

"My poor Em," Beth said under her breath. "How much more?"

"Nick, leave her alone," Decker yelled. His chair screeched as he pushed to his feet.

"Aw, I'm not gonna hurt her. I'm just gonna give her a little sugah. Women like her can't get enough attention. She wouldn't be showing herself off otherwise."

His fingers pulled her tank top out, revealing more of Emily. The corners of his mouth turned up. "These babes like to play hard to get. Well, I'm just playing their *game*."

Nick squeezed Emily closer and bent down to kiss her.

Emily's frown hardened. She squirmed. "You touch me, and so help me"—her voice turned guttural—"one of these days I'll drive a knife right through your heart." Spittle flew.

Nick yanked Emily's head down backward. Her knees caved. Her back bowed. His mouth covered hers, muffling Emily's moans.

Beth's blood ran cold. Nick had summoned her imagined horror to life. She sensed evil's presence—so potent, dark, and oppressing.

Run! Get out of here! She sprang for the door.

Decker grabbed her arm. "Not so fast, Missy."

Nick released Emily's hair and stood her up. "C'mon, let's get more comfortable." He gripped her arm and dragged her along with him toward the gaping doorway next to the fireplace.

Is he going to—

"Okay, Son, that's enough." Luke put a shaky hand on Nick's thick shoulder.

"Find your own girl, old man." Nick shoved Luke aside. "And I'm not your son."

Luke staggered and went into a coughing fit.

"I was wrong about you." Emily sounded indifferent.

"Oh yeah? I knew these lips would change your mind. Well then, c'mon, Baby."

"Pervert is too good a word for you. You are the lowest, most despicable slime to ever walk this earth. Just the sight of you makes me *sick*."

Beth froze in utter fear for her friend's safety. The room

hushed as though waiting out the calm before the storm.

Nick stopped. He turned to her. His face twisted with pain, then reddened with anger. All at once he raised his hand. "You heartless—"

"Hold it, Nick." Glenn's gun pressed against the brute's back. "Let her go."

"Yo, don't be pointing a gun at me unless you have a mind to use it." Nick released Emily with a powerful shove. "'Cause if you don't, you best not turn your back on me." With fists clenched and fury in his eyes, Nick rivaled a ticking time bomb about to explode.

Emily scurried to Beth's arms, trembling.

"Sorry, partner, but you would only listen to a gun." Glenn holstered his weapon.

Nick spun around and threw his fist into Glenn's face. The force flung Emily's "hero" backward to the floor. His hat flew off, revealing a headful of dark, wavy hair.

Beth tried to shut her ears to the terrible thud … to everything. But brutal reality traveled through the boards to the soles of her feet. The girls raced for the farthest corner, where they held fast to each other.

Beth squeezed her eyes shut to the violence that was so alien to her. Everyone was quiet. Why? Beth opened her eyes.

Glenn rolled over, shaking off the effects.

Nick grinned as he watched his victim struggle to his feet. While Glenn was still on his knees, Nick hurled a flying kick at his stomach.

Glenn's primal grunt burst with anger. He caught Nick's foot and yanked it up.

Nick went airborne for a second, then, with a huff, his back slammed against the floor.

Both men leaped up, bent slightly forward at the waist,

their arms out, fists eager, glowering at each other.

"*Errrr!*" Nick charged like a bull.

Decker hopped out of the way.

The charging crazy man rammed Glenn backward against the table. The wooden legs scraped on the floor.

Eyes bulging, Luke leaned in, ready to fight.

Nick swung his fist.

Glenn dodged the blow, bound aside, and faced his opponent. With eyes fixed on Nick, he waited. His mellow voice broke the silence. "We're even now. What's the sense in this?"

"We're *far* from even." Nick hurled his fist.

The cowboy caught Nick's wrist, jerked it down, and twisted it behind his back. Glenn wrapped his other arm around the brute's neck. "Ready to call it quits?"

After a moment, Nick gave a jerk of agreement. Upon being released, he straightened out his arm with a moan. His other hand held his shoulder.

Then he bolted headlong at Glenn.

Decker snagged Nick's arm. "Knock it off. I want to get across the border tomorrow. We can't do that if Glenn's eyes are swollen shut."

"Didn't I warn him never to turn his back on me?" Nick set his jaw like a pigheaded boar.

Beth drew in a long breath, trying to relax her rigid muscles.

Glenn's dark hair curled down his forehead. A drop of blood followed the downward sweep of his cheekbone. He wiped it with his cuff, snatched up his hat, and then clomped out, slamming the door.

The other men settled down as though nothing had happened.

Beth's hands shook. With so much nervous energy, she

busied herself with cleaning the sink.

"Go and see how Glenn is," Kathrin mumbled. She nudged Beth with an elbow. "Go *now*, Honey. I'll be out in a few."

Oh! The "plan." Beth had almost forgotten about it. She nodded slightly and headed for the door on wobbly knees.

5. One Easy Squeeze of the Trigger

"Where do you think you're going?" Decker's voice growled.

Beth's heart leaped to her throat. "I … uh … gotta go to the … you know, that little house."

Decker smirked. "Go with her, Uncle Luke."

Her body tensed.

"Glenn's out there," Luke said. "He'll keep an eye on her."

Decker nodded his permission.

The heavy door squeaked as Beth pulled it closed. Crickets sang their serenade. It seemed unusually loud.

When she turned around, the glorious moon greeted her. "Wow! It's beautiful," she said quietly.

In the distance, snowcapped mountains glistened with the moon's silvery beams. Millions of twinkling stars spread across the expanse. Shadowed pine trees dotted the hillsides; others huddled together in dark valleys.

Beth sighed in relief. *Good. I can kinda see all around me. But I don't want to do this.*

A nippy but gentle breeze swept across her face and arms. She knew it wasn't the night air causing her to shiver. She was alone in the black vastness except for wild animals and the outlaw … Glenn. "Where is he, anyway?"

She jammed her hands under her armpits and took a deep breath, trying to still her shivering. Her eyes swept across the clearing in front of the cabin. The horses grazed within the boundaries of a log fence. "What a peaceful sight."

She spotted Glenn. He was leaning with his forearms on the top fence rail, watching the horses. They moved slowly about the pasture with their heads down, chomping on grass and swishing their tails.

Oh no, the horses are in the corral. How in the world was she supposed to catch one? *This just isn't my day. Wait, one is missing.* Maybe it was in the stable.

Beth raced to the outhouse. When finished, she checked Glenn's whereabouts. He hadn't moved. She crept to the small, dark stable, lifted the latch, and shoved the rickety door open.

A stink rolled in from the blackness. "Hey, horsey, horsey, are you in here?" Beth used her childlike hide-and-seek voice. "Where are you?"

A muffled snort answered.

Beth turned toward the sound, straining to see the horse. Chomping noises rose from the black corner. "I'm just a friend. Nice horsey."

Her eyes adjusted to the dark. The moon glimmered through a window onto a rope and a lantern's glass barrel. She shuffled through the blackness toward the shiny object. "Yes, a cowboy's flashlight." A match book lay beside it.

Beth never would have guessed that watching all those *Rawhide* and *Bonanza* episodes with Grandpa could have prepared her for this night. She fingered the lantern. No sweat! A city girl could do this. She lit the wick and replaced the globe. A faint glow sputtered over the stable.

A horse watched her from its dark stall.

Beth made her way toward the animal. Long shadows, created by the lantern's glow, flickered like gray spirits reaching out at her. She hung the lantern on a nail which protruded from a web-covered post.

She stroked the horse's soft neck. "You're not going to hurt me, right?"

The horse flicked its ears back and snorted.

Beth peered closer through the dim light. "Oh, you have your halter on. Good."

She glanced around and spotted a saddle. Taking a deep breath, she lugged the heavy piece of tack to Horsey's side. Mustering all her might, she hoisted it atop the large animal.

Horsey jerked its head and twitched its tail.

"Hold still." The stirrup didn't cooperate. It got wedged underneath the seat. "Blasted thing!"

Beth's strength gave out. Wrestling a saddle was harder than she thought. She let it fall to the ground then gave it a swift kick. Horsey startled. "I don't need that stupid thing, anyway. I've already ridden today. I can ride bareback."

Beth ignored her aching thighs and slung the lead rope across the mare's shoulders. But how was she going to climb aboard? Maybe the stall railing? She clambered up the rough, wooden planks. Then she hung onto the partition, twisted her body, and reached out one leg until her ankle rested on the animal's back.

Horsey flicked his ears.

Beth flinched. Her leg stretched painfully across the gap. "I don't think I can do this. Horsey, would you mind getting a little closer to me?"

The creature didn't move.

"Is your father a mule?" Beth extended her leg and hip past the point of pain. Her foot pressed inward on Horsey's warm side. The mount shifted closer.

Beth hurtled herself, landing on the horse's back. "Ow! Oh my booty."

Her heart pounded. *Don't think about what happens next.* Her stomach fluttered. She closed her eyes and took in a calming breath. Then she shook the rope. "Back up."

Amazingly, the horse obeyed. "Now, giddy up."

Horsey sauntered lazily toward the door. A dark shadow loomed in the entrance.

"*Glenn?*" Beth gasped. She hadn't meant to speak aloud.

"Mm-hmm." Glenn leaned back against the door frame, arms and ankles crossed. "What do you think you're doing?" His tone was light-hearted and relaxed.

Beth stiffened. "How long have you been standing there?"

He walked up and seized the lead rope. "Let's see. At the kick. The mule thing. You're just too cute." Head tilted back, he smiled up at her, but his hat shadowed his eyes. "What are you doing with 'Horsey'?"

Beth kicked the animal's belly. Her mount stepped to the side and jerked its head.

Glenn stepped to the mare's flank and threw his arm around the rider.

"Get away from me!" She struck him with the rope.

Glenn dragged her off. Horsey pranced out of the way, pulling the rope through Beth's hand.

"Let me go!" She thrashed around, grunted, kicked, and pounded at him.

Glenn lifted Beth as though she were a small child. Her stomach landed on his solid shoulder.

With one arm gripping Beth to his large frame, Glenn lowered her to the ground. His free hand caught her flailing wrist and forced it behind her back.

She battered him with one fist. "Let go of me or I'll scream."

"I'll let go if you'll stop hitting me." He turned his face to dodge her knuckles. "If you scream, Decker will come."

The bashing stopped. Eyes wide, she glared up at him. With their bodies pressed together, Beth knew he could feel her shaking. He felt warm, sturdy.

"Decker will never know about this"—his voice softened—"unless you give me reason to tell him. And he's right, by the way. You could get lost in these mountains, especially in the dark."

One thought kept replaying in Beth's mind. *I've got to create a diversion for Kathrin, so she can snatch his gun.* The only things available in Beth's arsenal were one fist and one foot.

She used both.

Glenn grabbed her other wrist. They struggled, her strength against his. His hand seemed immovable. She whimpered in pain. With ease he twisted her arm around and held them both behind her back.

The outlaw towered over his captive. Encased by his brawny arms and body, completely at his mercy, Beth panicked. If he took her down, she couldn't stop him. He was too strong.

Her eyes burned with tears. *Kathrin, where are you?*

Still he gazed down at her. *Why is he not doing anything? Why is he just looking at me?*

Glenn drew in a deep breath and slowly released it.

Beth studied his face for his intentions. The moonlight and lantern allowed a faint glimpse of mildness about his mouth—no anger or wild look like Nick's. She glared up at him while he focused on her in silence.

A frightening intuition rushed in. He enjoyed being against her and wanted to kiss her … for a start. *Is that what Kathrin is waiting for? For him to kiss me? Oh no, that's it … a diversion.* Beth's fear rocketed into hysteria.

Glenn released her wrists and stepped back, but he was

between her and the door. Her struggle with Glenn wasn't over. His gun lay in its holster, and Kathrin may not come.

Beth searched for a possible weapon. She spied a shovel leaning against a wall covered with spider webs. Beth bound straight for it.

Glenn didn't try to stop her.

Baffled at his lenient behavior, she clutched the shovel and whirled around. He stood unmoving, obviously bewildered by her desperate actions.

"*Errr!*" Beth screeched, charging him with the weapon above her head. She expected him to take some kind of defensive action, but he didn't. She felt foolish.

Before him now, she braced her legs and swung the shovel.

In one smooth move, Glenn raised his hands and caught the makeshift weapon. They both gripped the handle. It felt like the shovel was cemented to a wall. She tugged and grunted. "Let go!"

Exhaustion hit Beth, but she couldn't let go. It was her last chance to escape. "I don't want to die," she choked. "You've got to let us go."

Through watery eyes, Beth glanced past Glenn's shoulder and caught sight of Kathrin creeping through the threshold. A breath of fresh hope filled her lungs. *Don't let on to her presence. Keep talking.*

"They're going to kill us," Beth said. "Please, you've got to help us." She looked into his shadowed face. Hot tears rolled down her cheeks. Clearly, he was moved by her plea. The muscles in his cheek tightened.

Kathrin slipped in behind Glenn and snatched his gun.

"What the—"

"Don't move," Kathrin commanded. "And put your hands up."

Glenn released the shovel and pivoted half-way around.

"I said *don't move!*"

He stopped mid-motion and slowly began to raise his hands. "Yes, *ma'am* ..."

Then in a flash, Glenn spun around. His raised hand knocked the pistol from Kathrin's grip. It landed in the loose hay beyond their reach.

The three burst into frenzied action. "C'mon, Beth, get it!" Kathrin strained to hold Glenn back.

Out of her mind with urgency, Beth bolted for the weapon. The handle felt good within her grip. She whirled back toward him. "Hold it!"

Glenn faced Beth and stood quietly. "Now what?"

Afraid to take her eyes off the outlaw, Beth clutched the heavy revolver in both hands and pointed it at his chest. "Put your hands up. Any more fast moves, and I'll pull the trigger."

In a calm, sincere tone, but with authority, Glenn said, "I can't let you take us in. We've got too much riding on it."

Annoyed at his confidence and selfishness, Beth braced her legs. "Well, we only have our *lives* riding on it. What do you think you are, bullet proof or something?"

To Beth's dismay, Glenn took a step toward her. "Maybe we're lowlifes, but we're not killers. If they intended on killing you, there would be no need for blindfolds."

"You, Beth, and Emily have already suffered Nick's madness." Kathrin moved to Beth's side. "He seems capable of murder to me."

Glenn's eyebrows rose. "What did Nick do to *you*?"

Beth gripped the gun to stop her jitters. "He punched me in the stomach."

Half a moment passed in silence before Glenn took another step closer. "You have my word. I'll make sure you ladies go unharmed." Another step. "I'll talk Decker into leaving you behind at the cabin while I show them the way to—" He stopped short. "Afterward, I'll come back and take you to the highway so you can go home."

Beth wished she could believe him, but it sounded too good to be true. She had to be more convincing and cold-hearted, but it went against everything inside her.

"I'm the one who tried to free you," Glenn said. "But I can't be much help to you dead."

Beth felt sick, but she forced out the words. "You won't be much hindrance either, and that's what you'll be—dead—if you take one more step." She swallowed hard, her palms sweating, her mouth dry.

Apparently, Glenn didn't believe her any more than she believed him. He kept coming.

Shaking, Beth took a step back. "I told you I'll shoot." Her voice quivered. "You're forcing me to choose between my friends' lives and yours. I swear—so help me—I will blast a hole right through your heart. Stop where you are."

She drew a deep breath to quit shaking. Then she tugged back the hammer and pointed the gun straight at the outlaw's heart.

For a long moment the cowboy stood staring at Beth. Finally, he sighed. "Would you *really* kill me?" A solemnness weighed his deep, steady voice.

Deep within, Beth felt a piercing stab. "If I have to." She couldn't believe she was standing there holding a gun on this man. She couldn't bear her inhumanity, but what choice did she have?

She studied the tall, dark figure. He was a living, breathing, feeling human being. His very existence was in her power. One easy squeeze of her finger, and he'd be gone … forever.

Beth focused in closer at the location of his heart. A picture flashed through her mind of the bullet tearing through him. He would suddenly fly backward, with blood spilling out all over him. She would be the one who took his life.

Her soul twisted with anguish. How could she kill this man … or anyone? It was true what he said. He might be their only hope.

Glenn resumed his slow, steady stride. In seconds, this living soul overshadowed her.

"Please, d-don't make me shoot you. I don't want to shoot you. P-please stop," she stammered. Tears trickled down her face. Sweat ran freely.

He kept coming.

Wait! I can wound him in the leg. Beth couldn't miss; he was so close. Her hands lowered the gun. She closed her eyes and squeezed the trigger.

The kickback made Beth jerk backward. Her ears rang. Then an unseen force yanked the barrel aside. Beth's eyes snapped open.

Glenn twisted her wrist backward. "Ow!" She crumpled to her knees and surrendered the weapon.

Kathrin jumped in and began to beat on Glenn, but he had the gun. He sprang a few feet away.

Beth whimpered, holding her bruised wrist. She hung her head in despair. Hot, bitter tears rolled down her cheeks. "I should have shot you when I had the chance," she growled. "You … you … *beast.*"

The beast stood over them in silence. He offered no comment and exhibited no wound. His gun dangled from his hand.

Kathrin knelt by Beth, hugging her. "It's okay, honey."

"What's going on?" Decker and Nick burst through the

stable's door and rushed up to the three.

With a listless gesture, Glenn pointed toward the open door. "Just some coyotes spooking the gals. I chased them off."

"Yeah, I heard. Did it occur to you to use a nice, quiet club?" Decker's gaze flicked from the three people to the lantern and then rested on the shovel. He pressed his lips together, cocked his head, and expelled a weighty sigh.

Glenn offered no excuse but holstered his gun.

Beth caught her breath. *Why is Glenn lying? The truth would have made him look good. Did he lie to protect us?* She wiped her tears and climbed to her feet with Kathrin's help.

"If you ask *me*, it looks like these two gals were fixing to get away," Nick snapped. "How come the mare's by the door?" He glared at Glenn and pointed a smudged finger at the horse. "Explain!"

Beth froze. How would they ever escape Decker's punishment if he learned the truth?

The skin on Glenn's knuckles stretched white. He marched up to Nick and got in his face. "My horse. My business. I don't have to explain *squat* to you."

"Whoa!" Decker stepped between the two contenders. He slammed his hands on their chests, power-driving them backward. "Knock it off. Both of you. I've had it with your constant fighting. You two are more trouble than you're worth."

He scowled at Glenn. "Take care of that horse." Then he turned to Nick. "You help me get these women inside and tie them up for the night."

Glenn and Nick glared at each other but did as they were told.

The two hostages trudged into their smoke-polluted log

prison. Beth plopped down on the bed next to Emily and shook her head in unspoken apology.

Decker sat at the table. "We're getting outta here by eight in the morning, sharp. Got it?" His round stomach interfered with untying his boots, but it didn't hamper his list of commands.

Luke leaned back on two legs of a chair. "What about the gals?" He tapped his cigarette ashes into an empty beer can.

Decker's silence unsettled Beth.

"Let's take 'em with us." With an evil grin, Nick sashayed up to Emily and gave her the once-over. "Since there ain't enough beds, this one and I could b—"

"Do you not learn?" Decker's voice sharpened with exasperation. "The cops are after us! You can have these and a thousand women like them *after* we're safe across the border. I've had enough trouble for one day. No more."

"They won't be any trouble. I'm fixing to tie them up." Nick stroked Emily's bare shoulder.

She recoiled as though a creepy spider crawled on her.

"Nick, this is the last time I'm going to explain this to you. I'm beat and my butt is killing me." Decker raised one side of his rear off the chair.

He took a deep breath and bored his dark gaze into Nick. "Tomorrow is another long, hard day in the saddle, so I could use some sleep. If you even *try* something, the women will scream and carry on. I can't sleep through that."

He waved an arm at Luke. "And do you think the bow-legged knights in cowboy hats will let you get away with it without a fight? This ends *now*." His fist slammed the table. Tin cups bounced, clattering on the wooden top.

Nick grinned. "Well, I'll be. Ain't I lucky to have such a sensitive boss?"

With that, the crisis passed. Beth stared at the men, amazed but too drained to react.

Glenn came in from taking care of Horsey. He selected a sleeping bag from the pile of gear in the corner and unrolled it.

Decker stood with pain-ridden effort. "Grab the bunks, guys. *I'll* secure the women." He turned to the hostages. "On the floor." A fat finger pointed to a large braided rug in the middle of the room.

"I reckon the boss gets the nice bed in the private room?"

Decker smirked at Nick. "Even an idiot could figure that."

With her hands bound behind her and a rope linked to her trussed feet, Beth wondered how she would sleep on the hard floor. She wriggled to find the least painful position.

I don't want to consider what might happen tomorrow. I just hope I can escape in my dreams for a while.

Beth's mind and body crashed.

6. Stampeding Black Stallions

In her dream, Beth's heart raced. The ground shuttered with the hooves of stampeding black stallions. They nearly crashed down on her. Their dark riders' eyes were consumed with madness.

Running, gasping for air, stumbling, Beth tumbled and rolled into blackness. Frantically, she reached out and clutched at empty space. Then in silence, she lay still.

A large hand rested on Beth's shoulder. She turned and looked up into the shadowed face gazing down at her. One of the dark riders. It seemed futile to escape his power, but yet—she felt he wouldn't harm her. Her ominous future, somehow, lay in his mysterious hands.

He swooped her up in his powerful arms, never taking his gaze from her.

She didn't know why—

Beth's eyes flew open. Flickering light danced against a wooden ceiling. Burning wood crackled and popped. Her nose wrinkled at a whiff of smoke.

Where am I? She felt lost, confused, sweaty. There was nothing familiar to help her feel grounded. It took a moment to shake off the coma of deep sleep and her disturbing dream.

This isn't my home. How did I get here?

Beth's stiff neck and sleeping arm and hip screamed a brutal reminder. She tried to move them, but the binding limited her. She cringed. *I'm a prisoner.* Her heart fluttered in fear at the memory. She cast her eyes about the room. *Where are they?*

Except for the snapping fire, the *drip, drip, drip* of a leaky faucet, and the faint noises coming from the dozing men, the room was quiet.

Beth peered through the dim light at the sleeping figures. Luke lay sprawled across the lower bunk, with his lanky arms and legs overhanging.

Decker's vibrating snore broke the stillness and rumbled through the doorway of the bedroom. Nick lay on the cot. Even in the firelight Beth could make out the lady tattoo on his stocky arm. The indistinct lump in the darkness of the top bunk had to be Glenn.

I wonder if the shadowy man in my dream is Glenn. With the dream still vivid, a strange feeling swept through Beth as she observed the blanketed bump. *But why did I dream about him carrying me?*

No answers came.

Despair threatened to suffocate her. *Why can't this all be just a bad dream? Will I ever wake up in my own safe bed?* A great longing blazed in her heart. Her eyes burned with unshed tears.

She lay awake for what seemed like hours, visualizing the foul things that could happen to her. They projected on the screen of her mind like a horror movie. Around and around her imagination spun. Beth slept fitfully.

She awoke expecting to see her home's familiar surroundings. Instead, the old cowboy leaned over, poking at the glowing coals.

A ray of golden sunlight beamed through the sectioned window onto the floor. Birds cheerfully sang. Why hadn't she ever noticed how pleasant that sound is?

Grumpy Decker looked comical. He stumbled from the

back room, sat on the edge of a chair, and attempted to bend over to lace his dusty boots. His plump cheeks puffed out and reddened from the strain.

On his way toward the hostages, Nick whistled the eerie notes. Beth finally put it together—*Twilight Zone's* theme song. Clutching a knife, he stepped up to her.

Instinctively, Beth squirmed to move away.

"Yo, I'm just fixin' to use this on your ropes. What'd ya think I was going to do, Bethie Baby? Hold this beauty at your throat and take you to bed? Well"—he arched one eyebrow and grinned—"I just might."

Obviously, Nick's entertainment was terrifying helpless women.

The bitter tang of disgust burned in her throat. "Go away, Nick," she muttered, as if she were bossing her younger brother.

To Beth's amazement, Nick backed off after cutting the rope.

The door swung open just then. The young cowboy swept in, bringing the bright, morning sun and a cool breeze with him. His silhouette reflected the sunny rays.

The fresh scent of mountain dawn filled the room, but only for a coveted moment. Too soon the door slammed shut.

Beth's gaze followed Glenn as he shed his jean jacket and black hat. His damp hair, supposedly from a bath, appeared black. Night no longer kept his looks a secret.

He glanced toward Beth with a cheery good morning.

Her heart nearly stopped. *Whoa! He is can't-help-but-stare gorgeous!* She delighted in his attractively shaped face and good-natured expression. A blue-plaid shirt accented his broad shoulders, and faded blue jeans fit him perfectly. But he wasn't wearing his holster.

Scanning the room, Beth saw it hanging on the back of a chair. Could she grab it before anyone noticed? *Maybe I could—*

Too late. Glenn set his thermos on the table, reached for his holster, and buckled the weapon around his narrow hips.

The girls huddled together by the fireplace. An iron rod leaned against a corner of the rock hearth. Luke had used it to rake over the coals, but it had possibilities as a weapon.

"You women hurry up and fix breakfast." Decker gathered up his gear.

"The fire's going out." Kathrin pointed to the embers.

"Build one in the wood stove." Clearly annoyed, he wagged his head. "Wonderful. I'm surrounded by idiots."

The hostages glanced at each other with pride-battered expressions.

"Okay." Emily sighed and rose to her feet. "Guess we'll need some matches."

Luke handed Beth his cigarette lighter. She studied it then looked up at Em. "How hard can it be? If a cow can catch Chicago on fire, we can handle this."

Beth kneeled before the cold, uncooperative-looking metal monster. It screeched as she forced open its dark mouth. She shoved sticks down its small, ash-laden throat. The wretch took revenge and blackened her hands with its sooty drool.

When she clicked the lighter open, Kathrin backed off as if anticipating the black monster to breathe fire. Beth concentrated on working the lighter. Nothing happened. She brushed the hair from her eyes then grimaced. "Uh-oh, did I get soot on me?"

A smile formed on Kathrin's pale face. "You've got a black-tipped nose and a stripe across your forehead." She stifled a giggle.

After repeated attempts and failures at producing a

constant flame from the lighter, Beth's patience wore thin. "What's *wrong* with this thing?"

The fire on the sticks went out.

Beth steeled herself. This metal monster would *not* win! After finally giving birth to what looked like a healthy fire, she began to close the door. The teasing flames disappeared.

"Blasted thing!" She slammed the chrome-plated door. Gray ash fell on her knees. "Err!" She threw her arms up in surrender.

Kathrin couldn't stifle her giggles any longer. The humor spread to Emily and some of the men.

Scowling, she looked up at the others. "What is so funny?"

They laughed harder. Even Decker smiled.

It dawned on Beth what she must look like. She rubbed her nose and saw her blackened fingers. Her lap was full of ashes. Disgusted, she turned around and brushed off the gray dust.

"Here, let me help," a deep but lighthearted voice said from behind her. Glenn didn't sound angry at her for attempting to shoot him the night before, so she scooted to one side. He bent down on one knee and handed her his handkerchief for her face. Then he went to work removing the sticks from the stove.

"I know how to do this," Beth protested as she moped her forehead. "It's just this crazy stove doesn't like me. Hey, what are you doing? You've got to have wood."

Glenn patiently explained how to pile the wood and open the damper. Before long he had the fire blazing. He shut the door.

Kathrin and Beth started for the sink. Glenn lifted the lid to the coffee pot that sat on the stove.

Kaboom! The blast shattered time and space.

The deafening explosion ripped shock waves through Beth. She ducked and covered her head. In her peripheral vision, the stove's small, black lid flipped through the air and rammed against the log wall, clanging onto the floor. Ash and small pieces of wood spewed from the top of the black beast. Glenn flew backward and slammed against the floor.

A shocked hush followed, except for the sound of burned bits of wood raining down. The charred pieces and a layer of ash covered the floor.

"Anybody hurt?" Luke's voice broke the stunned silence.

"We're okay," Kathrin and Beth answered in unison.

Not everyone was okay. Beth's gut twisted at the sight of the dazed, dust-covered cowboy lying motionless.

Glenn groaned and stirred. Sluggishly, he lifted his head and shoulders out of the blanket of ash and rolled to his side.

Luke hurried over. He bent down on one knee and rested his hand on Glenn's shoulder. "Are ya all right?"

Glenn nodded. Dust flew. He drew up one knee and sat upright. He lifted the pot—which was still in his grip—and dumped out gray powder. "Anyone want a cup of coffee? It has a slight kick." He blinked his ash-laden lashes.

Beth chuckled. Luke and Kathrin filled the room with laughter. Luke slapped his son on the back. A cloud of minute particles rose.

Tension left Beth's body. How good it felt to laugh!

"What caused that?" Decker brushed ash from his hair and fat belly.

"I'd like to know that myself." Glenn staggered to his feet, sweeping off debris.

"Looks like the beast doesn't like you either." Beth threw him a smile. A warm grin returned.

Nick charged through the door just then, wearing a wild

expression. "What happened?"

"Stove exploded," Decker explained.

Luke caught his breath from laughing so hard. "Well, I'll be. Look at this." He bent over, pulled something from the gray dust, and then lifted a shiny piece of thin, torn metal. "B-a-r-b-a-" He spelled out the letters. "Shorty must've thrown an empty can of shaving cream in the stove."

"What?" Glenn shouted.

Luke coughed and shook his head. "Has t' be. Shorty swore he'd get even with ya, Son. He's the only one besides you that knows the way here." He tossed the scrap away. "That's right! I remember now. He told me he was up here a couple weeks ago. Got ya good this time, ol' boy." He burst into laughter, slapping his knees. It ended in a fit of coughing.

"Some joke," Glenn muttered. Then the corners of his mouth turned up. "It'll take work to top this one."

Decker snorted his opinion of the joke. "Forget the mess. We gotta eat and be outta here by eight." Clearly short on patience, he grabbed his gear and lumbered outside to prepare for the trip.

Nick joined him. The door slammed shut.

Glenn found the small, round stovetop lid and replaced it. Then he started another fire—this time without mishap. All five cleared some of the mess while they waited for the stovetop to heat up.

Luke and Glenn retold stories of the pranks they and their friend Shorty had played on each other over the years. With hoots and knee-slapping, they relived some of their favorite times together.

Beth couldn't help but grin at the outrageous tricks the two men shared.

"That reminds me, Son," Luke said, wiping his eyes. "It's

clear t' me that ya don't want t' marry the boss's daughter, but I can't figure out why not. She's sweet on ya, ya know. Any one of those cowpokes at the ranch would jump at the chance t' marry pretty Brittany. They'd inherit the whole ranch someday. But *nooo*, not you. Opportunity flirts with ya, and ya pay it no mind at'll." He threw up his hands then went to wash off at the sink.

"I'm not in love with Brittany." Glenn scooped up the ash in a dustpan and glared at Luke. "And why do I need to be rich? God has blessed me already. I have all I want. What does it cost to sleep under the stars with your friends or have a picnic in a mountain meadow with your best gal? Give me a good horse, a guitar, and a good meal cooked over an open fire, and I'm satisfied. Can you see Brittany doing any of that?"

Luke shook his head. "Yer hopeless. Is that all ya want t' do the rest of ya born days and end up like me?"

Glenn leaned the broom and pan against the wall. He turned and joined the gaunt, old cowboy with an expression of respect and admiration. "I couldn't think of anything more I could hope for. Except maybe for a newer hat than that battered one of yours." He patted Luke on the shoulder in a friendly, light-hearted gesture.

"Like I said, yer hopeless." But Luke embraced his son.

Beth stood at the sink with Em. "He doesn't want much," she whispered in her friend's ear.

Em left for the outhouse while Beth scrubbed her face in the tepid water.

Glenn joined her. Wiping his face, he turned to her. "Would you like some help with the eggs?"

Beth looked up and lost her breath. Face to face in broad daylight, his crystal-blue eyes—framed by dark lashes—and striking good looks captivated her.

For a moment Beth forgot Glenn was a criminal. Instead, she seemed to be meeting a warmhearted, gentle man for the first time. She couldn't help but stare. A well-chiseled jawline and defined cheekbones outlined his tanned, strong face and wide-spread eyes. His smile gave away his apparent delight in gazing at her too.

Beth's face grew hot. Totally embarrassed at being caught admiring his looks, she turned away.

Decker and his sidekick barged through the door, ruining the mood. "Breakfast ready yet?" His eyes darted around the room, and he cursed. "Of course not!"

Beth and Kathrin quickly found the eggs and got busy.

During breakfast Beth studied Glenn from across the table. *Why does he have to be so annoyingly handsome? How can a crook have such a kind, gentle expression? When our eyes met, I would swear he wouldn't hurt me. I don't understand, but I don't trust him.*

While Beth stared at the cowboy, he stopped eating and looked up at her. Promptly, she turned away, not wanting him to read her thoughts, but she felt his gaze.

She blushed.

7. The Escape Plan

After breakfast, the women washed the tin plates as commanded, while the four men carried out perishables to load onto the horses.

No sooner had the door latched behind them when Emily drew close. "Kathrin told me what happened last night with Glenn. I have a plan that won't backfire this time. But we have to act quickly. They may be plotting our demise this very moment." She paused.

"Go on," Beth said.

"We could start a fire in the cabin. They'll be so busy putting it out—you know why … the money—that we could easily lift a gun."

Beth frowned. Another chancy escape attempt? "Hmmm, well, it's believable because the stove exploded, but we'd have to make it quick."

Kathrin jerked her hands out of the suds and barely wiped them on her jeans. "Yeah, hurry." She ran to the fireplace and picked up a short, sturdy branch from the stack of firewood. "We could hit th—Lord, have mercy—" She tossed the branch back on the stack. "Never mind."

"Yes, let's hit them with a club as they come through the door." Emily finished Kathrin's sentence.

They rushed around. Beth cut a clothesline into several pieces. Each of them kept a length. Kathrin added paper and some kindling to the woodpile and nestled a glowing ember into it. Smoke poured out. Emily pocketed the handcuffs and grabbed a sturdy branch. Beth selected the iron poker.

Beth took up her position behind the door. "What a violent person I've become. I *hate* it."

"But Beth, remember"—Em hugged the wall on the opposite side of the door—"they'll have no qualms about killing us." She raised her stick of wood as if she were going to bat. "We can't mess up, because after this they *will* want to kill us. So don't be squeamish about hitting them, all right?"

Beth nodded. Her body trembled. Every muscle turned to rubber. Stinky, suffocating smoke filled the room. Her eyes smarted.

Kathrin peeked out the window. "Okay, ladies. Ready to go home?"

"Fire!" Emily and Beth screamed.

Kathrin flung the door open and coughed. "Fire! The woodpile's on fire," she yelled, sounding frantic.

She's a good actress, Beth thought with a grim smile. *She's convinced me she's terrified.*

Smoke curled out around the top of the door frame.

"The money bags!" Nick shrieked. "Are they on fire?"

"I didn't see the bags," Kathrin yelled back. "Where are they?"

Beth's ears flooded with her pounding heart. Sweat poured down. It seemed an eternity before she heard footsteps echoing across the wooden porch. Her heart raced faster, harder.

Kathrin rattled on.

A man's shadow fell across the floor.

Beth's arms began their downward thrust. Shades of blue flashed by. Her heart froze. *No, not him!* But she couldn't stop the momentum. Everything seemed to move in slow motion.

The iron poker's impact with flesh and bone reverberated up Beth's arms. *Oh, dear God, what have I done?* Instant, stinging regret ripped through her heart.

Glenn's hat dropped. Knees caved. His body collapsed onto the floor.

Beth felt the vibrations of his crash. He rolled to a stop half on his back, half on his side. With one knee slightly drawn up, his eyes closed.

Nick dashed through the doorway. He paused just long enough for Emily to bash the branch into his stomach. He huffed and doubled over.

Emily grabbed his pistol and jammed it into Nick's back. "Hands behind your back! Any sound out of your mouth, and it'll be the last."

Nick froze then crossed his wrists behind his back. Emily slapped the handcuffs on him.

Beth looked back at the horrible thing she had done. Glenn's head came to rest against his shoulder. His forearm slowly slid off his body, settling beside him. He lay still.

She sucked in a jerky breath. *Did I kill him?*

She couldn't breathe. Unbearable remorse engulfed her. Tears spurted, and she dropped to her knees beside him. "I'm sorry," she whispered, settling a shaky hand on his shoulder. "I'm so sorry." *How could I do this to him?*

Emily's frantic whisper broke through. "Get his gun!"

Beth bent over Glenn's body, jerked the revolver from its holster, and jumped away.

Kathrin stood in the threshold and put on a good show. "It's too smoky. C'mon, girls. You need to get out. The guys will take care of things." She moved onto the porch.

Decker hustled toward the doorway. Kathrin's leg kicked out in front of his ankles. He tripped, hurtled forward, and slammed hard on the floor. *Ooof!*

"Oops, sorry." Kathrin said as she hustled to Decker's side, whipped out his pistol, and pressed it against the back of his head.

Luke stopped short in the threshold. He stared, clearly dumbfounded. His lips moved, but no words came out.

"I *will* pull this trigger," Kathrin threatened in her little-girl voice. "You don't want to test me. Decker, stretch your arms above your head. Luke, slowly hand me your gun—handle first—then go sit by the table."

Luke followed Kathrin's orders.

"Don't think this is over," Decker's voice growled from the floor.

"Oooh, you sound pretty scary." Keeping the pistol to his head, Kathrin plunked her dainty frame on the back of a man who probably outweighed her by 130 pounds.

Beth couldn't believe Kathrin's incredible strength of character packed in such a small frame.

"Y'all are going to regret this." Nick spoke as if he knew something the women didn't.

"Never, Nick, never." Emily strapped him to a chair, rubbed her smoke-irritated eyes then tied a damp handkerchief over her nose and mouth.

On her knees below the thickest layer of smoke, Beth's stomach knotted as she rolled Glenn's unresisting body over on his back. *Please let him be alive. But if he is, then I better restrain him before he knows what's happening to him.* She pulled his warm, hairy wrists across his flat stomach and looped the cord around them.

"Beth, can you dowse the fire?" Kathrin said between coughs. "Emily, would you come tie Decker's hands for me?"

"It's on my bucket list." Emily plucked a rope from her

pocket and hurried toward Decker.

Anxious to clear the smoke and get back to Glenn, Beth hurried through her task. The fire sizzled and went out.

Emily took over handling Decker. "Go sit over there. Any funny business, and you'll find yourself being prodded by the devil's pitchfork straight into hell." She jabbed the pistol into his back, forcing him to walk toward the chair.

The portly man arched his back away from the weapon. "Okay, lady, okay! Take it easy with that pistol." He cursed under his breath.

Kathrin joined Beth at Glenn's side, while Em anchored Decker and Luke to their chairs.

"He hasn't moved this whole time." Beth choked. "I must've … killed him." Tears brimmed over her lashes.

Kathrin checked his pulse. "He's just unconscious. Here … feel." She clasped Beth's first two fingers and pressed them on Glenn's smooth-shaven neck.

A steady *thump-thump* pulsed against Beth's fingertips. "Thank God. Funny how a barely perceptible thing can lift such a heavy burden."

Engrossed in examining the unconscious man, Kathrin didn't respond.

"You seem to know what you're doing," Beth said. "Are you a nurse or doctor?"

"I'm a student nurse," Kathrin replied.

Why do I find Kathrin's examination intriguing? Is it because Glenn is like a wild stallion, an untamed but beautiful animal? Since he's unconscious, I can get close to this stallion—even touch him—and he can't hurt me. Beth set a hand on his warm arm, in no hurry to let go. *Nor will he ever know.*

With a damp cloth, Kathrin carefully swabbed a small smudge of blood from Glenn's wound, blooding the rag. His thick, dark lashes didn't open.

Beth studied his quiet face. "His world is so different from ours. It's full of violence and greed. It's incomprehensible to me, frightening."

"Yeah," Kathrin said, preoccupied.

Beth continued in her thoughts. *No one can tell he lives in a violent world by looking at him now. His handsome face is peaceful. But last night—even today—I was the violent one. Glenn has been patient and kind toward me so far. What kind of man is he?* "Did I hurt him badly?"

"No, but he's likely to have a headache."

Glenn's chest moved deeper with every awakening breath. The muscles in his cheek drew tight. Sluggishly, he blinked and rolled his head away from his shoulder. He opened his eyes and stared up at Beth, as if puzzling over his predicament. His soft-blue gaze glimmered kind, captivating.

Wow! His eyes are stunning. Beth's face and arms tingled.

He tried to raise his arm. The cord stopped him. "What happened?"

Regret tortured Beth's effort to speak. "I"—she swallowed—"I hit you and grabbed your gun. Emily is tying up your friends over there."

Glenn stretched and turned to see the other men.

"Let's get him off the floor." Kathrin tugged on one arm. Beth took the other.

Glenn's dark brows knit as long legs bent and moved under him. He flopped into a chair and leaned back, eyes closed. One leg sprawled out before him.

"Hey!" Emily burst out. "We're going home! In one piece."

"If we leave right now, we'll sleep in our own beds tonight." Kathrin's arms stretched wide—just like her smile. She raised her head and said, "Thank You."

Beth clasped her hands together and hugged them to her chest. "Woo-hoo!"

The women cheered, congratulating each other with hugs.

Decker interrupted their celebration. "The day's not over." He annunciated each word with a sinister tone.

"Y'all have done made me mad." Nick scowled and bared his teeth.

Emily picked up her thick branch and patted his head on her way behind him. "Don't worry your dear little head, Nick. You will never manhandle me again." She raised her makeshift club and drew back.

"No!" Kathrin and Beth shrieked.

With a quick, vicious swing Emily smashed Nick's fingers against the chair back. *Crack!*

"Augh!"

Nick's agonized scream sank deep into Beth's psyche. Her stomach all but retched. She charged at Emily and yanked the club out of her grip. "Enough violence!"

Emily didn't fight her.

Nick gasped and moaned in torment. "You …" He cussed and spew a wicked name. Spittle seeped out the corners of his mouth. "You … will … *pay* for this." More cussing.

"Not if I get to you first." Emily eyes gleamed.

Beth stared at her friend in sickening wonder. Then squatting, she retrieved Glenn's hat off the floor.

Kathrin bent down and examined Nick's traumatized hand. He yowled at her touch.

"You probably caused permanent damage, Emily," Kathrin said. "The phalange bones in his left hand and the knuckles of the two middle fingers are broken."

"Good." Emily stuffed a bandana around Nick's mouth and tightened it. Thankfully, the outlaw's profanity was muffled enough not to recognize the words.

"Wait 'til we break free. You thought we were rough on you bef—"

Emily muted Decker too.

"Nick and Glenn need Motrin." Kathrin opened the door to the wall cabinet. "I saw a bottle in here."

Emily reached down for more clothesline curled on the floor. "After I tie Glenn to the chair, let's go outside. We need to talk."

Shortly, Beth, Emily, and Kathrin made an impromptu huddle in the brightness of the outdoors. The sun guaranteed a balmy day. Beth and Kathrin sat under an aspen tree.

Emily stood over them. "C'mon. Let's grab the horses and go!"

"I really don't want to wander for centuries in these mountains." Kathrin swatted at a bug.

"Glenn offered to take us to the highway," Beth said. She fidgeted with a small stick. "Maybe if we assure him that we'll set him free after we get to the highway, he'll take us there. And if we promise never to tell the police about him and leave the other guys tied up in the ca—"

"We could promise Glenn that, but then we need to tell the police the *truth*, Beth," Emily cut in. Her tone grated with superiority and demanding obedience.

Beth's neck and jaw stiffened. "I'm not stupid, Miss High and Mighty. I didn't say we should lie to the poli—"

"I don't want to lie to Glenn either." Kathrin interrupted. She dropped her gaze then looked up at Beth. "I *think* those could be effective promises, Beth, but . . ." Her voice trailed off.

"But what?" Emily paced.

Kathrin held Emily's gaze. "I think we need something

more to clinch the deal. Something Glenn couldn't resist."

Beth scratched her head. "Like what? He didn't seem to want much. Not even money. He's got a horse and a guitar. What were the other things he said?"

"And a picnic with a gal. Hmm ..." Kathrin stared into the sky, obviously deep in thought. A minute passed. Then another. "Maybe that's it. Yeah. Most men are a soft touch when it comes to a pretty lady they're interested in."

"Oh! I get it." Emily pitched her head back. "You want me to lure him into a good mood then convince him to help us. Pour on the charm. Sure, I don't mind. He's nice and"—she smirked—"sizzling hot. This could be fun."

Beth's eyebrows went up. Em had no trouble admitting she liked a crook. *Doesn't she worry that people will look down their nose at her and think her a fool?*

"You've got the right idea," Kathrin said, "but he's more interested in Beth."

Emily's mouth dropped open.

Beth gasped. She couldn't believe her ears. "What are you talking ab—"

Kathrin rested her hand on Beth's arm. "Glenn has that certain sparkle in his eyes when he looks at you. It's obvious he's attracted to you. A blind man could see it."

Peeved and disbelieving, Beth wagged her head. "You've got to be kidding! Are you saying that … that *outlaw*, that *criminal* is interested in me?" She jabbed her own chest with her finger.

"Yes, *you*, Beth. That's why you have an edge on convincing him."

"No." Beth's arm slashed the air. "He's probably the kind that looks at all women that way."

"He doesn't look at Emily or me that way," Kathrin

insisted. "We can use his feelings for you to our advantage."

Can she be right? He's interested in me? Really? A strange but pleasing sensation swept over Beth as Kathrin's words soaked in. She savored a growing interest in the high-risk, handsome man. Her heart puffed up a little, hearing that he chose average Beth over a voluptuous, lovely woman like Emily.

"But …" Beth paused. Her mind began to grow fearful of Glenn coming on to her.

"This could mean life or death for us, and you're depending on *Beth*?" Emily's hands moved in jerks. "She's so shy around men."

"I am not—"

"Maybe that's true, Emily." Kathrin cut Beth off. "But—"

"If she tried to act charming," Emily insisted, "he'd know it's all a ruse."

They argued about Beth as she stared, head bobbing back and forth, between contenders.

"I'm not going to lock horns with you about this." Kathrin set her jaw. "Glenn goes for Beth's type, and that's that."

Emily threw up her hands, shaking her head.

Kathrin turned to Beth. "You don't have to act. Just be yourself … only friendlier. He likes you." She skimmed over a few suggestions then added, "He already told you he'd help us escape, so it should be easy to convince him to go through with it. Isn't being home tonight worth it?"

Beth's mouth went dry. "Please, Kathrin," she begged. "Don't ask me to do this."

"Come on, honey. He's not that bad."

"You don't think he's dangerous?"

Kathrin patted Beth's shoulder. "Glenn's thunder. He's exciting but harmless. The lightening is the rest of those guys. We haven't got time to waste. We'll send him out to you. You do the rest."

Beth shuddered. "But I really don't want …" Her words clearly fell on deaf ears. She watched them step across the earthen path and disappear inside the cabin. She felt deserted.

"What'll I do?" She shook her head. "Kathrin actually thinks he likes me. *Sh-ee-sh.*" A short pause. "There's no need to be afraid. We have the guns."

Beth gripped the pistol.

"I can do this."

8. "Beautiful Wild Stallion"

A few minutes later, Glenn walked through the door. Kathrin followed behind with a gun at his back. "Sit on the bench swing. We'll be ready to go in a few minutes. Beth, would you watch him while we pack some food?"

"Okay." Beth dragged her feet to the porch. Once there, she sat down beside Glenn on the narrow wooden bench, leaned to the side, and placed the gun on the deck out of his reach. When she straightened up her thigh came down against his. Beth puzzled over why their close contact didn't bother her.

No time for that. I have to think about what to say. It felt so awkward.

Glenn leaned forward, his forearms on his knees, wrists tied together. A gentle breeze played with his dark, wavy hair, exposing his wound.

"I'm sorry for how horribly I treated you last night, and for hitting you this morning." Regret saturated Beth's voice.

Glenn massaged the side of his head. "You sure pack a wallop for a half-pint."

Beth brushed aside his rich-brown hair and inspected the injury. Her fingers moved to the nape of his neck and indulged in thick, silky strands, stroking again and again through his hair.

He closed his eyes and lowered his head. "That's easing the pain. Thanks."

Glenn and Beth continued in silence. Both, it seemed, took pleasure in their mutual contact.

After a while, Glenn opened his eyes, sat upright, and shifted his body toward Beth. His thigh rested against the full length of hers, awakening her senses. "Did you know that you're better than Motrin?"

Beth turned to him. "No, I—"

Her eyes met his. She stared. *His eyes are like blue gems. God is really showing off His magnificent work in Glenn.*

The gentle light of his eyes spoke softly of affection, filling every cold, lonely corner of Beth's being. An unexpected, pleasurable current coursed through her body.

She broke free of Glenn's gaze and turned to look at the horses tied to the fence rail. *Every female would stare at him*, she mused. *It's fun to look at beautiful people. That's all. There's nothing more to it.*

Beth took a deep breath. *Time to do this.*

She suspected Glenn might guess what she was up to, but Beth just wanted to get it over with. "Glenn, I … I mean … *we* want to thank you for lying to protect us and for rescuing Emily last night. You've been decent to us." She smiled up at him. "Thank you."

The corners of Glenn's mouth turned up. "You're welcome." His gaze followed Beth's every expression.

"I don't … I mean *we* don't want you to get into trouble with the law, so we thought"—Beth swallowed—"would you please take us to where we can see the highway, but far enough away so you're safe?" Her voice picked up speed. "We promise not to tell the police about you. The rest of the guys can stay tied up in the cabin. You can come back and free them when we're safely away."

Glenn didn't respond at first. He just looked at her. Then

he sighed. "Beth, if you lie or withhold information from the police, you'll be charged with obstruction of justice. Tell the police the truth. It'll be tough on you for a while because of us, but I hope that someday you can forgive me." He paused.

Beth marveled, *Wow, he's thinking of our well-being to the point of risking his own capture.*

"I will take you to where you can see a dirt road. It eventually leads to the highway." Glenn continued. "But I'll have to blindfold you the last mile. The others and I need time—at least until five o'clock tonight—before the police learn about us. It's important. Do you think you gals can make that work?"

Beth's mind couldn't wrap itself around this fantastic news. Astounded, she stared at him. "Yes, okay. We won't tell the police about you guys until five. So … you'll bring us to the road today? Right now?" She hung on his every word, every expression.

He grinned and nodded. "Mm-hmm, I will if you all give your word about tonight."

Beth's smile broadened. "Yes. Our word." She jumped up and threw her arms about Glenn's broad shoulders. "We'll be home tonight! Oh, thank you, thank you!" She pressed her cheek against his warm, freshly shaven face, giddy with hope. The faint, sweet-spice scent of his shaving cream infused into her memory.

A cord restricted his hands, so he patted her arm.

Then it hit her. She was hugging a criminal. But he didn't seem like an unpredictable animal anymore. He seemed human, a man with a compassionate heart. Still, she broke away and composed herself.

Beth held his kind, expressive gaze.

It was as though he kept nothing back but allowed her to

see his innermost feelings.

"Ya know, I used to think there's nothing cuter than a newborn filly with long, wobbly legs. But I was wrong. I hadn't met you yet." He beamed.

Embarrassed, Beth lowered her head, smiling. "I hate to tell you this, but you're uglier than an old frog." She stole a glimpse of him. Her face burned hotter. His lit up. *What an amazing smile he has!*

"A *what?* An old frog?" Glenn wagged his head. "Oooo! That's mighty ugly."

Blushing, Beth dropped her head again.

Out of the corner of her eye she saw Glenn lean toward her. He raised his bound wrists, lightly placed his curled fingers under her chin, and lifted her head.

She glanced up. Affection sparkled in his eyes. She drank it in.

Suddenly, Glenn's countenance changed. It was as though he longed to kiss her and sought her consent.

Oh my goodness! I wasn't expecting this. I don't even know him. If I pull away, I hope he'll stop. Beth's heart skipped. *But I wonder … how would Glenn's kiss feel?*

When Beth made no move to pull away, Glenn inched closer, tilting his head to reach her. His motions were docile. His curled finger and thumb, which cupped her chin, brought her mouth up to meet his.

Beth's heart hammered. She was somewhat afraid of him, but he treated her like an honored and cherished princess. She closed her eyes and felt his lips brush lightly against hers. Then his soft mouth covered hers in warmth and tenderness.

Beth's senses came alive. A lump formed in her throat, and her insides tightened. Like a taut bow launching an arrow, the sensation of blissful flying rushed in. In the magic of the moment, Beth forgot her fears. Instead, she soaked in his ever-so-loving kisses.

No one had ever caused such pleasurable feelings in Beth before. Why Glenn? He wasn't like anyone she had ever met. *How gentle he is! But these feelings are risky—*

Abruptly, Beth drew away. Not wanting him to see his effect on her, she kept her head down. Weakness washed over her. *This man is really getting to me. If he kisses me again I wouldn't want him to stop. But it would be a big mistake getting involved with a criminal.*

"I … I don't know what came over me." Glenn cleared his throat. "Uh … that's not true. I *do* know. I'm sorry if I frightened you." He let out a sudden, disgusted breath. "I guess I'm no different than Nick."

His words and tone, though, did not match his radiant expression.

Beth studied Glenn's well-sculptured profile. *Oooh, I caused that expression on that magnificent face?*

"I won't lay another hand on you," Glenn promised. "If I get too close, use that stick on me again, or whatever it was."

"You're not at all like Nick," Beth protested. "Not even close." She knew it would put Glenn on the spot, but she couldn't resist asking, "What *did* come over you?"

With an embarrassed grin, he glanced down for a second then looked back up at her. "First, I don't ever want to frighten you. After today, I may never see you again. That's heavy on my mind. But I'm not sorry I kissed you. I'll have this memory."

He took her hand in his rocklike, calloused hands and gazed into her eyes. "I've never met a gal like you—someone not spoiled by the world. It's refreshing. It takes a special kind of selfless person to face her enemy alone for the sake of her friends. And … Beth, you are so beautiful. I wanted to be close to you, to touch you."

Glenn's affection shimmered through the blue-velvet reflections of his secret mind, kindling an inner glow within Beth. She longed to dwell on it, but she dared not. *Don't look at him.* She dropped her gaze. *Forget about kissing him. You've got to stop enjoying him.*

That stung. Her shoulders slumped. It felt as though she plunged from a radiant mountain top into a lifeless valley.

Somehow, though, she had to survive in that barren land without him.

Glenn released her hand.

Beth took one last glance at his smiling, handsome face and turned away. "Oh, I see you're still an ugly, old frog. That fairy tale about kissing frogs must not be true. I'm never going to find my handsome prince this way."

Glenn laughed.

Beth grabbed her gun and stepped away. "I … I better go now and tell the girls you'll take us." She turned, stumbled, and then scrambled back to her companions.

The girls rushed out and huddled around her.

"Glenn agreed to take us to where we can see the road," Beth said, breathless.

They cheered in unison, and hugged each other. Beth glanced back and forth between Glenn and the girls as she listed his conditions. They agreed to his terms.

Emily stepped off the porch. "Where's the money?"

"I know. I'll get it." Kathrin started for the cabin door.

Glenn wrinkled his brow. "You're returning *all* the money?"

The women stopped, whirled around, and contemplated the outlaw.

"Yes, of course," Emily said flatly. "It belongs to the bank—to the people, actually."

Kathrin hurried over to Glenn's side. "This is about Sophia, Luke's granddaughter, isn't it? Luke was struggling to breathe a little while ago." She shrugged. "So I removed the bandana."

Beth's eyes widened. "And?"

"He told me about Sophia and the brain tumor." Kathrin glanced at Beth. "It's what we overheard when Luke explained to Glenn why he robbed the bank. For the operation, they need about a hundred thousand dollars. If Sophia doesn't get it, she'll die within a few months. Apparently, he has nothing. All his assets went for his wife's Alzheimer's care facility."

Kathrin touched Glenn's arm. "But don't worry, your dad and I worked it all out. Since no agency will help because it's an experimental operation, I offered to help by using that internet program and donations from people I know. Like you, Beth and Emily."

"Yes, I'd be happy to help." Beth became excited.

Glenn remained still a moment. Then he bowed his head, clasped his hands together and pressed them to his lips. Shortly, he looked up at them. "You would do that for kidnappers and thieves?" His voice was filled with gratitude and amazement.

"For Sophia we would." Emily placed her hand on her hip and shifted her weight.

"You gals are incredible. Thank you." Glenn spoke in an emotion-rich voice. "It means a lot to me."

"I'll get your hat." Kathrin started for the door again. "Oh … and Luke already gave me Sophia's info."

"C'mon. Let's go home." Emily stepped up on the porch and pulled on her prisoner's arm. "You walk in front of me, and no funny business." When he rose to his feet, he towered above his captors but relented to Emily's commands.

Glenn stopped close to the horses and turned to Emily. "We won't be needing the pack horse, but it shouldn't be tied up all day without water." He held out his bound wrists to her. "I need to unload it and put it in the pasture."

"Okay, but I'm watching you." Emily cut his bonds.

While Emily and Beth watched Glenn unload the pack horse, Kathrin approached Beth with an armload of money sacks.

Glenn's man-sized hat slide down Kathrin's head to her nose. Beth chuckled inwardly. How could she see out from under it? She reached out and lifted it off her friend's head.

"I could see the ground just fine," Kathrin said, then she lowered her voice. "He didn't get out of line, did he?" One sack almost slipped from her arms, but some quick fumbling caught it.

Beth shook her head. "He didn't even try to get the gun. He could have, just like he did last night."

"Good. I hated putting this on you, but you see now why it had to be you?"

"I do now." A smile slipped past Beth's control.

9. Has God Deserted Us?

In the mountains heading home

When Beth stepped up to the large, shiny black horse, she became awed by his size and magnificence. The animal proudly arched his neck, the coat soft and fuzzy under her hand. "You are a black beauty. You won't buck me off, will you?"

The horse swung his large head in her direction, blinking long lashes over pretty, bluish-black eyes.

Beth took this as a favorable response.

Glenn stepped into the saddle of his big, red mount. "These horses are well trained and ridden every day. They won't give you any trouble." His horse pranced about nervously. "I chose the most spirited one." Then Glenn gave the city girls a crash course on how to handle a horse.

Beth clutched the reins and *horn*—not *handle* according to Glenn—of her own mount and pulled herself up onto the creaking leather. The pain from yesterday's ride sharply hit her.

"You ready, horse? Let's go." Emily jiggled the reins of a golden mare.

Out of the corner of her eye, Beth saw Glenn's red horse bolt forward. The golden mare and a brown horse followed close behind.

Suddenly, without warning, the powerful black horse beneath Beth lunged into a full gallop. "*Oh, oh, oh!*" she screeched. The wind slapped against her face, and her white-knuckled fists choked the saddle horn. *Where is this animal taking me?*

The black horse followed his equine friends through the clearing that spread out in front of the cabin. The sight of the log hideout caused a strange but liberating feeling inside Beth. Her heart slowed, and she thanked God that this horrible chapter of her life was over.

She turned back into the wind. Her steed's mane tossed with the flurry of air and lightly feathered her hands. The gallop was smooth, but she clutched the horn for dear life.

How natural Glenn looked in the saddle. He wasn't hanging on to the horn like the rest of them, nor did he bounce all over. The big red's body stretched out. His mane and tail flew gracefully behind him, his rider one with his smooth motions.

What a spectacular vision they make together! One I don't want to forget.

The snow-capped, deep-blue mountain ridge provided the perfect backdrop. Without a doubt, this was Glenn's country. This was where he belonged, where he was meant to ride.

The four riders slowed to a walk and rode through some of the most awe-inspiring scenery Beth had ever seen. She swayed to the broad strides of the tall horse beneath her. She sighed with a great sense of relief and mirth. "We're going home. Wow! God answered our prayers and kept us safe."

"Yes, God is kind and good, even when He doesn't say 'yes' to all our prayers." Kathrin swung her arm out wide. "God does so much for us."

Beth basked in nature's splendor. She had lots of time to think. *I feel closer to God in this wide-open country than in the city. Life is a rat race in that man-made, black-tar maze. I'm not the same person anymore. This nightmare has changed me.*

Beth's thoughts drifted toward Glenn. When she looked at him, her heart wrenched. *Goodness, I can't even look at him without hurting.*

They traveled through the canyon. Then about forty minutes later they came to a brook. Emily stopped her animal like a pro. "Let's take a break."

Beth slid off her horse and tied him to a branch. Thick foliage surrounded the small clearing. The horses made quick work of devouring the grass around them.

"I'm taking the horses down to the stream for water." Glenn's voice came to Beth from about eight feet away.

She didn't look up but continued patting Black Beauty.

"Have you got what you need out of the saddlebags, Beth?"

"No, not yet, but I'd like to water him myself when I'm done here, if that's okay." Her fingers worked the buckle on one of the saddlebags.

Glenn didn't respond right away.

Is he waiting for me to look up or say something more? She kept to her task.

When he spoke, his tone hinted of sorrow. "Sure, whatever you want."

The *clop, clop* of the horses' hooves faded.

"I hate hurting him," Beth whispered to Black Beauty. She watched Glenn walk away. The other horses followed his lead.

Beth's heart dropped like a stone. "I don't want another painful meeting, so I better wait until he returns before I take you down."

She carried a bag of jerky to her friends. Before the man returned, the girls dashed to the bushes to piddle. Soon they sat on a crumbling, squashy log.

"I just realized I forgot to thank Glenn." Kathrin's hand wrapped around a thermos.

"Me too." Emily pulled some crackers from a plastic sack.

The memory of throwing her arms around Glenn made Beth smile. "I already thanked him."

Kathrin elbowed her with a grin. "Yes, we saw you *thanking* him."

Not wishing to discuss the subject, Beth sipped water from her thermos.

"Tell us, how was it?" Emily asked.

Playing dumb, Beth winced. "It tastes a little bit like coffee."

"Not the water, silly." Emily rolled her eyes. "How did it feel to be kissed by a handsome bad-boy like Glenn?" She crunched on a cracker. "It has to be more exciting than kissing your old boyfriend, Jeff."

"Is that all you think about?" Beth whispered her disgust as she offered jerky to the others.

"No, really. Was it exciting?" Emily eyes lit up with intrigue, her face glamorous.

Irritated, Beth sighed and tugged at her bolero. "It was okay."

Emily snorted. "I don't believe it was just *okay*. I saw you. It looked like you were really into it. You two kissed for a long time. C'mon, tell us. We won't tease you."

The forbidden, sweet memory came painfully back.

To Beth's relief, Kathrin interrupted them. "He's on his way back."

"Tell us quickly," Emily badgered in an undertone.

"I told you," Beth snapped. "Find out for yourself if you're so blasted curious. Go on. Kiss him, hug him. Do whatever you want. I don't care." She rose and stomped away before they could read her tortured heart.

"What's *her* problem?" Beth heard Emily ask.

Glenn was heading toward Kathrin and Emily. To avoid him, Beth walked faster in a different direction, back to the tree where her horse was tethered. She was grateful that she had an excuse to be alone and regain her composure. "Why can't Emily leave me alone? Why can't *everyone* just leave me alone?" She stroked her faithful steed's neck.

The large horse mouthed his bit. He obviously didn't understand why either.

"It hurts that Em can do whatever she wants with him, and I can't. She's only after a thrill. She doesn't care about Glenn like I do. She's beautiful and sexy. What man wouldn't want her, especially if she's chasing him? Who'd want plain ol' me when you can have *her*?"

She untied her large confidant and led him toward the stream. He followed along nicely. From the way he arched his neck over her shoulder, she figured he liked her. "At least I know *you* won't tell anyone."

When she raised her eyes to see which direction to go, she stopped short. Her mouth dropped open. Emily stood with her long, sexy fingers stroking Glenn's face. "I just wanna thank you." Then she caressed him in a long-lasting kiss. Glenn still held the horses' reins in his hand.

As far as Beth could see, Glenn wasn't pushing Emily off. "Men! They're all alike," she whispered to her horse. "They can't resist a pretty girl."

Kathrin rose to her feet. "You're a good man. Thank you, Glenn." On her tiptoes, five-foot Kathrin stretched to hug his broad shoulders and kiss a browned cheek. He returned her gesture by bending down and patting her on the back.

Beth started on her way again. Hiding behind the horse's

head, she passed the group and made her way carefully down the sandy grade to the cool, refreshing stream.

She watched the majestic horse's reflection in the creek as he nosed the water then took huge draughts. The sun's bright rays peeked through the shady red and yellow autumn leaves, sparkling like diamonds on the water.

"What a pleasant place for an escape." The tranquilizing rhythm of the rushing water against the rocks soothed Beth's soul. The air smelled of damp moss and reeds.

Suddenly, a strong, rough hand fell across Beth's mouth. Startled, she jumped. *What's Glenn doing?*

The loose rocks gave way under Beth's feet. She fell backward. The man flung another arm around Beth's shoulder, catching her. She landed against a squishy belly. His dark-green sleeve and fat, hairy hand told her who it was. Horror coursed through her body. *Decker!*

Decker's meaty palm muffled Beth's scream. His other hand whipped the gun from her pocket and thrust it under her chin. He forced her to back up and turn with him. "Up that hill." In a sort of awkward dance, they plodded up the sandy embankment.

Overwhelmed with distress, Beth wanted to scream. *Dear God! No. We're on our way home. You can't let this happen to us. I'm begging You. How did Decker get free? How did he come after us?*

The vision of Horsey popped into her mind. The pack horse! Why didn't we think of bringing it along, just in case?

The startled, frightened expressions on her friends' faces confirmed the stark cruelty of their fate. Their jaws dropped. Kathrin's piece of jerky fell from her paralyzed hand and into her lap. Glenn stared with a troubled frown. Next to him, Emily slipped her hand toward the gun lying at her side on the log.

"You'll toss those guns over here if you value your friend's life," Decker ordered from behind Beth. The hard, metal barrel dug into her temple.

She gasped and swallowed.

The captives surrendered their weapons.

"Everyone stay seated. Hand them over, little china doll, slowly and butt first." He thrust Beth aside, hurling her to the ground. "I told you this day wasn't over." One by one, Decker jammed the firearms in his worn out belt and into his pockets.

"How did you find us?" Kathrin asked Decker.

"Years of experience tracking illegals, horses leave tracks, and we came through here, yesterday." Decker turned his attention to Glenn. His face darkened. And you, McKlain, what a sorry piece of work you turned out to be. A real son"—he cursed—"and a traitor who turns on his family. That's the lowest in my book."

Decker wasn't finished. "These women are using you, but you're such a sucker for skirts you can't see it. They don't care a lick about you, you fool."

Glenn ignored Decker's raving and spoke quietly. "Why don't you let the gals go here? You know they're only going to cause us trouble, and we've wasted enough time already."

"And let them tell the police everything? His voice roared through the forest. "I'm not stupid like you."

Decker took a deep breath. "We can still make the border today. Secure the women. The cuffs and ropes are on my saddle. The gray's down by the stream. Don't think I won't shoot these women if you try something."

Beth's thoughts spun out of control. If Decker was worried they'd tell the police, why didn't he shoot them right now? Why was he keeping them alive?

Glenn returned, clearly irate. "What'd you do, Decker?

Run the mare into the ground?"

The animal following him, poor Horsey, was dull-acting and lathered.

Decker didn't answer. He grabbed the bag of jerky and devoured it.

Glenn cuffed the other ladies first, then he walked up to Beth. She put her hands out in front, but he hesitated. She raised her head and glanced into the alluring eyes she'd vowed never to look upon again. They spoke of regret. His brow furled. The muscles in his cheek tightened.

Sturdy hands took hold of hers. He held them for a long moment, his thumb stroking her skin. His touch sent a thrill up Beth's arms. Then he crisscrossed her wrists and tied them so loosely that the cord could be removed with little effort.

Soon they rode out. Beth sat in the saddle with Kathrin, and Emily and the men rode by themselves. Glenn insisted that the lathered gray carry no rider.

After many tiresome miles without conversation, they approached the hideout Beth thought she would never see again. Despondent and sick at heart she wondered, *Has God deserted us?*

The ruthless man Beth dreaded sauntered across the porch. With a sarcastic grin, Nick raised his hand above his head and rested it against the porch post. "Ya see now, don't ya? You'll never get away from us."

While they climbed off their horses, Nick continued as if he couldn't wait to tell them his plan. "You've used up your one and only chance to get *any* mercy from me." He held up his bandaged hand, shaking his head in slow motion. "Try it again, and it will have a much different outcome."

Beth suffered a numbness in her soul and her arms. Her legs went limp. Firelight beamed through the small windows and open doorway. Defeated, they shuffled into the hideout like zombies into graves.

The odor of smoke and something cooking reached Beth's nose. Luke's thin, stooped frame stood over a black pot stirring lunch. Decker plopped himself down into his favorite stuffed chair as though he'd done a hard day's work. The girls sat around the table. Glenn hadn't come in yet, probably caring for the livestock.

"After we eat, I wanna get goin'," Decker said. "We still have enough daylight to get to the border."

"Yeah, I'm tired of sitting around. Let's get this show"—then Nick yelled—"on the *road*." With his elbow supported by the mantel, Nick glowered at the girls.

It made Beth jittery.

"How'd it go?" Nick smirked. "They put up much of a fight?"

"Nah." Decker sipped a beer. "But can you believe that dumb cowboy was taking the women back to the city—or someplace? Ha!" He threw his head back in disbelief. "When I got there they were slobbering all over him. I don't trust him. He's too soft."

Nick perked up. "They *slobbered* all over him?" He let out a guffaw. "You mean they *kissed* him. They actually kissed that dirty, stinking cowpuncher?" He glared wildly at the girls and burst out laughing.

Beth stared at the table, afraid to move.

Nick raised his voice. "I bet he didn't even have to force y'all, did he? What's the matter? Ain't I as good as him?"

As if on cue, Glenn, the "culprit," walked through the door, zoomed in on the coffee pot, then sat at the table with the girls.

Nick began his vulture routine of staring at the women.

Irritated, Beth bugged her eyes out at him. Instantly, she regretted her childish gesture.

Nick walked up beside her. "Aw, what's the matter, Bethie Baby?" He stroked her hair and snickered. "I knew my baby was sweet on me."

"No, I'm not." Beth yanked her hair away from his palm. "Quit staring at me. My name's not Bethie Baby."

"All babes like men to stare at them, Bethie Baby."

"I don't."

Nick laughed. To Beth's surprise, so did Glenn.

"And why are *you* laughing?" she snapped.

Glenn shrugged and gave her a lop-sided smile. "It just struck me as funny."

"I'm not trying to be funny. I'm trying to be serious."

"It's hard to take anyone serious who has so many freckles." A playfulness hid in Glenn's approach.

Nick walked back to the fireside and kept his eye on the girls and Glenn.

"I don't have *that* many freckles."

Poker-faced, Luke briefly turned from his work to glance at Beth. "I haven't seen the like since my pa traded for that spotted Appy."

"He's just funnin' you, Beth." Glenn's eyes sparkled.

"I figured that." Beth fought back a smile.

"Actually, it was his pa's spotted mule," Glenn added. "It had so many spots that folks heard tell it had rolled in some tar and then was left out in a sandstorm." He leaned forward, propped his forearms on the table, and studied her with a cheerful countenance.

The cowboys' joking brightened the mood. Kathrin tittered.

Beth forced a grin. "No one left me out in a sandstorm."

Glenn smiled back. The warm friendliness they shared was clearly something they both treasured and needed. Was he as grateful for her presence as she was for his?

Decker's belching brought Beth back to her senses. *Stop. Remember, he's a criminal. They all are.*

"It's ready." Luke dropped tin platefuls of steaming canned stew onto the table with a dull bang.

Decker didn't move from his cushy chair so Luke handed him a plate-full.

A charged vibe hung over the meal. No one spoke. The firewood snapped. Silverware and tin cups rattled. People chewed and sipped. Clothes rustled.

Beth's knee bounced as she kept a vigilant watch on everyone.

The muscles in Glenn's cheek tightened. He finally broke the silence. "Dad, I want you to know that the girls and I had an agreement. I was going to come back and untie all of you. They weren't going to tell the poli—"

"I know ya better than ya know yerself, Son. No need t' say a thing."

Nick finished eating first. He stood, rested his hand on Emily's chair and peered down at the women. "It's good to have you babes back."

"Can't say it's good to *be* back." Emily turned away.

Glenn picked up his tin cup of coffee and stood at his favorite spot by the fireside.

Decker left the cabin.

"Now, don't talk like that," Nick whined. "You're not thinking. Don't ya realize with all that money I could show y'all a real good time? Acapulco, or maybe Rio de Janeiro? We could live it up, the finest motels, steak every night."

Nick was certainly worked up. His grin stretched from ear

to ear. He paced, arms waving with excitement. "Dancing, gambling . . . why, whatever your little ol' heart desires."

He paused for a response, but Beth and her friends didn't say a word. "Are y'all deaf?" With eyes suddenly wild-looking, Nick snatched up a chair and slammed it down. Spindles snapped. The broken chair skidded across the floor.

Beth flinched.

The fury in Nick's glare blasted the ladies. "I'm offering y'all the *world*."

Still no reply.

Nick's face darkened. His voice turned bitter, almost forlorn. "What's the matter? Ain't I even good enough to talk to?"

With kindness in her eyes, Kathrin raised her head. "We just want to go home."

Nick pounded his good fist on the table. Grabbing Emily's hair, he yanked her to her feet. "I could have killed you for crushing my hand, but I didn't. I offered ya everything. Do ya thank me?" With clenched teeth, he went nose to nose with Emily. "Y'all insult and ignore me. *You*, little girl, are gonna be nice to me one way or the other."

10. A Wounded Outlaw

In the outlaw's hideout

Emily glared at Nick. "You don't scare me, you creep."

"That's where you're wrong. Not only will ya be scared of me, but you're gonna find out I'm a better lover than all your college studs … or that hayseed over there."

Glenn, the hayseed, appeared unconcerned. He sipped his coffee while bracing his forearm against the fireplace mantle.

"You? A lover?" Emily exploded into a fit of mocking laughter. "You haven't a clue."

A brief, pained look morphed into rage. Then Nick cursed and yanked Emily's golden locks. "Don't get smart with me." A greedy mouth bore down on Emily's. She moaned and twisted, kicking him in the shins.

"Augh!" Nick sprang back, pressing his hand against his mouth. He cursed. "She bit me."

Luke sniggered. "Did ya say ya took a fancy t' tigers? Looks like that's what yer tanglin' with."

Glenn placed his cup on the mantle then turned around and watched.

Decker stepped through the doorway.

Nick wiped his mouth. Blood smeared his lip and hand. He stared at it. His body tensed, and his breathing grew harsh. "Girl, you're askin' for it!" Eyes blazing, he doubled his fists.

Emily spat in his face. The slimy mockery oozed down his

reddened face.

A silent explosion seemed to burst inside Nick's head. He grappled for his gun. Face drawn tight, he pointed it at Emily. "Nobody does that to me. *Nobody.*"

Emily's face drained of color. Her body stiffened. "Are you crazy?"

Beth couldn't move. She couldn't breathe. She wanted to run to Glenn and feel his strong arms around her, but her feet felt glued to the floor.

Luke jumped to his feet, shoving his chair aside.

Decker yelled, "Put that gun away, you fool!"

Nick shook his head. "Nothin' doin'." He stared coldly at Emily. "And to think ya could have had it so good." He pulled back on the hammer.

"Emily, duck!" Kathrin shrieked.

In the blink of an eye, Glenn suddenly appeared at Emily's side, forcing the gun barrel upward.

Nick squeezed the trigger.

The pistol exploded. The ear-splitting blast drove shock waves through Beth. Everything seemed to move in slow motion. She watched in horror as the bullet pierced Glenn, hurtling his body backward. He struggled to regain his footing, but to no avail. Arms reached out, but they grasped nothing. His body crashed to the floor.

Beth's hand flew to her mouth. She froze, staring. The other girls' screams pierced the air. The stench of gun smoke slapped Beth in the face.

With an agonized moan, Glenn's hand shot to his chest. He grimaced and rolled onto his side, as though he were trying to lessen the pain.

Beth's breath caught. *Did the bullet penetrate his heart? Will he die? Please, not Glenn.* Tears flooded her eyes.

Slow motion sped up to normal. The ringing in Beth's ears quieted, but her terror at Glenn's possible fate did not.

Kathrin squeezed Emily's arm.

Luke rushed to Glenn's side.

Nick cussed a blue streak then yelled, "He got in the way. I was just fixin' to scare her, that's all."

Decker flew at Nick, slamming his knuckles headlong into Nick's jaw. "You *fool*!"

Nick smashed into a chair and sent it crashing down with him.

Decker towered over the gasping man. "How do we find our way to the border *now*?"

Nick didn't answer. With his hand to his jaw, he scrambled to his feet and escaped outside.

Luke laid his hand on Glenn's shoulder. "Ya okay, Son?" Concern deepened his voice. "Where did he get you?" The old man rolled Glenn onto his back.

Beth pushed herself on wobbly knees to Glenn's side.

Kathrin knelt beside them. "I'm a student nurse. Want me to look?"

Luke nodded.

With visible effort, Glenn spoke between short breaths. "I'm sure … there must have been … a better way." His facial muscles tightened.

Blood soaked the plaid material near Glenn's left shoulder. Kathrin unbuttoned his shirt and pushed back the flannel from his tanned chest. Dark-red blood engulfed the wound. His chest rose and fell with quick, shallow breaths.

Beth bit down hard on her lip to keep from crying out. *He seems defenseless, so much at risk.*

"The bullet has t' come out, doesn't it?" Luke looked at Kathrin with worry-worn eyes.

"Under the right conditions, that would be best," Kathrin answered, checking her patient.

"Then ya best get t' hustling and take it out here and now."

Kathrin sucked in a shocked breath. "I can't do that."

"Yer a nurse, ain't ya?"

"A *student* nurse, yes. But this man needs a hospital, where it's sterile and well-lit and—"

"I'll fetch my propane lantern."

"That's not enough!" Kathrin insisted. "He needs a surgeon, surgical instruments, anesthetics, probably some blood. There's no way I—"

"You can use this-here knife." Luke pulled one from inside his boot. "There's whiskey in the cupboard."

Glenn's blue eyes glistened up at them. "If you'll help me up, I think …" He rolled over and pushed himself to a sitting position. Beth and Kathrin helped. He flinched. "I can make it until … we get to a doctor."

No sooner was Glenn on his feet, when he turned pale and unsteady. Luke grabbed his arm and led him to the cot. Cringing, Glenn eased himself down onto the mattress. He lay back and sighed.

"Would you please free my hands so I can clean the wound and bandage your son?" Kathrin asked.

Luke removed Kathrin's restraints then Beth's.

Beth gathered the rags and soap Kathrin requested, while her mind worked to grasp it all. *That mysterious outlaw took a bullet for Emily. I've got to rethink things.*

Items in hand, Beth raced to Glenn's side. His eyes were closed, his head turned away. "Is he going to be all right?"

Kathrin sopped up the blood. "His breathing is shallow but rapid. His pulse is weak. How far away is a doctor?"

Luke rubbed his brow. "A good day's ride."

"I don't think he could last a full day on a horse." Kathrin looked up from her work into Luke's worry-creased face.

"He wouldn't. That's why *yer* taking the bullet out."

"I'm not experienced with a scalpel, much less a pocket knife. That bullet could be lodged in his lung or next to an artery. There's no blood on hand … nothing. He could die."

"His chances are better here with you than riding. Now get to it." In three strides, Luke drew near the fireplace. He squatted and held a roughly used blade over red-hot coals.

Decker dragged a hand across his beard, studied Glenn then shook his shoulder. "Wake up. C'mon."

He received a muffled, "Huh?"

"Tell us how to get to the border—in case you croak after these women get through butchering you."

Glenn opened his eyes.

Decker bent low over Glenn. "C'mon, man! Tell us what route to take. Uncle Luke, write it down."

Luke searched for a notepad and pen. Ten minutes of strained conversation with Glenn, and the task was done. He closed his eyes.

"All right, let's get outta here." Decker snatched the directions out of Luke's hand.

"I ain't leavin' 'til I know Glenn's gonna be okay." Luke glared at Decker.

"Fine." Decker headed for the door. "But I'm not hanging around 'til the cops find us." Before he shut the door, he glanced back at his uncle. "Are you leaving today then?"

"Yeah, after the operation. I'll catch up."

Decker nodded. The door closed.

Like a whirlwind, Nick burst in and snatched up a couple of thermoses. He stopped short in front of Beth. "Gotta go, sweet thing." He pecked Beth on the lips.

Beth stepped back and shuddered. Her hand shot to her mouth.

"See ya around, Bethie Baby." Then he whistled his eerie notes and rushed through the doorway.

Beth spit and scrubbed off Nick's kiss. "Yuck! Am I ever glad he's leaving."

"Maybe they *aren't* going to kill us or take us with them," Em whispered.

Kathrin leaned in closer. "And I doubt Luke will."

Beth and her friends stood at the dingy window and watched two of their kidnappers ride off with two horses in tow.

Guarded relief flooded Beth.

Tied to the rail, the brown horse whinnied and pulled on its rein. Luke's gun still hung at his side, but Decker had taken all the other weapons.

Old Luke's frail figure faded into the shadows of the far side of the room, where a little door squeaked as he removed a heavy, slightly used bottle of whiskey. He handed the substitute anesthesia to Beth. "Give this t' him now. I'll fetch the lantern." He placed his knife in Kathrin's palm.

Beth poured the whiskey into a tin cup. Kathrin lifted Glenn's head and shoulders onto her lap. He looked too big and heavy for her. "Drink this."

Glenn sipped as the liquid slid down his throat.

After a while, the whiskey appeared to be doing its work to dull the pain. Glenn's face and body relaxed. Eventually, he opened his eyes. The corners of his mouth turned up.

Kathrin responded in a like manner.

"How did I get so lucky to be served this way by a nice, little gal like you?"

"Aw, you're just drunk." Kathrin's smile widened. "I bet

you say that to all the girls."

"No, only the nice ones."

Beth hid a smile behind her hand at Glenn's amusing behavior.

"Finish this." Kathrin offered another cupful.

After a few more drinks, Glenn struggled to look around. "Where's ... Beth?" His words slurred.

"Over there." Kathrin pointed, but Glenn was clearly too plastered to recognize her.

His words ran over one another. "Beth's so sweet ... I love her. Take care of her, would you?" His eyes closed, and he was out cold.

Beth felt her cheeks blaze with embarrassment, but she was deeply touched. Adoration spread through her as she gazed on Glenn's quiet face. His appreciation not only delighted Beth, but it also gave her a greater sense of value.

Kathrin eased Glenn's head down on the pillow without waking him.

Luke brightened the shadowed cabin with a camp lantern. The clothes line cords dangled from his other hand. "Here. Best tie him down. There's no more whiskey than what's left in the bottle, and it won't keep him under for long. He'll be squirming soon enough."

Beth helped bind Glenn's unresisting, limp body to the bed frame. He lay shirtless, unconscious, bound, and bleeding. *He's going to die if no one helps him!* Beth thought. *It's up to us women to save his life.*

Kathrin drew a deep breath, then pulled a red bandana over her nose. "Lord, please guide my hands and give me wisdom. Please, heal him without any complications or infection." She turned to Emily. "Keep the wound clear of blood and check his vitals often. Beth, you hold him still whenever he begins to come around and feels the knife."

Beth placed her cold hands on Glenn's biceps and fuzzy chest. Her knees weakened when Kathrin sliced into Glenn's bleeding shoulder. The contents in her stomach threatened to rise. She turned her head.

The substitute anesthesia only worked for a few minutes. Too soon the patient's breathing became irregular. His muscles tightened. He moaned.

"Emily, sop up the blood." Kathrin sounded alarmed. "Quick!"

Beth caught a glimpse of Glenn's red blood pouring out around the knife as it dug into flesh. Immediately, she refocused on his face.

Glenn's dark head turned away from its fluffy support, and his once peaceful brow furrowed. The muscles in his cheek and temple grew tight. His body tensed up beneath Beth's hands.

Thick, long, lashes opened to liquid-blue eyes, the eyes Beth feared she might never see again. He tried to raise an arm but couldn't. He stared, clearly confused. Suddenly, anxious distress and an urgency to escape marked his face and strained his muscles.

"Here, Son, bear down on this." Luke put a leather piece in Glenn's mouth.

Sweat beaded his skin as he flinched, gasped, and strained against the cords. The veins in his temple and neck swelled. "Water," he croaked around the leather piece.

Glenn's defensive lurches made it difficult to retrieve the bullet. "Beth, would you hold his head and shoulders still?" Kathrin's voice sounded intense.

Beth got down on her knees and wrapped her left arm around his head, running her fingers through his thick, silky hair. A faint iron smell of blood reached her nose. Her fingertips pressed the other side of his drawn face. His skin was cold and clammy.

Glenn's efforts to escape became weaker. The leather fell from his mouth. His head lolled to the side.

Beth felt the stirrings of desperation. Glenn was too dear to lose. She began to pray but was brought back by the sound of Glenn's faint, broken voice pleading, "Please"—a tortured pause, a fast breathe of air as if it were all he could do to force out the words—"stop."

Compassion and a fierce desire to relieve Glenn's suffering overwhelmed Beth.

Engrossed in her work, Kathrin didn't seem to realize the hell she was putting Glenn through. "Stop it," Beth pleaded. "We're killing him." She held back her burning tears.

"I've just about got it."

"If ya don't take it out, my son will have suffered fer nothing." Luke's voice was heavy with grief. "It must come out."

Beth caught a glimpse of a hand jabbing and twisting the shiny blade like digging a rock out of a garden. Glenn yelled in torment, stiffened his body, and pressed his head into the pillow.

Beth's eyes flooded, her heart breaking.

Glenn uttered a muffled sigh, then his body went limp. His face relaxed, his head settled on the pillow, and his doubled fists opened, no longer fighting the ropes.

Beth couldn't see his chest moving up and down. She saw only Glenn's unnaturally pale face and red blood spilling all over the knife. "Oh, dear God, no! Kathrin! Did we kill him?"

Luke rushed over. Bony, wrinkled fingers touched the side of Glenn's neck. It was an insignificant gesture that held so much importance.

Beth held her breath.

"He passed out."

"Thankfully, he's not suffering anymore." Kathrin continued digging.

Beth curled her hand around Glenn's. How cold and lifeless it felt!

She shuddered. *Please God! If You're up there, please don't take him.* Tears gushed. *He's not such a bad guy. I know it's not right that I come to You only when I'm in trouble, so I can't blame You if You don't listen to me now. After all, why should You? But I hope You are listening. And I pray You'll let Glenn live. Please, God.*

11. A Search Plane

"I've got it!" Kathrin rejoiced and held up the lead culprit, which dripped with Glenn's blood.

Chills ran up Beth's spine.

"Thank God it wasn't in a critical place." Kathrin said. "Now, if no infection sets in, he should be okay."

Kathrin mopped up Glenn's blood and wrapped a strip of sheet she'd torn around his shoulder and chest. Her patient's unconscious face held a worn-out expression, but at last it was over.

Luke retrieved his knife from the make-shift operating tray on the chair. "Ladies, I thank ya kindly for yer help." He picked up a pen and paper and left the cabin for a time.

When Luke returned, he grabbed a thermos and lunch, went to his son's side, and curled a wrinkled hand around Glenn's. After a moment he brushed the side of Glenn's face, and then tucked the blankets in around him.

"Take care of my son for me, please." Luke kept his eyes on Glenn. "He's—" His voice cracked. "He's a good man." Luke turned and walked stiffly out the door.

With the old cowboy and horse still in sight, Beth and her friends stepped outside and watched him ride off into the woods.

"Wahoo!" Kathrin threw her arms up in celebration. "We're alive. And free. Thank You, God."

"Hurray! We can go home." The girls squealed, high fived,

jumped in the air and hugged each other.

"I thought for sure they would rape and kill us." Emily's slate-gray eyes stared blankly for a second. Then with a tone of urgency, she said, "We should leave now, before they come back."

"What about Glenn?" Beth's brow wrinkled with concern.

"What about him?" Emily shrugged.

"Glenn can't travel. Not yet, anyway. And we're certainly not going to leave him here to die alone and without a burial." Kathrin gave Emily a disbelieving look. "Lord have mercy, girl."

"How long before he can travel?" Em twisted her watch.

"A week, ten days, I'd say."

"A week or ten days?" Emily shouted. "Are you kidding? I'm *not* waiting around for those monsters to come back." She threw her arm in the direction they'd last seen their kidnappers. "I'm leaving *today*." She cast a pleading gaze on Beth. "You'll go with me, won't you?"

"No. I don't want to get lost. I'll wait for Glenn to show us the way. Maybe a rescue team will find us before that."

"Yeah, *maybe*. He'll probably die after we've waited a week for him. It'll be all for nothing." Sparkly lavender fingernails dragged through Emily's golden locks. "There's hardly any food left. Don't worry, the crook won't die alone. We birdbrains will die along with him."

Wow, Beth thought. *Em's sure working herself into a tizzy.*

"It's because of *them* we're in this dilemma," Emily raged, pacing. "Why do *we* have to die?"

Beth stomped up to Emily and got in her face. "Because you'd be the one shot if it hadn't been for that *crook*. Is this how you thank Glenn for risking his life for you?"

"Okay, okay! All right already."

"I need a bath. Hey, you want to take a dip in the stream?" Kathrin brightened. "C'mon. Let's get some towels and soap."

Before long the young city dwellers tromped through a mountain meadow. Four steps into it, Em said, "I'm leaving my clothes on in case those crazies come back."

Beth glanced around. It was her first real chance to take in the beauty of her surroundings. Across the valley to the south, jagged rock cliffs burst into view. To the north, a mountain range sheltered their valley. The sun's brilliance reflected off the dazzling snowcaps, cutting a crystal-clear sculpture against the blue sky.

Beth looked behind her. The log cabin lay nestled at the base of the mountain range, basking in beauty. It added a cozy touch to God's masterpiece—not at all like a dreaded prison.

A quarter mile down the slope, the sound of water rushing over rocks enlivened Beth's spirit. The girls raced each other. Em lagged behind. Before them golden aspens hugged a sparkling stream.

Beth became energized by the adventure of exploring a winding tunnel of cool shade trees overhanging a staircase of rocks and water cascading down. The air swept cool against her cheeks. She and Kathrin laughed like children and hopped from rock to rock set above the clear, glittering water.

The booming pound of a waterfall grew louder as they climbed. Soon they couldn't hear each other's words. Their faces—even Em's—shone with excitement.

The girls rounded a corner and gasped. A thundering, massive volume of water poured from above, plunging into the fluid depths at their feet. The sun peeked through the trees, causing bright ripples in the churning water.

Beth felt the pounding waterfall through the rock where she stood. Its fine, cool mist on her face and arms invigorated her and enticed her to plunge into its depths.

Beside her, the bold, Swedish beauty dove into the shimmering pool. Fast-flowing ripples from Em's dive glistened in Beth's squinting eyes. Then Beth and Kathrin jumped in.

Icy water flooded Beth's ears. Completely submerged, the sound of the waterfall mellowed to a full-bodied rumble. Bobbing up, she faced her friends with a smile. Droplets rolled off their lashes.

The girls squealed and laughed in their hideaway paradise, trying to dunk each other while they splashed and chased around in the water. Finally exhausted, they lay back and floated.

Beth shut her eyes, relaxing in the buoyant waves. She welcomed the sun's heat as it peeked through the branches down onto her skin. Soon, Beth swam to the rock, grabbed the soap, and rubbed it across her clothed shivering body.

What a heavy, slow-moving struggle it was to pull herself up onto a rounded, warm rock! Beth sprawled out on it. It felt good to be free from those awful men.

Kathrin yelled above the rumble, "Isn't it great to be alive?" She rolled onto her elbows. "Funny how we don't appreciate life as much until we come close to losing it."

"I wonder"—Em began—"if Mom and Dad think—"

"Wait! I hear something," Kathrin shouted.

Beth held her breath and cocked her head. She heard a faraway rumbling noise. It became increasingly audible, but the thunder of the waterfall disguised it. "What is it?" she asked, quivering and wide-eyed.

Emily jumped to her feet and scanned the sky. "It's a plane! They're searching for us." Her countenance burst with joy and relief. "We're down here," she shouted at the plane.

Through the leafy canopy, Beth caught the sun bouncing off shiny, silver wings. They cheered and jumped, waving their arms. The aircraft, now overhead, buzzed right on by—that quick.

"They can't see us," Beth cried out. "No!"

Helplessly she watched the tail of the twin engine disappear over the tall trees. Her face went slack, and her shoulders drooped. It felt as though fate had played a cruel, sadistic joke on them … again. The sound dissipated, along with her hopes.

"Come on!" Emily cried. She scrambled up the embankment. Beth and Kathrin followed. Perhaps there was an outside chance the pilot would circle around and make another pass.

He didn't.

Left behind and speechless, the girls strained to hear the sound of an engine well after the plane had vanished.

"It's *possible* they saw us." Kathrin's optimism never quit. "Or maybe they'll search here again."

"We'll be home sooner or later." Beth turned and headed toward the cabin. In its wake, the airplane had stirred up painfully sweet memories of her city home. She returned to the hideout quiet and pensive.

Back at the cabin, Glenn remained unconscious. The bandage was only tinged with blood.

Fearing the return of the three stooges, the girls latched the door. "We've got to get out of these wet clothes," Kathrin suggested. "There might be something we can use in the closet." A moment later, she pulled out two of Glenn's shirts on hangers. A man's pullover sweater lay folded on an upper shelf under a straw hat and jeans.

Kathrin rose up on her tiptoes and inched the sweater out with her fingertips. Hat and jeans toppled down on her head and to the floor. She strained to replace them on the shelf. Same results—toppling garments. With a flustered grunt, she kicked the jeans into a heap on the floor.

Beth and Em chuckled.

While Beth buttoned up, she marveled that two of her could fit inside one shirt. The flannel hung down to her knees. "I didn't realize how much bigger he is than me."

Shortly, their wet clothes were drying on chairs pushed near the fireplace.

After dinner, Emily passed by Glenn. He moaned. "He's waking up," she called to the others.

Kathrin rushed over with a cup. Water spilled down her hand. Beth peered over her shoulder.

Glenn's ashen face hardly changed from his state of unconsciousness. He didn't move. He opened his eyes and stared with a lifeless daze. His expression was empty of emotion, except for suffering and weakness. Soon, his eyes closed, but no other muscles moved.

Kathrin slid her hand under Glenn's head and lifted it. "Here's some water."

He didn't respond.

Kathrin drizzled enough water to wet his lips. "Come on, Glenn. Wake up and drink this."

He opened his eyes only long enough to take a few sips. His head lolled, so Kathrin lowered him onto the pillow.

The cool night made the fireplace all the more welcome and cozy. It wasn't long before everyone was preparing for bed.

Every night from then on, the girls braced a chair under the doorknob—just in case. For defense they took glass bottles and a paring knife to bed with them. Em and Kathrin chose to sleep in the bedroom, but Beth wanted to be close by Glenn in case he needed something. The lower bunk worked.

Thoughts of life and home circulated in Beth's mind, but the dancing glow of the firelight soothed her to sleep.

In the night, the howl of wolves woke Beth. The wind kicked up. It whistled through the pines, banging something outside. The wind and the wolves howled a lonesome wail. The gusts shrieked through the fireplace chimney, causing the fire to flicker.

Beth shivered and wondered how her friends could sleep through all the noise. It left her with the ghostly sensation of being the only one left alive in the whole world.

Heavy with sleep, Beth's mind shut out the noise and dozed off.

12. The Night in a Tree

Somewhere in the Pacific Northwest's forest

The bright sunshine woke Beth. Rubbing her stiff neck, she scrutinized the wounded man across the room. He lay still.

Her feet hit the cold floor and closed the distance between them. Somehow, Glenn didn't appear as worn out as he had yesterday. His face seemed more relaxed, as if pain had eased its grip on him. Or … could it be that he was free of life's hold altogether?

Beth touched his neck and sighed in relief. Glenn was still warm. After locating the right place, she felt a slow, weak *thump-thump* against her fingertips. "Thank You, God," she whispered.

His jaw had become bristly with black whiskers, giving him a more mature, rugged look, but still attractive.

"He needs a shave, doesn't he?" Kathrin came up behind Beth. "Sorry, I didn't mean to startle you. Is he all right?"

"Well, his heart's beating."

Kathrin nodded. "Good. I'll check on him as soon as I get back from the privy."

Beth leaned on the window sill and followed Kathrin's familiar, slight figure as she jogged down the dirt-worn path. Beth waited her turn.

When Beth returned, Kathrin held up her wrist and

pointed to her watch. "Beth, do you realize it's ten-fifty?"

"That late? We must have been tired. I don't think we slept well while those guys were here."

Emily dawdled out of the bedroom, her hair disheveled. "What else is there to do around this dump anyway, but sleep?"

Kathrin checked on Glenn. "Good, he seems to be improving."

At breakfast, Beth paused between bites. "I wonder why God allowed us to be kidnapped."

"I don't believe in God." Emily sipped coffee then set it down. "Why don't we work on SOS signals this morning?"

They stepped off the porch and out into the sunshine and fresh air. Birds did what they always do … chirped cheerfully.

Like chickens pecking at grain, the girls bent down and gathered rocks. Kathrin carried an armload to the SOS site. "I believe God has a reason for everything, including our abduction," she said. "And He can make good come from bad."

Beth did not ask what possible reason God could have, but continued collecting in silence.

On her hands and knees, Kathrin positioned the rocks until they formed the word 'HELP' in large, capital letters. "Sometimes I wonder if God is paying us special attention," she mused. "Like right now. There's a gentle breeze. Is that His loving touch? I wonder if the beautiful songs of birds might be one way He sings His love to us."

Em chuckled. "Yeah, a hideous vulture could be perched in the dogwood outside our kitchen window instead of a finch."

"I started working on a poem about God," Kathrin went on as if Emily had not spoken. "Can't remember it exactly, but it goes something like this. 'Did you ever think that He's kissing you affectionately with each delicate touch of a fragile snowflake that melts like unto His heart as soon as it feels the warmth of your cheek? And the bright, pink sunrise—sprung from the dreams of God—was created out of His longing to show you His joy in you. As great and big as His mind is, His heart is also.'"

"That's beautiful, Kathrin," Beth said. "God being involved in the details of my life and feeling about us in such a close, loving way is new to me."

"Oh, *how* He loves us." Kathrin's eyes sparkled.

Beth put the last rock on the P and rubbed the dirt off her hands.

After lunch, the girls spent the rest of the afternoon trying to devise some snares like they'd seen on TV. They dug a hole and covered it over with small branches and leaves. Three city girls stood around their poorly camouflaged hole. "I've got to make it better, because I am *not* going to be so vulnerable ever again," Emily vowed.

Kathrin left to check on Glenn. She returned saying, "He's sleeping like a baby."

The girls searched for possible weapons a short time, but twilight was already upon them. They plodded back to the cabin. When they walked inside, it looked as if Glenn hadn't moved. Kathrin checked Glenn's vital signs while Emily stoked the fire and heated up some soup.

Beth collected the things Kathrin requested to change Glenn's dressings.

"Beth, please hold him up so I can wrap this bandage around him." Kathrin held out a strip of torn sheet.

It took all of Beth's strength to lift Glenn's upper body to a sitting position. He moaned and then slipped into semi consciousness. His head fell back. "Goodness, he's like a heavy rag doll." She grunted with effort.

Once Beth got Glenn into place, his head came to rest against her shoulder. His hair lay silky against her neck. *This is nice holding him and taking care of him.*

Kathrin washed his wound and wrapped the bandage around his chest.

"He's coming around," Kathrin announced. "Would you give him this"—she handed a cup of water to Beth—"while I get him some broth? It would do him good."

"Come on, Glenn." Beth brought the water to his mouth. "Wake up and drink this, sleepyhead."

Glenn's long, dark lashes slowly opened. Half-awake, he slurped the water, then the broth. "I gotta go," he mumbled.

The three girls tugged Glenn to this feet. He wavered and leaned so heavily on Beth that she thought they were going down.

"Whoa, Glenn," Emily pulled him upright. "Stay with us." With effort and time they accomplished the task and then put Glenn back to bed.

That day's strenuous physical labor motivated the women to crash early.

Beth slept hard and woke up refreshed.

Thank goodness there was no lineup at the outhouse. Making fast tracks for the door, Beth didn't notice any change in Glenn except that dark whiskers now concealed his jaw.

On her first step outside, Beth paused. Even though the valley was still in pre-dawn darkness, the mountain's snowy tips were aglow with a glorious pink hue from the sun's first rays.

Shortly, the girls raked the coals in the fireplace, added

wood, and prepared for the day. The noise woke Emily and Glenn.

Beth helped Glenn recline. She offered him water and thought, *Good his bandage has only a tinge of blood. It's great to have him back. His new look is appealing, but I hope he shaves.*

Beth sat down carefully on the edge of his cot. "Do you realize you've been asleep for almost two days? You must be Rip Van Winkle in the flesh."

He blinked and gazed up at her.

His azure eyes affected her every time.

With a slight head shake, Glenn asked, "What day is it?"

"Sunday."

Emily entered the cabin from her early morning jaunt.

Glenn slowly turned his head to search the room. "Where is everyone?" His gaze became pained, obviously worried and puzzled.

A sympathetic cord struck in Beth's heart. "Oh, you mean Decker, Nick, and Luke?"

He waited.

"They're gone," Emily said, "and good riddance. Your friends packed up and left Friday afternoon."

Glenn studied Emily then turned back to Beth. His eyes searched hers as though he didn't believe Emily and wanted Beth to deny it.

Beth rested her hand on his arm. "Yes, they left … with all of the horses."

"With the money and guns too." Emily drew near.

Glenn's eyes widened; a tanned brow furrowed. "Dad left? Why?" He spoke with a disbelieving voice, and wincing he sat up. "Why didn't he stick around at least until I woke up?" He swung his legs over the bedside.

"I don't know." Beth swallowed. "They thought you

wouldn't make it, you know, riding a horse."

Briefly, their eyes met. Her hand found its way to his warm, hairy wrist as she tried to comfort him.

Glenn looked away and stared in silence a moment. "Did Dad leave a message or anything?"

"Mmm, no." When they began to walk away, Glenn attempted to get out of bed.

Kathrin hurried back to his side and restrained him. His infirmity made it easy for her to push him down. "What are you doing?"

Between wrenches, he asked, "Would you look to see if Dad left something … in my coat pocket or in my hat?"

"Like what?" Kathrin asked.

"If you'll let go of me, I'll find out."

"No. You stay here. We'll look."

After rummaging through his pockets, Emily said, "I think I found something." Holding a piece of paper, she ambled toward the cowboy and read aloud.

Glenn, Son,

Ya couldn't be closer t' me had ya been born t' me. So it doesn't make my leeving any easier. Yer not like the rest of us, and I'm sorry I got ya involved in the first place. The only way I can correct it now is t' leeve ya behind. Without me I know you'll go strait if ya can ever get out of this mess I got ya in.

The way yer hurt we both know ya wouldn't have lasted 2 days on the trail. You'll be best right here with them nurses a-tending you. I'll be asking God t' look after ya, and remember I'm the one who's supposed t' meet Him first. Don't be fretting bout me. I'd have told ya this face t' face, but you've been out the whole time. Besides, this way I don't have t' put up with yer goll-dang wrangling t' go with me.

Ya know ya really rate with me if ya get a note, especially one this long. I haven't writ one like this since Germany when I asked Harriet t' marry me. Well, the ol' boy is chomping at the bit so's I better git. Take care of yerself for me. Yer a good man, my Son. I couldn't be prouder. I wish ya all the best.

Love, Dad

Emily handed the good-bye note to its rightful owner.

Glenn stared lovingly at the paper as though he were holding part of the author. A bittersweet sadness filled his eyes as they traced across the paper. It appeared now that his wounds were more than physical.

The thought of never seeing his dad again had obviously affected Glenn deeply, but he tried to disguise his feelings with a few casual words. "It's surprising Mom could read his proposal"—his voice mellowed—"the way Dad spells." Obviously, he strained to hold back his emotions.

Before Beth looked away, she caught a glimpse of tears brimming his eyelashes. To give him some privacy, she started breakfast. It didn't take long to prepare jam and bread.

Later, the girls took inventory and discovered that the food supply might last a week if they rationed it carefully.

Emily perked up. "Why don't we go pick berries? My grandma and I used to pick them in the mountains together."

"Sounds like fun." Beth agreed.

"Yeah." Then Kathrin asked, "Glenn, do you know where there's any berries around here?"

He blinked. "Huckleberries grow at the base of the snowcapped mountain a couple of miles from here."

"I know what huckleberries look like." Emily stood tall.

"Thanks, Glenn. We're kind of bored, so we'll do some exploring as well. We'll be gone most of the afternoon." Kathrin checked his bandage. "Do you think you'll be all right alone?"

"I can stay with him," Beth volunteered.

"No, I'm okay." Glenn sounded confident. "Go ahead. I'll probably sleep."

Kathrin warned him of their "snare," the camouflaged hole.

He smiled.

The girls put food and water within Glenn's reach, gathered containers for berries, and left. They rounded the corner of the building and headed for the mountain. When they'd traveled about two miles, they split up.

Beth searched the wooded area for some time and began to wonder. Finally, Emily discovered the huckleberry patch and called the others over. The berries were a nice change from cowboy cuisine. With a potful and a belly-full, the girls explored the area. Tired, they headed home, singing as loudly as they wished.

The setting sun dipped behind the tip of the mountains, its rays beaming around the peaks. Beautiful, but with a warning of darkness soon to fall, the sun's light was disappearing faster than they had anticipated.

"We'd better hurry!" Beth said. "It's a long way back."

They stepped up the pace, but in no time darkness was upon them.

Beth could feel and hear sticks snapping under her feet. She smelled the damp, fallen leaves, but she could hardly make out the form of her friends. It was as though they had vanished in the blackness. She shivered.

"If we don't find the cabin in the next five minutes, we'll have to stay out here tonight," Emily said. "We could really get lost if we just wander around."

Emily was right, but the thought rattled Beth.

All at once, Beth stopped short. The distant howl of a

coyote—or was it a wolf—echoed through the night. Wide-eyed, she flung out her arms, seeking the comforting touch of her friends. Their silence screamed fear. "What are we going to do?" The dread in Beth's hushed voice hung in the air.

"We're going to climb a tree." Emily sounded brave.

Through the blackness resounded another bone-chilling howl. "I think they're getting closer." Kathrin's grip restricted the circulation to Beth's arm.

"All you have to do is put those strong hands of yours around their throats, Kathrin, and they wouldn't stand a chance."

"Oh, sorry." She released Beth's tingling arm. "They're way too close. I'm climbing a tree."

"Me too," the others said in unison.

A few moments passed. "Ouch! Stupid tree." After several scratches and a couple of bumps on her head, Beth perched herself several branches high in a tree that had lost some leaves. No matter how much she wiggled to get comfortable, nothing worked. A broken-off twig stabbed her in the backside. "Hey, uh, is anyone close to me?" she called out, ignoring the pain in her tush.

"I'm over here." Kathrin's soprano voice sounded close. "I'm still trying to get into this God-forsaken tree."

"Yikes!" Beth yelled. "Hurry! They're coming."

"I would be, but this twig won't let go of my pants." After a few grunts and groans, Kathrin yelled, "I'm up."

For some time the three city slickers sat quietly, listening and shivering.

"The wolves must be circling us. I don't know about you, but I'm freezing." Kathrin's disembodied voice reached across the blackness.

"Yeah, my nose is running and my fingers are icy," Beth

said. "If God helped us survive abduction, surely He doesn't intend for us to die like frozen vultures in a tree."

"Funny you should choose vultures, creatures of death. Why not eagles?" Emily's far-flung voice sounded far off in the distance.

"I don't feel majestic right now. I feel more like a vulture hunched over in the night, with the cold wind blowing through my sparse feathers and bald head."

"Very funny, Beth." Emily's words found their way through the dark to Beth's ears.

The moon rose over the eastern horizon. Scattered, black clouds slinked across its glowing face. "Creepy. Even the clouds are sneaking around." Their spooky sight, the cutting wind, and the proximity of the wolves' howl sent chills up Beth's spine.

All at once a riotous fluttering mixed with squeaks, and a hair-raising scream resounded through the black forest. Beth jumped, almost falling out of her tree.

"Something hit me," Kathrin screeched. Her cry was followed by the sounds of panic and wrestling.

Heart racing, Beth crouched down and stiffened. She looked around wildly. "Kathrin, are you okay? Is it a bear?" A helplessness overcame her.

"What hit you?" Terror gripped Emily's voice.

"Ooh! Claws … caught in my hair." Kathrin shrieked. The flapping and rustling continued. Then the noise stopped.

"Lord, have mercy!" Kathrin exclaimed. "They're gone. I think it's bats."

Beth drew in a deep sigh, but before her nerves had time to settle, Emily burst out, "What's that?"

"Stop scaring me," Beth protested. "What's *what*?"

"That over there."

"Where? I can't see where you're pointing."

"I thought I saw a flash of light."

A glimmer of hope welled up in Beth. "Do you think it's the cabin?"

"I don't think so. It disappeared. But it was a light." She paused. "There it is again, way down there. It's moving."

"Moving?" Beth asked.

13. A Light in the Distance

Did you hear that?" Kathrin used the same urgent tone. "It sounds like a man."

Beth strained her ears and eyes into the blackness. She spotted the faint light, flickering in the distance. "Yes, I see it." Hope swelled.

"Maybe it's a search party. We're over here!" Emily shouted.

From the far expanse of darkness came a faint voice. "Kathrin, Emily?"

"Over here!" Kathrin called out. "We're going to make it. Lord, You are so good. How can I thank You enough?"

They all cheered.

"Listen." Beth shushed her friends. "I think it's Glenn." "Glenn?" she shouted.

"Beth?"

What sweet music to my ears. Her heart expanded. They had reached out to each other through the infinite night. Beth couldn't help but love him.

"Yay, Glenn!" Kathrin and Emily shouted.

A sudden fear pierced Beth. "How did he get here with that hole in his shoulder and being so weak?"

"Who knows? Maybe we're closer to the cabin than we thought," Emily answered. "Who cares? I'm getting down out of this birdhouse."

A few more scratches descending through the branches

and Beth planted her feet on the ground. Concerned over Glenn's condition, she suggested they head toward the light.

Kathrin agreed. They grabbed up their huckleberries, found a primitive blind-man's cane, hung onto each other, and edged their way inch by inch toward the light.

Beth called out Glenn's name, but only crickets answered. "Why won't he respond?" Her stomach churned.

"He's probably too weak or"—Kathrin's voice jerked. "Ouch! I tripped. My toe."—a second of muted moans—"or maybe he passed out or something."

All sorts of horrible *somethings*— even bears—came to Beth's mind.

Dozens of tiny nowhere steps farther, they rounded yet another clump of trees. On the ground in the middle of utter blackness, the camp lantern sat burning brightly. Glenn's hand rested close by it, but his body lay motionless.

Beth and Kathrin ran to his side. "Glenn, are you all right?"

No response.

Beth's knees weakened. She dropped onto her haunches beside Glenn.

Kathrin grabbed the lantern and joined her. She raised the light, allowing them to see his face. He lay sprawled on his stomach, his head to the side with one arm above. Kathrin checked him over. "He passed out. He should be okay once we get him back inside the cabin and warmed up."

Beth tipped her head back and closed her eyes. "Thank God." Gazing at Glenn again, she added, "It's amazing that he would rouse himself from his sickbed to look for us?"

Together, the girls turned him over. Blood soaked his shirt. Had all that activity reopened his wound? Would he recover? Beth studied his calm, attractive face and begged God's mercy on the outlaw.

They lifted his head and hefty shoulders. The movement stirred him. "How are you feeling?" Kathrin asked.

Glenn blinked then opened his eyes. His hand rushed to hold his wound. "I must have blacked out. Is everyone okay?"

"Yeah, we're just cold." Emily rubbed her arms.

"But thanks to you we'll be fine now." Beth touched his shoulder.

Kathrin held the lantern, while Beth and Emily helped Glenn to his feet. When Beth wrapped her arm around his warm, solid waist, a fondness flooded her, but she didn't fight it.

"This way," Glenn murmured and led them through the blackness. Then he draped his arm over Beth's shoulder and hugged her tightly to his side. Whatever his reason, it helped her to stop shaking from the cold.

They slowly made their way down a timbered embankment. Before long, the cabin's lantern lights became visible, shining not far in the distance.

He leaned heavier on them, and at times he lowered his head as his stride became more unstable. A few feet from the door, Glenn stumbled. Beth blocked his fall with a quick hand slapped against his chest.

He sucked in a sharp breath.

"Sorry. The door's right in front of us," Beth assured him.

His body shook.

"I think he's cold," Beth said. "He's shivering."

"We've got to get him inside … quick." Kathrin urged.

Step by step, they hauled Glenn up the porch stairs and into the cabin. Kathrin ran ahead and pulled the footstool away from the rocker. "Let's set him by the fire on the footstool while I clean him up."

"He's still trembling a lot, Kathrin." Beth said.

"Hypothermia and weakness from blood loss could cause shock and shivering. We've got to warm him quickly. Would you get him some broth and coffee, Beth? Emily, would you put wood on the fire?"

Kathrin pushed Glenn's shirt open, and cleansed the wound. Before they helped him back to bed, she rewrapped his shoulder and changed his blood-stained shirt.

Glenn gulped down two cups of broth, then coffee. It didn't take long before he fell asleep.

Kathrin tucked the blankets around her patient. "He should have been in a hospital, instead of searching for us in the forest." She yawned. "Ben Franklin once said, 'My feet are dead. Let's go to bed.'"

"I think it was 'Early to bed, early to rise.'" Emily checked out her reflection in a small mirror and fluffed her hair.

"That's what Ben rewrote the next morning when his mind was clear." Kathrin headed to the back bedroom. Emily followed.

The room grew quiet except for the restful sounds of the snapping fire and crickets. The howling wolves—or coyotes—that had frightened them earlier posed no threat, thanks to the log walls.

An oil lamp glowed on the table. Beth was grateful for its light, wishing to etch Glenn's features in her memory.

I can't do this when he's awake. This is my only opportunity. After all, he'll soon either be in the slammer or a fugitive on the run. Beth walked to his bedside and enjoyed watching him sleep to her heart's content.

Memories of Glenn's kiss rushed in, provoking the desire to kiss him again. Beth bent down, her face within inches of his. Their lips almost touched. Instead, she lifted her head and returned to her study of Glenn. *Is this what falling in love is like?*

Goodness, it's powerful.

I would love to know him better. It hurts to think that after this, I may never see him again. A terrible hollowness gnawed inside. There seemed no way to change things. Any future together looked impossible.

Beth crawled between the cold, lonely covers of her bunk. Imagining her future without the kind-hearted fugitive seemed empty. She wanted to be there when he was laughing, hurting, or lonely, but she wouldn't be.

Accept the fact that there's no future with him, and stop torturing yourself.

Tears rolled down Beth's temples into her ears and dampened her pillow. She snagged a tissue from her pocket. "I got along fine without you before I met you, Glenn McKlain, and I can survive after," she whispered. "But I don't know how I'm going to do it."

Grief poured from her breaking heart. With the most gut-wrenching decision of her life settled, Beth battled to be strong and get some sleep. She fell asleep between tears.

After a long, rough night, morning arrived. Beth dragged herself from the bunk with a moan. A headache pounded behind eyes that felt like sandpaper. She didn't allow herself one glimpse of Glenn.

"What's the matter?" Kathrin asked.

"I've got a headache."

"How about some Motrin?" Kathrin offered.

"We better save them for Glenn." It felt good to say his name, even if Beth dared not acknowledge his existence.

Beth skipped breakfast and escaped outside to the

refreshing morning air. After trying to shake off the effects of last night's inward struggle, she took a deep breath then pushed forward to face life.

When she returned, Emily set her coffee cup down. "We should hike up the mountain this morning. We may see a city or something familiar. Then we'll know which direction to go."

"Magnificent idea, but let's be back in the cabin before sundown this time," Kathrin said.

"You think?" Emily gave her a side glance.

Kathrin checked on Glenn. "On second thought, I should stay behind and take care of my patient."

During the hike, Beth rarely entered into conversation.

"You still have a headache?" Emily asked.

"It's gone." Beth kept her eyes on the path. "I just want to go home." Her voice cracked, and her eyes burned.

"So do we all."

The climb up the mountain face was more difficult than both of them had anticipated. After trampling through crusty snow with inadequate shoes, Beth's feet were cold, tingly, and wet.

Once on top, the view took her breath away. At this altitude Beth could see bright turquoise lakes settled among the white peaks. She felt as if she were standing on the top of the world. She stretched her arms out at the expanse of mountain crests as far as she could see. After looking around and seeing no sign of civilization, the women retraced their steps.

Their noisy entrance into the cabin woke Glenn. A quick glimpse told Beth he had gained strength, for which she was grateful. He sat up on the bed, swung his legs over the edge, paused, and then walked to the stuffed rocker, gingerly lowering himself onto it.

"I'm feeling better," he said in response to Beth's

surprised expression. "I've already been up and around today with Kathrin's help." He pointed to his chin and grinned. "See? I shaved."

"But you still need to rest after last night's forest wandering," Kathrin insisted.

Emily and Beth stood before the fireplace, reaching their hands out to the heat. Once warmed, Beth and Kathrin prepared dinner, while Emily recounted their adventures to a male audience of one.

When dinner was ready, Glenn insisted on sitting with them around the table. They ate by the twinkling light of the fireplace and the lamps. Beth kept her attention on her soup bowl to avoid eye contact with Glenn.

A few bites later, she drew in a long breath. *It's not working to pretend Glenn doesn't exist.* She couldn't help but enjoy his company. *How will I ever get over him?*

Emily also made the best of Glenn's presence. She flirted with him like she did with all men, but he barely responded. Deep down, it hurt Beth to see how friendly and how much fun her friends were having with him. She longed to let go and join in, but she had to keep her distance. Otherwise, it would hurt all the more when they went their separate ways.

The wind kicked up, howling through the trees and banging the stable door. The flames in the fireplace flickered and roared with each burst of air gusting down the rock chimney.

Lightening flashed, and a deafening crack of thunder sent them reeling from their seats. A torrent of rain pounded the roof.

Emily swung the door open. The fresh breeze chased away the odor of lamp oil and smoke, replacing it with the fresh, sweet smell of rain. Bucketsful beat down on the porch and the roof. Beth and her friends peered out into the wet darkness, only to be splattered by the cool, refreshing raindrops bouncing off the porch's wooden floor and railing.

"Does it always come on so fast up here?" Emily asked.

"Sometimes." Glenn leaned against the door frame.

The chilly wind blowing on Beth's damp arm sent a shiver though her.

"Ohhh! I'm cold." Kathrin returned inside to the warmth of the fireplace. The others followed.

Emily spotted an old-time popcorn popper hanging on the wall near the fireplace. Glenn pointed out the bag of kernels, and the cabin soon seemed all the more homey with the aroma of popcorn teasing their senses.

The rain calmed down to a soothing *pitter-patter* on the roof. The cabin that Beth first knew as a dreadful prison had now become a cozy shelter. They sat around the hearth, munching on the treat. Firelight flickered on their faces.

"Let's sing," Kathrin suggested. "There's a guitar over there." She pointed to it. "Is it yours, Glenn?"

"It's Dad's."

"Do you play?" Kathrin asked.

"Not very well."

"I bet you're just saying that. Would you play for us? I'll get it." Kathrin didn't wait for an answer but jumped up and took hold of the instrument. She handed it to Glenn.

A crooked smile formed on Glenn's face. "Dad's much better at this."

Beth sensed he didn't really want to play. Maybe he was timid. He turned away and blew dust from the guitar. Then holding it in position, he slowly strummed across the strings, tightening the knobs. "I should give you fair warning. I play mostly to calm the cattle."

He rose from the rocker, moved to the footstool, and rested the guitar on his thigh. The three women sat at his feet.

The cowboy plucked some cords, hummed along, and then strummed his melody. He stopped. "Don't you recognize it?"

"I don't listen to that country stuff." Emily waved a tactless hand.

Glenn looked at Beth and began a beautiful, heartfelt rendering of his song.

> "You give your hand to me, and then you say 'hello,'
> And I can hardly speak … my heart is beating so.
> And anyone can tell, you think you know me well,
> But you don't know me.
> You don't know the one who dreams of you at night,
> And longs to kiss your lips, and longs to hold you tight.
> To you I'm just a friend. That's all I've ever been.
> 'Cause you don't know me."

Beth sat mesmerized with the gentle sway of Glenn's deep vibrations. It was apparent that the sparkle in his eyes flowed from the same heart as the sincerity in his voice. He never turned his face from Beth's.

She blushed and smiled, pleased with his sweet attentions.

Glenn closed his eyes as he sang, "No, you'll never, never know …" Blue eyes opened and looked straight into Beth's. "The one who loves you so. No, you don't know me."

Beth relished his every heartfelt move.

The others clapped. "Bravo! Encore."

"Thank you, Glenn," Beth said. "That was beautiful." Then she thought, *But you're not helping me get over you.*

He acted like he didn't even hear Kathrin and Emily, but as though he and Beth were the only ones in the room. He gazed at Beth with affection, but his eyes held a trace of sadness.

They sang songs for most of the evening, until Emily stood. "I need to ask you something, Glenn. What are your plans now that the others are gone? Are you staying in the cabin, or giving yourself up, or what?"

The room became quiet. Their future hung upon his next words.

Glenn leaned the guitar against the wall. "I'll take you gals to the highway under the same agreement, except Dad doesn't need the hundred grand any longer. Dad took what he needs. After that I'll lie low for a while, I reckon. It would be sweet if I could visit my sister in Ireland, but I'm not sure yet."

Beth beamed. "You'll still do that for us?"

"Mm-hmm."

"In spite of everything, I'm glad I met you." Kathrin patted his knee.

The rest agreed.

Glenn lowered his head, clearly unprepared for their appreciation. "I owe you, anyway, for doctoring me and sticking by me."

Beth sat back on her heels and laid her hand on Glenn's forearm. "You saved our hides more than once too, and we're grateful."

They spent a few more minutes discussing the hike down to the highway.

After some small talk, they decided it was time to curl up under their covers. The rain composed a soothing beat on the roof, lullabying them to sleep. The glow of the firelight danced on their drowsy faces.

In the middle of the night Beth awoke with a start to the sound of footsteps on the porch. Wide-eyed, she bolted upright. *Nick and Decker! No!*

The footsteps stopped. *What are they waiting for? Are they looking in the window?*

Beth scanned the shadowed room, afraid of what she might see—afraid of who might burst in. A scream stuck in her throat.

Shivering, she waited for their next move.

14. Footsteps on the Porch

In the mountain cabin

The door handle didn't jiggle, nor was anyone peering through the glass. Beth crept out of bed, grabbed the poker, and tiptoed to the wall by the window, pressing her back against the logs.

The footsteps moved again.

Beth thought her heart would pound out of her chest. She knew she had to look, but she was too scared.

What are they doing out there?

Gathering all her courage, she peered out the window and gasped. Beth and two deer leaped backward, away from each other. The startled animals bounded off the porch, their hooves pelting the boards.

Beth's hand flew to her chest. She exhaled a sigh of relief. "Oh, thank God," she whispered. She climbed back under her warm covers, but took a long time to fall asleep.

Morning came bright and cheerful. Beth awoke to birds singing, welcoming the new day. Upon raising her head, she discovered everyone was still asleep. Golden light flooded the world outside.

Eager to experience its newness, Beth tiptoed through the threshold. What fun to sneak out and be the first! The rain had washed everything clean. She sat upon a step. Freshness and a sweet fragrance rushed to her. God's creation comforted Beth.

It wasn't but a few minutes later when the heart-breaker came through the door. "Beautiful morning, huh?"

"Yeah." Immediately, her nerves set on edge.

Glenn sat down beside Beth on the step. A moment passed. "I've been thinking. I'll probably be able to take you to the highway tomorrow."

"So soon?" Beth forgot she should be anxious to go home. She glanced at his attractive face, dark with stubble. She couldn't look long. His glistening blue eyes affected her. She ducked her head. "I mean, uh … are you sure you feel up to it?"

"Mm-hmm. Beth … I…" His voice trailed off. He was clearly grappling to find the right words.

Beth feared he would say something sentimental, and she'd lose it. Quickly, she switched to small talk. "You know, I really don't know anything about you."

"What do you want to know?"

"Uh … uh …" She paused and shot another speedy glance at him.

His face radiated with amusement. "All right, I'll start then. You're in college, right?"

She nodded.

"What do you want to do after you graduate?"

"Become a teacher or a social worker." She fidgeted with her necklace.

"You'll be good at that," Glenn said. "Wish my teachers had been as sweet-natured as you are. A couple of mine were quick with the ruler." He leaned forward and stared at the ground, his forearms resting on his knees.

Beth studied his profile. "You got the ruler?"

"'Fraid so."

"You were one of those kids who got in trouble?"

Still leaning forward, Glenn looked over his shoulder at her. The corners of his mouth turned up. "I don't think I ever grew out of it."

When she remembered he was a lawbreaker, she reddened. "Oh, yeah." She studied his tanned face. "Would you like to … umm … grow out of it someday?"

"Once you have a reputation, you can't escape it—even if you want to."

Enlivened by the few insights he'd allowed Beth to see, she forgot her pledge not to get involved with him. "What if a friend gave you a good recommendation? Or was there to encourage you and help you start over in another place? It can be done, Glenn. I'll help you."

Glenn closed his eyes, and the muscles in his cheek tightened. He propped his chin in his hand and said nothing. Several seconds passed.

Then he swallowed … hard. "You really want to help me?"

"Yes, I do. I meant it."

He looked at her. "You're an amazing woman, Beth. There's no way to express how much you've touched me. That you would care about my life, especially after all we've put you through."

"Then you'll let me be in your life and help?"

His expression turned sad. "I've already messed up your life enough. Besides, I have to do it myself. Your family must be worried about you."

"Yes, I'm sure they're quite worried, but thanks to you they won't be much longer. And don't change the subject. You did *not* mess up my life. You protected me. Yes, I do care very much about what happens to you. Your family must be worried about you too."

He turned away, as if there were painful, dark corners in

his life that he didn't want her to see. "Besides Dad, there is one other who probably worries about me."

"A wife or a significant other?"

A slight twitch of his head. "No, I'm not married or in a relationship. She's my biological sister."

Beth pondered then asked, "If I'm not getting too personal, did Luke adopt you as a baby?"

Glenn rubbed his hands together, staring at them. "My birth parents were killed in a car accident when I was eight. That's when Luke and Harriet took me in. They were my parents' close friends."

Sorrow and sympathy pierced Beth's heart. She laid a tender hand on his back. "I'm so sorry, Glenn. I shouldn't have asked."

He sat up and pivoted toward her. "That's okay. I don't mind telling you." A strong hand covered hers. "Beth, we don't have much time. And I want to tell you how—"

Palms sweating, she began, "But—"

Firm, hot fingers pressed against her lips. He didn't seem angry. On the contrary, his eyes shimmered with delight. "Beth, you have touched my life in a special way. I'll never forget that cute smile of yours." He dropped his fingers from her mouth.

Beth lowered her head. She couldn't bear to gaze into his captivating eyes a second longer. *Whoa! I have such strong reactions to him.*

Glenn was still talking. "And the way—" His index finger and thumb cupped Beth's chin and lifted her face. "Look at me please, Beth."

Beth looked up into radiant blue eyes. His kindhearted expression melted her. Her brain turned to mush.

"And the way you look at me…" Glenn paused. His eyes

wrapped her in abounding love. "I don't want to ever forget that."

His sentiment dove deep into the core of Beth's being. He'd opened an inner sanctuary no one had ever touched before. It was a depth that even she had been unaware of.

"Since I can't ever see you again after this," Glenn was saying, "I want you to know how much I"—he paused—"appreciate you … and your concern for me."

His words *can't ever see you again* tore Beth to shreds. Her emotions surged. "Please don't," she pleaded. Her eyes burned. She closed her eyes, trying to hide the tale-telling tears, but droplets squeezed out and rolled down her cheeks.

Glenn became quiet.

Beth knew he had figured it out. *So, now he knows. In a way, I'm glad. It was getting too hard to carry alone.*

"My sweet Beth," Glenn said ever-so-softly as he pulled her close. He wrapped his strong arms around her and held her against his warm chest.

Glenn's compassion dissolved what little control Beth had left. She buried her aching heart in his arms and her face within his soft flannel shirt.

Hot fingers stroked her temple then moved through her hair. How comforting his nearness and loving manner. She soaked in his affection and solace. He laid his head on Beth's, surrounding her with himself, kissing her hair, her forehead. His scratchy chin grazed her skin. Neither of them spoke until Beth had her sniffles and emotions under control.

She sat upright and wiped the tears. "I don't want to think that I'll never see you again—"

The door swung open. Emily came up behind them. "Oh! I wondered where you two were. May I get through? I've got to visit the john."

Glenn rose to his feet and let Emily by. When she was out of hearing range, he reached his hand out to Beth. "Let's go for a walk down by the corral."

It sounded romantic and peaceful, a place where they could be alone. Beth wanted to go with him, but part of her knew she shouldn't. He waited. With pounding heart, she looked up into his patient face. Somehow, she knew if he kissed her again, there would be no turning back.

I wouldn't be able to fight my feelings after that. I barely can now. Nothing has changed. It only tortures me.

She suddenly knew she must run from him. "I can't. You don't understand." She jumped up, spun around, and tripped up the stairs.

"Beth! Wait. Help me understand."

It was dark inside. Beth's eyes strained to adjust to the dim light. She went right to work busying herself with the dishes—anything to keep her mind off Glenn.

Kathrin turned from making the beds. "I think I'll take a dip in the freezing cold stream later this morning."

Footsteps echoed on the porch. Emily burst through the door, smiling from ear to ear. "Glenn says he can take us back tomorrow! Yahoo!"

Just then, Glenn edged his way around Emily and headed for his favorite coffee pot. He grabbed a can of coffee on the way.

Kathrin's eyes grew big. "Tomorrow? Really?"

"Mm-hmm." Glenn filled the pot with water and scooped in the coffee.

"Yay! We're going home tomorrow." Emily and Kathrin squealed, but not Beth. Emily's gray eyes danced.

Kathrin placed a hand on his arm. "Thank you, Glenn."

"We're square," he answered. "I owe you my life."

"Well, you're sweet potatoes in my book. But are you you're feeling up to it?"

"Mm-hmm," Glenn assured her. After setting the coffee to boil, he settled back into the stuffed rocker.

Emily dashed to his side, rested one hand on the chair back, and leaned her shapely frame over him. "Thanks, Glenn, for rescuing me from Nick, for taking us home, and for everything else," she said in a silky voice.

"Sure." He shrugged, but his countenance turned troubled.

In one, swift, unexpected motion, Emily bent down and covered his mouth with her own. Her fingers twined through dark strands of Glenn's hair then slid down into his shirt.

Beth winced. Every throb of her heart bruised its raw, wounded walls. Jealousy flared into a bonfire.

Glenn shoved her away. "That's enough, Emily."

"But we're just getting started." Emily leaned forward to kiss him again.

"No." His expression sharp, Glenn pushed against Emily's shoulder. His voice hardened. "Stop it."

"But why don't you want to kiss me? Is it because of that mousy Beth?"

"She's one reason. You could take lessons from her. She's a gentle dove."

Shocked and furious at Em, Beth cocked her head to one side and turned her palms up. "Hey, I can hear you." She marched straight at Emily. "I'll show you mousy."

Emily began to straighten up.

Beth grabbed Emily's arm and wrenched her to the floor. "How's *that* for mousy? And keep your greedy paws off Glenn."

"Ow! You hurt me!" Emily glared up at Beth. "And I didn't see any Beth label on him."

"It's hidden." Beth turned and walked away.

"Mm-hmm, I keep it under my belt." Glenn leaned back with a grin and tucked his thumb under the leather.

Emily jumped up and lunged at Beth's back. Together, they crashed to the floor. The impact bashed the wind out of Beth, stunning her. Emily clutched a handful of long brown hair and gave a vengeful yank, scratching Beth's neck.

Beth yelped but recovered quickly. She'd been born with a naturally tough head and had spent her youth wrestling with her brother. It paid off now. She twisted around and dug her nails into Emily's fists. They struggled and rolled on the floor until Emily let go of Beth's hair.

Emily winced, squeezing her hand. "You're mean, Elizabeth Farell."

At some point during the fight, Glenn had risen to his feet and sat half-way on the table, arms crossed, watching. Now that things had calmed down, he chuckled and raised an eyebrow. "I take it back. Beth's no gentle dove. She's a wildcat. Better not mess with her."

Kathrin laughed.

Glenn stood and offered Beth a hand up. His lips brushed her ear, and he whispered, "It's kind of nice being fought over, my little wildcat." He smiled and pulled her to her feet.

Then his voice returned to normal. "I don't know about the rest of you, but I'm famished." The women prepared breakfast, while Glenn shaved.

After breakfast, Glenn leaned his chair back on two legs like Luke had done and began to whittle on a solid stick with the kitchen paring knife.

"What are you making?" Kathrin asked.

"A spear in case we run into any of Decker's bears." Glenn quickly added, "But they usually run off when they see us."

Kathrin turned to Beth. "Since we're going home tomorrow and since it's a beautiful day, want to take a bath in the stream with Emily and me?"

"Sure. Go ahead. I'll join you in a few."

Kathrin finished gathering towels and soap. "On second thought, maybe you should stay with Glenn and make sure he doesn't join us." With a stern expression, she turned to the man. "You are not invited, Glenn."

"What makes you think I'd do that?" But he had a mischievous smile.

"Kathrin, you're a killjoy. It could have been fun." Emily closed the door behind them.

In the now-quiet cabin, Beth studied the cowboy. He kept whittling, not saying a word or looking around. They were alone together and neither one spoke. *Does he even know I'm here?*

She dropped a tin cup. It clattered noisily to the floor, but still he whittled away. "Glenn?"

After a time, he answered mildly, "Yes, Beth?" He paused his all-important whittling to turn a distracted gaze on her.

"I'm sorry I ran from you this morning."

"That's okay." He returned his attentions to that miserable stick of wood.

"Glenn," she began again, "I was wondering . . ."

He didn't stop.

Beth moved closer and raised her voice. "What do you think about giving yourself up?"

No response. He steadily chipped away at the make-shift spear *and* at Beth's patience. Finally, he looked up and shrugged. "Huh? Oh, I don't take to jails very well."

Beth boiled inside. He'd callously blown to pieces any future they might have had together. *He won't even stop and listen for one minute. Won't even consider it. I wasted all those feelings and all those tears on that—cowboy.*

Sweet revenge came to mind. With a slight push of her foot, the chair balancing on two legs crashed backward to the floor. The stunned look on Glenn's face as he gasped and flung out all four limbs made Beth giggle. He sat spider-style on the back of the chair and stared up at her, clearly bewildered.

"Now that I have your attention." Beth stood above him with her hands on her hips. "Do you realize that with seven thoughtless little words—'I don't take to jails very well'—you blew any chance we had of a possible future together?"

He still looked confused.

No matter how angry she was, his big, blue eyes affected her. "You don't even know what I'm talking about, do you?"

"No, ma'am." He climbed to his feet.

"I hate being called 'ma'am.' You, Mr. Glenn McKlain, wouldn't give me the courtesy of stopping for one blasted minute to discuss it with me, either."

"Discuss *what* with you, Miss Elizabeth Farell?" He brushed shavings from his clothes.

"Ohh!" She clenched her fists. "Men!"

15. Love Confessed

Glenn chuckled, which infuriated Beth. How could he take her feelings so carelessly? She grabbed the nearest object—an unlit candle from the table—drew back, and flung it at him.

Glenn ducked. The wax smashed into the log wall behind him then dropped to the floor and rolled away. He brightened. "You're so dang-blasted cute when you're angry."

Beth couldn't believe his audacity. "*Cute*? You want more *cute*?" She whirled, snatched a tin cup out of the sink, and threw it at him.

He laughed all the more.

Turning to the sink again, she snagged another cup.

Too late.

Glenn's right hand gripped her wrist. He stood at Beth's back with his arms around her, pulling her close. With his head over her shoulder, he pressed his cheek against hers and said softly, "Beth, I'm a fugitive and a felon. I can't even *consider* a future with you."

"Yes, you can." She turned around. "Why do think you can't?"

He stepped back, held her forearms, and looked her in the eyes. "Because it wouldn't be right to drag you down to my God-forsaken kind of life."

"It wouldn't be dragging me down"—Beth said in haste—"if you turned yourself in. You shouldn't have to serve *any* time. And it is right and good because I love you."

Glenn gaped at Beth.

Beth reddened. "I can't believe I blurted that out. I had no intention of telling you. But surprisingly, it feels good." It wasn't just a fairytale in her mind anymore. *After it sinks in, I wonder how he'll feel.*

Tenderness flooded his expression and filled his eyes until they nearly spilled over. He blinked and swallowed.

"Can't argue with that one now, can you?" The corner of Beth's mouth quirked up.

A gorgeous smile formed on Glenn's face. He seemed sensitive to her every word and gesture.

I think he's opened his heart to me, Beth mused, *and it wouldn't take much to hurt him.*

Glenn released her. He took a deep breath and stepped up to the window, facing the world outside. "What am I going to do?" He sounded as though he was torn up inside.

Beth contemplated his sturdy, straight back. "You can let me into your life and future, and you can tell me how you feel about me."

"Come with me." Glenn reached out his hand. "Kathrin's right. It's a beautiful day."

Why doesn't he tell me how he feels? Beth gave him her hand.

Glenn held it snuggly, grabbed his Stetson, and dashed out the door with Beth trailing behind.

He never went outside without his hat. *Will I ever be as much a part of his life as that hat?*

Beth panted to keep up. *Where is he taking me?* She hoped he wasn't thinking about making love. She wanted to wait for her honeymoon.

He raced toward a hill, pulling Beth with him.

"Where are you taking me?" she hollered. "And why are

we running?"

"Up this steep hill." He glanced over at her with a joyful expression. "And I don't know why we're running."

They both laughed. Their hearts were flying as high as the refreshing wind in their faces.

On the embankment, there was no time for speaking. They were too preoccupied with climbing and giggling. Glenn stumbled, probably from weakness, then laughed. Soon they rounded the top. Hand in hand, they hiked among sparsely timbered cliffs.

Glenn finally stopped at the edge of a high precipice. A green valley stretched out below Beth's feet. Not far, rock formations masqueraded as castles. "This is spectacular."

Glenn cradled her from behind. Together, they gazed upon the scene's beauty and harmony. "You're the only one I've ever shared this place with," he said.

"Really? Why?"

"I wanted to save it for someone special to me, and it would be our secret place."

A sensation of floating high above the earth inspired Beth to turn to the one she treasured. They stepped back from the cliff's edge, and enfolded into each other's arms.

All at once, a whirlwind propelled leaves. They took flight, skittering across the grass and bending the shoots. Suddenly, the leaves swirled around the couple, wrapping them in vigorous energy.

Beth's long tresses whisked in the air. She squealed with delight and held tightly to Glenn's waist. Then she leaned back and closed her eyes.

Suddenly, just as it had come, the whirlwind raced through the pines and disappeared. The leaves settled.

Glenn placed his large, brawny hands around Beth's waist.

"Hey, world," he shouted blissfully. "I love Elizabeth Farell ... with all my heart." His deep voice echoed through the canyons repeating *I love Elizabeth Farell with all my heart* until it absorbed within its walls forever.

That's why he wanted to come here—the echo. Even the hills are telling me of his love. Her heart sang.

Their merriment resounded through the canyons. The bright sun smiled upon their joy.

Glenn's gaze never left her. He brought strong arms around Beth and held her against him.

What exhilaration! She looked up into his face, and longed to relive his kiss. His eyes reflected the same.

All the love for Glenn that Beth had crammed down inside came bursting forth.

They drew closer. Beth shut her eyes. Then in a magical moment, his warm mouth tenderly embraced hers. Tingling electrified her. She felt weak and on top of the world.

Glenn touched his hot face against hers. "I never knew I could feel this strongly for anyone."

Beth was deeply moved, not only by his words but also by the heartfelt way in which he said them.

Glenn's mouth curved into a smile. "We better get going before ..." His voice trailed away.

"Before what?"

"Before I forget you're not mine to love." He moved a few wayward strands of Beth's hair from her eyes.

Beth beamed. "I don't want this day to ever end."

A faint, distant voice came to Beth's senses. She lifted her head, straining to hear. Glenn cocked his head and listened too. It sounded like a feminine voice, but the words were indistinguishable.

"It has to be Em or Kathrin," Beth said. Teasingly, she

nabbed the Stetson off the cowboy's head and placed it on her own. Then she took off for the other world. She pressed down on the hat to keep it from flopping.

"Hey!" Glenn set out after her.

By the time Beth approached the edge of the slope, she'd spotted her friends walking toward the cabin. "Em, Kathrin, we're up here." She waved the hat.

They turned and watched her bound down the hill, hat in hand. Glenn was not far behind. Once on flat ground, Beth replaced the hat on her head without missing a step. She jogged up to the others.

Emily's brows drew together. "Why are you running from Glenn? Did he force himself on you?"

Beth could hardly speak, she was breathing so hard. "No, of course not. He never has. I was … keeping his hat … from him."

Emily planted her hands on her hips. "What were you two doing up there?"

"Kissing."

Glenn caught up just then. "Beth, you were coming off the slope pretty fast." He wasn't even winded.

"But you didn't catch me." With a smirk and a wink, Beth stretched up and plopped the Stetson on its rightful owner's head.

"My stomach says it's half-past lunch." Kathrin said. "Care to join me?"

Everyone started out for the cabin. No longer concerned about what her friends might think, Beth held her arm snugly around Glenn's slim waist. His arm encircled hers too. Beth felt cherished and bonded to him.

After lunch, Emily tried to tease Glenn into taking a bath. "Not that you stink, but just saying …"

"I planned to take one. You gals will stay in the cabin?"

They agreed, but Emily crossed her fingers behind her back. All the while, she studied Glenn with a gleam in her eye.

Em must be getting bored, Beth thought. *I wonder if she regards Glenn as a fun challenge to pass the time until he can show us the way out.*

With soap and towel under one arm, Glenn took off for the stream.

He had barely disappeared over the hill when Emily said, "I don't know about you, but I'm going to tease Glenn." She winked and took off across the clearing.

Beth and Kathrin watched her.

"What if her teasing crosses a line?" Beth bit her lip. "Shouldn't we try to stop her?"

"Or at least warn Glenn what she's up to?" Kathrin tugged on her. "Let's go."

Beth and Kathrin jogged to catch up to Emily.

Upon discovering Glenn's whereabouts, the three stood behind a large boulder while Emily strategized. Bushes between them and the stream camouflaged their presence.

Emily pointed to Glenn's western duds spread out on a rock by the water's edge. The sun shimmered off the water as Glenn soaped up. Before long, a dark head ducked under water.

Emily dashed down to the rock and snatched his clothes.

Glenn surfaced, shaking water from his head. He apparently noticed the empty rock and Emily making a getaway. "Come back here with those! *Emily!*"

Emily ignored the furious cowboy and scurried back to where her friends waited. With an armload of western duds, Emily explained, "I left his towel hanging on a tree for bait." Mischief sparkled in her slate-gray eyes. "It's far enough away that he'll have to get out of the water to reach it."

"We'll give him the towel before he gets out, won't we?" Beth pressed her lips together in disapproval.

"*No.*" Emily wrinkled her nose at Beth. "What fun is that? C'mon, let's go down and tease him." She trotted down the slope, ducking under the branches.

"Wait, Em. I don't think we should ..." Beth's voice trailed off.

Kathrin chased after Emily.

Shaking her head, Beth followed.

When they arrived, Glenn was swimming toward the towel hanging in the tree.

Emily held up his jeans and shirt. "Looking for these?"

He gave her a lopsided smile. "Why do I get the feeling that I'm not going to get them back that easy?"

"Oh, you can have them. I'll give them to you. Honest."

"Why don't you just put them back on the rock?"

"Okay." But she piled them on the back side of the large rock, out of his reach.

Then Emily sauntered back to join her friends. "Okay, Glenn, they're on the rock. You can come get them now."

"I will if you go to the cabin where you promised to stay."

"But why? Aw, c'mon, Glenn." Emily's face glowed with mischief.

He began to swim toward them, his wet hair appearing black.

"No, Glenn," Kathrin called. "Emily's only joking."

"No, I'm not," Emily said.

"This water is freezing. My legs are cramping up. If you want a show, hey, right now I don't care. I just want out of this water." Glenn was close enough to shore that he could walk on the bottom. Water swirled around his waist. Droplets sparkled off his brows and thick lashes.

Beth liked what she saw, but she yelled, "Wait, Glenn. I'll get the towel for you." She ran for it.

"Oh, *come on,* Beth!" Emily protested, "Don't."

Glenn pushed through the water in their direction. Beth rushed back with the towel and splashed in the stream toward Glenn. His next step showed the waistband of his dark boxers.

Kathrin and Beth laughed.

"Oh, Glenn." Emily sighed her disappointment. "Just when it was getting interesting."

He wrapped his towel around narrow hips then rescued his clothes. His recent gunshot wound showed dark and swollen. "Show's over!" He headed for home, chuckling.

Beth hurried back to the cabin and reached it before him. She opened the cabin door and glanced back to see Glenn stepping up the porch stairs. His wound looked sore and oozed blood. She winced on his behalf. *He really overdid it this morning.*

Without a word he pulled clean, dry clothes from the closet and shut the door to the bedroom.

Kathrin ran up and met Beth on the porch. "Are you taking a bath now? I'll go with you."

Beth nodded.

Emily walked up behind them just then, so Kathrin turned to her. "Would you stay here, Emily, and make sure Glenn doesn't try to take revenge on your practical joke?"

"Sure, I'll stay." Emily's eyes gleamed.

Beth and Kathrin turned around and headed back to the stream. They were nearly there when Beth asked, "You brought the soap, right?"

"No, I thought you had it. Isn't it wrapped in the towel?"

Beth checked. "No."

"Maybe it fell out. Sorry."

Beth sighed, flipped the towel over her shoulder and started back for the log home. Kathrin kept right at her side.

Just as they rounded the corner to the cabin, Beth heard her name. She froze. *What's up with Emily and Glenn?* Putting her finger against her lips to silence Kathrin, Beth tiptoed closer.

This time, Emily's words came through loud and clear. "Why not? Beth won't find out."

Beth gaped at Kathrin then strained her ears to hear more. The door hung open a crack.

Beth crept up to where she could watch without being seen.

16. A Tough Decision

A glowing oil lamp created two silhouettes standing face to face. "Aw, c'mon, Glenn," Emily was saying. She latched onto his hand with both of hers. "Come to the bedroom with me. Don't you want to?"

Beth's throat went dry.

Glenn yanked his hand free. "No, I don't." His voice was hard. Cold.

Emily pouted. "But why not?"

"I'm not attracted to gals who chase after me," Glenn said. "But mostly it's because I'm in love with Beth." He turned abruptly and marched toward the door.

"Aw, Glenn, *stay*." Emily whined like a little child who wasn't getting her way.

Glenn stepped through the threshold and stopped short. His face reddened at seeing Beth. "Did you"—he cleared his throat—"Uh … how long have you been standing here?"

"Long enough." Kathrin's voice held admiration for the faithful cowhand.

"I came back for the soap," Beth explained.

"Oh." Glenn nodded. Head down, he started out for the stable.

Kathrin squeezed Beth's shoulder. "You stay out here, and I'll get the soap." She hurried inside.

Beth remained like a statue. Her mind could hardly process Emily's attempted betrayal. If it hadn't been for Glenn's staunch refusal, well … Beth shook her head. She didn't want to think about what-ifs. A sadness swept over her as she grieved the loss of a friend.

As for Glenn ... Beth's heart soared. He had proven his loyalty and his love. She grabbed the soap and headed back to take her long-awaited bath. Kathrin came along. Beth had no worries about leaving Emily and Glenn alone together.

She smiled. *None at all.*

The time it took to bathe and return to the cabin helped Beth recover enough to deal with Emily. She stood in front of the fireplace and let its radiating heat drive the chill from her bones. "Thanks, Glenn, for lighting the fire."

"That stream is fed by snowmelt. I know how cold it is." His voice was kind.

The tension between Beth and Emily was so heavy it was almost tangible. The lack of conversation around the table seemed comical. Glenn kept his eyes on his plate. Emily acted as though she had every right to her behavior. Kathrin tried to start a conversation regarding the hike home in the morning, but it fell flat.

After the meal, Beth asked Glenn to accompany her outside. Without a word he followed.

The cool of the late afternoon felt fresh on Beth's cheeks. They moseyed toward the corral, down the very path Glenn had wanted to take that morning. *Weird. My goals have done a one-eighty since then. I'm not running from Glenn any longer.*

A few steps into their stroll she reached for Glenn's hand and curled her fingers around it. They turned to each other for a moment.

Glenn looked at the ground. "I'm sorry you had to see that display between Emily and me."

Beth touched a finger to his lips. "No need to apologize. It wasn't your fault." She smiled. "You honored me. Thank you."

A quiet moment passed as they approached the split rail fence. Still hand in hand, they faced each other. "Glenn, you are the best thing that's ever happened to me." She giggled. "Which is a paradox, considering how we met."

Dark eyebrows rose, and his throat bobbed. Her words had clearly impacted him. He dropped her hand and studied her intently. "The best thing that's happened to you?"

"Oh, yes."

Glenn shook his head, as though he couldn't believe her words. "Beth, you are a sweet, compassionate young lady raised in high society. I'm just a"—he paused—"well, we're on opposite ends of the spectrum. At best, my annual income is probably your dad's monthly income. I smell of horse dung and sweat. At worst, I'm a criminal."

His face screwed up in disgust at himself. "*I helped your kidnappers.* Why would you want anything to do with me?"

Beth placed her hand over his heart. "What matters is a person's heart, and yours is like pure gold. My goodness! You risked your life for us. Don't discount that. And hey, it worked for Tarzan and Jane, and for Prince William and Kate. She was a commoner."

Glenn snorted, but his downtrodden expression began to clear.

Beth looked into his eyes. "High society has its problems. A fancy degree, money—none of that guarantees happiness. *You* are what makes me happy, Glenn McKlain. That other stuff never has." She embraced him and murmured, "I love you. I want to spend the rest of my life with you."

She leaned her head back and looked up at him. "There's no reason why you should serve time, but if it looks like you might have to, my dad's an attorney for Jets Without Borders.

He could probably get you off with three years. That isn't too long, is it? Then we could be together if … if you want to be."

Glenn's expression clouded with sadness. "Beth, you are the most lovable gal I've ever met. Any man would want you in his life." He sighed. "But it's more likely they'll give me ten years for all the things they can slap on me." His cheek tightened.

He let go of her. "You don't realize what you're asking—to give myself up. I can't take that chance. I'd rather run than throw away *ten years* of my life in prison." He shook his head. "And if I do end up in prison, I don't want anyone waiting for me."

"I don't want anybody else," Beth insisted. "What if I'm still single when you get out?"

"What kind of job can an ex-con get to support a family?" Glenn argued. "All I know is ranching."

"You can be a rancher, and I'll be a teacher. Living in this cabin with you and our little Glenns and Beths would be heaven." She chuckled. "Well, solar panels and a satellite dish would be nice additions."

He released a deep breath. "Do you think I could live with myself, seeing how I've dragged you and our kids down through an ex-con's kind of hard life? God help me if I haven't learned this lesson. I found out the hard way doing wrong out of love for someone doesn't make it right."

"You're talking about your dad, right?" Beth asked.

Glenn nodded. Then he spoke in a quiet, calm voice, stroking the side of her face. "No, Beth, you deserve much better than that. You belong in a magnificent home with a fine, upstanding young man who can give you and your children peace and respect and all that you ever wanted." He paused. "You'll get the opposite with me."

"But Glenn, no. That's not—"

"Forget it, Beth. It won't work." His voice dropped as he turned aside. "You better go now."

Stunned, Beth's heart shattered. *This can't be the end. I won't let it. I can't let him go.* She clutched his arm and swung him back toward her. "Listen to me, Glenn McKlain. People are always making decisions for my life"—she drummed her chest—"but this time *I* want to decide for me. Not you"—she poked his chest—"or anybody else."

Beth softened her voice. "For better or for worse, I want a life with *you*. You are well worth the wait, Glenn. You are everything I ever wanted, and a whole lot more. I know this isn't an easy decision, so please think it over first."

She stretched up on tiptoes, kissed him on the cheek, and dashed away before he could say no again.

After a couple of paces, she glanced back. He stood as though at the crossroads of his life, staring at her.

In spite of the darkness, Glenn didn't come inside for over an hour. During that time, the three women discussed their return to society.

Emily couldn't get comfortable on the stuffed rocker. "I hate it," she burst out. "You know what everyone must be thinking, don't you? That we were all raped."

At first, no one replied. The silence spoke of its sickening effect on them.

Then Kathrin leaned forward. "I suppose if they are talking about me, then someone else is getting a break."

Glenn finally sauntered through the door with a couple of canteens hanging off his shoulder. He busied himself filling them with water. Then he stuffed sacks with crackers, dried fruit, and such. He lacked his usual warmth and vigor, which attested to the burden he carried.

Glenn's melancholy mood tore at Beth's heart. *Without him I know I'll always feel hollow. It hurts too much to imagine never seeing him again.* "Please make him want to give himself up. I don't know how I'll live without him," she mouthed to God.

"We've got gazillions of miles to travel tomorrow," Kathrin said. "We better get our rest."

"Yes, *gazillions.*" Beth winked at her friend and prepared for bed.

Glenn went outside again. Beth wasn't sure why. It wasn't long before Emily and Kathrin were sawing logs. Beth fell asleep before Glenn returned.

The next thing Beth knew, birds were singing. She opened her eyes. Sunshine streamed through the windows. *But this day is different,* she thought sadly.

The idea of never seeing Glenn again after that day caused more heartache than she thought she could bear. She had to speak to him—alone—and learn his final decision.

The wooden door swung open just then. The bright morning sun rushed in, along with Glenn. *What a pleasant sight to wake up to every morning.* His countenance wasn't his typical upbeat expression, but it wasn't solemn as it had been the night before.

At breakfast, Glenn barely glanced in Beth's direction. *Uh-oh, he's avoiding looking at me. What is it about this kind outlaw that can overturn my world so?*

"Glenn, is your wound bleeding?" Kathrin squinted at a dark spot on his plaid shirt.

Glenn unbuttoned his shirt and pulled the material out to check. "Mm-hmm, a little."

"Here, let me see." Gingerly, Kathrin peeled the shirt off his shoulder. Dark-red blood smeared his skin. "I'll clean it up," she offered, "but you really need to see a doctor."

She cleansed his shoulder then wrapped a few layers of torn sheet around it. "And it didn't help your wound to be running around with Beth all over these mountains yesterday." She scowled at him so darkly that Glenn chuckled.

After breakfast, everyone rushed to prepare for their long journey home. Glenn swung the canteens over his right shoulder, then closed the door on this chapter of their lives.

They set out across the clearing, four figures eclipsed by the magnificent mountain range. Beth turned and silently said good-bye to the now-abandoned hideout nestled in the peaceful meadow. Her mixed feelings about her precarious future unsettled her.

I can't wait to be back with my family and for them to meet Glenn … hopefully. I know they won't approve until they hear what happened. Then they'll be grateful.

Half an hour rolled by. "If you look to your left"—Kathrin swung her arm—"you'll see the most awe-inspiring works of art, compliments of the unsurpassed Artist in the sky. Made with you in mind." Their tour guide's voice echoed off the nearby canyon walls. Water trickled and splashed down its sides.

Since their food supply was low, they pushed on past hunger pangs and through a green, picture-postcard valley. After a while Beth no longer marveled at the beauty surrounding her. Her sore calf muscles cramped with every downhill step. "How much farther?" She looked up. The sun was not yet at its zenith.

Glenn turned his attention to Beth. "You should be on the dirt road within the hour."

They crested a small hill. Below glistened a refreshing stream. All four bolted for the water. They sat in a row on rocks and swished their burning feet and calves in the soothing stream. Afterward, they munched on their snacks beneath an old cottonwood tree.

Glenn broke off twigs with red leaves from a nearby bush. Then while reclining against the tree, he twisted the sprigs together.

So far, Glenn had been silent about his decision. "Glenn," Beth said, "would you please come with me a minute?"

"What? Now?" Emily frowned. "We haven't got time for side trips."

Beth ignored Emily and stretched her sore, stiff muscles to an upright position.

Glenn studied her in a hesitant, doleful manner as he rose to his feet.

"Come on," Beth urged, taking his hand.

"Ten minutes, and we'll start without you," Emily threatened.

"Go ahead and get lost," Beth threw back.

Glenn and Beth tromped several yards through the trees. They both remained solemn and quiet. "You know why I want to talk with you," Beth finally said. "Did you decide? Am I in your future?"

Glenn didn't answer. He stopped and stared at the ground. A moment passed.

"Glenn, tell me, please." Her voice trembled.

Finally, his luminous blue eyes met hers. They were compassionate as always, but to Beth's despair, they also looked forlorn. "I decided to trust God and not run—for my own sake."

Beth gasped and threw her arms around him "Awesome! It really is for the best." *Thank you, God!*

Glenn didn't reciprocate her hug right away, which was uncharacteristic of him. Then he embraced her. His hand rubbed her shoulder, and he rested his head against hers. They lingered without words.

Why is he hugging me for so long? Is this our last embrace? The way he's swallowing ... is he fighting back tears?

He kissed her temple and let go.

"Here, Beth. It's for your pretty hair." Glenn held out a circle of the little red leaves entwined together.

She stared at their loveliness in his rugged hand. "Oh my goodness. It's beautiful." *Wow!* She thought. *He created it because of what he's feeling in his heart and by his own hands*. Beth cherished it. Smiling, she glanced up at him.

He moved close and placed the crown upon her head. Fondly, he stroked her brown locks between his fingertips.

Beth felt honored. "Oh, Glenn, thank you. I wish I could keep it forever."

"Sometimes what we wish for cannot be." His strong hand gently touched her flushed cheek. "Please think a minute, Beth. People sometimes talk about being treated like a criminal. If you saddle yourself to an ex-con like me, you and your children would be outcasts. I can't mess up your life like that. Someday you would regret—"

"No!" Beth cut in. Her heart raced. "I'd *never* regret marrying you. No matter what happens." Beth squeezed his arm. She shook her head in denial.

"Why are you refusing to face reality?" Glenn asked. "It won't be like it was up at the cabin." His sorrowful eyes searched Beth's for understanding. "I'd rather leave you with those memories than take the chance of making you regret you ever met me."

Glenn's words crushed Beth's heart into a thousand pieces. "I could never regret having met you. I thank God I did." Tears welled up. "Nothing could devastate me more than what you're saying right now."

His expression collapsed. "Then I better get out of your life now, before I hurt you again." He pulled his arm from her grip. "I'm sorry, Beth. I never meant to hurt you." He turned and walked away.

Beth darted in front of him and set her hands on his chest. Drops overflowed his eyes and trickled down his cheeks.

"No, no! It's the *absence* of you that hurts. There's nothing that could possibly hurt as much as that." Her voice cracked. "Please, Glenn! Please don't shut me out of your life—"

Beth was interrupted by Kathrin's frantic voice. "Someone's coming!"

17. Captured

Somewhere in the forest

Glenn wrenched his head around. His eyes searched the forest.

Kathrin and Emily raced to the couple. "I think it's the police," Kathrin whispered.

Beth clung to Glenn's arm. The four waited, stock-still, like frightened deer in a hunter's scope.

Horses' hooves clomped; reins jingled. Men's voices echoed, but their words were unclear. Shades of brown and blue moved through the trees as familiar shapes of horses and riders took form.

Closing in, two law enforcement officers shouted, "Hey there! How's it going?"

Birds squawked and fluttered away.

"Doing okay. Great morning," Glenn greeted them in a friendly manner.

The deputies' expressions remained calm.

Why so casual? "They're looking for *us*, aren't they?" Beth whispered to Kathrin. She felt it in her gut.

The deputies dismounted. Their bay horses flicked their tails and ears. "On a hike?" Before anyone could respond, he continued, "Say … a couple days ago a local resident, Shorty, reported two of his friends missing."

All four kept quiet. Beth rubbed her wrist. *Maybe they're not looking for kidnapping victims, after all.* She relaxed.

"We're heading up to a cabin where Shorty thought we might find them." The deputy pulled a wrinkled paper from his pocket, unfolded it, and handed it to Glenn. "On your hike, did you happen to come across these guys?"

Beth peeked at the paper. It was a fuzzy image of a smiling, younger Glenn. Standing beside him was a healthier-looking Luke.

"The photo was taken a few years ago so they may look a little different now."

"Shorty is my friend," Glenn said. He peered at the officer's name tag. "It appears, Officer Dalton, that I'm not missing any longer." He grinned and handed back the paper.

Both deputies squinted at Glenn, clearly unsure how to proceed.

Dalton cleared his throat. "Hmm, I see." He stuffed the photo back in his pocket. "What about the other fellow? Luke something?"

Glenn shrugged. "Oh, we were at the cabin together. You can save yourself a long hike by taking my word that he's fine. I'll tell Shorty when I get back."

Silence.

A strong breeze whipped up, catching a lock of Beth's hair. She shoved it back and noticed her hand was shaking like a leaf.

The deputy who hadn't spoken yet whispered to Dalton.

Dalton scowled. He looked from Glenn to the girls and seemed to be pondering his next move. Then it appeared as if a light turned on in Officer Dalton's mind. He seized his gun and aimed it at Glenn.

The other officer followed suit.

Beth gulped.

"Down on the ground!" Officer Dalton's tone turned gruff. "Now. All of you. You three"—he waved at the girls—"over there." His gun pointed to a spot several feet from Glenn.

All four dropped to their knees and sprawled out on the pebbly ground. Beth shook. She cranked her head to one side.

"Why are you treating us like criminals?" Glenn demanded.

Officer Dalton kept his gun trained on Glenn. "Murphy," he barked. "Secure him."

Officer Murphy cautiously stepped up to their captive. He grabbed Glenn's wrists from behind and locked on handcuffs. Then he body searched everyone who lay on the ground.

"All of you. Get up … slowly."

The four climbed to their feet. The girls brushed dirt off their clothes.

The physically fit Deputy Murphy mirrored Dalton's stance. White-knuckled hands clenched his weapon, zeroing in on Glenn.

"Is there anyone else around here besides you four?" Officer Dalton studied their faces.

"No," Emily answered for them all.

"Are you ladies okay?"

"We're all fine, thanks to Glenn," Beth declared boldly.

"This is Glenn McKlain?" Dalton jerked his head in the prisoner's direction.

A look of resignation settled over Glenn's face.

"Yes," Beth and Kathrin said in unison.

Officer Dalton requested their names. Afterward, he nodded. "I suspected as much. You're the hostages from that bank robbery over on the west side."

"We were." Kathrin raised her voice. "But *all* of our kidnappers rode off Friday and left us in the cabin."

"Glenn didn't kidnap us," Beth put in, hoping to clear his name. "He helped us."

"The cabin belongs to you, Mr. McKlain, right?" Dalton asked while scribbling notes.

"Mm-hmm, yep."

"Then how did you happen to come upon these hostages?" Dalton turned to Glenn.

"I want my attorney present for any and all questioning." Glenn gazed at the ground.

Dalton flinched his head back slightly. Obviously confused, he stared at the four a moment. Then he asked the girls, "How did McKlain come upon you?"

The ex-hostages summarized their story.

Dalton turned his attention back to Glenn. "I'm afraid we will need to detain you for questioning."

Glenn nodded.

Officer Dalton twisted his head toward the radio on his shoulder. His thumb pressed a button. After identifying himself and Murphy, he gave their coordinates. "Let the FBI in King County know we've detained a person of interest for questioning in their kidnapping-bank robbery case. He's Glenn McKlain from Okanogan County. All three hostages are with us and appear unharmed.

"The FBI will probably want us to transport them at least half way, maybe to Wenatchee," Dalton continued into the radio. "Find out, though." He paused. "Send backup, but McKlain is coming in on his own free will. He doesn't appear hostile."

Beth was grateful that she and the other girls were allowed to ride the horses. Beth and Kathrin rode double. The deputies held the animals' reins, and Glenn led the procession.

Beth's mind couldn't rest during the journey back to

civilization. Everything seemed unpredictable and alien to her. *I wonder what Glenn's thinking. I know that he won't let me in his life. Oh, don't start crying! Not now. C'mon, get hold of yourself.* She took a deep breath, then slowly let it out.

About an hour later, a dirt road came into view. Several sheriff department cruisers and SUVs were parked in the road. A few officers stood watching. Others barreled up the hill and surrounded Glenn. Not wasting a moment, they escorted them all to the road.

Deputies Dalton and Murphy led their horses to a horse trailer hitched to a pick-up. The girls dismounted. Beth watched as other officers led Glenn away to their cruiser. Her chest weighed heavy with sadness.

Dalton and Murphy took the girls to an SUV. Once inside, Dalton handed Kathrin a cell phone. "You ladies may call your families to let them know you're safe. No more than a one-minute conversation, understand? The FBI will want to question you before they release you to your families."

"Yes, thank you." A relieved smile stretched across Kathrin's face.

When Beth dialed her father, he broke down and cried. So did his daughter. He kept asking, "Are you all right?"

"Yes, Dad. I really am." A wonderful sensation of heat radiated through Beth's chest. "They said you can pick me up at the Federal Detention Center. But it'll be several hours. We're somewhere on the east side of the state."

Father and daughter conveyed their love for each other and then hung up.

The SUV whisked the ex-hostages away, with Glenn two cruisers ahead. Exhausted, Beth dozed off and on for most of the trip. The FBI met up with them in Wenatchee. They took the women in one vehicle and Glenn in another the rest of the way to Seattle. Two other SUVs filled with agents followed.

Hours later, the parade of federal SUVs drove into a very full parking lot. They rolled up behind a large, white building and parked. Beth remembered the place. Her attorney father had taken her to the Federal Detention Center before.

People were everywhere. When they saw the caravan pull in, they raced toward it. Beth nervously scraped a hand through her hair. An agent opened the back door. Wide-eyed, Beth and Kathrin stepped out but stuck close to the vehicle. Emily stood tall. She rolled her gray eyes and released an exasperated sigh.

An uproar of questions greeted them. Shutters clicked. Video recorders rolled.

FBI agents surrounded the SUV that carried Glenn. An agent threw open the back door. With his hands cuffed behind him, Glenn climbed out. Again, shutters clicked amid the hubbub. Agents gripped the captive's arms.

Beth kept one eye on the horde of people as the agents escorted the four of them along. The media acted like starved buzzards yearning for a juicy tidbit. They seemed anxious to pick bones clean and leave nothing uncovered.

Sheriff deputies and FBI agents did their best to barricade the four people from the on-rush of reporters.

A cacophony of voices rose. "Where did they take you? Were you abused?" Disorder broke out. The mass of people shoved in on each other, crowding the new arrivals.

Beth's steps wobbled.

"Move back!" the law officers bellowed. They braced themselves with legs spread. Their arms pushed against the crowd.

Alongside Glenn, an angry uprising swelled. "Let us have that—" Someone cursed.

"He doesn't deserve to live," another shouted.

The throng strained against the human barricade. Their fists struck at Glenn's shoulders. He swerved and ducked.

Terror suffocated Beth. Would the angry crowd break through the line and beat Glenn? "He's handcuffed! He can't protect himself." She screamed, frantic to help him.

A uniformed man demanded though a bullhorn, "Stand back or you'll be arrested for disobeying a lawful order."

That cooled the crowd's vengeance.

Control partially restored, the law officers steered Glenn and the ex-hostages toward the detention center's doors.

From among the unknown faces inside the building, Beth spotted her parents. They looked worry-worn but were smiling at their daughter. How reviving to see their faces.

"Dad! Mom!" Beth pushed her way to them. Instantly, it felt like fifty pounds lifted off her shoulders. She flew into the security of their arms and hung on tight. She wanted to make all the bad go away, like she had done as a child.

"Are you sure you're okay?" Dad asked close to her ear. "We were so worried about you."

Like many parents in their fifties, Dad and Mom carried extra weight. When Beth hugged them, her head landed on her Dad's shoulder and on top of her Mom's head. Beth forgot how stylish her mom looked with short, black hair. She cherished Dad's attentive gray eyes, his fair complexion, and even his receding gray hair.

"Yes, I'm okay. Better now." Beth stepped back and gazed into her Mom's black eyes. "I'm really home, aren't I?"

Dad pulled her close. "Yes, you're safe with us."

Emily's and Kathrin's families were with them also. A man in military uniform—probably her husband—hugged Kathrin. Beth had forgotten the commotion of the half-dozen reporters who had been allowed in the foyer. She ignored their questions and searched for Glenn. *Aw, there's his Stetson.*

"Are you looking for someone?" Mom asked.

Glenn's entourage of lawmen waited a moment for the crowd to clear as flashes brightened the room.

"Are you one of the kidnappers?" a man demanded of Glenn.

Dad squeezed Beth's arm. "Don't worry, Kitten. He can't hurt you anymore. I'll make sure he pays for what he did to you. The electric chair is too good for his kind." His voice grated with hostility and vengeance.

Beth gaped at her father. She had never heard him talk like this. Little did he know how his words stung. "No, Dad." She shook her head adamantly. "He wasn't involved in the robbery or the kidnapping. He didn't hurt us. He rescued us. He saved our lives."

Dad stared at her in shock and disbelief.

Miraculously, every reporter hushed the second any of the girls spoke. Two microphones popped before Beth's face. "You're Miss Farell, right?" He didn't give Beth a chance to confirm or deny it. He rushed right along. "Did you say that the suspect saved your life?"

"Let's go." An FBI agent took Beth by the arm. "We've got to take their statements. You understand." He tugged on her arm.

But I want the reporters to know Glenn's a good guy. Beth turned to face the reporters. "He's *not* a suspect," she said confidently. "And yes, Glenn rescued us. He was good to us."

One male reporter crowded out Beth's parents and shoved a mic under Beth's nose. "What hap—"

"Can we figure out from your face and words that you have feelings for him?" a female reporter interrupted.

Beth's face grew hot. *Oh no, I can't let them find out. They won't understand. They'll think I'm a fool for having anything to do with a potential kidnapper.* She dropped her head, barely shaking it. Instantly, it dawned on her that Glenn might see. She looked up.

Beth caught a pained look on Glenn's face before he broke eye contact.

"Come along now," the agent interrupted. He eyed the reporters. "They'll answer your questions later."

All the way down the hall, Beth tried to swallow the huge lump in her throat. *How could I have denied Glenn like that? I feel awful. He must think that our relationship embarrasses me.* She cringed. *I didn't even know it did … until now.* Her eyes watered. It felt as though she carried a hundred pounds through the narrow hallway.

Beth kicked herself mentally. *My stupid, stupid fear of what people might think!* Didn't Glenn mean more to her than what those people might think? *He deserves better. How in the world can I make him feel better about this?*

There seemed no way to right this horrible wrong. *I hurt him. Right now he's probably thinking, 'Beth feels that I'm not good enough for her.'* Beth shuddered. *Ugh! I really blew it.*

A stern-faced woman in a button-strained uniform escorted the ex-hostages to a stale little room. A table, half-a-dozen chairs and a two-way mirror decorated the space.

No sooner were they seated when two FBI agents and a tall, forceful-mannered man with graying temples stepped in. He closed the door to the world outside. From the way he acted—all alpha male—Beth surmised he must be important.

The alpha male plunked himself down in one of the empty chairs and introduced himself as Chief Agent Bradrick. He peered at the girls through narrowed eyes. "We are thankful to have you all back in what appears to be good health. I'm sure you're anxious to go home, so with your cooperation we can probably be done by eight."

He took a deep breath. "Because of the seriousness of this case, we need each of your statements, including complete details from the time you were in the US Bank until now. Don't leave *anything* out, even if you think it's not pertinent. After all, we've got to stop these men before they harm any other pretty ladies like yourselves. Vanderhoff, you interview Ms. Farell. Agent Perez will take the other girl's statement. Ms. Jacobsen will remain with me."

Agent Vanderhoff ushered Beth into a cubical. He waved her into a wooden chair beside a desk piled high with files.

I wonder what Kathrin and Em will say about my feelings for Glenn. Her stomach rolled and fluttered.

Devoid of emotion, the plain-clothes man with a long face and dark hair shoved a recorder before her. "State your full name, address, and birthday." After Beth's reply, he asked, "Did you know or have you ever met any of the suspects before your abduction?"

Beth shook her head.

"The recorder needs a verbal response, please."

Beth blushed and chuckled nervously. "No."

"Do you have any idea of their whereabouts?"

"No. They talked about going to Canada, but I don't know where in Canada."

"Tell us what happened right from the beginning."

Beth did her best to advocate Glenn's case without revealing her love for him. She spoke in generalities of Nick's advances toward Emily, being careful not to humiliate Emily. After all, Emily was the one who insisted Beth tell the police the truth.

Beth finished with a loud sigh.

Agent Vanderhoff looked her in the eyes. "Is that everything? You didn't leave a single thing out?"

Did he know she was hiding something? She squirmed. "That's all the important things."

Vanderhoff left the cubical and returned a few minutes later with a stack of papers in hand. Photos of six different men were on each. "Can you pick out your kidnappers from these?"

"I'll try." She gave him a wane smile. Then she gaped. To her amazement, Decker's image—in Border Patrol uniform minus the beard—graced the top sheet of papers. "Then he really *is* a Border Patrol agent?"

"This is an on-going investigation. We can't discuss it."

"That must be how he had access to the uniforms, equipment, and the van." It all was starting to add up in Beth's mind.

On the last sheet of paper, Beth discovered Nick's smug mug. "That's Nick." She poked his sneering face.

"Good. How about the others?"

"No." Beth handed the photos back to the agent.

An hour later, the three ex-hostages were reunited in the stale room. "Would you please describe the man Luke to our artist?" Vanderhoff offered the artist his chair and watched from behind.

When Chief Bradrick entered the room, Vanderhoff presented the profiles and drawings to him.

Bradrick handed Vanderhoff another profile. "Ms. Jacobsen found him in the Okanogan County records."

Wait. Who are they talking about? Beth stretched to see the profile.

"Want to see what this pretty-faced hero of yours is *really* like?" Agent Bradrick set the photo in front of Beth.

Beth felt herself grow hot with embarrassment. *That Emily!*

She must have squealed. And I tried to protect her reputation. She is so not my friend. Leaning forward, Beth studied the photo of an attractive teenager.

Everyone was too quiet. She knew they were all watching closely, as though they were all silently screaming, *"I told you so."*

It was his stunning blue eyes that gave Glenn away.

Beth's stomach soured as she scrutinized the contrite expression on the young face. The name, McKlain, Glenn Michael, age sixteen, was typed underneath. Alongside the mugshot, "misdemeanor: obstruction of justice: record expunged" with a line of fingerprints. To see it in print hit her hard.

Beth scratched her temple and stared at the photo. Confusion clouded her mind.

"Don't talk to anyone else about the events of last week, except the assistant US attorney. We'll be questioning you further, and you will be called to witness for the prosecution." Bradrick's mind was obviously preoccupied with his new-found discoveries. "You may go."

The moment they stepped through the double doors Beth was instantly blinded by bright lights. Raucous voices fired questions all at once.

The whole world is watching. Too worn out, Beth began to shake. Her jaw ached from clenching so long.

"Are you all right? You look unharmed." An older female reporter asked with compassion.

"We're extremely exhausted, but yes, we're unharmed." Kathrin's voice came out strained. "The FBI told us not to talk to anyone. So please …"

"They didn't harm you?" Suddenly, a mic appeared before Beth's face. A thin, young man peered at her, lifted a single brow, and cocked his head. "They didn't hit you or violate you in any way, even though you were together for a whole week?"

"Weren't you listening? *No talking* to anyone. So move it, buster." Emily took the lead and barged through the clamor of rude people and the sea of hand-held mics.

Once the ex-hostages stepped outside, the night air refreshed Beth. The unusual tie that bound the girls no longer existed. They said their good-byes and joined their anxiously waiting families.

Not long after Beth settled into the family car's back seat, Beth's father recommended she see a doctor.

Too tired to argue, Beth consented. "Okay, if it'll put your mind at ease."

They only asked a few questions. Most of the time was spent with her mother telling Beth about her long, harrowing story of last week's events—the media, people staring, and the horrifying rumors.

Beth's mind was too weary to think or listen. Her body could relax now. It was no longer necessary to be on guard. In a daze she stared at the city lights. The city's constant hubbub of people, cars, horns, and music seemed much louder than she remembered.

Finally, they pulled into their garage. Beth's two siblings greeted her with long, healing hugs. It was so good to be home, surrounded by caring family.

Their home boasted of wealth. Beth viewed it through different eyes, as if for the first time. The log cabin could have fit inside the Farell living and dining room. Her mom liked expensive, elegant things and lots of windows. Dirt didn't stand a chance in that house, but that was because of a hard-working maid.

Mom gave Beth a sleep aid—her first ever.

"Dad," Beth murmured, "would you please double check and make sure all the windows and doors are locked? And may I borrow your cell phone tonight? Nick smashed mine."

His wrinkled brow revealed that questions plagued his mind, but a fatherly hand held out a phone to her. "Sure, Kitten, I'll do that for you. And here, take my personal cell. I use the firm's mostly. I'll get you a new, girly phone tomorrow."

"That would be great. Thanks, Dad."

Exhausted, Beth excused herself. She carefully removed Glenn's circle of red leaves from her hair and lovingly placed it on the nightstand. A short shower relaxed her. Then she collapsed onto her own comfy bed and set the cell under her pillow within easy reach.

She sighed. "Love these modern conveniences."

Then a deep, hard slumber overcame her.

18. Was It All a Dream?

Beth parent's home, Auburn, Washington

The urgent, screaming ring of a phone jerked Beth out of a nightmare. Her eyes popped open. She bolted upright. *Was that a gunshot?* Again the phone shrieked its blaring demand.

Then it stopped.

Beth's heart pounded. She teetered between reality and a dream-like state, struggling to make sense of things.

Dusky as it was, she recognized her bedroom.

I was dreaming about a gun firing and bank robbers abducting me. And I fell in love with one of them?

"What a strange dream. But it seems so real." She rubbed her head. That sleeping pill was powerful. "I wasn't"—she couldn't say the word aloud—*abducted.* "That doesn't happen. Not to me, anyway. And I wouldn't fall in love with a criminal."

Wait. Then this Glenn guy doesn't exist? The thought saddened her. *Why do I feel heartbroken over a dream?*

In the silence of her room, Beth whispered, "Or was I really that close to evil?"

She shuddered. Dread grabbed hold of her as denial began to lose its grip.

She searched her darkened room and saw the circle of leaves.

"No!" Beth drew her knees up to chest and pulled the

covers up to her eyes. She stared at the leaves on her nightstand then poked them. They were real.

"It's not a bad dream. It *did* happen to me." *My world's dangerous.* She spent several minutes processing this horrible reality.

"I fell in love with a *criminal?*" *Fear and love are powerful emotions, but how can they co-exist?*

Beth remembered now. Glenn was a good guy. She was grateful for such a man in this world. Warmth spread out from her inner being. She threw back the covers and slipped on her robe.

Coming on the heels of her bad dream, last night's scene with the media replayed in Beth's mind—the embarrassment, her denial about Glenn. She paced the floor with a heavy heart. "If I were Glenn, I know what I'd say"—her arm slammed down—"'Who needs you?'" A lump formed in her throat.

Actually, I think he's better than me. He obviously doesn't worry about what people think of him. That's healthier, braver. "But me?" She shook her head. "I want people to think good of me, but they won't. Not if I'm hitched to their preconceived version of Glenn. But I don't want to lose him."

Beth plopped down on the bed feeling lost and torn. "I don't know what to do. I hope he can forgive me."

She grabbed her dad's cell and called the Federal Detention Center in hopes of talking to Glenn. After waiting on hold for what seemed like forever, a crisp voice said, "He can't talk to you," and hung up.

Beth pondered. What now?

Glenn's arraignment! She would call and find out when it would be. With that small task ahead to keep her mind busy, Beth felt ready to face the world again. She could hear her mother conversing on the phone.

By the time Beth poured tea and scarfed down a banana, her mother had hung up. "Morning, Mom."

"Good morning, Elizabeth. How did you sleep?" Her tone was polite but aloof.

Beth flinched. Why did Mom's tone bother her today? *She always uses that tone with me…except when we're in public. Was I expecting a little more warmth and happiness because I'm home safe? I should have known better.* She frowned.

"I slept unbelievably hard. That sleeping pill was *potent.* It took me a while to come out of it."

Beth made her call to the courthouse before Mom could respond. While she waited for the clerk to answer, she checked the clock on the microwave. "Whoa! Almost ten."

The clerk answered. Beth inquired about Glenn's arraignment and hung up.

"What's that about?" Mom pursed her lips.

"I'm going to Glenn's arraignment tomorrow."

Mom stiffened. "You're not serious! The one they arrested last night?"

"Yes."

Mom began to cry.

Filled with compassion, Beth wrapped her arm around her mother's shoulders. "What's wrong?" Crying was not a common occurrence from Mom.

Mom sat on a bar stool and sobbed. She pulled out a tissue and wiped her nose. "It was awful … so frightening. It made me physically ill."

"What? My abduction?"

"Yes. We couldn't get away from the questions. Everywhere we went—the police, the FBI, the media, people, even the kids at school. The students pointed and stared at poor little David. He's too young to have to deal with this,

Elizabeth. He's only fourteen."

Beth brooded. It was always about her 'little' five-foot-six brother. The favorite child was embarrassed. Poor David suffered so much. Beth's blood pressure began to rise, but she squeezed her lips shut.

Mom wiped her eyes. "I told your father we shouldn't send David to public school, but he never listens to me."

Her red-rimmed eyes glared at Beth. "Elizabeth, why were you at the bank with Emily that day?" Her voice turned hard. "I warned you that friend of yours was trouble, but you never listen to me, either. She's not in your class, Dearie. This family has *never* had such a shameful thing happen to us."

Heat flushed Beth's body. "You're blaming *me* for being abducted? I'm sorry, Mom, for all you and David went through. I'll try not to get kidnapped again."

Beth clenched her fists. "But what about *me*? How about what I went through, or do you care enough to ask even one question?" She threw up her fists.

Crash! A vase shattered into a hundred pieces on the floor.

Mom gasped.

"No, wait!" Beth yelled. "What am I thinking? You've never cared about me. Why should I expect an ounce of compassion from you now?" Beth turned to charge out of the room.

"I *do* care." Mom took a deep breath. "Is it possible that you might be pregnant?"

Beth stopped in her tracks and whirled on her mother. "*What?* That's your one question? Unbelievable. What compassion. No, Mother, they did not violate us. Don't worry, you won't have to be embarrassed in front of your precious Bridge Club or saintly friends." She spun around and stomped to her bedroom.

A long shower and preparations for the day calmed Beth down.

Later, the front door opened and closed. "Beth, oh Beth!"

"Heather!" Beth flew down the stairs.

The two sisters hugged. "I'm so glad you're home safe with us." Heather teared up a bit and laid her hand on Beth's shoulder. "You look good. No one would guess what you've been through."

"Thanks." Beth exhaled with a slight moan.

"It's my lunch break, but I wanted to see you." Her older sister, the whirlwind, hopped onto the couch with a remote directed at a flat screen.

Beth always thought of Heather as her pretty counterpart because of her sister's cute, turned-up nose and nice long legs.

Mom entered the room with chicken-salad sandwiches for her daughters.

Beth wanted to slam it into the garbage, but her growling stomach overruled. A sandwich never tasted so good.

"Those reporters are still on the front lawn," Heather said. "They're so rude. I had to fight to get to the door."

The newspaper lay folded on the end table. On its front page were color photos of Glenn and the three girls. Just as Heather inquired of her well-being, the newscaster listed the ex-hostages' names.

Beth didn't answer. She broke out in a cold sweat and stared at the TV as yesterday's events flickered across the screen. She found her face among the crowd. The circle of leaves adorned her head.

"We look like we've been dragged through hell," Beth whispered. "It's awful seeing yourself on the national news."

The camera swung to the angry mob striking out at Glenn. Though the picture was unsteady at times, Beth caught a number of clear glimpses. Love and compassion burdened her heart, just as it did in real time.

Meanwhile, the indifferent newsman shared their private nightmare with the entire country.

Bigger than life, the mug shot of Glenn's kind face and captivating eyes displayed across the screen. "Pictured here is suspect Glenn McKlain of Okanogan County. The victims also identified these three others." After showing their names and photos, the news anchor revealed law enforcement's objective to continue in their search for the fugitives.

When the topic changed to the senate vote, Heather turned to her little sister. "You must have been scared to death. The expression on that Nick fellow is disturbing, but the one they caught sure is cute. Glenn, right?"

"Yes, it was terrifying. You're right about Nick, but Glenn was good to us." Beth ached to tell Heather the whole truth.

The clock announced it was time for Heather to "scoot."

When her sister left, Beth escaped to her room with the newspaper under her arm. She closed the door, unfolded the paper, and enjoyed the close-up of Glenn. She pored over the article then hid it.

Beth felt inspired to compose a letter to her beloved and to include her picture. Before tucking it into the envelope, she reread the last sentences to herself. "I'll go on with my life, like you want. But even if you're 110 years old when you're released, you'll see a white-haired, old lady—with lots of freckles and a big smile—standing by the prison gate. Approach her with caution. She'll most likely cover you in kisses."

She stuffed the letter into a plain business envelope. She hoped this would ensure that Glenn would open it.

The conversation around the dinner table that night seemed stilted. Beth sensed her family's discomfort. David wobbled a fork between his fingers and picked at his food. Mom tugged at her clothes. Dad straightened his tie. Then he loosened it and unbuttoned the top button of his shirt.

Beth doubted her family was ready to hear about the love of her life.

After dinner, everyone retired to the living room except David. He headed to his room to finish his homework.

Heather muted her phone and plunked down next to Beth on the couch.

Dad sat in his recliner with his legs crossed at the knee. "You look thinner, Kitten."

"I am. There wasn't much to eat there."

Beth looked around. "It feels like there's a big elephant in the room. I suppose it's because you're wondering what happened?"

Dad nodded. "If you're up to it."

"You know we're supposed to keep this under wraps—Chief Bradrick's strict instructions."

Her father nodded. "We will."

Beth began her story. She expected to remain in control as she had done with the FBI, but reliving the abduction in front of her family left her shaky and tearful.

Silence fell.

"I'm sorry for all you went through." Heather squeezed Beth's hand and held it for a minute.

Beth nodded. Tears stung her eyes. She avoided eye contact with her family.

"Something doesn't add up." Dad stared at the floor, his

brow furled. "I can't put my finger on it. It's that McKlain character. He doesn't figure. He helps his adopted father and cousin escape and takes a gun away from you. But then he helps you ladies escape too?"

He shook his head. "Well, as long as we never have to lay eyes on him again, it doesn't matter."

Beth snickered to herself. *If I have my way, you will do more than lay eyes on Glenn, Dad. He'll be your son-in-law.* "I couldn't figure him out at first, either. He has some good in him. After all, he saved our lives."

"I wouldn't go that far, Kitten. Most likely his motives were corrupt and self-seeking. Playing the hero to get a lighter sentence. He probably fought Nick because he wanted you for himself. Any halfwit can figure that would win you and the other girls over. Who could know he'd get shot in the process?"

From a winged-back chair, Mom joined in. "They'll say what they think you want to hear, Dearie, but you can't trust them."

"Decker held a gun to my head to make Glenn comply. I'm glad he complied or I'd be *dead.* And as far as winning us over, he never claimed his prize."

"Why are you always defending that degenerate?" Mom's glare bore holes through Beth.

"Maybe she has a little defense attorney in her like our father," Heather joked.

Nobody laughed.

"Would *you* risk your life the way he did for people you hardly know?" Beth's words came fast. "That's certainly not self-seeking. If you had been there, you would see it differently."

"Why won't you answer my question, Elizabeth?" Mom

demanded with a darkened expression.

"I don't understand your brick wall." Frustration filled Beth's voice. "I defend him because you don't seem the least bit grateful." She ached, longing for them to like Glenn.

Mom leaned forward. "Don't seem grateful? How can you possibly expect us to be *grateful*?"

"I deal with his type all day long." Dad sat on the edge of his seat. His voice grew more irate. "I'm not interested in discussing that demented barbarian, but I'll tell you why we're not grateful. Should I thank him for ruining my daughter's life, for the mental anguish she's suffered, for brainwashing her, and for God only knows what else? The only thing I want to hear is his pleading when the Feds fry him for what he's done to our Kitten."

At a loss for words, Beth gaped at her father. Then she found her voice. "You want to hear Glenn *plead* when the Feds fry him?" Her father's sick words ricocheted inside Beth's wounded heart. Just as quickly, anger heated to a boil within her. "They didn't even *try* to brainwash us. Glenn didn't cause any of those things. Weren't you listening?"

Beth had more to say, but her family probably did not want to hear it. *Too bad.* "I was going to break it to you easy, but because of your hard-nosed, high-and-mighty attitude, I'm going to tell you straight out. I love Glenn McKlain." Her voice rose to a shriek. "So if you want to fry him, then you'd better fry me too, because I don't want to live without him."

Her parents' faces washed white. Heather's jaw dropped.

"Glenn is as good a man as you are, Dad. He gives a person a fair chance." Beth's sadness poured out in hot tears. "I intend to marry him someday if he'll have me."

She bolted, choking back her sobs. She slammed her bedroom door, flopped onto the bed, and smothered her anguished wails into the pillow.

A half hour later, someone rapped on her door. "It's Heather."

"Come in."

At Beth's invitation, Heather plunked herself down on the edge of the bed. "Sis, you know we all love you. That's why Dad is so concerned. You weren't there when the police told us you had been abducted. We all lay awake night after night, frantic over what might be happening to you. Were you being tortured? Were you freezing in the rain, bleeding, terrified? We had no idea what those dreadful men were doing to you. We couldn't help imagine the worst—that we might never see you again, or ever find out what happened to you."

Beth rolled toward her.

Heather's eyes glistened with tears as she rubbed Beth's arm. "It broke our hearts. Dad paced the floor by the hour and made himself sick with worry."

"I didn't realize how hard it was on you guys," Beth whispered. "I'm sorry. I wish I could've spared you the worry, but there were no phones. But, Heather, Glenn is a kind, gentle man. He doesn't deserve to die."

Heather chuckled. "That's quite a bomb you dropped on us, you know."

"Yeah, I know."

They ended the conversation with Heather agreeing to give Glenn a fair chance.

"I can't wait for you to meet him." Beth's eyes brightened.

A crooked smile formed on Heather's freckled face. She squeezed her little sister's hand and left.

Beth didn't want to face the rest of her family, so she stayed in her room. That night, sleep was elusive for Beth. Exhausted, she tossed and turned.

19. Irrational Fears

Federal Detention Center, SeaTac, Washington

The next afternoon, Beth planned to visit Glenn before his arraignment.

She felt like singing as she threw on a baseball cap, pulled her ponytail through the hole in the back, and grabbed a pair of sunglasses.

The mudroom door leading out to the garage and the automatic garage-door opener gave Beth the chance to back out of the driveway without having to deal with reporters. She and Kathrin planned to ride together, so she set out for her friend's apartment.

For the first time since their abduction, Beth and Kathrin were on their own in the big city. Kathrin's husband had been ordered to return for deployment at 0600 that morning.

Upon their arrival at the detention center, Beth couldn't shake the feeling they were being watched. She scanned the parking lot before flinging open the car door. The hair lifted on the nape of her neck.

She jumped out and grabbed Kathrin's hand. Together, they speed-walked along the street toward the entrance. "That jail house never looked so good," Beth said.

Once inside the building, a corrections officer led Beth to the visitor's room. Kathrin stayed behind, her nose buried in a text book while she waited.

A guard appeared from behind a locked metal door.

Beth sat upright. A big grin stretched across her face. Her heart leaped with excitement.

"McKlain doesn't want to see you."

His words sliced like a searing knife through Beth's heart. Her smile slid into a frown. "Wha… Did he give a reason?"

"He said you should go home."

Beth stared in disbelief as she watched the guard disappear behind the door. *Is Glenn done with me because I hurt him? If not that, then why? Goodness, can't I even visit him? I will see him at his arraignment—but he doesn't want to see me.*

Thirty minutes later, Beth sat beside Kathrin in a federal courtroom. The high ceiling caused footsteps to echo on the tiled floor. A clerk raised her voice over a constant buzz of commotion. She read the case details from a clipboard and handed it to the judge.

Her and Glenn's future happiness depended on the decision made within this cold place of judgment. Beth shivered.

At his podium, the assistant US attorney, an African American, presented his case against a man who stood before the judge.

Meanwhile, the side door opened. Three men stepped into the courtroom. The light bounced off a US Marshal's badge on one man's suit. The two prisoners with him were dressed in street clothes.

Glenn was one of them. He appeared like a sacrificial lamb being led to slaughter.

Beth's chest expanded with excitement at the sight of him. *Please look at me*, she pleaded silently.

All at once, Glenn's eyes met hers.

For a moment no one else existed. The same glowing

sensation he'd caused in Beth earlier rose anew. His eyes gleamed, unblinking, and his face softened. He gave Beth a barely perceptible nod before the marshal pushed him forward.

Beth's heart skipped a beat. She couldn't take her eyes off Glenn. *He forgives me!* Or perhaps he hadn't heard the reporter's question. She drew a deep, satisfying breath. *Either way, we're still good.*

Distracted, she didn't hear the proceedings, but was brought back when the judge hammered his gavel and barked, "Next."

The same fast-paced process was repeated for another man. Another bang of the gavel. "Next."

"Docket number 87753," the clerk said over the commotion. "Accessory after-the-fact to armed robbery. Accessory after-the-fact to three counts of aggravated kidnapping in the first degree."

Glenn and Mr. Willheight—plainly his counsel—walked up and stood before the judge.

"Do you understand these charges against you, Mr. McKlain?"

"Yes, Your Honor." Glenn's voice remained steady, respectful.

The judge peered over his glasses at the accused. "How do you plead?"

"Not guilty."

"We ask that the defendant be remanded," the US attorney said without emotion.

"Your Honor," Mr. Willheight's voice pleaded, "Mr. McKlain was in the process of bringing the hostages home when he was apprehended. We ask that bail be set."

"His father and suspected partners in crime are still at large," the US attorney argued. "He's a flight risk. We ask that he be remanded without bail."

"So ordered." The judge hammered his gavel. "Next."

The arraignment was over. The marshal took the other defendant and Glenn promptly from the room.

Beth stumbled from the courtroom as tears burned her eyes. After dropping Kathrin off, her mind couldn't rest. She was so consumed in anxious thoughts that she was taken by surprise when her driveway came into view. *What happened to the last five miles?*

Beth charged through the mudroom door, ran straight for her room, and shut out the world. After hours of internet research—plus an interruption for dinner—she learned Glenn might have to serve ten years if he was convicted. She would be almost thirty, and he would be thirty-three by the time he was released.

"The best years of his life behind bars," she mourned.

Their future together looked grim. *If he even wants a future with me.*

It appeared on the surface that Glenn and her parents were right. Beth's dream of a life with Glenn was just that—a silly dream. Beth was devastated.

Beth tried to call Glenn again. This time the officer said, "He doesn't want to talk to you."

He doesn't want to see me or even talk to me. Her eyes stung. *Maybe never again.*

Beth dropped on her bed and wept. Night came, but not sleep. The noticeable absence of crickets and crackling firelight added to her grief. She ached to be back at the cabin with Glenn.

The awful longing changed nothing. Beth's heart felt raw, and it would be like that for a long, long time.

She tried to imagine what Glenn was going through. Was

he lying awake in his dark cell? Surely he must be despairing. Was he thinking of her?

More than likely, he's staring out at the stars and freedom from between iron bars. He's accustomed to wide-open country. What's the scope of his freedom now? Maybe four steps. His cell can't be much bigger than that.

Beth's heart broke for him. Tears gushed. After a while, she grew numb.

Dawn dispersed the darkness, but it did little to chase away Beth's swollen headache or puffy eyes. "I don't know where to turn or what to do."

No one else in the house was up. The clock explained why: 6:37. Beth peered out the window. The sun still hid below the horizon, but the sky was painted pink with empty promise.

She dragged herself outside on the deck. A brisk breeze blew through her hair. The constant drone of traffic a few blocks away nearly drowned out the faint chirp of a few birds.

A waist-high rail encircled the deck. Beth collapsed to her knees. Fingertips hung onto the railing. Her forehead pressed onto the back of her hands. "How am I ever going to live without him?" Tears came. "Dear God, please help Glenn … and me." Drops rolled down her cheeks and splattered on the deck.

Over the next couple of days, Beth trudged through the house in a zombie-like state. She sheltered memories of Glenn in a corner of her heart, and would only treasure them in the sanctuary of her bedroom. There she could lie on her bed, enjoy his image, hug her pillow, and think about Glenn without interruptions or comments of concern.

Oh how she missed him during those times! But at least in her room she didn't have to put on a smile or hide her pain.

The next day, the doorbell chimed. Kathrin greeted her and introduced the young woman at her side. "Beth, this is Ashley. She helped solve my computer problems at college. We've been hanging out."

Beth nodded. "Nice to meet you."

Ashley was dressed in tight clothes that revealed rounded curves. Mid-length, light-brown hair gathered in a ponytail, showing off a round face, wide smile, and squinty, bright eyes.

"Let's go for coffee," Kathrin suggested.

Beth shrugged. *Why not?*

They found a popular espresso stand permeated with the aroma of coffee. A dozen people conversed in muted tones.

Kathrin sipped her latte then set the steaming cup down. "How are you doing, Hon?"

"Fine."

"Really?"

Beth nodded her lie. It pierced.

"I called Emily, but she couldn't join us," Kathrin said. "I think it's good to reintroduce ourselves to the world before facing our classmates at college tomorrow, don't you?"

"Nothing can prepare me for tomorrow," Beth said. "Emily and I haven't remained in contact. I guess we agree that we're too different to be friends."

"I've met Emily." Ashley never stopped smiling. "How are you different?"

Beth shrugged. "She's direct, I guess."

"Yeah, no doubt." Ashley leaned forward. "That snob called me a fat cow. I am *not*—" Smiling, she raised her head with pride. "I am a huggable teddy bear." She burst out laughing with a slap to her thigh.

From across the shop Beth noticed a skittish-acting teenager. He stared at the girls and whispered to his companion, a young man dressed like himself.

"What's with those two punks? They're staring at us. Do you think they have guns?" Beth dug into her purse for pepper spray. A familiar sensation of shrinking in fear swept over her.

"Those kids? My gut feeling is that they don't. We're both suffering from being abducted. It's normal. But I'm tired of being spooked, so I made an appointment for tomorrow with Jennifer, my counselor."

Kathrin's idea had merit. Beth perked up a tiny bit. "I think I need to see her too. Could I have her number?"

"Of course." Kathrin brought up Jennifer's number on her cell and handed it to Beth.

When Ashley left for the restroom, Beth confessed, "I don't know what to do, Kathrin. You know Glenn won't see me. He won't respond to my calls or letters, either."

"Has he ever said anything that might explain why he doesn't?"

Beth stared at her empty hands. "He said that he doesn't want to mess up my life and"—she choked back tears—"to forget it."

"It's probably not easy for him to keep turning you away. In his mind he can't have you—though he'd like to. And you are a reminder that he's just wasting away in jail. So you're making it hard on him." Kathrin's small soft hand rubbed Beth's.

"I don't want to make it hard on him." Sadness overwhelmed Beth. Her chin quivered.

"Who knows what the future holds? For now, though, you need to let him go."

Kathrin's words stung. Beth sopped her tears with a

napkin. "I can't let him go."

"Well, let's say you did … today. If he's convicted and does time, then when he's free you and he can start over. You never know."

Beth sniffled. "Why does life have to be so hard?"

"I don't know." Kathrin rushed to Beth's side and hugged her shoulders. "It won't always be like this, Honey." She reassured in a kind, upbeat voice as she briskly rubbed Beth's shoulder. "You'll be happy again. You'll see." Then she sat down. "Are you going to be okay at college tomorrow?"

"I don't like all the attention. If students say anything mean, I have no fight left in me." With Ashley heading back toward them, Beth hurried to compose herself. "How about you?"

"I don't know if I'm ready, either," Kathrin said. "I'll pray for God to rescue me. Knowing how much He loves me helps. We'll be old news soon. Want me to pray for you?"

"Yes, please. You're a good friend." Beth patted Kathrin's hand.

Ashley pulled out her chair, sat down, and asked in her cheerful way, "What are you guys talking about?"

Kathrin toyed with her cup, turning it around. "It's private."

"Oh, okay, sorry." The words rolled off Ashley's tongue. She didn't seem to mind.

They finished their lattes, and Kathrin drove them home.

Beth's first step on campus the next morning was met with stares and whispers. She slipped her hand in her pocket and curled her fingers around the comfort of her pepper spray.

Upon entering the classroom, Beth thought, *What I wouldn't give to be invisible right now.* Forty pairs of eyes turned to gawk at her. She held her chin high and took wide, easy steps, but she couldn't get to her seat fast enough.

"Nice to have you back, Elizabeth." The professor smiled.

A quick once-over of her peers' faces showed no sign of rejection. *What a relief.*

The restroom cubical was Beth's oasis between classes. In there no one asked questions; no eyes stared.

At 3:30 sharp, Beth fled to her car. With the campus retreating in her rearview mirror, she sighed. "I made it. Maybe I can survive tomorrow."

A live report of Decker's and Nick's transport to jail flashed on the TV screen the next morning. Beth jumped to her feet. "Yes!" She grabbed her cell and texted Kathrin and Emily.

"Thanks to a tip and night-vision scopes," the pretty anchor woman was saying, "suspects Nick Thoren and John Decker were apprehended by Border Patrol agents while riding their horses across the Canadian border west of Nighthawk at 2:00 AM this morning. Two-thirds of US Bank's stolen money has been recovered."

Luke must still be out there somewhere with the rest of the money, Beth mused.

The criminals' capture stirred up public interest, but Beth's classmates paid it no mind.

The following evening, Heather looked up from her cell. "Your kidnappers pled not guilty."

"No surprise there," Beth said in disgust.

"They'll be tried in Federal Court." Heather's eyes moved across her phone's tiny screen. "This report also explains why Agent Decker was fired from the Border Patrol in the first place. He tested positive for alcohol. Conduct unbecoming an officer." She laughed. "And exceeding weight restrictions."

Beth chuckled and gave Heather a fond smile. She was a

good sister. She'd made her laugh during a time when Beth found very little to laugh about.

Beth, Emily, and Kathrin were interviewed by Mr. Phillips, the US attorney, including uncomfortable questions about Beth's attachment to Glenn. "All the information we've gathered has to be disclosed to the defense team," he said. Then he prepared them for trial. "… so you'll know what questions we're going to ask."

Before being released, Mr. Phillips warned the girls, "You will be subpoenaed as witnesses for the prosecution."

"No." Beth shook her head. "I don't want to testify against Glenn."

"If you don't, you'll suffer serious penalties."

After that unpleasant surprise, life slid into something resembling normalcy. Beth wrote Glenn a second letter. It would be the last one, she decided when she mailed it the next day.

Every day for a week she dashed to the mailbox, hoping Glenn would respond. He didn't. Beth's life clanged as empty as the metal cubical. From then on she passed by the mailbox with no more than a wistful glance.

Then one afternoon Beth reached into the mailbox. An important college correspondence was due to arrive, and she didn't want to miss it. To her surprise, she saw the letter she'd addressed to Glenn. It had been returned unopened, stamped with "return to sender."

Hopelessness drained the life out of Beth as she stared at yet another rejection. "At least my first letter never came back," she said weakly, fighting to hold onto hope. *Maybe because my photo was in it, and he wanted to keep it.*

Beth puzzled over another envelope in the mailbox. The lock-up's return address disclosed where it came from, and her address was hand printed. *Can it be from Glenn?*

Her hopes soared. *Maybe he changed his mind and wants to keep in touch with me, after all.* With a grin stretching across her face, Beth ripped open the envelope and pulled out a hand-written note.

"Don't worry, Bethie Baby," the note read. "We'll see each other soon. I'll pick you up and make you mine."

20. Public Display

Federal courtroom

Beth gasped. She flung the note away as if it were a viper. Her limbs weak and shaky, she stared down at the paper on the walkway.

"Nick knows where I live." Wide-eyed and on the verge of panic, Beth scanned her quiet suburban neighborhood. Then she snatched up the note, raced into her home, and locked the doors and windows.

She dropped onto the couch and reread the threat. "How did he get my address?" Trembling fingers snatched up her cell and tapped out Kathrin's and then Em's phone numbers. Kathrin hadn't received one, but Emily had already opened her note.

"Mine says, 'I'll find you, and I'll kill you.'" Em snorted. "I'd rather be dead than be his."

"Me too. It's gotta be Nick."

"It's his MO, all right. He terrorizes and tries to control us even from behind bars. Unreal."

"Yeah. Be careful, Em."

"He's in jail, where I hope he stays for a hundred years. What can he do? Bye."

Beth was not as confident. She stopped in at the US marshals' office, where Deputy Johansen reassured her that as long as Nick was behind bars he couldn't harm her. However, they couldn't stop him from sending her notes.

The deputy's fat fingers hunted and pecked on a keyboard while he talked. "Who has your address besides friends, family, organizations, clubs, and educational institutions? I assume you don't put that kind of information on social media?"

"Of course not." Beth frowned. But the officer's questions rolled over and over in her mind. *How did Nick get my address?*

Several weeks passed. People paid less attention to the ex-hostages. New stories captured their attention. Christmas came and went. Beth could not bring herself to enjoy the holidays, however. The calendar was rolling closer and closer to Glenn's trial.

It had been three, long, drawn-out months since Beth had last seen Glenn. It took all her energy to hide her excitement at seeing him again.

At last, the day of Glenn's trial arrived. Interest in the kidnapping had clearly revived after the holidays. People filled every seat in the courtroom. Whispers buzzed.

The three ex-hostages were together again for the first time since Glenn's arrest. Emily acknowledged Beth with a polite but aloof nod. Her five-inch heels, classy skirt, and sharp-looking blouse were more conservative than usual. Beth and Kathrin wore low-key but smart dresses. They sat together, with Ashley on the other side.

"It's nice of Ashley to come," Beth whispered to Kathrin.

"Yeah." Kathrin answered, but she was obviously distracted. "I hope I don't exaggerate when I'm questioned, like saying gazillions. It's such a habit."

"You'll do fine." Beth grabbed her friend's hand and

squeezed. "Hey, in just a few minutes I'll see Glenn."

Shortly, the side door opened. Glenn stepped into the courtroom well-groomed, and dressed in a suit and tie.

Beth couldn't stop smiling. *Those stunning blue eyes. How could anyone not notice them? Every female in here must find him attractive, especially in that well-fitted suit he's wearing. It's easy to see he's not full of himself. I love that about him.*

Glenn focused on the defense table and headed straight for it.

Please, Glenn, look at me.

He didn't. He pulled out a chair and sat down.

Beth's happy spirits faded. She stared at the back of Glenn's dark head and broad shoulders. Preoccupied with trying to understand his behavior toward her, she didn't hear the "all rise" from the clerk, but she rose when everybody else did.

The twelve jurors could have been picked at random off the streets of Auburn, and probably had been. After lunch, the jury concentrated on the opening statement from the assistant US attorney. Every so often, they glanced at the defendant.

Beth brought her attention back to Mr. Phillips, the assistant attorney. He was spinning what sounded to Beth like an impossible tale during his opening statement. "Don't let his looks fool you. Some found the serial killer, Ted Bundy, attractive too."

Beth cringed. It never occurred to her that Glenn's looks would play a negative role in his trial.

Glenn's court-appointed attorney, Mr. Willheight, delivered a solid opening statement that would surely put reasonable doubt into the jury's mind. He painted Glenn as the hero he truly was. The hero never lifted his head.

Mr. Phillips moved right along presenting his case. First,

he invited Luke's doctor to the witness stand.

Mr. Willheight objected. "Relevance?"

Beth didn't quite catch the reason for the doctor testifying, since Luke was not on trial, but the judge appeared satisfied with Mr. Phillips' reasoning. "Objection overruled."

The physician went on to describe Luke Lazaro's terminal cancer.

"If Mr. Lazaro were caught and convicted today, how long would the defendant's father be slowly dying behind bars before the cancer took him?"

"A few months."

A specialist spoke about Sophia's experimental brain surgery that insurance doesn't cover. A representative from social services also confirmed that this type of surgery was not funded by the state.

What is the prosecutor up to? Beth scratched at her temple. *Is he trying to show that Glenn had motive to get involved in the robbery and to keep his dad out of prison?*

The judge adjourned for the day.

The next morning, Glenn stared at the defense table just as he had the day before. The prosecutor's witnesses came and went. Even Glenn's friend Shorty was called to the stand.

Traitor! Beth thought, but she knew Shorty had no choice but to answer the questions truthfully—questions about Glenn's relationship with the other suspects, his remote cabin, the horses, and his other means to carry out the accessory crime.

Thankfully, the defense lawyer got a chance to let Shorty testify of Glenn's good character, and that Glenn had been told they were going on a hunting trip.

Beth's emotions rode a roller coaster. Up and down. Prosecutor and defense. Hope and despair.

Deputy Sheriff Dalton from Okanogan testified about Glenn's capture and the hostages' rescue. A bright spot occurred when Mr. Willheight's cross-exam came around, and Beth's hopes took flight again.

"The hostages did not appear terrified or anxious to get away from him. Instead they seemed appreciative and defensive of him." Office Dalton said.

"Did Mr. McKlain try to escape?"

"No. He didn't run, hide his identity, or resist arrest."

"No more questions, Your Honor."

On the third day of the trial, Beth's roller coaster ride of emotions crashed.

"I would like to call Elizabeth Farell to the stand," Mr. Phillips announced.

Beth did her best to rise and glide across the courtroom with poise. *Okay, calm down, deep breaths.* When she settled onto the smooth wooden chair, all eyes were staring at her—except two blue ones.

Mr. Phillips' questions were easy at first. They stilled Beth's frazzled nerves, and she began to relax. Then he got down to business.

"Please identify the man who guided your kidnappers to the remote mountain cabin where you were held hostage."

Beth pointed to Glenn, proclaiming his guilt, but he didn't even twitch. He stared at the tabletop.

"Let the record show that Ms. Farell identified the defendant, Glenn McKlain," Mr. Phillips said. "Did you know or have you met the defendant or any of your kidnappers before your abduction?"

"No."

Then Beth answered questions about the battle in the stable for Glenn's gun.

"During this conflict," Mr. Philips began, "what did Mr. McKlain say—*his* words please—that revealed what he thought you would do with the gun?"

Beth blinked rapidly and licked her dry lips. She glanced at Glenn. He didn't look up.

"Answer the question, Ms. Farell," the judge broke in.

Beth's chest ached. *I hate incriminating him.* "He said—"

"Speak up."

She glanced at the judge's tightened face and gulped. "He said something like, 'I can't let you take us in.'" She looked at Glenn again, not caring if the jury saw her sorrow.

"Anything more?" Mr. Phillips wouldn't quit. "Like *why* he couldn't let you take them in?"

Beth slumped. "He said something like they had too much at stake."

The US attorney faced the jury. "'I can't let you take us in. We've got too much at stake.'" He sighed. "This sounds like someone committed to helping his family escape."

"Objection!" Mr. Willheight yelled.

"Withdrawn." But Mr. Phillips' lips twitched in a confident smirk.

The judge picked up his gavel. "We will adjourn for lunch. You may finish questioning this witness when we reconvene."

Beth let out a breath of relief. She needed a break.

When she returned to the witness stand after lunch, the judge reminded Beth that she was still under oath.

Mr. Phillips fired questions at her like a machine gun. By the time he was finished, the jury knew about Glenn's love and loyalty for his dying father and niece, including the pressure Luke had put on his son to help them.

Apparently satisfied with Beth's answers, Mr. Phillips withdrew. "Your witness."

Mr. Willheight stood tall and imposing. His height, big-boned structure, and the way he glared down at Beth would have made Goliath cower.

Beth quailed and hugged her body.

The cross-examination began.

Beth testified that Glenn had wanted no part of it right from the beginning. Her testimony was consistent with Shorty's regarding Luke's fabricated hunting trip.

"What compelled Mr. McKlain to finally agree to help them?"

"Decker held a gun to my head and said he would kill me if Gl—Mr. Mcklain didn't help them." Warmth spread through Beth's body. *It feels good to speak up for him at last.*

"We need to clear up an earlier statement regarding the gun," the attorney said. "You stated that my client took it away from you."

Beth nodded.

Arms crossed, Mr. Willheight's gaze pierced her. "Why did you shoot at him?"

"I only shot at him because"—she cleared her throat—"I wanted to keep the gun so we could escape. But I didn't want to hit him. Mr. McKlain helped us."

The defense lawyer leaned closer to Beth. Obviously annoyed, he raised his voice. "Don't you think being shot at is reason enough to take a gun away from you?"

"Yes." Beth lowered her gaze.

Glenn moved restlessly in his chair.

"Now we get to the truth." Mr. Willheight shouted. "Did my client ever do *anything* to warrant being hit over the head and knocked unconscious?" His angry tone filled the room as he swung his arm toward his client.

Beth winced. "No, he—"

The screeching sound of a chair being shoved back interrupted the courtroom theater. Glenn stood, his face tight. "The only truth is that she was kidnapped," he snapped. "What would you expect her to do?"

A shocked murmur went through the bystanders. Defendants did not speak in court. They especially did not rebuke their own attorneys.

"*I'm* on trial here, not the witness. Stop harassing her." Blue fire blazed in Glenn's eyes.

The judge hammered his gavel and roared, "Sit down or I'll have you removed from this courtroom—defendant or not."

Glenn sat, but Beth could see his hands shaking in anger.

What a sweet, caring man. Her heart overflowed with love.

"The jury is instructed to disregard the defendant's last remarks," the judge ordered. "They will be stricken from the record. Proceed, Ms. Farell."

Beth finished her testimony in a numbed daze. "… we were only trying to escape."

The court adjourned until Monday. Thank goodness for the weekend. It gave Beth time to recoup.

First thing Monday morning, Mr. Phillips summoned Emily to the witness stand. She leaned back in her chair and answered the questions without emotion, as if she were describing a day at the grocery store.

Through his questions, the US attorney painted a picture of Glenn readily participating in the crime. "Did Mr. McKlain ever try to help you ladies by calling 911?"

"No, but—"

"Did he use his hunting rifle against the perpetrators?"

"No."

"Other than what's already been testified, did he in any way try to frustrate his family's plans of guiding them to the remote cabin?"

"No."

After more detrimental questions, Mr. Phillips sat down.

Mr. Willheight repaired the damage done. Besides Decker's death threats, Emily told of how he had seized Glenn's phone and weapons. Then she explained how Glenn had been shot while saving her from Nick.

The next day, after Mr. Phillips rested his case, Mr. Willheight called Kathrin to the stand. She testified that twice Glenn was in the process of taking the hostages home when he was interrupted—once by Decker, once by the police.

Kathrin was the defense's star witness in Beth's opinion. She confirmed that Glenn didn't accept any of the stolen money. She gave numerous examples of Glenn's sacrifice, heroism, and honorable character.

The US attorney tried to tear apart her testimony. He was unsuccessful.

Beth felt a spark of hope ignite inside her. Perhaps the jury would see Glenn as she and Kathrin saw him: a good man caught up in a situation beyond his control.

After the attorneys presented their summations, the judge instructed the jury and sent them to deliberate Glenn's guilt. The court adjourned.

21. Perjury or Suffer Disgrace

The jury reached their decision in two days.

Beth sat with Emily between Kathrin and Ashley in the anticipation-charged courtroom.

Her mind turned to Glenn. *Surely he'll be acquitted. But if he isn't, then this could be the last time I'll see him for ten years.* An empty feeling contorted in the pit of her stomach.

Her mind relived their sweet moments together at the cabin.

The judge's words brought her back. "Would the defendant please rise."

Glenn stood at the same height as his attorney.

The court clerk brought a folded paper to the judge. He opened it, read it, and returned it to the clerk. "Members of the jury, have you reached a verdict?"

A balding man in the jury box rose. "We have, Your Honor." He unfolded the paper the clerk had returned to him.

"On the first count of accessory after-the-fact to aggravated kidnapping in the first degree, how do you find the defendant?" the judge droned.

"We find the defendant not guilty."

The judge repeated the question for the other two counts of accessory kidnapping. All were not guilty.

Beth's heart sang. *Not guilty! Not guilty!*

"And on the one count of accessory after-the-fact to armed robbery?" the judge asked. "How do you find?"

"We find the defendant guilty."

Beth's heart dropped to her stomach. *Guilty?* How was it possible? How could the jury find him not guilty to one accessory crime and not the other?

And it wasn't over yet.

The judge set the sentencing date and adjourned court. Beth would have to agonize for several more weeks until she heard Glenn's ultimate fate.

Her heart wept.

The day of Glenn's sentencing arrived, bleak and gray. Rain poured down. Beth scurried to her place in the courtroom to hear what would become of the man she had grown to love more than her own life.

The judge peered over his wire-rimmed glasses at Glenn. "Ordinarily, Mr. McKlain, I would sentence you to ten years, with fines up to $10,000, but your efforts to come to the aid of these young ladies has worked in your favor. In consideration of time served, you are hereby sentenced to not more than six—but not less than four—years in minimum security at the Federal Detention Center."

The gavel struck, and it was over.

The US marshal led Glenn through the side exit and out of Beth's sight. The door closed. She stared at it for several moments, not wishing to start her life without him.

"Come on, Honey," Kathrin encouraged. "Let's go."

Dazed, Beth let her friend pull her toward the double doors. She ignored the reporters.

That night, Beth lay awake in the dark. Tears ran down from the corner of her eyes, pooled in her ears, and dampened the pillow. *I miss Glenn so much. If he doesn't let me into his life four or six years from now, I don't think I'll ever be free of this ache, this horrible emptiness.*

The first rays of dawn spilling into the window caught her eye. There were still classes to attend, peers to face.

At breakfast Beth skimmed the *Seattle Times*. Photos of her, Kathrin, Emily, and Glenn made the front page. An article that included Glenn's outburst during his trial asked, "Why did the defendant reprimand his own attorney and fervently protect Elizabeth Farell? Could it be the felon, Glenn McKlain, and the female hostages became friends during that horrific week?"

Dad read the newspaper next. He slammed it down on the table in front of Beth and dashed off to work without finishing his breakfast.

Nick's trial was slated for three days later. When it rolled around, the court summoned the ex-hostages to testify.

The closer the time came to facing Nick again, the more Beth's insides quivered.

Moments before the trial, Beth leaned over to whisper in Kathrin's ear. "I used to be excited to go to court—you know, to see Glenn. But today feels too much like going through the abduction all over again."

She shivered. Nick's words, *"I'll pick you up and make you mine,"* turned to ice in the pit of her stomach.

Beth clasped and unclasped her hands in her lap when Nick entered the courtroom. After he and his lawyer took their seats at the defense table, Nick twisted around in his chair and leered at her.

Beth dropped her gaze. Bile bubbled up into her throat.

The jury had been selected the day before. The opening statements proved Nick's defense attorney, Ms. Hill, to be a shrewd one. She was a tight-skirted, pretty blond woman. It was too bad her hardened expression stripped her of her natural loveliness.

After their statements, assistant US attorney, Mr. Phillips, called Kathrin to the witness stand. She pointed out the man who had robbed the bank and kidnapped them.

Kathrin also gave grim testimony of Nick's assault and battery. After lunch, she finished up with her eyewitness account of Nick's molestation and assault with a deadly weapon.

Nick hissed and wagged his head every now and then.

"Your witness, Ms. Hill," Mr. Phillips said.

The defense attorney's quick, sharp, forceful tone intimidated Beth—even in the spectators' gallery. She dreaded being questioned by her.

"In a trial where alleged molestation is introduced," Ms. Hill said, shooting a look at Emily, "we need to consider enticement."

Through Kathrin, the jury heard about Emily's skimpy attire.

"Did any of you pretty women ever voluntarily show affection to the four men who allegedly kidnapped you?" Ms. Hill probed.

"*Three* men kidnapped us," Kathrin said, as if to remind the haughty woman that Glenn had been acquitted of that crime. "No, we did not show affection to any of the men who kidnapped us."

Through clever questioning, Ms. Hill insinuated that Emily had been malicious and promiscuous. Not only was she dressed immodestly, she had crushed Nick's hand.

"No more questions." Ms. Hill's five-inch heels clacked on the tiled floor as she strutted back to her table and sat down.

Court adjourned for the day.

The next morning, Mr. Phillips called Emily to the witness stand. She substantiated Kathrin's testimony. The female jurors seemed to react most when Emily described Nick's personal attacks on her.

Nick grinned as though he were proud of it.

Under cross-examination, Emily readily admitted to insulting and threatening Nick. "He wasn't taking 'no' for an answer," she explained. When Ms. Hill accused her of felony assault with a deadly weapon, Emily said, "It was supposed to be a deterrent. I wanted him to stop manhandling me, and—"

"That's enough, Ms. Jacobsen," the attorney snapped. "Just answer my questions."

But Emily didn't stop. "It was self-defense. He tried to kill me."

After several more questions, Ms. Hill was finished with Emily.

The trial adjourned for the weekend.

Monday morning, proceedings began like a mirror image of the previous court days.

A number of other witnesses testified against Nick until the US attorney was satisfied and rested his case.

Judge Marcelli formally passed the baton to the defense.

"I would like to call Elizabeth Farell to the witness stand."

Dread squeezed the breath out of Beth. The last place she wanted to find herself was in the witness chair on behalf of Nasty Nick. But a subpoena was a subpoena. Knees wobbling, she feigned courage and made a beeline for the witness stand. Once seated, her eyes made a wide berth around Nick.

Ms. Hill jumped right into her questions. "Ms. Farell, in regard to your abduction, is it true that Glenn McKlain was charged with"—Ms. Hill held up a document and read from it—"accessory after-the-fact to three counts of aggravated kidnapping in the first degree?"

Beth bristled. "*Charged* with? Yes. But he did not kidnap us, and he was found not guilty."

"Was Mr. McKlain at the cabin during the time you were held hostage?"

"Yes."

"Before your abduction, did you ever meet any of the men?" Ms. Hill asked.

"No." *So far, so good.* Beth thought.

"So they were all strangers to you."

"Yes."

"On just the second day of your abduction, with which of the four men did you laugh and joke?"

"I laughed at Mr. McKlain," Beth said. "The stove exploded," she hurried to add. "Ashes went everywhere, and—"

"Who is this?" Ms. Hill shoved a photograph in front of Beth.

"Glenn McKlain."

Ms. Hill showed it to the jury. "He's a handsome man. Did any of you three lovely ladies show any signs of affection to him?"

Beth scanned the courtroom. Fifty pairs of eyes bore holes through her. She felt naked.

Why is she asking that dumb question, anyway? Somewhere in the back of Beth's mind, she knew the questions she would be asked, but the reality of answering out loud made her face grow warm. "Yes." *There goes my good name.*

The room hummed.

"You did? All three of you?" The lawyer acted surprised. Beth knew she wasn't. It was all part of the lawyer game. "Exactly what kind of affection did you show him?"

"We thanked Mr. McKlain—and *only* him—with a hug and a kiss for protecting us from the kidnappers and for taking us home." Beads of sweat dampened Beth's skin and clothes, intensifying her discomfort.

"Did my client, Mr. Thoren, know that you three were affectionate to his partner?"

Beth nodded. "He heard about our gratitude."

"Did he act jealous?"

Nick slid down in his chair and leaned back, arms sprawled.

"Yes."

"Ms. Farell, did you fall in love with Mr. McKlain while you were at the cabin together?"

A sour taste rose up in Beth's mouth.

The room buzzed.

"Quiet." The gavel slammed down.

That question wasn't on the disclosure list. Beth squirmed in her chair. *I could lie. No one would know.*

Mr. Phillips objected. "Your Honor, how is this line of questioning relevant?"

Beth held her breath.

"Approach, Your Honor?" Ms. Hill requested.

The judge nodded, and the two lawyers hurried to the bench. They leaned close in quiet discussion.

I wonder what the penalty for perjury is. Beth felt ripped in two. *Worse, Glenn will find out if I lie about this. I can't hurt him.*

After a moment, Judge Marcelli turned to the Beth. "Objection overruled. You may answer the question, Ms. Farell."

The room waited, deathly still.

"Umm …" Beth's tongue was sticking to the roof of her mouth. "May I have some water?"

"Just answer the question." The gray-haired judge's dark

gaze pierced her.

It's Glenn or me—trashing my life forever or hurting him. Her pulse raced. "He's good-hearted and kind. He risked his life for—"

"Just answer yes or no, Ms. Farell." Ms. Hill scowled.

My whole world is falling to pieces. A sinking feeling roiled in her stomach.

Beth kept her eyes on Kathrin, drew a deep breath, and answered slowly. "Yes, I love Glenn McKlain."

22. Capture Bonding

The room buzzed with astonishment.

Glenn deserves my sacrifice, and for once in my life I acted unselfishly. But what about my good name? Mom and Dad are going to kill me.

"Order in the court." Judge Marcelli pounded his gavel. When everyone was quiet, he nodded at Ms. Hill. "Proceed, Counselor."

"Besides Mr. Thoren, did anyone else notice your little romantic adventure with Mr. McKlain while Nick was still at the cabin?"

"Kathrin did."

Ms. Hill leaned on the railing toward the jury. "Mr. Thoren clearly had reason to be jealous and want in on the romance. If a hostage can laugh and joke and fall in love, then perhaps—"

"Objection." Mr. Phillips barely cleared his chair.

"Sustained," Judge Marcelli said. "Save it for the summation, Counselor."

"That's all for this witness, Your Honor." Ms. Hill sauntered back to her table.

Beth felt Nick's nasty gaze on her all the way back to her seat. She glanced at the people. Some turned their faces away. Others shot her arrows of disgust.

Beth felt like crying. *Is this how the world is going to treat me, like something disgusting the cat threw up?*

Emily wore a poker face, but Beth's faithful friend,

Kathrin, smiled compassionately.

Beth paid little attention to the next witnesses. Her mind was too busy swirling with doubts and questions. When Ms. Hill finished her case, Mr. Phillips sought a rebuttal.

Permission was given, and the judge called it a day.

The next morning, the US attorney called a psychiatrist, Dr. Beckridge, to the witness stand. "Please explain to the court what Stockholm syndrome is."

"Yes, sir. Stockholm syndrome—also called capture-bonding—is when victims of abduction develop positive feelings toward their captors. Sympathy—even empathy. They defend and identify with their captors. It's a strategy for survival on the victim's part."

"Is it possible that a hostage might believe she's in love with her captor?"

Dr. Beckridge nodded. "Oh, yes. The survival instinct is strong. This is all born out of fear and has nothing to do with real love. It's pure terror."

"Thank you, Dr. Beckridge." Mr. Phillips pivoted on his heels and shot the defense attorney a hard smile. "No more questions."

Stockholm syndrome? What's that? Beth's thoughts were fixated. *How could I not know my own mind?*

Mr. Phillips took his seat. "The prosecution re-rests its case, Your Honor."

After lengthy summations from both lawyers, the jury was dismissed for deliberations, and court was adjourned.

Like before, reporters swooped down on the three women the moment they left the courtroom. Emily squeezed around everyone and left.

A blond reporter sidled up to Beth. "Do you believe capture-bonding played a role in your feelings toward Mr.

McKlain, the defendant?"

Before she thought it through, Beth found herself answering. "Absolutely not. Glenn helped us. He did *not* kidnap us or hold us captive, and the jury agreed. He's a hero—not a criminal to be scared of."

The blond reporter's eyes sparkled with interest. "What's he *really* like?"

Beth couldn't help but smile at the thought of Glenn. A camera snapped, forever capturing her expression.

After Beth described Glenn, the reporter asked one more question. "How do you feel *now* about falling for a friend of your kidnappers?"

"It's not my favorite way to meet someone, but life sometimes has more imagination than we do."

Once home, Beth headed straight for her room and searched the internet for Stockholm syndrome. After much research, she flexed her stiff muscles. *Maybe I'm in denial, but I don't believe this Stockholm syndrome theory applies in my situation.*

Before breakfast the next morning, Mom ran to the store for milk. Beth was pulling plates from the china cabinet when Dad stomped up behind her. His face was rigid with anger. He thrust a newspaper in Beth's face and waited without a word.

The picture captured Beth's glowing expression. The headline read, "Hostage Falls in Love with Kidnapper." Underneath, and in smaller print, it read, "or was it capture-bonding?"

"He's *not* a kidnapper!" From skimming over a few sentences, it was obvious the press was milking this story for all it was worth. The first line read, "Handsome Glenn McKlain captured Elizabeth Farell more than physically—he captured her heart."

"*Now* are you satisfied?" Dad's harsh voice assaulted her.

Beth set the paper on the cool, stone counter. "They didn't get it right, Dad. I'm sorry. I never meant for this to happen."

"I'm sure you didn't, but why did you have to tell the world? Couldn't you have said something else?" The veins in Dad's neck bulged.

"Lie on the witness stand?"

"Yes. They can't prove a thing like that. You're a fool to throw your life away over some loser and to continue in this idiotic fairy tale of yours. You're my daughter, and you are *never* to speak to him or see him again." He slashed the air with his hand.

Beth shook her head. "You can't order me around anymore, Dad. I'm leaving." She grabbed the newspaper, spun around, and marched to her bedroom.

"Elizabeth Farell, get back here!"

Beth kept going. Through blurred vision, she dragged out her suitcases and pitched in some clothes. *How can something as beautiful as this love I feel for Glenn cause such heartache and strife?*

"This world may turn on me," she whispered to herself. "But please—Mom and Dad—not you too. I need you now more than ever. Can't you see that?" Her heart twisted.

A few minutes later she wiped her tears, lugged her suitcases to the Honda, and backed out of the garage. She glanced up at her dad, who watched from the kitchen window. A sharp pang pierced her. Then she drove away.

Beth picked up Kathrin on the way to the courthouse. When her faithful friend heard about the confrontation, she consoled Beth. "Why don't you stay with me? I'd love it. My husband won't be through with his deployment until July. I'm alone in my gargantuan apartment. Stay with me, Beth."

"I'd love that." Beth squeezed her hand. "You are an

amazing friend, Kathrin."

The girls arrived just in time for the court's time-honored opening proceedings. The jury's verdict, "guilty on all charges," made Beth's heart explode with joy and relief. Nasty Nick would be put away for a long, *long* time.

She grinned at her friends, and they embraced.

As the marshal was escorting Nick away, he glared at them. "Y'all can't hide from me," he yelled at the top of his lungs. "I'll kill you for what you've done to me!"

Then he was gone.

Eerie chills raced up Beth's arms.

"Aw, he's all talk." Kathrin patted Beth's shoulder. "He'll be behind bars."

Back at Kathrin's apartment, while Beth unpacked her suitcases, she confided in her friend. "I'm not just an ex-hostage anymore. To people I'm probably a naïve twit who tried to keep her love for her so-called kidnapper a secret. Things could get ugly. I don't know how to begin to prepare for that."

"God will be with you, Honey. Call on Him." Kathrin smiled. "Text me and—just like Him—I'll come running."

It was another night of fitful sleep for Beth. Unfamiliar, new noises kept waking her.

The next morning, Beth's shaky legs slogged through a crowd of classmates. She kept her head down, hoping to go unnoticed. To her surprise, her college peers treated her no differently. They walked with friends side by side, focused on their cells.

A couple of weeks later, between classes, Kathrin ran up to Beth and grabbed her arm. "Did you hear?"

"Hear what?" Judging from Kathrin's furled brow, it wasn't good news.

"Nick held a marshal at gunpoint with the marshal's own gun. He escaped before he was transported to prison."

"*Escaped?*" Beth gulped. Wide-eyed, she did a quick three-sixty of her surroundings. Was he around the corner? Would he barrel down on them at any second?

"Nick would want to get light years away from here," Kathrin assured her. "I don't think he's stupid enough to try something in broad daylight with all these people around."

"Oh, I don't know." Beth gave the campus another once-over. "His ego overrides his common sense."

"True. I'm texting Emily." Kathrin's thumbs flew across her phone's display. NICK ESCAPED. WE'RE GOING 2 THE POLICE 2 ASK 4 PROTECTION. WANT 2 MEET US THERE?

Kathrin's phone vibrated. Emily declined their invitation and mentioned her dad, the retired cop.

The girls drove to the police station. After speaking with a deputy, Kathrin and Beth tromped out of the station.

"Randomly sending a patrol car by your apartment won't be enough to protect us." Beth's voice trembled. Her leg muscles tightened, ready to run.

"I'm sure they're doing all they can." Kathrin glanced over her shoulder. "It's up to us to do all *we* can too."

"Like carrying a gun and taking classes in—"

Bang! A loud noise shattered the air.

Beth jumped, screaming, "Nick!"

The girls ducked down and raced for the Honda. Breathing heavily, they jumped inside, slammed the doors, and fumbled the door lock button. Beth scanned the parking lot and wrapped her fingers around the pepper spray.

Not far away, an old lady bent over and peered at a dent in a parked car. It appeared as though she had backed into it. When the girls realized the bang was only a collision, they laughed at their irrational fear.

From then on, Nick plagued Beth's mind. She never knew if or when he'd find her and—

And what? Beth trembled.

23. Nick's Spy

Two weeks later
Portland, Oregon

By luck or skill, Nick had so far managed to avoid the authorities.

He hid in the shadows near the railroad tracks on the skid row side of Portland, Oregon. Nick watched druggies and boozers staggered down the backstreet.

He slipped his wallet from a back pocket. Stocky fingers pulled out a worn newspaper clipping of Beth. He stroked the image of her lips and grinned. "One of these days, I will lay one on those sweet, juicy lips. After me she'll forget that hayseed."

Laughter caught Nick's attention. A couple of good-for-nothings had dug around in a dumpster and come up with a half-eaten burger. The fools acted like it was Mama's fried chicken.

Against a graffiti-covered wall, another lowlife lay sprawled on a pile of full-to-bursting garbage bags. Nick snorted. "That's gotta stink to high heaven."

The two dumpster divers went their way.

Nick studied the passed-out bearded man. *I'm piddling my time away.* Some of the bums were so filthy that no one could tell what they looked like underneath. *That poor excuse for a man on the garbage sacks, for instance. He'll do. Yeah, he could pass for me.*

Even better, he looks so stoned that he'll never know—or care—what happens to him.

Nick waited until nobody was around but the bum. He cautiously approached the garbage pile. "Hey, you!" He kicked the unconscious form and waited for a response.

Nothing.

When another, harder kick produced the same *nothing* response, Nick chuckled. "Like shooting fish in a barrel."

He slipped his hand into the drunk's filthy pocket and drew out a skinny wallet. He dropped it into his own coat pocket and landed a parting kick. "Thanks, buddy." Then he headed for the pick-up truck he'd lifted earlier.

No one yelled. No one followed him. "Man, you're the *king*," Nick complimented himself. He slicked back his hair and started the truck. It came to life with a roar.

At the first stop light, he took a moment to open the wallet and pull out the I.D. "Robert Grady. That'll do. I just need to grow a beard. Now I can get on with life and go anywhere I please."

A few blocks down the street, Nick turned into a parking lot and shut off the engine. He pulled out his cell and texted. U ALONE?

Finally, *bzz, bzz.* "Ashley" appeared on the display. YES. U OK?

HOW'S SPYING? Nick studied his reflection in the rearview mirror.

CAN'T GET CLOSE 2 BLONDIE, BUT WAS E-Z GETTING FRECKLES' & BLONDIE'S ADDRESS FROM CHINA DOLL.

THEY DON'T SUSPECT WE R RELATED? Nick grabbed his beer out of the holder.

I PLAY IT SMART.

HOW DID BETH REACT 2 THAT NOTE FROM ME?

SHE WAS RATTLED flashed on the screen.

Nick smirked. GET BETH'S CELL # & C IF SHE MOVED.

JUST FRECKLES THIS TIME? U R INTO HER AREN'T U?

SHE'S INTO ME. Nick grinned. His fingers flew across the screen. SHE GAVE ME THE LOOK. AGAIN SAY IT'S 4 U.

DONE. I'LL KEEP MY EARS OPEN & LET U KNOW.

Nick tossed his cell on the seat and drove off.

John Decker's trial went the way of Nick's, with one difference. The assistant US attorney put forth that Decker used his former law enforcement position as a means and opportunity for criminal activity. Mr. Phillips also presented evidence of Decker's vengeful reaction to his discharge from the Border Patrol Agency.

When he was pronounced "guilty," the judge lectured Decker on how far wrong he went, and the honorable conduct Supervisor Special Agents should have.

"The judge really slammed him," Beth told Kathrin as they walked out of the courtroom. "I am *so glad* these trials are finally over."

Kathrin agreed.

One late afternoon, Beth leaned over the dining room table scowling. Calculus hurt her brain. She sighed and puzzled over the example again.

The vibration of Beth's cell rescued her. Without thinking, she reached for it. Her mind and eyes still concentrated on calculus. "Hello."

"Beth?"

"Yes. Who is this?"

"It's good to hear your voice again, Bethie Baby."

Nick! Beth's heart slammed against her ribs.

"I've missed you." Nick's lewd tone slinked into her ear. "You looked sexy in that little pink number you wore yesterday. The one with the flower-shaped buttons down the front."

Beth sprang to her feet and severed the connection with a jab of her finger. She sent the phone sailing across the table.

Bzz, bzz. It vibrated again.

A sudden chill hit at her core. Beth backed away from the table, never taking her eyes off the cell.

Kathrin looked up from chopping vegetables. "What's the matter?"

"Nick!" Beth felt dizzy. Black spots swam before her eyes. She slumped into the chair.

The buzzing wouldn't stop.

"*What?*" Kathrin headed in her direction.

Eyes wide, Beth left the phone and fled to her room. She leaped onto her bed and hugged her pillow, trying to calm her pounding heart.

Kathrin followed her.

After talking it over, Beth decided to report this harassment to the authorities. She would also change her phone number and move away from Auburn.

"The world's not safe anymore. How does he know so much about me?" she wailed to Kathrin. "Where I live, my cell number, and what I'm *wearing*? I feel violated. But I am *not* going to let that jerk make me an invalid. I am going to live a normal life." Her tone was forceful, but underneath beat a quailing heart.

"I think I'll ask Ashley or Mama if I can stay with them a few weeks," Kathrin said. "I'm sure they'll welcome you too."

Beth shrugged. "Maybe." But something inside warned

her to get farther away than Kathrin's friend or mother.

Later, Marshal Quinn took Beth's report and then studied his computer. "Sorry, the number traces to a burn phone, which of course tells us nothing."

He shook his head. "Unless something comes up that must be attended to, we'll coordinate with the police department and park at your home for about a half hour every now and then until you move. It would be a good idea to relocate ASAP. When would that be, do you think?"

"As soon as I find a place." Beth's mouth felt dry. "I'll call you."

That night, sounds in Kathrin's apartment spooked Beth more than ever. She got up after Kathrin had gone to bed to check the doors and windows before she could fall asleep. She was spiraling out of control into a dark, scary place, but she couldn't do anything to stop it.

The next morning Beth called her grandparents and explained her dilemma. They invited her to stay with them.

"Thanks Grandpa. Moving to Olympia should help." Beth told no one except Kathrin and Dad. The two friends promised each other never to reveal their new locations to *anyone*.

Since Beth had an important test that morning, she postponed her move for a couple of hours. Kathrin had classes all that day so she took her own car, leaving Beth to drive alone to the campus. On the way, a chilly tickle scratched her mind. *Stop it!* But she couldn't stop panic.

A white van appeared to be following her.

Beth's eyes flicked between the mirror and the traffic ahead. To test if this silly fear was real, she made a quick right, bumping and bouncing over a curb. Surely the van would keep going straight.

It didn't. It followed her, and the driver didn't seem to care if Beth knew it.

Perspiration beaded her forehead. She squeezed the steering wheel, but she couldn't stop trembling.

Beth stomped on the accelerator to change lanes, cutting off a Prius. It honked.

The van swerved into the same lane.

She barreled through a yellow-turning-red light, hoping that would discourage her stalker. Nope.

"I'm tired of being afraid of you!" Beth yelled, glaring at the rearview mirror. *What should I do?* She fumbled in her pocket for her cell, hit 911 and burst out, "Nick Thoren is chasing after me. He's wanted by the FBI." She described the van and her location. "Please hurry."

After asking a couple questions, the dispatcher said, "Stay on the line."

Beth felt a little better. Two blocks down the street, police cars with sirens blaring and lights flashing surrounded the white van.

Beth pulled over too. She jumped out of her car but kept her distance from the van. "Whew, they got him." Giddiness swept over her.

Guns drawn, police stood behind their car doors and shouted, "Driver, get out with your hands up."

A gray-haired man with a confused expression did as he was ordered. His license confirmed that he was not Nick.

Beth was on a first-name basis with the officers at the front desk. Standing before them she grimaced, bit her lip, and apologized for her mistake.

A female deputy handed her a brochure about stalkers. "You've changed your phone number, but you should change everything else too—your city, your vehicle, your college, and any place you frequent. Wear nondescript clothing, change your hair, and maybe all but one of your friends—at least for a while."

The deputy's gaze bored into Beth. "Most importantly, do not tell *anyone* about these changes, except one or two trusted people. Okay?"

"Okay. Thanks." Beth clutched the brochure. "I feel I can *do* something now."

Beth skipped classes and made major changes in her life that very day. Thank goodness, Dad dropped his agenda, picked her up at the police station, and escorted her to the places she needed to go.

First, she went shopping for an entirely different wardrobe. Later, with Dad at her side, Beth walked out of the mall wearing glasses and her hair in a ponytail. A gray hoody hid most of her face.

Dad waited while Beth met briefly with her counselor.

Not long into her story, Beth began to tremble and fight back tears. "I feel like I'm losing it. I'm afraid of almost every man. I'm afraid they may stalk me or kidnap me. I feel helpless, like Nick's always watching me. Every morning, I wonder if this will be the day he finds me and grabs me."

Jennifer's compassionate counsel and prayers calmed Beth a little—for a while.

Dad took her first to Kathrin's to pick up her clothes. Then he drove her home and helped her pack. A police cruiser sat parked across the street the entire time, just as Edward Farell, Esq. had requested.

A car dealership was next on Beth's list. She became the owner of a nondescript Ford Taurus. *The most boring car on the road. There's so many.* Beth decided with a little smile.

Dad went back to work.

Beth breathed easier when she left I-5 that afternoon and pulled up to her grandparent's townhouse an hour later in Olympia. She didn't waste any time calling South Puget Sound Community College and having her classes transferred mid-quarter. Under the circumstances, the administration was very helpful.

"All the changes and isolating myself from almost everyone has lessened my anxiety somewhat," she told Kathrin over the phone that evening. "But I'm grateful for any degree of relief. Are you staying with Ashley?"

"It was either Ashley's cement couch or Mama's luxurious spare bed." Beth heard Kathrin's little chuckle. "So I'm at Mama's. Ashley and some others have asked about you, but I *only* told them that you're doing all right."

"Thanks, my friend."

Several weeks passed, and still Beth glanced in the rearview mirror as much as she did the front windshield.

In Olympia, sunshine was as elusive as Bigfoot, but on one particular day it was shining brightly. So when Kathrin took the time to drive and see Beth, they stepped out on the back lawn to soak in the rays and relax.

With little grunts of frustration Kathrin struggled to open her lounge chair and sit on it without tipping it over sideways.

A smile tugged at Beth's lips. She had missed her friend's cute, bumbling ways.

Kathrin finally succeeded and lay back on the lounge chair next to Beth. "How's your stay been?"

"Good. My grandparents are the best. Do you realize it's been over five weeks now, and it appears that all my changes have worked."

"That's fantastic." Kathrin cheered.

Beth smiled. "I hope so, anyway. When I wake up in the

night, I still feel compelled to see if the doors are locked. Peace keeps running from me, no matter how hard I chase after it. Ha. I'm starting to wax poetic. Your influence, I'm sure."

Laughter provoked a tap on the arm between the girls. "It feels good to laugh," Beth said.

"You know, Kathrin, I just realized something. My mind has been so preoccupied with Nick that I haven't had time to dwell on Glenn. I think this whole thing—as awful as it's been—has actually helped me heal a little from losing Glenn."

"Oh, I'm so glad." Kathrin patted her arm.

"There's nothing I can do to keep Glenn in my life, anyway. He won't let me." Beth's expression sobered. "Like you said, it's best if I let him go. It'll hurt like—well, like you know what—but I've *got* to do it."

Kathrin nodded.

Beth drew in a deep breath and closed her eyes. "Okay, Glenn McKlain, it's official. I totally let *go* of you"—she cringed—"for now, anyway." Beth took a mental survey of her pain and then opened her eyes. "It hurts, but from what I can see, it didn't kill me." She wiped her watery eyes.

"Whatever happens four to six years from now, I'll deal with then. Glenn will need a friend when he's released. I wonder who that will be. Shorty? Maybe his sister will be back from Ireland. I wish it could be me."

"God is in control. If He wants you and Glenn to be together, He will make a way where there seems to be no way." Kathrin winked at her.

PART TWO

24. The Missionary

Four years later
Malawi, Africa

Beth Farell, World Relief's newest team member, pondered over what to pack for her first field assignment in Malawi, Africa. She tossed a couple pairs of shorts and three tank tops into her suitcase. "What do you think, Rosie?"

"I've been told that the ladies in Malawi wear dresses," Beth's fun-loving friend advised as she tucked her curly red hair behind her ear. "Only prostitutes wear pants." She grinned at Beth's shocked look and slurped her soda.

"Then dresses it is!" Beth dumped her suitcase upside down and made a mental note to buy some lightweight dresses. "I certainly don't want men to think I'm a prostitute." A slight chill shot through her.

"Me neither," Rosie replied. "And I haven't been kidnapped and stalked."

Beth nodded. "It took me a couple of years not to break out in a cold sweat whenever a man just *looked* at me. Now I'm going to Africa with you and Bob—*a man*." Beth wrinkled her nose. "Thank goodness Bob and I have worked in the office together before this project. I've discovered that he's trustworthy and protective."

Laughter hit Rosie just as she took a mouthful. Soda spewed out. "Is *that* what you call it?" She swiped soda off her sweater. "Sweetie, that old man is possessive of you and me."

"And jealous of any man who looks at us."

Rosie nodded.

Beth pulled out the hoody that had disguised her for too long. "I'm sick of wearing this thing." She tossed it back in the drawer. "Hey!" She grinned. "I don't have to hide from Nick in Africa."

The girls cheered, and then Beth finished packing.

Several days later, after many more preparations, Beth, Rosie, and their boss—big, balding Bob—touched ground in Lilongwe, Malawi, after a full day of traveling. From the very first step off the aircraft, heat blasted Beth, but neither the temperature nor jet lag dampened her excitement.

Their work took them to several orphanages in northern Malawi for two weeks. Then the small city of Chikwawa became their headquarters in the south.

Beth's ground floor room in Hotel Chikwawa was fairly modern, except for the toaster-sized power converter. Instead of a coffee pot, a French press sat on the counter. Mosquito netting draped down from the bed's canopy, giving the room an almost elegant touch.

She wandered onto the patio. The porter followed.

"Oh, it's very pleasant," she commented. "Nice view of the plains. I'll be spending time out here." As soon as Beth handed the patient man a tip, he left.

Curious to know what lay just beyond the patio, Beth leaned over the three-foot high railing.

She gasped and jumped back. A sharp drop fell into a deep ravine. She looked to the side. The adjoining room had the same short railing.

It must be a temporary fix, she mused. *A railing this short can't be safe.*

Other than this unpleasant surprise, Beth found the room comfortable.

After Rosie and Beth unpacked, they met outdoors for tea on the deck of the hotel's lounge.

They began their conversation with small talk, but somehow they ended up chatting about their first loves. While Rosie described her romantic adventure, she gazed up at nothing, as if lost in a delightful daydream.

Then she turned to Beth. "How about you?"

Beth skimmed over the details of her life four years ago until Rosie was completely caught up. "Enough time has gone by that I seldom think about the abduction, or about meeting and falling in love with Glenn."

Rosie's almond-shaped green eyes opened wide. "I'm blown away. You never told me about Glenn."

Telling her story had aroused a melancholy mood in Beth. "Whenever I picture Glenn's loving eyes, it feels like a sword pierces me." She pressed her fist against her heart. "He might not want to see me when he's released. Until he's free, I'll go on living my life. This job helps."

On their third day in Chikwawa, Beth, Rosie, and Bob watched the locals from an open street café.

The sounds of the city and a foreign tongue surrounded them. The streets bustled with people. Many women were dressed in bright-print wraps and balanced a pot on their heads.

Cartoon-cute, overloaded trucks bulging in all directions paused for the crowd to move out of their way. They didn't even honk or shout at them.

Beth chuckled. "Is it a game to see how much they can pile

on their truck without tipping it over?"

Her friends shrugged.

The three sipped flavorful coffee, unexpected in such a poor country. After a relaxing time, Bob left to pay the bill.

One Caucasian man stood out among the sea of black faces and bodies. Several African children were clustered around him. Beth's gaze rested on his tall, lean frame and broad shoulders. His dark hair almost covered his ears, but his beard was nicely trimmed.

Unlike many around him, this man apparently could afford to take care of himself. His short-sleeved shirt hung over his shorts, and he wore sunglasses and sandals. The children didn't.

"There's a white guy over there." Beth pointed in an inconspicuous way.

Rosie's eyes twinkled with exuberance as she scanned the crowd. "Where? There's so many people, but a white guy should be easy to—oh, I see him." She smiled broadly. "Hey, he's attractive. Looks like he's buying ice cream cones for the local children."

They watched in silence. Then all of a sudden, Rosie grabbed Beth's arm. "Do you want to meet him"—her words came fast—"and see where he's from? I'll stay here and wait for Bob."

"What? No. I'd feel awkward and forward." Beth shook her head. "And he could be a jerk, or worse, a predator or something?" She shivered, as if the sun had gone behind a cloud. *No!* She told herself. *I will not slide back into fear.*

"Pfff." Rosie flapped her hand. "That's silly."

"You go," Beth challenged.

Too late. The man with his small crowd of chattering followers ambled down the hard-packed dirt street. When they weren't licking ice cream, they were jabbering and smiling. The little troop piled into an older model, open-air jeep and pulled into traffic.

Beth tried to read the insignia on the driver's door, but it was no use. Dirt plastered it.

Bob came up behind them just then. "Let's go."

The three field advisors hopped into their rented SUV, then Bob drove onto the main street heading north. It wasn't long before he veered onto a side street.

They stopped at an orphanage in downtown Chikwawa. The visit was routine, with little or no concerns. The nurse practitioner, Rosie, examined the orphans and inoculated them. Bob gave the children lessons in hygiene, and Beth filled out the necessary reports.

Everyone looked forward to the playtime that followed, including the visitors.

Early the next morning, they were scheduled to visit an orphanage out in the country, The Shepherd's Little Flock. This orphanage lay within proximity to three small villages.

Six miles out from Chikwawa, Beth and her coworkers lost their cell service, so the valued phones were shoved into the glove box. Only a few more miles, and they found themselves on a mud-hole infested road. The tires seemed to hit every hole, jostling the travelers and causing them to hit their heads on the roof.

Rosie and Beth laughed at their new adventure. Bob and their Malawian guide and interpreter did not.

"Au-to-mo-biles do not keep well or long here." The guide pronounced each syllable clearly and with care.

On the way, Beth 'had to go,' so they found a bush to accommodate her. *This is really roughing it*, she thought. *But so far I'm enjoying every minute of my time here.*

Many miles later, their SUV pulled into a small village. Curious youngsters ran up and mauled the car in their eagerness to greet the visitors.

Beth watched from the window. The kids all wore the same crew cut, so it would have been impossible to tell the girls from boys if it wasn't for their tattered, faded dresses. A couple of the children suffered with distended bellies. Beth's heart tugged.

Without waiting for an okay from the field advisors, the Malawian guide decided to stay in this village and visit his relatives. "An English-speaking missionary is at orphanage, about thirty-five minutes down this road." The guide pointed to the only road.

Deep mud holes plagued the travelers the rest of the way to the orphanage. Rosie's and Beth's sore necks and tired muscles no longer saw the humor in it.

About three isolated, rough miles later, Bob turned off the road that followed the tree-lined river. Under The Shepherd's Little Flock sign, everyone clambered out of the SUV. Beth straightened up and stretched her back.

Bob walked around the car. "We've lost five lug nuts and a rim and dented another. Some were probably missing when we rented the thing."

A few yards from the sign, someone had dug a well. The red, iron hand pump marked its location. One lonesome-looking straw hut sat in the middle of the wide-open plain dotted with young trees. A short, grass-walled enclosure stood several yards behind the hut.

Bob pointed out a primitive baseball diamond. "Baseball!" He grinned.

The difference between the urban hubbub and the country quietness struck Beth. A few chickens clucked and pecked the bare ground. In the distance, children's squeals and laughter brightened the silence.

"They must be on the other side of the hut." Bob motioned the girls to come along. The chickens fluttered out of their path as the three made their way toward the festive sound.

Under a tree, several small black bodies wrestled in the dirt on top of a white man. The children giggled and screamed. The man lay mostly on his side, laughing along with them. In their merriment, the little flock clearly didn't notice the visitors approaching.

"It's a happy, carefree place," Rosie whispered to Beth.

"They obviously enjoy each other." Beth agreed. "I've heard that not many white men will take the time to play with children, especially in a poor, third-world country."

An adult female national in a brightly colored printed wrap stood by. She smiled at the newcomers then turned back to the wrestlers. "Teacher!" she called.

The teacher didn't respond. He kept roughhousing with the children.

Rosie's elbow poked Beth in the ribs. "Look." She nodded toward the grass hut. The jeep they had seen the day before rested in the shade of the hut.

Rosie bent close to Beth's ear. "He has to be that handsome guy we saw in the city."

It made sense. Children climbing all over him in Chikwawa. Children climbing on him here.

Beth smiled.

One of the orphans suddenly sprang to his feet and started rattling off something in what Beth figured must be Chichewa—their language. Immediately, the rest of the children abandoned their wrestling partner and raced toward the new arrivals, whooping with gaiety.

The man sat up, dropped the football, and replaced his sunglasses and baseball cap. Once on his feet, he brushed off the dirt.

Beth grinned. He'd missed a dark smudge on his cheek.

Two children smiled broadly. Then they stood formally and faced the visitors. "Good afternoon, ladies and gents," they recited together in a British accent. The poorly clad boy bowed in a proper manner; the little girl curtsied in her frayed dress.

Even my mother would be impressed with these children's perfect decorum and accents, Beth thought. *Contrasted with their destitute poverty, it's charming.*

Beth expected a British accent also from the white man, but he surprised her. He spoke like an American or a Canadian. It was the same man, all right—tall, lean, broad shoulders, dark hair, trim beard. Now that they stood face to face, it was easy to see that he'd inherited a well-chiseled jaw line.

A young girl—maybe three—tapped his leg and raised tiny arms to him.

Instantly, he scooped her up into his arms. Pink ribbons adorned her short pigtails. She grinned shyly at the visitors, and then reached out to Beth.

"I'm Bob Gregory," Bob was saying. "This is Elizabeth Farell and Rosie Manchester."

Just then, as the tall man was introducing, the pigtailed girl hollered, leaned over, and snatched a lock of Beth's waist-long hair.

Startled by this unexpected move, Beth drew back slightly. The tot dropped the brown hair.

"I'm sorry," the teacher said in a husky voice. "She has never seen such beautiful, long hair like yours."

Beth lowered her head to hide her blush. Her pale-yellow dress caught her eye. *I'm glad I wore this today*. "That's okay. She can hold it." She tilted her head forward. Brown strands spilled over a freckled shoulder.

A corner of Teacher's mouth turned up. He said something in Chichewa to Pigtails.

Eyes dancing, the toddler grinned. Her little fingers felt Beth's hair. Squealing, she gave her opinion of such a marvel.

The woman from the orphanage translated. "She says, 'Ma'am, your hair feels soft as corn silk.'" The woman gestured with her hands.

"Oh, thank you, Hon." Beth smiled at the girl.

Never losing her grin, the toddler leaned into the man's neck and giggled.

Teacher placed a tanned hand on the national woman's shoulder "This is Cosi and her two children, Buseje and Chikumbu." He moved his hand to Pigtail's head. "And this is Amie." He pronounced it *ah-mée*, the French word for friend. "And this is Kenta, Jekél, Jemba, and Ramo."

"We're from World Relief," Bob said. Then he explained the reason for their visit. "Do you have about an hour?"

"Yes"—hesitancy lingered in Teacher's voice—"but a nurse gave them vaccinations and examined the children two months ago. And we already teach them hygiene."

"Good. Then we only need to have Elizabeth go over the questionnaire with you." Bob turned to the two ladies. "Instead of waiting around, we should take advantage of the daylight. Rosie and I will go back to the neighboring village to find some lug nuts. I don't want to lose a wheel in the dark. There's not one street light." He grimaced. "Actually, there's *nothing* out here."

While Rosie chatted with the missionary, Bob whispered

to Beth, "Will you be all right for an hour? I need Rosie to come with me. She's strong."

Beth glanced at Teacher. Did he look like someone she could trust? *No fear!* she ordered herself.

Then she turned back to Bob."I'll be okay. But hurry back, please. He *could* be dangerous. You just never know. "

"They wouldn't let him work with the kids if he was dangerous," Bob assured her. "We'll be right back."

Beth nodded. She tried to push down a rising, irrational fear as she watched her friends drive away.

I'm alone now. God, please protect me from this stranger, this man and from the wild animals. Please bring Bob and Rosie back in just a few minutes.

25. No Place to Escape the Darkness

Many miles from small city of Chikwawa, Africa

There were no chairs in the orphanage, so Beth sat on a blanket next to the teacher-missionary in the shade of a tree. She was afraid to look at him for fear of giving him encouragement.

Without pleasantries, she jumped right into the report. "Name of proprietor/missionary in charge?"

"Andrew Powell." His fuzzy forearm rested on his upright knee.

Beth scribbled away on her clipboard. "Okay. What is your last completed level of education?"

"Mine?"

She nodded.

"One year college."

Beth tried not to show her surprise at his lack of credentials for this career and quickly moved on to the next question. "What tangible or licensed experience do you have working with children?"

"Not much. I trained for two weeks as a middle school retreat counselor." He smiled.

Beth wasn't sure she should bother to write that down, but for the sake of not embarrassing him, she filled in the blanks. "Have you or anyone here ever been convicted of a crime against children?"

"No."

"Do you teach them to read, write and speak English?"

"Yes, and they teach me how to speak Chichewa. They understand more English than they speak."

After several more questions about the curriculum, Beth moved on to the children's health.

"Cosi can better answer those questions," he said. "She's been with the children most of their lives. We have two other orphans—brothers—but they are visiting with their sponsors for a couple of weeks. And we're expecting seven more children next month."

The missionary/teacher, whose name Beth finally knew—Andrew—rose. "An orphanage up north has too many, so they're moving some here." He wandered over to where the children were playing. "Hey, Cosi," he hollered. "Could you answer this young lady's questions about the kids' health?"

Cosi's accent made it more difficult to communicate, but after about fifty minutes Beth's report was finished.

"Where is your husband, Cosi?" Beth tucked her pen in her pocket.

With an empty stare, Cosi said, "He working in Blantyre. Make more kwacha—dollars—in city."

Energetic Kenta, probably twelve, acted like an older brother and corralled the other orphans. Soon they were quiet, seated on the dirt in a semi-circle at their teacher's sandaled feet.

Wearing his sunglasses and ever-present cap, Andrew sat on a flat-topped rock before them.

Cosi smoothed a brightly colored blanket over the ground in the outdoor classroom. With a bashful smile, she invited Beth to join her. The Malawian was mother to a four-year-old and an infant, who stayed tucked snuggly in a bright-colored cloth sling on his mama's back.

The lesson began. The teacher held out a large picture book and pointed to where Israel was in relation to Malawi. He briefly explained Israel's early first-century political and religious climate. Then he picked up a small Bible and told the story of Jesus.

"No matter what we've done"—he paused at the end of each phrase so Cosi could interpret for the orphans—"or who we are, Jesus paid the price with His life so we could go to Heaven. Trying to be good enough won't get us there, but trusting Jesus will. Do you know why Jesus did that?"

After a quick pause for translation, Kenta and Jekél yelled out, "Because He loves us!"

"Yes, Jesus loves *you*." Andrew poked one shoulder at a time and said, "and you," until all were included—that is those who were awake.

Beth smiled when it was her turn.

While the youngest children slept on the others' laps, Kenta, Jekél and Jemba prayed a simple prayer, asking Jesus' Spirit into their heart. Andrew hugged the three children and spoke to each one. The commotion awoke the others.

Beth made mental notes of Andrew's gentleness, his obvious desire to encourage, and a sincere love for the children. A wish to become better acquainted with him budded within her.

"On this special occasion of having a guest visiting, we invite Elizabeth and Baby Ramo to play a game of softball with us," Andrew said.

Beth jumped at the chance. So did Baby Ramo. He wasn't a baby. He was close to three years old, and his limp didn't slow him down any.

The afternoon sailed by.

Beth hadn't given any thought to how much time was passing. Under a partially cloudy sky, she became engrossed in a lively game of softball with the two adults and six children.

Goodness! I haven't laughed this hard and felt so carefree since I was a kid. The cares of the world didn't seem to exist for anyone in this small orphanage.

Andrew never came across as forward or bossy, but rather as the gentlest of souls. Beth began to feel more comfortable around him. The warmth of his smile touched her innermost being, the part she'd locked away over the past four years.

This stirring means nothing. No one stands a chance compared to Glenn.

After the game, Beth gladly rested and delighted in a picturesque lone bilbao tree silhouetted by the waning, orange sun. The air against her skin was cool and pleasant.

"Please, come eat dinner." Cosi approached from behind. Her tone was always reverent.

"Dinner?" Beth jumped up. "Why aren't Bob and Rosie back? They said they'd be gone for only an hour." She glanced at her watch. 5:50. "It's been almost five hours! What's happened to them?"

Cosi shrugged. She didn't seem concerned.

But fear swamped Beth like an ocean wave. *Did the wheel fall off or did the SUV break down?* She pushed back other, darker imaginings.

None of Beth's thoughts cheered her, but she followed Cosi to the cooking area. A pot of rice and a pan of mouthwatering chicken sizzled over a small wood fire on the ground. The oldest girl, Jekél, who appeared about eleven, stirred the pots. With enthusiasm in her big, brown doe-eyes, she grinned at Beth.

By now, darkness blended land and sky. Beth scanned her

surroundings for an outhouse. "Cosi, where's the restroom, please?"

Brows knitting, Cosi struggled to pronounce it. "Rest … room?"

"Sorry. The loo … water closet?"

Cosi's face perked up. She nodded, then pointed to a four-foot high grass enclosure some distance away.

"I'm amazed," Beth told Cosi, "that I didn't need the water closet all afternoon."

"It is because it is hot here." Cosi dropped her head with a shy smile. "The body uses most the water we drink."

"Interesting. Thanks." Beth hurried over to the four-foot high spiral-grass wall. Staying between the straw walls, she followed the path the walls took her. The curious path always curved to the right, winding around in ever smaller circles until she came to a hole in the ground in the middle of the spiral. She was grateful for the privacy when she squatted down, and it didn't reek as much as an ordinary outhouse.

When Beth returned, someone had added wood to the crackling wood fire. The others filled their plates and found spots to sit on the dirt around the fire. Beth joined them.

They bowed their heads and closed their eyes.

"Father, thank You for always listening to us," Andrew prayed. Cosi translated. "It's amazing that You do. We want to thank You for bringing Elizabeth here. Please keep her and her friends safe and give her peace of mind."

Goosebumps covered Beth's arms. She felt honored.

"Father," Andrew was saying, "You said, 'All good things come from You,' so we want to thank You for all that You do for us and for this meal. You are so good."

They ate the messy, sticky meal with their fingers. Beth wasn't sure what parts of the chicken she was eating, but it was truly finger-licking good. She smiled at the thought.

During the meal, only Cosi and the kids were chattering in their own tongue.

As darkness descended further, Andrew stuffed his sunglasses into his button-down shirt pocket. Humming, he gathered the plates. Without being told, the children pumped water and began to help wash up.

In spite of Andrew's prayer and his relaxing hum, concern for her missing friends and fear of spending the night here robbed Beth of her peace.

Heavy clouds now shrouded the starlight. Darkness closed in around Beth. Her heart skipped a beat. There was no place to go. No place to escape it. *It's unnerving.* "Wow, it sure gets dark here all of a sudden. Toto, we're definitely not in Kansas anymore."

Andrew chuckled. "That must be why it's called 'darkest Africa.' But when the sky is clear, the stars shine, and everything appears brighter."

They gathered once again around the fire, the only source of light in this dark place.

Beth sat two orphans away from Andrew. The glow of the firelight gave her a sense of safety and some light. The people, though—and everything else—were shadowy figures.

"What could have happened to Bob and Rosie?" Beth was on the verge of tears. "Are there any dangerous men or animals around?"

"Most likely no one had the right size lug nuts, and someone had to take them to the city." Andrew's soothing, husky voice flowed with compassion and assurance.

But it didn't help much.

"Not many nationals have vehicles," he continued. "I've never heard of any dangerous men in that village. I'm sure they're fine, Elizabeth. If they did go to the city, they won't be back until tomorrow afternoon."

He smiled at her. "If they don't show up tomorrow, Kenta, Jekél, and I will take you back to the city early the following morning."

"I would be grateful if you would."

He nodded. "Cosi says she would be honored if you would stay in the hut with her and the young ladies tonight. The gents sleep outdoors."

"Maybe Rosie and Bob will still show up tonight." *If they don't then I'll have to stay the night here. Alone. Please, God, I don't want to. It's a scary place.* Beth checked her pocket for the mace. *What if the car overturned because a wheel fell off, and Rosie and Bob are lying in the road badly injured or d—*

"Elizabeth, do you have a favorite song? If I know it, we can sing it." Andrew, the only other white person for a hundred miles and fluent in English, rescued her from her torturous "what ifs."

When Cosi, smiling, translated Teacher's words, Kenta hopped to his feet and brought back a guitar. The children fired off their favorite songs.

"Let's allow our guest to go first." Andrew strummed his guitar with surprising skill. Once in a while he drummed on it with his palm. Each child had their own drum and kept a fitting beat. Cosi's babies slept through it all.

"I can't think of one right now," Beth finally answered.

Excitedly, the children requested "Drummer Boy" and began to beat their drums in unison.

"We practiced that song *a lot* for Christmas"—Andrew explained—"and you can tell it's still their favorite."

Kenta sang in English. "Come, they told me"

"Pa rum pa pa pum," everyone sang.

"A newborn King to see"

Everyone followed with, "Pa-rum-pa-pa-pum."

Their little fingers kept the beat.

Andrew took a turn with a solo. His deep voice softly sang, "Mary nodded … pa-rum-pa-pa-pum."

"The ox and lamb kept time … pa-rum-pa-pa-pum."

The three youngest sang a trio: Five-year-old Jemba, Amie, and Baby Ramo. Their young, sweet voices and round faces endeared them to Beth's heart.

Enthusiastically, she clapped and cheered at the end. Their faces, reflected in the firelight, lit up the night.

"Old McDonald!" several children yelled, waving their hands and wriggling in place.

Andrew threw Beth a comic grin. "They enjoy taking turns making the animal noises."

The girls stroked Beth's hair while they sang. She laughed with the others.

"Thank you for getting my mind off my worries," Beth said a while later. She smiled at Andrew. She could barely make out his face in the dying firelight.

"It's what we do every night. Different songs now and then." A deep chuckle came through the night. "Once the fire goes out, we turn in."

"I'm tired, anyway." Beth yawned. "It's so dark I don't think I can find the … uh … water closet."

Cosi spoke quietly to Amie in Chichewa, to which the little girl nodded. "Amie wants to help you, E-liz-a-beth."

With a grin, Amie's small hand slide into Beth's, and she led her through the blackness to the spiral restroom. It was slow going, but Amie's infectious giggles made it enjoyable. Even though Amie's language was unfamiliar, her tone communicated love and kindness.

Later, lying on a thin mat on the dirt floor in Cosi's hut, Beth listened to the rhythmic breaths of the sleeping children and her hostess. She couldn't hear the gents outside, only the peculiar, foreign sounds of the African animals and insects.

The earth and her flat pillow smelled faintly of dust. Above her hung mosquito netting, which Cosi had lowered from the same branches that held up the thatched roof.

Beth wanted to turn this day over and over in her head, but she was too tired.

Sleep won out.

Faraway hushed singing woke Beth the next morning. She groaned. Every bone and muscle ached.

This bed is so hard. Where am I? She opened her eyes. The first warm rays of the morning sun streamed in between the hut's branches and straw and onto her face.

She sat up. Snoozing, peaceful faces surrounded her. *Oh! I'm in an orphanage hut in the middle of Africa.*

A man was singing, only it sounded far away. Beth slipped past tangled arms and legs and dark bodies and ducked through the doorway. The boys' huddle outside revealed that one person was missing—Andrew. The rest were still asleep.

Beth's curiosity took her to the top of a rounded hill that dropped down to the river's edge. Excitement prickled up and down her arms and legs as she pushed her way through the leafy branches. The sun glistened off the water, making her squint.

Andrew stood at the river's edge. He sang with his head and arms upraised.

"All that You've done is so overwhelming,

I delight myself in You, in the glory of your presence.

I'm overwhelmed. I'm overwhelmed by You.

And God, I run into your arms, unashamed because of mercy."

Whoa! Beth was caught off guard. *He's a beautiful singer, with such depth of feeling. I love it.*

She quietly lowered herself onto the cool, sparse grass under a tree on the hillside. His voice spread velvety smooth across the new dawn.

Not wanting to be caught watching and listening to this private moment, Beth pulled herself away before he finished. She climbed up the short embankment, grinning from ear to ear.

Why am I smiling? she wondered. *There is something about this missionary that I like. I wish I could have the joy and peace he has. He's certainly devoted to God. I really don't know Andrew. Should I be afraid of him?*

Beth had no more time to contemplate. Already, a few of the children trotted toward her, full of new-day cheer. Jemba and Amie grasped her hands. They swung their arms, causing hers to swing.

Beth laughed and skipped down the path with the children. Her long, tangled hair flopped against her back.

Soon, everyone gathered for a cornmeal mush breakfast and ate with eagerness. Cap and sunglasses in place, Andrew approached Beth. "Would you like to help the younger children learn to count in English, while I work with the older ones? The kids would be thrilled."

Beth agreed. It would certainly distract her from worrying about Bob and Rosie's absence, or when they would arrive.

Jekél rang a cowbell, and the school day began.

Just before noon, wide-eyed Jemba pointed behind them

and said something.

Beth turned to look. Heavy, dark clouds loomed over the horizon. Thunder rolled in the distance.

The children's faces gleamed. The wind kicked up. The papers in Beth's hands flapped, and one sailed away. Her students giggled and chased after it.

A sudden, booming clap of thunder brought everyone else to their feet with gasps. The children laughed, except for the very youngest. Eyes wide with fear, Baby Ramo dove into Beth's arms and hung on tight.

It felt good and natural to Beth, like a mother bird covering a frightened chick with her wings. "Shh," she soothed the little boy. "You're safe. It's just thunder." She rubbed his back.

Baby Ramo might not understand Beth's words, but her tone made his body relax.

Amie ran to Andrew's protection, and Cosi's daughter to her. Andrew wrapped his arms around Amie. "It's just a loud noise, *mon amie*. You'll be fine."

Large raindrops plopped onto the ground. Andrew stood up. "Let's get inside. The rain's coming."

Too late.

The sky suddenly opened up and dumped on the little group. Before they could escape to their sanctuary, they were drenched. The hut seemed suffocating with ten people crowded inside. Andrew's head touched the ceiling.

Droplets blew in through the open, glassless windows, tickling Beth's arms. The sweet scent of wet, thirsty earth filled her nose. Never had Beth heard such a deafening pounding. Rain back home in Auburn drizzled and occasionally poured. But it never came down like this!

Concern covered Andrew's face. He made his way to the hut's door, removed his sunglasses, slid them into his shirt pocket, and buttoned it down. He peered outside, his gaze apparently fastened on the southern horizon.

The rain thundered too loudly for normal conversation. They waited for it to pour itself out, but it kept dumping. A few minutes later, Andrew caught his breath and pointed. "*Flood!*

26. The Flood

A long ways from civilization, somewhere in Malawi, Africa

Everyone in the jeep. Run! Run!"

Like the climax of a horror movie, a bank of muddy water was surging toward them, swallowing everything in its path. It swirled and uprooted trees.

Shock gripped Beth. She felt glued to the ground. She stared, openmouthed, as the deluge advanced.

Andrew snatched up Amie and Baby Ramo in his arms. He glanced back at Beth. "Now! *Move!* Then he bolted for the jeep.

Andrew's shout prodded Beth into motion. She grasped Jemba's and Jekél's hands and tore out after him. Her heart hammered.

Just behind her, the oldest child, Kenta, sprinted to keep up.

She and Andrew flung the children into the cargo area and back seat. Then they leaped into the front. Amie climbed onto Beth's lap.

Through the torrent of pouring grayness, Beth caught a glimpse of Cosi's long, print dress. She was carrying her children and leaning into the onslaught.

But she was charging in the wrong direction—up a slight hill behind the hut.

"Andrew!" Beth screamed and grabbed his arm. She pointed at Cosi and her children.

Andrew glanced in Cosi's direction. "Hang on!" He yelled to Beth and the kids. He yanked the steering wheel and flattened the accelerator to the floorboard.

Beth and the children were flung backward. They hung on for dear life. Hope dared to rise as they sped after Cosi.

Beth glanced behind her shoulder. A wall of roaring, churning water and debris slammed into the back of the jeep. Beth lurched forward.

The flood hurled them off the ground and into its control. Bone-chilling water overfilled the floorboards. The rushing surge pitched the jeep forward, thrusting it to and fro, and up and down.

The children screamed and clung to each other and to the adults.

Beth's eyes widened. *How will we ever survive this!*

She tightened her grip on Amie and prayed for mercy as the floodwaters carried them away from Cosi and down, down, down . . . into the quickly rising river.

When the jeep hit the river, the engine sputtered and died. Andrew struggled to use the wheels like rudders against the current in an attempt to keep the jeep upright.

Lightning flashed across the sky. *Boom!* Thunder rattled Beth's insides.

Terrified at the thought of losing Amie, Beth strained to hold fast to the jolting vehicle and the precious little girl. Too soon, her worn-out muscles screamed in pain. She couldn't hold on much longer. The relentless torrent sloshed over them.

The jeep smashed headlong into a giant boulder near the edge of the river and stuck fast. Everybody flew forward. Beth and Amie slammed into the dashboard, the impact lessened only by Beth's outstretched hand.

Baby Ramo screamed and hurtled through the air. Arms

and legs waving like a windmill, he fell into the water and disappeared. In a flash, Andrew vaulted over the door and dove in after him.

Water continued to gush into the jeep. A large tree lay wedged between the boulder and the embankment, creating a precarious bridge to land and safety.

"Quick," Beth ordered. "Climb on that tree!" She pointed and pantomimed to make the children understand.

Kenta obeyed at once. He grabbed Jemba by the hand and yanked him onto the tree trunk. Like quick, lithe cats, they glided across the bridge with no trouble.

Thankfully, the river's surge kept the jeep shoved fast against the boulder. Beth grabbed Aime and Jekél and followed Kenta. She shot a frantic glance behind her shoulder when her feet touched solid ground. Where were Andrew and Baby Ramo?

There they were!

Andrew bobbed with the swell of the current. He kept Ramo's head above water with one arm and swam with the other. Lightning lit up the grayness; thunder rumbled.

Beth and her precious charges clawed their way on all fours up the muddy, soaking embankment. Rain pelted their backs. When they reached the top of the ridge, Beth straightened up. Heart pounding, she scanned the brown, swirling water.

Jemba yelled something in Chichewa. A small index finger stretched toward the river.

Beth squinted through the downpour. Water dripped off her nose and lashes. What sharp eyes Jemba had! A little ways downstream, Andrew was pulling himself and Ramo onto the embankment.

But something didn't seem quite right. "Stay here." Beth signaled with her palm outstretched before them. "Watch them, Kenta."

He nodded.

Beth bolted in Andrew's direction. Bushes scratched her legs as if they were trying to keep her from the two. *Hurry, hurry!*

It took several glances overlooking the ridge before she spotted them below. She plunged down the steep bank. Mud sucked at her heels. She tripped and fell, then righted herself and kept going. "Andrew!" she screamed.

He didn't appear to hear her. He sat on a muddy shelf, where the violent current beat against its bank. With each wave, another chunk broke off and tumbled into the river. Rocking back and forth, he held Ramo's limp body against his chest.

"No, no!" he wailed. "Please, Father, no." He pressed Ramo's tiny face against his whiskered cheek. "R-ramo."

Beth rested a gentle hand on his drenched shoulder.

Andrew turned his head up into the rain. It was evident on his face—his heart was breaking. He glanced at her and then lowered his head again.

"I'm so sorry." Compassion poured from Beth. Hot tears ran down her cold face.

All at once, the ground beneath them gave way. Dirt, rocks, Andrew, Baby Ramo, and Beth collapsed into the cold, churning river.

Underwater, everything turned muffled. Beth couldn't see a thing.

The flood swept her downriver, its power too fierce. Beth kicked and thrashed until her head broke the surface. Her lungs gasped for air. The murky water seemed resolute in dousing her face. It stung her nose and choked her. She fought for her breath and to keep her head above the boiling swells. The tree-lined bank raced by.

Not far away, a surviving tree grew close to the bank. Water from the deluge reached nearly to its leafy crown. To Beth it was a lifesaver in the middle of a raging ocean.

She wrestled against the current and swam toward it. Her left hand stretched and snagged a flimsy branch. It cracked. Panicked, Beth flung her other hand closer and grasped it. The wispy branch snapped in two.

"Help! Help me." The current started to snatch her away.

A strong hand suddenly locked onto her arm. With one arm anchored to the tree, Andrew strained to pull her toward him.

Beth kicked against the surge. Soon, she was hugging the trunk, high in the tree but barely above water.

"Are you okay?" Andrew yelled above the flood's roar, the pouring rain, and the rumble of thunder.

Beth tried to turn around to look at him, but her face was too close to the trunk. "Yes, thanks to you." Hope washed over her.

"Are the kids all right?"

"Yes, they're waiting on the river bank, high above the water," she shouted back. She kept her cheek pressed against the rough bark.

"Good. We can't stay here."

"Why not? I like this tree," Beth joked, giddy with the realization that she might not die in that river.

"The river is calmer here in this inlet. We can swim to shore." Andrew's voice sounded at ease. "Do you see that root hanging down on the bank? It's a little downstream."

"No." Beth shivered from fear as much as the cold.

"It's about three feet above the water's edge." Andrew pointed. "See it?"

"Okay, now I see it." Her chin and her voice quivered.

"We can use it to pull ourselves up the bank. But it's too high to reach if we're just treading water. And from here, the bank looks too step to climb without the root. I need to find out how deep and swift it is over there. Be right back." Before she could beg him not to go, he dropped down and disappeared under the muddy water.

The bank might as well have been a mile away. Beth was too scared to let go of the tree. *But I have to let go eventually.*

Andrew's head bobbed up next to the shore. He treaded water, drifted downstream in this calmer section, and apparently calculated the possibilities. Then he swam above water toward Beth.

Once there, he latched onto the tree's branch and wiped the excess water from his face.

Through the downpour, Beth caught his beautiful smile.

"You're choking the life out that tree. Ease up on it before it turns blue." His voice came light-hearted.

Andrew's effort to calm her helped. She relaxed a bit and raised her voice above the turbulence. "Thank you for coming back to help me instead of just calling me over." Appreciation and trust swelled in her.

"You're a strong swimmer, Elizabeth. I saw you. You can do it. I'll stay right with you. C'mon, Sweetheart, let's go."

Beth blinked to squeeze out the raindrops and dropped down from the branches into the cold river.

Before he released the branch, Andrew wrapped his hand around Beth's upper arm. "When we get to the bank, I'll stand on the ground. It's not too deep. Then if you sit on my shoulders, you'll be able to reach that root. Can you do it?"

Trembling, Beth nodded. *I have to do it! We have to get back to the children.They must be terrified, thinking we've drowned.*

She clenched her jaw, took a deep breath, and let go. Panic washed over her, but she swam forward in spite of being stiff as a board. With Andrew on the downstream side of Beth, they swam together toward the shore. *I couldn't do this without Andrew.*

The torrential rain pelted the river.

Once in position below the root, Andrew explained, "The water is up to my mouth when I'm standing on the ground. I'm going to drop down under you now and lift you up on my shoulders. I'll hang on to you. As soon as you're on my shoulders, grab that root and pull yourself up to the top, okay?"

Beth jerked her head yes.

Andrew swam behind Beth. Large, cold hands wrapped around her waist. Then he dropped under the surface. At once, he rose again, lifting her partly out of the water.

Beth's upper thighs landed on his shoulders. In haste, she grasped hold of the large, muddy root and pulled herself up off his shoulders. Loose dirt fell onto her from above as she planted her feet against the bank. Her hope now refreshed she glanced back at her rescuer, who watched from below.

"Can you pull yourself up?" Andrew sounded pleased.

"Yes!" Beth grappled her way up the bank. *Only two more feet. I'm going to make it.*

A sudden, muffled thud and a splash alarmed Beth. She twisted around to look behind her. A small tree floated downriver where her rescuer had once been. He wasn't on the embankment, either. She scurried the rest of the way up.

"Andrew! Where are you?"

No answer came. Only the continual roaring of the floodwaters.

Lightheadedness threatened Beth. She searched the violent waters. Should she jump back in to search for him? Or was Andrew climbing up the bank somewhere? Did that floating tree hit him? Was he unconscious underwater?

It seemed as if time stood still. Beth waited.

And waited.

"It's been too long and no sign of him." The horror that Andrew was gone … drowned … stunned Beth. Her eyes and heart stung. Something deep inside her could not cope with the thought of losing this kind teacher.

With a heavy chest, she sat and stared at the angry river that had stolen Andrew and Baby Ramo.

The rain—now dripping mildly on her back—felt as if it had joined her with tears from Heaven.

Andrew was a wonderful man. Why didn't I realize how dear he was to me?

All at once, another horrible reality struck Beth. She was alone … in Africa.

How in the world could she protect the orphans? How would she get them back to civilization? Her body trembled uncontrollably. "Dear God, I don't know what to do." With her head down and her hands over her ears, she sat, overwhelmed, weeping. "Help us … please, God. Help *me*."

Beth didn't know how many minutes passed before a thought came to her mind. *Follow the river. It's where people live.*

She took a deep breath to settle her nerves. "How do I tell the children about Andrew and Ramo?" Robot-like, she pushed off the ground and trudged back to her charges.

It took Beth a long time to make her way upriver to where she had left the children. When she saw them—trembling and forlorn—her heart broke. She picked up the pace and knelt down to let them engulf her in their shaking embraces.

With a watery gaze, Jekél asked, "Teacher? Baby Ramo?"

Beth stroked Jekél's cheek. "I am so sorry. Ramo drowned in the river. He died. But Teacher?" She shook her head and shrugged her shoulders in the universal gesture that meant "I don't know."

It was clear Kenta understood a little English. He spoke in their native language to the others.

Jekél's voice rose in a wail. When the rest of the little children began to wail, Amie's eyes filled with big tears. They rolled down her cheeks.

Beth pulled all four children close to her until their weeping subsided.

The rain had finally stopped. The sun peeked through the clouds and warmed Beth's shoulders. She gazed at the sky and pointed. "Look. A rainbow."

The children sniffled and looked up.

"Looks like the sun's coming out." Beth tried to encourage the youngsters. "It will dry our clothes." She knew they probably understood only one word out of five, but it was her tone that counted. Cheerful. Upbeat.

"We … go," Kenta said in his British/Malawian accent. "Village. Not stay here. Not good. Go village."

Beth stood and shook her head. "Teacher first. Ramo first." Her next words stuck in her throat. How could she make them understand? She made the motion for digging with a shovel. "Bury them." Her eyes watered.

"No!" Kenta's voice cracked. He shook his head violently. "Teacher say … go village." He pointed upriver.

"Follow the river?" Beth asked in a flat voice. She pointed too.

Kenta nodded.

The Malawian children headed for the trees along the river bank. They stepped within easy reach of the tree's foliage and sipped the rain that had pooled on the leaves. Beth followed their example.

Slightly refreshed but heavy in heart, Beth and the children set out on their journey in silence. For the next two hours—like Beth—they grieved the loss of Teacher and Ramo. Walking alongside the children, Beth tried to anticipate every threat they might encounter—and how to escape it, but she knew nothing about the African bush. These little orphans probably knew much more.

Suddenly, out of the blue, a man's voice called out from behind.

They stopped and spun around. Panic-stricken, Beth scanned the shadows of the trees. Yes, there he was. Were there more men obscured by the shade? *They could be dangerous. Maybe the children should hide.*

One man walked toward them, but he was too far away to perceive his intentions.

27. A Battle with Wild Beasts

Again he spoke, but Beth couldn't figure out what he said.

With a squeal, Amie took off running toward him.

What is she doing? Beth bolted after her. She felt she would burst if she didn't stop the little girl. She stretched out and grabbed her arm.

Amie skidded to a stop. She shook Beth off and said "teacher" in her little voice.

Beth scrutinized the man who sauntered out of the shadows. *Yes, that's Andrew's walk!* All the tension flushed out of Beth's body, replaced by a tidal wave of giddiness. Her hand pressed against her heart. *Andrew's alive!* Tears welled up.

The rest of the orphans dashed by Beth, cheering, "Teacher! Teacher!"

Andrew squatted down as his flock jumped into his arms. Everyone laughed. He appeared in good shape except for dirt, a tear in his sleeve, and scratch near it. Even his ever-present sunglasses had managed to survive in his pocket and now rested upon his nose.

Andrew spoke briefly in Chichewa. The children's faces lit up. Then he stood and faced Beth.

"Thank God you're okay." Beth sprang to him.

They embraced like long-lost, treasured friends. He was a head taller than her, solid, and a lot for her arms to hug.

"Are you all right?" Beth whispered. "What happened?"

"My shoulder is sore where the tree hit it." Andrew released Beth and rubbed his shoulder. "Otherwise, I'm fine. The river swept me down for quite a ways. I couldn't get out. When I finally did, there was a rock cliff posing as a river bank."

Beth gasped.

He grinned. "It was impossible to climb it, so I had to go all the way around. It's a good thing you can't walk any faster than Amie." He tugged on her pigtail.

Amie's cherub-like face turned up to his. When man and child beheld each other, their expressions changed to one of mutual adoration.

"Thank you for rescuing me from the river," Beth said.

The corners of Andrew's mouth turned up, and then he nodded.

Each one told their side of the story while Andrew and Kenta dug a hole close to the river. "The water's muddy, but it's safe to drink," Andrew explained. "The ground purified it."

Beth, imitating the children, squatted down, filled her hands with the cool liquid, and sipped the dirty-tasting water.

"Where Ramo?" Jekél asked again.

Andrew stopped sipping and released the water from his hands. He gathered the children in his arms. Using English, Chichewa, and sign language, he explained that the river had washed Ramo's body away, and that he couldn't find him. "God took Ramo to Heaven."

Kenta translated. They didn't react with surprise, only sorrow.

After a time of comforting embraces, the little group headed south under the bright sun.

They hadn't been walking long when Andrew stopped and studied the sky. "We have about thirty minutes of daylight left before dark. We need to prepare for spending the night out here."

Just the thought of sleeping in the wilds of Africa sent shivers through Beth.

Andrew turned to the children. Again in half-English, half Chichewa, he motioned to the children. "Thorn bushes. Find them." He made digging motions. "I'll dig for drinking water."

The Malawians grinned and took off. They clearly knew where to look.

At twilight, Beth and the children, using extra caution, dragged a number of thorn bushes back to their makeshift camp. Andrew had dug another hole close to the river for water.

Everyone gathered rocks and sturdy sticks. "To use as weapons if need be." Andrew explained each time.

Later, they pulled away a thick layer of rain-soaked leaves to expose the dry dirt underneath. "Makes a dry bed for us," Andrew said. They arranged the thorn bushes around the dry earthen patch. "The thorns will protect us from wild animals."

Beth gave Andrew and the children a wan smile. She appreciated Andrew's calming presence and survival skills, but wild animals?

I hope he's right about the thorn bushes, she thought with a shiver.

Night came too soon, with no matches and no luck finding dry sticks to start a fire. The scent of the damp earth and vegetation permeated the cool night air. Starlight allowed Beth to recognize shadowed forms and movement.

Andrew herded his flock and Beth into the circle of thorn bushes.

Beth sat down on the dirt and drew her knees up to her chest to stay warm.

"*Ouoo*, cold." Jekél's voice trembled, which started a chorus of complaints among the youngsters.

"Teacher, I hungry," Jemba said in plain English.

"I'm sorry," Andrew's voice came through the darkness. He shook his head. "Shh. Tomorrow."

The orphans talked to each other in Chichewa for a short time then lay down in a row. Andrew settled himself next to the children, with his back facing the outside.

"You warm, Teacher. Good." Kenta snuggled closer.

Beth sat by herself in the cool night air. *What do I do now?*

"Come here with us, Elizabeth." Andrew's deep, soothing voice invited her from the shadowed ground.

After a slight hesitation, Beth chose the far end of the orphans, opposite from the man. Amie shoved her way in next to her. Her little body helped warm Beth.

The exertion and emotional strain of that day had exhausted Beth. The children were already taking long breaths, including the deeper, husky sound of Andrew.

The soft chorus of *zzzz's* lit an inner glow within Beth. She smiled.

Why am I smiling again? I barely escaped a terrifying, flash flood today. I'm in darkest Africa, with no civilization for a hundred miles. There is nothing between me and wild beasts except thorns. I'm with strangers in a foreign land—a citified female—and I'm smiling?

Beth's eyelids closed out the starry night.

Snuffling and quick running feet next to Beth's head jolted her awake and set her heart racing. Unknown beasts panted and darted close to her, just outside the thorns. Their foul breath and wet-dog stink intensified the horrifying reality.

Freakish shadows of slope-backed, dog-like animals worked to get at her. Inches away, clawing feet dug at the dirt beneath the wall of thorns.

Beth shrieked. "Something's trying to get in under the thorns."

The children screamed.

Andrew leaped to his feet and charged at the beasts. "They're hyenas." He lashed out with a downward swing of his arm.

A hyena yelped and limped away. Hair-raising whoops came from the shadowy creatures as they paced around them.

Beth shook. Her pounding heart felt like it would explode.

Jekél held Jemba and Amie. Kenta snatched up a thick branch and joined Andrew at the thorn wall.

"Wait." Andrew laid his hand on Kenta's club and shook his head. "The wall," he warned. "Don't hit the wall."

Beth scoured the blackness. A hyena suddenly leaped into the wall. The barrier shook. Beth shrieked and burst into hysterical tears. "Make it go away! Make it go away."

Amie left Jekél's side and rushed to Beth. Her little hand patted her leg, clearly longing to ease Beth's suffering. "Okay," she murmured. "Okay."

Beth bent down, scooped Amie into her arms, and held her small body tight.

Another hyena began digging on the opposite side.

Andrew shot over and swiped at the creature's paw. It bolted away, whimpering. The others followed it. From the darkness an eerie laughter mocked the humans.

Prickles of fear raced up Beth's spine. Never had she heard such an alien, macabre sound. She wanted out of here. Even though the panic and weeping subsided, the trembling didn't. Her voice quivered, "Will they come back?"

"I don't know," came the honest answer. "But we'll give them more of the same if they do."

Everyone stood wide-eyed for the next half hour, listening. The night squalled with the strange trill and drone of insects and the croaking of hundreds of whatever else was out there.

After a while, they surveyed the thorn wall the best they could in the darkness. Apparently, it had survived the onslaught.

"Good." Andrew patted the orphans on their shoulders. "Brave kids." He encouraged them in a few words of Chichewa then sighed. "Go back to sleep."

Andrew lay down, and the children lined up beside him like firewood. They kept their makeshift clubs ready on the ground above their heads.

Beth kept standing in the dark. A cool breeze had kicked up. She shivered. *It's too scary to lie at the end of the line again. What should I do?*

"Let Kenta sleep on the end," Andrew suggested, clearly sensing Beth's distress.

"How about I sleep between the girls?" she squeaked.

"Of course," Andrew agreed.

Without words, the children seemed to understand and made room for Beth. Jekél rolled closer to the boys.

Beth settled herself on the ground between two dark shapes. Little Amie lay between her and Andrew. His warmth comforted Beth.

Soon she rolled onto her side. When Beth draped a cold arm over Amie, her hand landed against Andrew's warm chest. Instantly, something like a mild electrical jolt traveled through her. *It must be because I wasn't expecting to touch him. It just startled me.* She thought to move her icy hand but changed her mind, his heat was most welcome.

After a few moments of feeling his chest rising and falling with his every breath, she began to calm down.

"So, I'm not as scary as the hyenas, eh?" Andrew gave a soft chuckle in the dark.

Beth giggled. It felt good. "You better not be, or you'll be sleeping on the *other* side of these thorns."

He laughed.

Beth marveled. *I just met this man yesterday and now look at me! It's a bit unnerving to sleep this close to a man I hardly know, but I do feel protected.*

Quiet moments passed. Amie's and Jekél's warmth chased the chill from Beth's body.

The children were soon asleep. Andrew rolled onto his back.

Beth's shoulder and hip complained of the hard ground, so she followed Andrew's lead. The brilliant, twinkling stars grabbed her attention.

"Aren't the stars bright?" Andrew's hushed voice traveled through the darkness.

"They're beautiful. They seem much brighter than back home in Auburn. Perhaps it's because there's not even one light here." Beth searched the heavens. "But where's the Big Dipper and the North Star."

"We're on the other side of the world. There are different constellations here, but just as stunning. There's the Southern Cross." Andrew pointed. "Do you see it over there?"

"Oh yes. Those stars are *bright*." Beth felt a lightness in her chest. Andrew could have made her feel dumb, but he hadn't. His voice was kind, and he sounded intrigued. The stars winked at her, as if they were flirting. "It makes me realize how far I am from home," Beth whispered, "and how foreign this place is. Everything, is so different."

"In a frightening way?"

"Not the stars. No, in an exciting, adventuresome way."

"Good."

"How did you stop the hyenas from digging?" Beth wanted to know.

"With my pocketknife."

"The children didn't seem as terrified as I was. I can't believe they're already asleep."

"They see hyenas quite often."

"How long will it take us to get back to civilization?" Beth asked.

"Civilization? Uh, it's not quite civilized in Western thought, but we should get there by tomorrow, maybe late afternoon." His calming voice turned drowsy. "You won't have to spend another night with any beasts."

Beth smiled in the dark. Her thoughts turned to the first time she'd seen this man on the street in Chikwawa. *If Rosie had told me then that Andrew and I would be together in this situation, I would have said she's crazy.*

She smiled wider. *God, I don't know why You arranged this, but I'm grateful I met him. I don't know where this is going—if anywhere—but You've got my curiosity. I'm beginning to become interested in a missionary—a missionary! He's different and a kind, good man. I wonder what he thinks of me.*

Time passed without further conversation. Gradually, Andrew's breathing became deeper. He was asleep.

Beth's last thoughts before dozing off returned to her first love—a friend of her kidnappers. Deep in her subconscious, she began to feel disloyal to Glenn.

She shook off the troubling thoughts. Glenn had never given Beth the slightest hint of a possible future with him—not after his arrest, and not after his heartbreaking trial. He wanted her to date other guys, not wait for him. *I should know within this year—after he's set free—if I even have a future with Glenn. Oh dear God, he's just got to let me in.*

And if he doesn't... Beth felt a deep painful stab.

Oh, that still hurts. She sighed. *My heart is torn. But if Glenn says no to me then it's time for some permanent healing. Is it possible Andrew might be part of that cure? Maybe Andrew and I can keep in touch as friends.*

Beth yawned. She would have to deal with the situation later, when and if the time came, but right now she was too tired. Sleep came in spurts. A couple hours before dawn, night noises startled her awake every few minutes.

Beth woke—not refreshed in the least—to first light in the eastern sky. She turned her head and discovered the slumbering children beside her, the thorn "door" closed, and a missing Andrew.

Her skin was cool, but the air was calm, milder than yesterday. She sneaked through the prickly doorway and headed for a bush. A few moments later, she left the bush behind and set out for the river, expecting to find Andrew.

At the end of her brief journey, she found Andrew standing by the water's edge. Like the day before, his melody rose on the morning dawn.

"God on high ... hear my prayer."

Andrew's song suddenly reached to a very high note, causing Beth's soul to soar.

With skill and tenderness, he sang,

"In her need ... You have always been there.
Beth is young ... she's afraid.
Let her rest ... Heaven bless ... Bring her home.
Bring her peace ... Bring her joy."

Beth caught her breath. *He's singing a prayer for me? It's beautiful.* Tears filled her eyes. She felt like she was floating. The sun glistening on the water heightened this unforgettable encounter. She stayed this time, not concerned if he caught her listening.

Andrew finished his song. He titled his head and brushed his palm against his cheekbones. Looking up, he quietly said something … to God, more than likely.

Andrew turned and discovered Beth watching from under a tree. He hesitated then ambled toward her. On his way he ate some leaves he plucked from a nearby bush. A bronze forearm reached out to Beth. Dark-green leaves lay in a calloused hand. "They taste like lemon. They're edible, anyway."

Beth picked up the foliage and sampled a small bite. "Not too bad. Gotta plant myself one of these back home." Hunger drove her to the bush to make breakfast out of a few more of the leaves.

Andrew followed.

"Thank you for praying for me," Beth said softly. "That was incredible. You're just as good a singer as those who sang the original in *Les Miserables*. I was touched."

"I thought you would still be asleep after our animal encounter last night." He paused. "I meant it, you know. Those words." His quiet voice resonated with sincerity.

Surprised at his tone, Beth stopped eating and turned to glance up at him.

Andrew stood close to her, almost touching. He wasn't wearing sunglasses, nor did he avert his gaze.

Beth's breath caught. His darkly framed blue eyes captured her in their beauty and adoration. The sparkle of the river glistened in them. She wanted to stare at him as he lovingly gazed upon her.

Andrew lightly stroked her jaw with his fingers.

Shock waves rippled through Beth. Before she could analyze her feelings, Andrew lifted her chin closer to a magnificent face and brought his mouth down to meet hers.

Andrew's going to kiss me!

Anticipation electrified her. Just as quickly, a feeling of uncertainty washed over her. She pushed it aside and closed her eyes, waiting.

An instant later, Beth felt the light brush of Andrew's lips against hers. A pleasureful shiver traveled through her being. She waited for more, but nothing happened. His curled fingers remained under her chin. She opened her eyes.

Andrew's face was within inches of hers. He seemed to be searching for her consent.

Beth's expression must have given him the green light, because Andrew's broad hands moved to cradle her head. Then his warm mouth embraced hers, soft and haltingly, as if savoring their intimacy.

The nape of Beth's neck tingled.

Andrew broke away then enfolded his arms around her. In the quiet of the morning, he held her for several long, treasured moments.

Beth soaked in their closeness. Feelings awakened inside, feelings she had tried to shut out for four long years. Her stomach swirled. *Andrew surprises me. This religious guy isn't a cold fish. He has emotion and sensitivity and . . . what a kisser! I haven't felt like this since—*

Her thoughts came to a screeching halt. Sharp pangs of guilt stabbed deep into her.

This is more than friendship with Andrew. How could I feel this way about another man? I only want Glenn in my heart. Her chest tightened. *And if Glenn says no?* She sighed. *I don't know what to do.* In the depths of her core more tried to surface, but what?

She couldn't put her finger on it.

"It's so hard to let you go." Andrew whispered. His breath brushed against her forehead.

The children ran toward them.

28. Who Are You?

Kenta elbowed Jekél and grinned. With sideway glances toward the couple, they giggled and chattered to each other in Chichewa.

The children made breakfast out of lemon leaves, and then it was time to continue their journey upriver. The sun beat through Beth's dress, but a slight breeze made the trek pleasant in the early hours. Except for her little friend Amie, the children walked with Andrew.

This gave Beth opportunity to think. Her mind whirled. *Andrew reminds me of Glenn.* She shivered. *It's uncanny. Those eyes!*

"Can there be more than one handsome man with striking blue eyes in this world?" she murmured softly. "Or do I look at every man and see Glenn?"

Amie turned her big brown eyes up to Beth, as if she wanted to understand.

Beth's head wagged. The corners of her mouth turned up. "Sorry, Honey. I'm just talking to myself." Her finger pointed to her heart. "In here."

Amie grinned.

Beth's thoughts rolled on, silent this time, so as not to confuse Amie. She focused on the differences between these two striking men. *Andrew is thinner than Glenn, and maybe an inch or so shorter. And there's Andrew's beard, of course, and his longer hair. Glenn stayed clean shaven and neatly trimmed.*

She furrowed her brow and picked up her pace. *Andrew's*

voice is different too. Husky. Almost raspy. She smiled. *Until he sings, and then—*

She felt her face glow with the memory of his morning songs.

"And the most important difference"—she chuckled—"Glenn is in prison for several more months, not including probation." She shrugged. "Or longer. I wouldn't know, since I haven't heard a peep out of him this whole time." She sucked in a cool morning breath. "This is *Andrew*. This is *Africa*."

Beth watched the mysterious missionary/teacher as he carried chubby-cheeked Jemba on his shoulders and sang along with the children.

What about the way Andrew kisses? Beth wrinkled her forehead in concentration. She tried to remember Glenn's kisses, but four years later, the memory had faded. *From what I do remember, Glenn and Andrew kiss the same way.*

Beth tried to wave that idea away with a mental shrug. *Their kisses have the same thrilling effect on me.*

A prickling crawled up Beth's spine. "Could this man"—she swallowed—"could he be Glenn?"

She studied Andrew's back and stride. His short-sleeve, blue-checked shirt flapped open with the breeze. *Was that what my subconscious was trying to tell me? That Andrew is really Glenn?*

Her heart skipped a beat. *No! Surely he would have told me right from the start!* She frowned. *If he is Glenn, then he lied when I was filling out the report. Why wouldn't he tell me?*

Beth's heart raced. Her emotions knotted into a ball of confusion. It was too much of a coincidence to run into him in Africa, of all places. *He cannot be Glenn.* Her heart settled to normal. "Still," she murmured, "I need to ask some questions."

Beth pulled gently on Amie's hand and pointed to the group far ahead. "Run?"

Amie's answer was a quick grin. Giggling, she pulled Beth along until they had caught up.

"Thought we'd lost you," Andrew teased, clasping Beth's hand.

After a few steps, Beth cleared her throat. "I was just thinking." She paused. "I don't know anything about you, Andrew, and I would like to. You sound American or Canadian. Where are you from?"

Andrew broke his stride. He turned to Beth but didn't hold her gaze.

Why can't he look me in the eye? Is he feeling bad about something?

Andrew's face reddened. "You"—he paused and cleared his throat—"you must have assumed that I was the proprietor/missionary when you filled out the review."

"You're not?" Beth blurted.

"Andrew is the proprietor. He's on furlough in the States and should return next week. I'm just filling in for him."

Beth's mouth dropped open.

He shrugged. "You asked who the proprietor was, and I told you. You assumed and"—his voice filled with remorse—"I never corrected you."

Did he just say he's not Andrew? Beth's mind raced, searching for answers. *Then who is this man? I have called him Andrew for two days.* Her stomach fluttered. "You're not Andrew? Then who are you?"

He didn't answer for a minute. Clearly, whoever-he-was was allowing time for this big mistake to sink in.

"It seems unbelievable that we'd meet again here, but I'm Glenn." He took a breath. "Glenn McKlain."

Beth reeled. Her stomach turned over, and she broke out in a cold sweat. No! It wasn't possible. "I feel fai—"

She felt herself spinning, knees buckling, her emotions out

of control.

Then everything went black.

Beth became conscious reclining in someone's arms. The blood flowed back into her head. Footsteps crunched pebbles. Her body swayed in time with someone walking.

A deep, husky voice came to her. "Let's rest under this tree."

Blinking against the bright sunlight, Beth murmured, "I must have fainted."

"Mm-hmm. You haven't had enough to eat or drink in this heat. And the shocking news didn't help you any." He laid her down on the cool sand and rested her head on his lap. "I'm sorry."

He waved Kenta to him and made digging motions. "Water, please."

Kenta jumped right to it.

The mystery man stroked her hair in silence. A few minutes later he said, "I should have told you the first day." His eyes filled with adoration mixed with sadness. "I really am Glenn McKlain."

The older children rushed up to Beth. Each held a straw-like stem, their fingers covering both ends. "For you."

"It's water from their hand-dug well," Glenn explained.

Beth smiled. "Oh, *thank* you." She sat up, took Kenta's, and released the water into her mouth. Jekél's was next.

Kenta and Jekél took the stems and darted off for refills.

Beth struggled to make sense of things. "Why"—she swallowed—"why didn't you tell me?"

Glenn sighed. "I thought you might be afraid of me, so I

planned to tell you that first day right before you left, but you didn't leave." His eyebrows drew together. A pained expression hinted of regret. "Are you frightened of me, Beth?" Concern hung heavy in his voice.

"No." Beth's answer and smile came without pause.

"Good." The ex-con released his breath.

The two younger children drifted off to play.

"You look different. Those clothes, your beard, and your longer hair. You wore sunglasses until this morning." Beth's hand limply gestured. "Why would I expect to meet you again in darkest Africa? Your voice is huskier, and you act so different."

Beth paused then continued. She might as well get it all out at once. "You seem happy, carefree and—I don't know—at peace. And"—she grinned—"you're religious."

Glenn's mouth turned up. That statement clearly amused him.

"So, you escaped from prison and that's why you're here?" Beth blurted. "Because you're on the lam?"

Glenn smiled wider. A chuckle escaped his lips. "On the contrary, I was released early for good behavior. My parole is finished too. I'm here in Malawi because the prison chaplain, Pastor Lewis, arranged it with a missionary acquaintance, Andrew. Pastor Lewis is a great guy and a close friend."

Beth's eyes widened. Prison chaplain? Good behavior?

"In prison I met a guy who had been a voice and music instructor," Glenn continued. "He trained me for the three and a half years I was incarcerated. Pastor Lewis thinks my voice sounds husky because I used it so much in prison. I sang all the time. He thought I should have it checked out, in case there's a nodule on my vocal cords."

Beth sat still, fascinated with this revealing recital. That would explain why she didn't recognize Glenn's voice.

"My throat's been improving little by little." He shook his head, clearly amazed about something. "I thought prison would be a waste of a good part of my life, but even there God blessed me."

He rose and helped Beth to her feet.

A little woozy at first, she hung her head.

"Are you all right?"

"Yeah, I just need a second." When she felt better, Beth looked up into the beautiful eyes she loved and had missed so much. Joy surged through her. "I can't believe I'm actually talking to you, Glenn McKlain." She put her hand on his chest. "Yep, you're real. It's been so long. I was afraid I'd never see you again. There must be a God." She raised her eyes heavenward. "Thank you, God."

Glenn's face began to beam. His mouth curved into a new smile, but then his countenance changed, softening. His eyes filled with an inner glow as he stood quietly a few seconds, focusing on Beth. Dark brows lifted. "After all—" Swallowing hard, he regained enough control to speak. "After all that's happened, you forgive me and want to see me?"

"Not only do I want to see you, I want to *be* with you." Happy that she could, Beth played with his hair. "And the only thing you need to be forgiven for is not being honest with me about your identity."

Glenn ducked his head. "I know, and I'm truly sorry. I was just afraid . . . well, that you would not want to be with me."

"You're forgiven," Beth said. "But you won't keep secrets from me anymore, will you?"

Glenn raised his head and looked into her eyes. "I won't keep anymore secrets from you. Except maybe for your birthday and Christmas."

"My birthday?" Beth grinned at him. "Okay, good."

Glenn reached out and caressed the side of her face. "There's another reason—a more serious one—why I wasn't totally honest with you."

Puzzled, Beth wrinkled her brow. "And what's that?"

"I read that the psychiatrist at the trial said it was because you were afraid of me that you thought you were in love with . . . " His voice trailed off.

Beth filled in. "That I thought I was in love with you." Her fingers formed quotation marks around the word *thought*.

"Mm-hmm. I didn't want Stockholm Syndrome to play any part in our relationship this time."

Beth chuckled. "No worries. You're doing fine on your own without any silly Stockholm Syndrome to help you out." Her heart felt light for the first time in years. "I knew from the beginning that capture-bonding had nothing to do with my feelings for you. I wasn't scared of you after that first day. You made me feel safe."

Glenn let out a long, satisfied breath. "Good. I—"

Screeching and laughter interrupted his response. The two youngest bolted for Glenn and held fast to his legs. They scrunched up their shoulders to protect their necks.

At their heels, the two oldest—growling and acting like humped-back monsters—charged stiff-legged at them. They stretched their arms out in front with fingers curled and spread. A playful tussle ensued, with much growling and laughter.

Later, after quenching their thirst, they returned to their primary task—to get home. They trudged upriver while hunger gnawed at Beth's belly.

They had traveled quite a distance when Jekél stopped along the high river bank. With eyebrows drawn together, she examined the soggy land across the river. "Where home?" Her head gave a slight shake, a black hand covering her mouth. "Home gone!"

The others rushed up beside her, contemplating the muddy terrain. Only a well pump and flat rocks could be seen. "Where Cosi, Baby Chikumbu, and Buseje?"

The little group stared, without a doubt trying to understand what this all meant. The two younger children took ahold of Kenta's and Jekél's hands. Long-faced, the orphans stood together, overlooking the ruins of the only life they knew.

Beth's eyes stung. *They had so little before. Now they have nothing.*

Glenn's face mirrored Beth's grief.

He went down on one knee between his flock, placed his arms around them, and gathered them to himself. They hugged a long moment.

"Where Cosi?" Jekél's dark eyes filled with worry.

"I don't know, Jekél." With a soothing tone and a compassionate expression, Glenn stroked her ebony cheek and spoke a few sentences of choppy Chichewa.

He turned to Beth. "I told them we'll try to find Cosi and her children when we get to the village."

Glenn stretched his arms wide to indicate a hut shelter. "We'll build a new home, a bigger one. God is with us." The muscles in Glenn's cheek tensed.

Beth's heart turned over. Whenever Glenn had been under emotional turmoil, his jaw and cheek tightened. *It's amazing that I remembered that about him!* She nearly burst with pride. *Glenn, the cowboy, the ex-con, caring for these dear, homeless waifs in Africa. But then,* she reminded herself. *He's always been caring and protective.*

Once they resumed the final stage of their long journey,

Glenn eased the orphans' apprehensions. His tone gave them peace, and they resumed their chatter. A spring returned to their steps.

With the children put at ease, Glenn and Beth caught up on each other's lives.

"I'm still trying to get it into my head that you are Glenn McKlain. It would help if you dressed like him."

"I have some stuff in storage."

"It would also help if we discussed the first time I met you. Do the kids know?" Beth asked.

He shook his head. "Not the details."

They discussed their time together at the mountain cabin. Beth remembered his wound. She placed her hand on his forearm and stopped walking. He turned, blinked, and then gazed at her. "What's the matter?"

Beth pushed the open shirt off his shoulders. Without asking for explanation, he stood before her wearing only shorts and sandals. She reached up and touched the scar on his shoulder. "You *are* Glenn."

She glanced at his bearded face, then back at the old wound. Delicate fingertips lingered there. Her mind relived his suffering when the bullet was cut out. Beth sucked in her breath.

Glenn's deep voice resonated above her. "This wound didn't hurt nearly as much as my defense attorney raking you over the coals." He lowered his head, his expression solemn. "I have regrets about what happened to you because of me."

Beth raised her head. "Oh, Glenn, please don't. It was *not* your fault. I wouldn't have met you otherwise. And you are worth it."

"How can you say that?" He pulled his shirt back over his shoulders. "Every time you're around me, you go through some horrific, traumatizing danger."

"Maybe God puts you there when I need you most to rescue me, which you did both times." *Where did that thought come from?* Beth wondered. *That's not like me.*

A moment of silence passed. Glenn was doubtlessly considering his role in a new, favorable light. Adoring eyes met hers. "You amaze me, Elizabeth Farell." A rock-hard hand rubbed her arm with gentle affection, slid down, and then wrapped around her hand.

Something good stirred in Beth. She embraced him. Two young orphans hugged their legs. Then Beth, Glenn and all the orphans stood in a huddle in the blazing sun.

Wow! I'm hugging Glenn. It feels good to hold him again. What an endearing mixture he is, a kindhearted, wild stallion.

Glenn let go of Beth. "Jemba and Amie could use a short nap, and we could all use some water." They gorged themselves with the muddy water from another small hand-dug well.

A large, sweeping tree offered welcome shade, and its trunk a backrest. The air beside the river was pleasant. The sand cooled Beth's legs. Her toes dug in. Kenta and Jekél left to search for food. Jemba and Amie fell asleep a little ways from the adults.

Beth leaned against Glenn's chest. He cradled her with his arm, shoulder, and upraised knee.

The Shire River mesmerized Beth with its constant movement and sparkle. Its cadence and the rustling leaves were a soothing melody to her ears. "Funny how the river is not our enemy anymore, but a friend who gives us water and shade."

"Mm-hmm." Glenn stroked her arm. "Your skin is silky soft."

Joy bubbled up in Beth. "I haven't been this happy since

the first time I met you, Glenn. Even your touch is electrifying."

Glenn kissed her temple.

"Isn't it remarkable that I became interested in you all over again," Beth went on. "And not knowing it was you? Even in disguise, there's just something about you." *Oh, my goodness, Andrew's thrilling kiss was actually Glenn's.* She smiled inside and turned to glimpse his face. His countenance reflected her own heart full of gratitude.

After a quiet moment, Glenn said, "The first time I saw your expressive, brown eyes and those cute freckles over four years ago, I fell in love with you."

Glenn ran strands of Beth's hair through his fingers. "Then the other day when the kids and I were wrestling around on the ground, and you stood close by—I thought I was hallucinating. When I realized I wasn't, I wondered how you'd found me. My heart was pounding so hard, I was sure you'd recognize me. It didn't take long to figure out you didn't. When I introduced myself, Amie interrupted which worked out well—at least for me.

"I don't know how all this happened"—devotion filled his eyes—"but I thank God for giving me another chance with you."

Slowly, he leaned down toward Beth. An empty feeling fluttered in her stomach. She thought, *I have dreamed of this moment for so long. Now the moment is here.*

29. The Village

Outside the small village of Kambalame, Malawi

Glenn drew Beth close, and kissed her with tender feeling. She melted at his touch. In the middle of their kiss, Glenn dipped her back as in a romantic dance.

Beth's heart skittered. Warmth spread through her as time suspended in the closeness that they shared.

Glenn raised her shoulders again. "I've missed you," he whispered. Their eyes met.

"You kiss like you sing." Beth took pleasure in watching his expressions. "You put your feelings into it, so moving and beautiful." Her fingers caressed his lips. "I used to wonder what our reunion would be like. You by far surpassed my dreams."

Glenn grinned. "My imagination didn't come close either."

Jemba sat up. Little fists rubbed sleep out of his eyes. A fuzzy head turned to scan his whereabouts. "Teacher." He bounded full steam at Glenn.

Beth scooted out of the way.

Jemba dove into Glenn's arms, flattening him to the ground. On the way down, Glenn stiffened his arms straight up. The child dangled, giggled, and grinned down at his teacher. Drool dribbled on Glenn's forehead. He flinched. All three laughed.

Awakened by the merriment, Amie joined in.

The young Malawian food-gatherers walked up and proudly held out handfuls of dirt-covered roots. Once they were cleaned, Beth thought they tasted pretty good.

On the last leg of the trip—no matter how hot the sun—a hope and lightheartedness settled in Beth's soul. The miles gave the happy couple time to get reacquainted.

Glenn turned to Beth and spoke in a soft tone. "I read how you testified in court that you loved me." They stopped walking a moment and faced each other. "I'm sorry you had to go through that." With the gentleness of a falling leaf, calloused fingers stroked Beth's arm. "You were brave. Did it cause you problems?"

"Actually, not that much. Maybe people understood. You're a kind old frog. What girl wouldn't fall in love with you?" They both laughed.

"By the way … I kept the news article." Bright eyes searched hers. "Please, tell me about yourself now."

It didn't take Beth long. Then she asked about Luke and Sophia.

"Shorty told me that Dad only lived four months after"—Glenn stared ahead with a distant gaze—"after I last saw him at the cabin. When he left, he didn't meet up with the other two. Dad thought they must've taken a wrong turn and wandered around before they found the border and were caught."

Beth nodded.

"Sophia only lived another two years after the operation." Glenn's head dropped.

"You helped to bring her two more years."

Glenn nodded.

They walked in silence until Jemba asked, "Teacher, how

much more we have to go?"

The sun rested on the horizon by the time they heard the sounds of a village. Huts followed the slope of a hill across the river. Inhabitants milled about, clearly unaware of the thirsty travelers until Glenn, Beth, and the children shouted, jumped, and waved their arms.

A crowd gathered. Soon, a young man jumped into a narrow canoe and rowed toward them.

Glenn turned to Beth upon the canoe's approach. "There isn't room for all of us. Why don't you, Jekél, and Kenta go first?" He gave Beth a tight hug and then turned to the two oldest. "Please, take care of Elizabeth?"

"Yes, Teacher," Kenta said in his precise English. "It is my pleasure." He smiled and bowed.

Kenta hurried to the canoe and spoke with the oarsman. The burly man nodded. Beth and two orphans climbed into a rocking watercraft. The African heaved on the oar, and the little canoe lurched forward.

Beth didn't take her eyes off Glenn. Glenn, Jemba and Amie watched from the shore. The distance between them grew farther and farther.

What if for some reason we become separated, and I don't see Glenn again for a long time? I couldn't stand that. I can't lose him again. All the while Glenn's image grew smaller, the ache in her heart gripped tighter.

The river waters passed by, lapping against the boat while the Malawians conversed in their language. After a time the canoe pitched and ran aground. The passengers stepped from it onto solid ground.

Many black faces surrounded them. They talked at the same time. Young village children fingered Beth's clothes and hair. Beth kept her hand over her button-down pocket to safeguard her wallet. It contained her ID and money.

Loud chaos reigned for over ten minutes. Many chattered intensely at the visitors. Jekél and Kenta did their best to respond, but judging from the tone, Beth sensed things were out of control. Panic wanted to overtake her, but she fought it back.

The oarsman stood waiting.

Why isn't he going after Glenn? Is he planning to leave him there? What'll I do?"

Jekél pushed the youngsters' hands off Beth and scolded them in a harsh voice.

Kenta said something Beth's ears understood. "E-liz-a bet, give *kwacha* to man. He go get Teacher."

With relief Beth dug through her wallet, pulled out a few *kwacha*, and held it out to the oarsman.

The Malawian studied the money. Then with a darkened expression, he glared at her.

Beth figured he was taking advantage of their crisis. She removed a few more slips of money and frowned. He took it. She pointed in Glenn's direction, pretended to row the canoe, then motioned for him to go.

He nodded, folded the wad, and disappeared into the crowd.

"Please God," Beth whispered again. "Make him *go now* to get Glenn and the children."

The commotion settled down. Thankfully, the burly man was on his way across the Shire River.

Beth turned her attention to the sparkling river and Glenn, who sat on the opposite bank. Just the sight of him lightened her heart. She waved. The three responded. Beth thought that if she kept her eyes on him maybe she wouldn't panic. Glenn had become too important to her. It felt as though she couldn't live without him.

The moment Glenn stepped out of the boat onto land, he gazed at Beth. A beautiful grin formed on his face. Beth threw her arms around his neck and hung on tight. He hugged her to himself, lifting her off the ground. Overwhelming gratitude and love washed over her.

The tribal leaders and chief asked the visitors to sit with them. A few had already met Glenn and the orphans a couple months ago. Communicating through Kenta and Jekél, and Glenn's limited knowledge of the language, the leaders made them understand how one teen had gone missing since the flood, and how the water washed away a hut and three goats.

Worse news came to Beth's ears when Glenn told her only Cosi had survived the flood. Her baby was still wrapped up on her back. "Cosi is with villagers downriver. Death is commonplace here."

The orphans stared at the ground with grief-stricken faces. Without words, Glenn and Beth held them.

Afterward, Glenn offered to cover the cost of fuel and their time if someone would take them to the city in the morning. A man grunted his agreement in Chichewa. With business out of way, the chief invited the visitors to their social gathering that night.

At dinner, everyone, including Glenn and Beth, sat cross-legged in the dirt eating *nshima*—corn mush—with their fingers. Half starved, Beth savored every bite.

No sooner had Beth set her plate down, then the socializing began. Around a blazing fire, singing, drumming, and dancing filled the night. The orphans joined in from the start. The strong scent of smoke masked the smell of dinner and sweat.

Many hands drummed a harmonious beat. Other villagers

whacked sticks together in perfect unity.

Beth's foot kept rhythm until Glenn handed her some sticks. They gave the sticks a try, but their clumsiness only sparked peals of laughter.

Two young women pulled on Glenn's arms, wanting him to dance. He studied their foot and arm movements, and then attempted to follow. At first, he was out of step but before long his movements blended with the others.

Beth and the women giggled.

Glenn swaggered up to Beth. With a slight bend at the waist, he reached out his hand to her. "May I have this dance?"

"Oh no." She wagged her head.

"Oh yes." He pulled her to her feet. With full smiles and full hearts, they held hands as they endeavored to keep in step with their Malawian friends. The orphans beside them danced with mirth and with all their might.

Later during the night, only a couple of people moved about. The fire sustained a low flutter. The orphans slept nearby. On the ground, Beth sat with her back resting against Glenn's chest. She could feel the rise and fall of his breathing. His arms around her kept her toasty warm and content.

"When we were separated by the river, and the guy wouldn't go get you at first, I realized I couldn't stand to lose you again. I don't ever want to live without you." Her voice quivered.

After a moment, Glenn spoke quietly. "I love you, my little Darlin'." His words and deep, tender voice quickened a rush in Beth. She turned her head up to him. The glow of the firelight on his face laid bare his sincerity.

"And I love you, Mr. McKlain."

Their souls and lips met in an exhilarating bond.

Glenn let out a deep, long breath. "We'd better stop, or I'll have to apologize."

At first, a corner of Beth's mouth quirked up. Then her sentiment changed to one of deep respect. "I am touched that you want to safeguard my honor."

Glenn didn't respond.

Against the backdrop of a serenade of insects and a crackling fire, Beth reflected audibly, "Hard to believe it was just this morning when I thought I was kissing Andrew."

They chuckled.

"But I'm a better kisser than that guy, right?" Glenn asked.

"Uh … You're better looking." She felt his chuckle against her shoulder. "But I think I need more test runs on the kissing. Are you up for another try?"

"So long as you don't give that Andrew guy any more test runs."

Playfully, Beth swatted his arm. "Are you jealous?"

"Green," Glenn answered. Gazing at each other, their smiles could not be contained.

Beth yawned. "I'm getting sleepy."

"Then good night, my little Darlin'." They lay down on the hard ground. Beth snuggled into his arms and dozed off.

In the first light of dawn, Beth found Glenn and the youngsters asleep all around her.

Glenn began to stir. He raised an arm, blinked and turned up a corner of his mouth. "Mornin', Darlin'. Excuse me." Hair tousled, shirt wrinkled, he rose to his feet and took off for a Malawian outhouse.

About half an hour later with the day promising to be hot, the orphans, Glenn, and Beth bathed fully clothed in the river.

It was more horseplay than bathing.

The promised driver passed by. Glenn called to him. "When are you leaving for town?"

The driver perked up. "Anytime from now." He continued to amble along between the cluster of grass huts.

Since the kids were playing in the water, Glenn and Beth strolled hand in hand on a path that took them outside the village. A grove of scrub trees between them and the settlement provided privacy. Rock outcroppings sloped against the grassy, rolling hills like a painting in a gallery.

They stopped and turned to each other. "I never imagined that a human being could feel such powerful love for another as I feel for you." Beth stroked Glenn's tanned, bearded cheek, which inspired a kiss under the morning sun.

While still in their embrace, Beth rested her head on his shoulder. "Glenn, where do we go from here? I mean our near future?"

"What would you like?"

"More than anything? A hamburger."

Glenn burst out laughing.

"No, really, I want to be with you." Beth poked a finger at his chest. "My job is exciting and rewarding. I hope to keep it for a few years. What would you like in *your* future?"

Glenn's sun-browned hand rose to play with her hair. "I thank God for bringing you back into my life. I want *you* in my future too. All else is gravy. I enjoy ranching, music, and teaching children in situations like this. But if God wants me to dig ditches or build huts for Him, it'll be my honor."

"This religious stuff isn't just head, is it? It's heart."

"Mm-hmm. Only, I like to call it 'relational stuff.' It's kind of like our relationship. It's not just knowing facts about Elizabeth in my mind. I prefer having a relationship with you through two-way communication and experience. You're right. It involves my heart, not just my mind. It's the same with God. He wants to have a relationship with us—spiritually as well. It seems strange to think that if I hadn't gone to prison, I still might not realize the difference."

"You learned that in prison?" Beth asked.

"Actually, I put my faith in Jesus about a year before I met you, but I didn't understand everything. And I'm still learning." Once in a while, refreshing gusts of wind tossed and rippled their hair.

"I feel an emptiness sometimes." Beth's voice dropped. "Maybe that's what's missing."

"He's here with us, Beth. He hears you."

Good shivers ran up Beth's arms. "You have about a week left of caring for The Shepherd's Little Flock, right?"

Glenn nodded.

"Would you like to go with me on my next two trips? On me, that is. I have to go to Kenya and Botswana before I head home to Auburn."

"It would be my pleasure." Glenn's eyes gleamed. "I'll pay you back soon as I can."

"Wonderful!" She pecked him on the cheek. "I have to fly to Mozambique early Thursday, but I'll be back Friday noon. What are you going to do while I'm gone?"

"Build a new hut."

The driver called out that he was ready, so off they went.

A few hours later, the old pickup pulled in front of Beth's city-style hotel.

Beth registered Glenn and the orphans for one night at her

hotel—compliments of World Relief. While Beth waited for the desk clerk to work out the details, she treasured the look of wonderment on the children's faces as they marveled at the modern conveniences and luxury.

Curiosity provoked Jemba to raise chubby fingers and push a button on the wall. The elevator door opened. Bugged-eyed, Jemba bounded away. From behind his teacher, he peeked around at the incredible moving wall.

Glenn and Beth stifled their laughter. The moving wall seemed harmless, so Jemba had to give it another go.

The desk clerk interrupted Beth's fun distraction. "Ma'am, your friends gave to me your cell phone." He slid it toward her.

"Oh, awesome."

Glenn took Beth's hand. "Would you accompany me to dinner tonight?"

"Yes. That sounds fun." Beth squeezed his palm. "Since there are three hours before dinner, a nice, long, hot bath, seems in order."

Glenn agreed.

Before long, Beth reclined in her tub with suds up to her chin. Her mind revisited all that had been said and done the past week. Her heart filled with gratitude to God. The thought that she could have a relationship with God drew her to consider praying. *What could it hurt?*

"God, Jesus, I know I haven't done right at times. Forgive me and please send your Spirit into my heart. I want to have a close relationship with You, like Kathrin and Glenn have. Thank You, Jesus, for dying for me, for rescuing me, and for Glenn."

Beth waited. Nothing. No bells went off, but there was a new uplifting sense of worth, peace, and a happy anticipation.

Beth knew she couldn't put off calling her parents any

longer. Wrapped in a towel, she picked up her cell and hesitated. *I can't tell them about Glenn.* "They'll have a fit."

Beth's parents sounded relieved. Their tone was more loving than usual. Before Beth began her story, they relived the trauma of hearing about the flood, but not hearing from her.

Next, Beth hit Kathrin's number. Her friend's sweet voice lifted her spirits. They talked of the flood. Then Beth told of meeting Glenn again. "It was such an unlikely thing—to run into Glenn here. I wonder … did you have anything to do with it? Just asking." She waited.

"Besides praying for you to meet Glenn again? Yes, I put feet to my prayers this time."

"What? Are you saying that you *did* orchestrate it?" Beth held her breath.

"Yes, I did," came the answer from across the ocean.

"No way!" Beth flopped backward onto her bed, eyes wide, mouth slack. "I never would've guessed you would or could pull it off." The phone picked up Kathrin's quiet giggle. "How did you do it?"

"Well ... When Glenn was in prison, one day I called him—just that one time—to get informa—"

"You *what*? You called Glenn?" Heat flushed through Beth's body. "Why didn't you or Glenn tell me?" Anger escaped in her voice.

From across the miles, Kathrin calmly said, "We both wanted to give you a chance to fall for someone else—free of past encumbrances—but since you didn't … Honey, I called him to get information so that I could orchestrate this for *your* sake. None of this would've happened if I hadn't."

Kathrin continued. "I kept up on his parole hearings and release date. And the day I called Glenn, he mentioned his prison chaplain, Pastor Lewis. I knew you were going to

Chikwawa, so I asked Pastor Lewis if he had a connection in Chikwawa that could use Glenn as a temporary missionary for orphanages. Maybe my prayers helped Pastor Lewis find one. It certainly didn't hurt that he thinks highly of Glenn."

"Did Glenn know about you arranging this?" Beth tensed up, ready to be ticked off.

"No. No one told him. We weren't sure that Glenn would agree to it. We wanted to give you and Glenn a second chance, but it never entered my mind that you wouldn't recognize him. To fall in love with the same man says something."

"Yes. How cool is that?" Beth's muscles relaxed. "Thank you, Kathrin." After a few more minutes, they hung up their treasured connection. Beth sat on the bed and processed all that she had learned.

There was one more call to make, but Bob and Rosie didn't answer.

Beth went to the closet and drew out an elegant, pale-coral dress. Later, the mirror and clock agreed that she was ready.

When the elevator door opened to the main lobby, Beth searched for Glenn and the kids. Only a tall man gazed out the window. He stood decked out in a gray Stetson, blue jeans, blue-plaid, western-fitted shirt, and boots. His thumbs were tucked into his jean pockets.

It's Glenn. He granted my wish.

Beth couldn't stop smiling. She stepped up beside him. Glenn's boots made him taller, a bit over six-foot-two.

He turned to her, and his face lit up. "Evenin' little Darlin'." He tipped his hat. "You are *beautiful*."

"Now you look like the Glenn I met on the mountain." A slow, pleased grin formed on Beth's face. "It's not just the clothes. You got a haircut, and you shaved off your beard." The mild but sweet, spicy scent of aftershave heightened her excitement for the evening. "Where are the children?"

"They said they're tired, but most likely it's the TV. They don't have many chances to watch Bugs Bunny."

They walked out of the hotel together. Glenn hailed a taxi and opened the door for Beth. Seated together on the backseat, he took her hand in his and rested them on his thigh.

Beth burst out with the news of their sneaky friends' collaboration.

"I'm glad we have sneaky friends." Glenn's eyes softened. "They went through a lot of trouble for us, didn't they?"

A moment of silence passed. Then Glenn rubbed his hand up and down his thigh. His gaze became pained. "One reason I took Kathrin's call—the call that she just told you about—was because the thought crossed my mind that something might have happened to you, and that's why she was calling. That's the only time she called me. Do you understand why I wouldn't take your calls or communicate with you?"

"You took her call and not mine because you like her more than me?" Beth ribbed him. "Just kidding. I do understand, but you wasted four years. No one could ever take your place. Did Kathrin tell you about me?"

"She said she wouldn't tell me anything about you, only if you got married."

The taxi parked at the entrance of a modern Asian restaurant—in Blantyre. They stepped up to a hostess.

She looked up from her work and gaped at Glenn. Her countenance lit up. "Hi." She blinked. "D-do you, uh, have a reservation?"

Glenn nodded. "McKlain for two, please."

The hostess led them to their reserved table, which was outside on a second-floor, private balcony overlooking the city. A fragrant bouquet of pink lilies and a flickering candle decorated the table.

"This is wonderful, Glenn. So romantic." Beth felt lighter than air. "You thought of everything—a setting sun and the perfect temperature."

After *nshima* and rice for three days, General's Tao chicken gratified their taste buds. For dessert, the waitress dropped two fortune cookies on their table. Glenn reached for his, accidentally knocking Beth's clutch onto the floor. "Sorry."

"That's okay." Beth bent down and scooped it up.

Upright again, Beth picked up a hard cookie with a broken corner. "Let's see what my fortune is." She broke it open and read aloud. "Beth …"

She stopped. Her eyebrows drew together as she traced across the words in silence. Her mouth dropped open. She held the little strip of paper closer to the candle light and read the words again—aloud this time.

Beth, will you marry me? Love, Glenn.

30. A Surprise

Beth's eyes widened. A whirlwind of thoughts rushed at her. She was too excited to think straight. She looked up into Glenn's shining blue eyes.

Glenn shoved back his chair and dropped on one knee before Beth. "Little Darlin'," he asked, his countenance radiant, "will you marry me?" A rugged hand held a glittering diamond ring in a velvet box.

"Oh, wow! Yes, Glenn. Yes, I'll marry you."

Glenn stood.

Beth threw her arms around his neck and kissed his soft mouth. "I love you so." A warmth radiated through her body. "Oh my goodness! You want me to be your wife." Eyes teary, she leaned back to peer into the windows of his soul.

Joy flooded Glenn's glistening eyes. He raised Beth's hand as though it were a delicate rose and slipped the diamond onto a white finger. The back of her hand felt his warm kiss. "Beth, you make me the happiest man." After another loving kiss and a long embrace, he asked, "When and where do you want to get married?"

"The sooner the better!" Beth said.

"It would be perfect if the kids were included." Glenn half sat on the balcony rail.

"What a great idea. Let's get married here." Beth clasped her hands. Then they sat at the table to make plans.

Glenn's face beamed. "The jeweler said that we both need

to register together at the district office. It takes about a week to receive our international marriage certificate. He also said that maybe a bribe would hasten things along."

"A bribe?" Beth snickered. "Okay." After a short discussion, they agreed that the following Saturday would be their wedding day. "Next week we'll be Glenn and Elizabeth McKlain. Feels like a fairytale. I don't usually receive and accept a marriage proposal on my first date. Not usually."

They laughed. Excitement charged the air.

"But then," Beth mused, "nothing about our relationship has been ordinary. If the newspapers catch wind of this, they'll sensationalize it. How do you feel about that?"

Glenn took her hand. "It's not going to change our relationship. The rest doesn't matter."

"It's going to be hard to leave the orphans." An idea popped into Beth's head. "Hey"—she grinned—"can we adopt them?"

"Let's look into it."

Beth lowered her head. "Uh … several years ago you didn't want to marry me because you thought it would mess up my life." She looked up at him again. "You must have changed your mind. I'm glad you did."

Glenn's expression sobered. He blinked, rose to his feet, and stared out at the city lights.

Beth moved to stand before him.

"It about killed me to turn you away." The grim set of Glenn's mouth conveyed pain. "I loved you even then, and"—his voice softened—"I hurt you." His eyes watered. "I don't have it in me to do it again. I love you too much."

Beth threw her arms around him. They held each other in silence for a healing moment.

From above her, Glenn's deep voice communicated what

obviously burdened his heart. "You're going to have difficulties being married to an ex-con," he warned her. "But I've learned that in the hard times I'm more aware of God's hand helping me. Darlin', I pray it will be the same for you so that you'll feel God's love for you more and more."

"I appreciate you helping me to understand," Beth murmured. "Now, I also know how much you have always loved me."

Glenn smiled.

After talking it all out, they decided to register in the morning and use the week to finalize wedding preparations. The rest of the evening they celebrated with a favorite activity—dancing, topped off with waltzes.

Beth relished being in Glenn's arms. Her head rested on his shoulder. "I feel intoxicated with happiness."

"Me too, Darlin'."

But the clock struck midnight, and their "pumpkin"—the taxi—awaited.

It was hard for Beth to separate from Glenn. They kissed outside her room, then said, "Good night."

"I'll wait outside your door until I hear you lock your door." Glenn said.

With a wide grin, she thought, *Chivalry isn't dead. It thrives in Glenn's DNA.*

That night Beth floated to sleep.

By two o'clock the next afternoon, the couple had completed the wedding preparations they needed to do together. This left Glenn time to rent a pickup and shop for the needed building materials for the new hut.

"I have to leave tomorrow morning to pick up Andrew from the airport before heading back to the orphanage site," Glenn explained to Beth as he drove to the hotel. "Andrew is coming earlier than first scheduled to help rebuild the orphanage hut and to perform our wedding." He glanced over at her with a warm smile.

That evening, the engaged couple had dinner in the hotel restaurant with Rosie and Bob. Rosie kept sneaking glimpses of Glenn, acting all silly around him. It seemed that Glenn didn't notice.

Halfway through dinner, Beth announced their wedding plans.

"What?" Bob's brow furled.

"Seriously?" Rosie's eyes held an incredulous stare.

Beth couldn't contain her grin. She nodded.

"Congratulations!" Rosie cheered. "How romantic." She jumped up and hugged their shoulders.

Bob remained quiet. His eyes appeared cold and dead.

After a while, Jemba began rubbing his eyes, and Amie yawned. Since it was past the little ones' bedtime, Glenn and the orphans left for their room.

No sooner had the troop left the dinning hall when Bob said, "Are you crazy, Elizabeth? You've only known this joker a few days."

Beth didn't tell him anything different. "Nothing we say to each other, Bob, will change either of our minds. So there's point in trying."

"Then I might as well leave." Bob shoved back his chair and marched out.

"He'll be okay," Rosie said. "Uh … Who did you say was your first love?" Her brows squished together. "It starts with a 'g'—Greg?"

"No. Glenn." Then Beth told her the rest of the story.

Later that evening, once Beth was in her room, she tapped her parents' cell number. *I might as well get this over with and make someone else unhappy, like I clearly did with Bob.* After the usual niceties, she blurted it out. "Mom, Dad, I have something to tell you."

"Yes, what is it?" Beth heard the dread in their tone.

"I'm engaged to be married. I would love it if you would fly out here for my wedding, which is this coming Saturday. I would like you to give me away, Dad. Would you do that?"

"You're *what*? Getting married this Saturday?" Her father's voice sounded restrained.

"Yes. Would you—"

"Hold on a minute." Dad raised his voice. "Why so soon, and why in Malawi?"

"My job takes me away from Chikwawa next week. I've come to love the orphans here and want them to be part of the ceremony."

"Is it Bob?" Mom asked.

Beth chuckled. "No."

"Then you've only known this man a couple of weeks. Do you think that's wise, Elizabeth? Who is this guy, anyway?" Dad asked.

"It's the guy who saved my life in the flood. The teacher at the orphanage."

"Is he uh … a Malawian national?" Mom asked.

"No, he's Caucasian, an American."

"Oh,"—her voice brightening—"I'm glad to know that you finally got over that criminal."

"I didn't get over him, Mom. That's who I'm marrying this Saturday."

The silence couldn't have been more deafening.

After a moment, Mom scolded, "That's not funny, Elizabeth."—a pause—"Really, what's the teacher's name?"

"The teacher's name is Glenn McKlain. I'm not kidding.

I'm marrying Glenn, the same Glenn from four years ago."

It was Dad's turn to sound harsh. "Isn't he in prison? Did he escape?"

Beth's explanation didn't seem to help their bad attitude. "Tell you what. I'll let you get used to the idea, and I'll call you back in the morning—about six PM your time."

She hung up. "I'm *so* frustrated with them. What is their problem? Why do they dislike Glenn? If it wasn't for him, I'd be dead. Oooo!" She growled and threw her sandal across the room.

It took a soak in the tub to settle her down.

In the morning, when Beth called her parents back, they sounded more than a little strange over the phone. *Are they still upset?* "What's the matter? You sound different."

"Maybe it's because I just got this new cell, and you're on the speaker phone. I probably did something wrong." There was an uncertainty in her father's tone.

"Oh, okay. I hope you feel better about Glenn and me getting married. Since it's this Saturday, there's not much time for you to make arrangements. So I was thinking … the corporation might let you take their jet. It can fly to Blantrye—can't it? That's the closest airport. Because I really want you here to give me away, Dad."

"I will try, Kitten. Whether we get there or not"—a short silence—"just know that we love you and want the best for you." Dad's tone had changed to a blend of love and sadness. "Sorry, I've got to go now. Bye, Kitten."

The cell went dead.

"Dad … Dad …" Beth listened then slowly dropped her arm. Her gaze clouded as she sat on the edge of the bed. *He must be sad because I'm marrying Glenn. He almost sounded final, like he'd written me off.* "Hope not. But he did say he'd try."

She called her parents again, but no one picked up. Beth shrugged and gave up. If they came to the wedding, wonderful. But if not? Nothing would prevent her from marrying Glenn.

Glenn stopped by with the children before they left for the airport. The couple kissed, smiled, and kissed again. Beth leaned against the door jam, beaming as she watched her fiancé saunter down the hall, hand in hand with his little flock.

Preparing for her wedding, Beth zigzagged her way through many dark faces on the crowded street. "I know I saw a flower shop here, somewhere. Where'd it go?" she muttered to herself. Her eyes scanned the bustling street.

A familiar white face stopped her cold. A bearded man with a stocky build and sandy hair was weaving his way through the swarm of people. Beth gasped. *Nick!*

Her heart jumped into her throat. She stretched to see over the tall people passing in front of her. A kid scooted by bumping her arm, momentarily distracting her. When she turned back, there was no sign of the white man.

Can't be him. Nick certainly wouldn't come all the way to Africa to stalk me. How would he get through customs? He's a wanted man. I really can't be sure anyway because of that guy's beard.

Beth laughed. "It's ridiculous." It had to be someone who just looked like him, but her nerves wouldn't settled down.

Just before twilight, Beth arrived at the hotel and stepped up to the front desk.

"Good evening, ma'am," a middle-aged Malawian clerk said with a heavy accent.

Beth greeted him with a smile. "Any messages for Elizabeth Farell?" While waiting for the man to look through his notes, she asked, "By any chance have you heard from or seen my parents, Ed and Carla Farell? I had asked that my adjoining room be reserved for them."

"Yes, they come here. They ask for adjoining room 104, next to yours. A note for you is here too." A bony hand reached out with a piece of folded paper.

"Oh my goodness, they came!" Beth's joy bubbled over. "Thanks." She unfolded the paper and read the scrawl. "See you at the wedding, Bethie."

Beth caught her breath. Prickles of fear raced up her spine. No signature—she turned it over—still no signature.

Only Nick called her Bethie. *Then was that Nick I saw?*

Just his name set Beth on edge. A terrible feeling washed over her—a feeling of barreling down a railroad track, sensing disaster ahead and not being able to jump off the train.

31. Freakishly Quiet

Hotel Chikwawa in Chikwawa, Malawi

What did the man look like who wrote this note?" Beth asked.

"I come to work at five." The clerk didn't look up. He continued shuffling papers. "The note is already here."

Maybe Rosie or Bob wrote it. They don't know about Nick's 'Bethie.' Beth no longer held her breath, but she couldn't shake a growing dread. She took a few steps and called her parents' room. No answer. Maybe they had gone out to eat.

A large hand grabbed Beth's shoulder. Her heart leaped. She gasped and whirled around.

"So sorry, ma'am." The hotel clerk's black eyes expressed regret. "I do not wish to scare you. The clerk on duty this mornin' ringed. Straightaway I ask him. He say the man who wrote note is white. He come here with one white man and one white woman."

The clerk didn't know anything more. When Beth asked if he would accompany her to her room, he said he couldn't leave his desk.

Beth swiped her cell for Bob's number. No answer. Was he still angry at her? *He probably wouldn't come anyway. He'd think I was just being paranoid.* She drew a deep breath. *I wish Glenn was here.*

All the way down the dimly lit hall to her room, Beth's

senses stayed on high alert for sudden movements. Her doorknob refused to turn in her shaky hand. *Good. It's locked. No one can get in.* Rotating her key in the lock, the click echoed through the hallway. She pushed the heavy door open enough to peek inside the shadowed room. No one was there.

Beth sighed with relief, stepped inside, and dead bolted the door.

A new scent hung in her room, yet it was distantly familiar. Without moving her head, she threw sidelong glances and listened intently. An open bottle of beer sat on the edge of the entertainment center. Condensation trickled down the side. She gasped then gulped her breath to stay quiet.

Eyes wide, Beth twisted her head around to the door of her parents' adjoining room. It was ajar. She froze. *Stop overreacting. Everything's fine. Maybe the clerk let Mom and Dad into my room. But Dad prefers wine. Maybe he had a taste for beer today.*

Beth stared at the door, gathering courage, and then tiptoed into their darkened room. The floor creaked, but the room seemed freakishly quiet. "Mom? Dad?"

Silence answered.

Beth had a weird feeling someone was in there, but with the light-blocking drapes closed it was too dark to see. The bottom of the drapes swayed slightly with a breeze. *The patio door must be open.*

All at once from behind her, an eerie whistling jolted Beth into a tailspin. She lurched forward, screaming. *No, not Nick!* she begged in her mind.

A powerful arm whipped around Beth's chest and jerked her backward against a broad, rock-hard chest. It was a man. One hand held a gun. He slapped his other hand over her mouth, but the fingers were oddly stiff.

The memory of Emily smashing Nick's hand at the cabin

flashed across Beth's mind and yes the musk after- shave.

"You know better than to scream," Nick said in the drawn-out, sinister voice Beth thought she'd never hear again. His breath whisked her hair.

She wrestled to get away. Her nails dug in as she wrenched on his hand.

"Yeah, Baby, squirm. I like it."

She stopped, but questions and dreadful imaginations swirled in Beth's mind.

Nick freed her mouth, dropped his arm from around her chest, and jabbed the gun into her ribs. Then he reached behind and with a forceful shove slid the patio's heavy drapes open. The last rays of the sunset poured in.

"Fancy meeting you here, Bethie Baby," he murmured. "I was having a little visit with your parents when you called about the jet. Y'all gave me a way to Malawi. Hot"—he used his favorite cuss word—"I *knew* you wanted to see me."

Beth's stomach curdled as the buried memory of Nick's Southern drawl rose from the depths. She scanned the room. Her parents sat with tape over their mouths and cords binding their upper bodies to their chairs. Dread and worry formed creases in their brows.

Nick snickered. "Your parents are a little tied up at the moment."

Trembling, Beth struggled to find enough breath to speak. "Are you all right, Mom and Dad?"

Dad nodded. Mom's voice was muffled through the tape.

Nick spun Beth around and held her at arm's length. "Let me get a look at you. Yo, Baby. I do declare, you're a sight for sore eyes." His beard couldn't hide Nick's self-satisfied smile.

That was him on the street. "How did you know where I live, and how did you get in Malaw—"

Nick's booming laugh spiked Beth's anger. "Oh, that's easy, Bethie. I have a little spy—my cousin, Ashley."

Fuzzy, racing thoughts of Ashley's involvement in their lives rammed together in Beth's mind.

Nick was saying, "Kathrin couldn't wait to tell her that you and Glenn were getting married. I saved you just in time."

"Saved me?" Beth wrinkled her nose and backed away. "From what?"

Nick stepped toward her. "From marrying that no-good goat roper. Baby, that dog won't hunt." His head moved from center to side and back again as he spoke.

"I *want* to marry Glenn." Sweat beaded on Beth's skin.

Nick wagged his head. "Aw, now, you don't have to play hard to get anymore."

"Wha—"

"I saw how you looked at me at the cabin. I know what y'all want. You're just tense, Bethie, but I can help."

What? He must be insane. "I've *never* been interested in you." Beth's racing heartbeat thumped in her ears. "You need to go, Nick." She flung her arm out and pointed at the door. "Just go. Leave." Beth tried to sound stern, but her voice trembled.

"Don't be ugly. I'm not done. Girl, you still think y'all have options." Nick lunged forward, long arms snatching out at her.

In terror, Beth gasped. She skittered backward onto the patio until the back of her thigh touched the far railing.

But now she was trapped.

Nick's mouth stretched wide. His teeth gleamed. "I didn't know my baby liked to play rough." His hands seized her upper arms.

The more Beth struggled, the tighter his hand gripped her.

"Ow, you're hurting me."

"Then stop pitching a fit."

Beth tried to calm down. "Why are you here?"

"Funny you should ask." Nick's fingers relaxed their grip. "Well, I've a mind to show ya." He smirked and yanked her close. Sloppy-wet lips pressed hard against hers.

Teeth clenched, Beth rammed both hands against Nick's chest.

A hand shot out and tightened around her throat. Nick's strong fingers painfully choked off her air.

Beth gagged and wrenched at the vice-grip hand. *Nick's going to kill me!* Her insides felt sluggish, heavy.

Nick's crippled hand slid down Beth's chest and under her blouse.

Her outrage exploded into flames. She kicked with all her might. But it wouldn't do any good in the end. Even now, her oxygen-deprived brain was struggling to retain her fading consciousness.

A shuffling sound came from behind Nick. Was Beth imagining it in her semi-conscious state or was someone approaching? She forced her eyes open and saw her father.

With the chair still anchored to his backside, Dad had risen as high as the chair allowed. Bent over like a bull, he waddled headlong toward Nick.

Hurry, Dad, hurry! Beth's mind screamed.

Nick noticed this new threat as quickly as Beth did. He released Beth, snagged his pistol from his back waistband, and spun around.

Beth jammed her foot behind Nick's knees as he turned. He teetered. Her hand hooked his shoulder, and with all her strength, she heaved Nick backward.

At the same instant, Dad head butted Nick in the stomach.

Nick flung out his arms while attempting to step back. But there was no place to go. The porch rail stopped him. It knocked him off balance into further backward motion. The gun hurtled through the air.

Blindly, Nick scrambled for something to save him. He caught Beth's sleeve. His momentum dragged her upper body over the rail.

Beth gasped as she plunged head first. Two bodies tumbled over the barrier, both screaming. Beth's jaw clenched in terror. Her heart beat out of control.

In frenzied desperation, four hands grappled for the railing. Beth's palms slammed the wood. Her fingers clawed and latched onto it.

Nick's crippled hand floundered. "Ahhh!" He flailed wildly, dropping. He snagged Beth's dress. His weight dug the material into her shoulders.

Beth cried out in fear and pain. The dress ripped.

In a flash, Nick grabbed hold of Beth's ankle.

The thought of plunging into the deep ravine below played like a horror video in Beth's mind.

Her muscles strained. It felt like her joints were being pulled out of their sockets. *I can't hold him.* "Let go! Let go," she screeched, kicking at his hand with her free foot. His lame left hand wasn't able to stop her.

Nick's grip slipped. "If I can't have you, no one will."

This is how I die? Being murdered. The mental picture of Glenn grieving over her death broke her heart. *I am so sorry, my love.*

"We're going to die together, Bethie."

32. Crazy Man

Beth panted, straining. "No, we are *not*."

Her tormented muscles knotted and cramped. She was weakening fast. Her free foot kicked wildly at Nick's wrist. She felt his hand slip again. Encouraged, her assault gained force and speed.

Nick's stranglehold slid off her ankle. He gasped and whipped around, clutching at the air. "Bethie! Bethie." His voice trailed off as his body plummeted. "Bethiiiieee." It wasn't angry, only sad, begging for help.

Nick's body thumped against the hill and into the rocks. Then he lay still at the bottom of the ravine.

Beth's muscles felt like rubber, fast growing too weak to hold her own weight. Terrified that she was next to plummet to her death, her feet skidded and kicked into the dirt bank, trying to find a toehold. Sweat poured down as she whimpered and fought for her life.

Dad peered over the rail at his daughter. Gray eyes filled with anxiety. He moaned, helpless to lend her aid.

To one side, Beth's foot hit on a small rock protrusion. It enabled her to push her body up—just enough. Her elbow hooked over the rail. Then the second elbow. With that, it seemed almost easy to flop over the partition and roll onto the floor at Dad's feet.

"I made it. I made it." Tears flowed down her cheeks. "Thank You, thank You, Lord."

She peered up at her dad in the waning light and started laughing. A puzzled expression emerged on his face. She caught her breath. "You looked so comical walking with that chair on your rear. But you saved us all. Thank you, Dad."

His eyes wide and filled with visible frustration, he moaned something, but the duct tape kept his thoughts a secret.

Beth pushed to her feet and picked up Nick's gun. She looked over the balcony partition and searched for the one who had tormented her. Because of the encroaching darkness, she could no longer see into the ravine.

"How did I end up so close to that crazy man?" Her body shuddered. Now that the crisis was over, more tears poured out. Beth took a moment to pull herself together, then with a ragged breath said, "I'll feel better when they find his body. Then I'll know for sure that I don't have to fear that creep ever again."

Beth flipped on the lights. Dad and Mom grimaced and yelped when Beth stripped the duct tape off their mouth.

"We could have been killed!" Mom shouted with jerky head movements and red-faced. "I've never been so terrified. Will this *ever* be over?"

"It *is* over, Mom. Nick could not have survived that fall." Beth pulled the ropes off Mom as she thought, *Mom doesn't get to me like she used to. Good. I must have succeeded at letting Mom off the hook, thanks to Jennifer.*

"It's far from over," Mom was saying. "We'll be ridiculed and made a laughingstock because you're going to marry that kidnapper of yours, Elizabeth."

"Aw, give it a rest, Carla." Dad shot her a stern look.

"You'll be fine, Mom. You're strong." Beth rested her hand on her mother's shoulder.

Dad didn't wait for Beth to finish untying him. "I was so

scared I was going to"—his voice cracked—"to lose you. I wouldn't survive that, Kitten. But I see you can take care of yourself pretty good, and now you have Glenn."

His gray eyes watered. "I'll try not to be so controlling. While we were held hostage, I decided being in control is only an illusion, anyway."

Beth's eyes filled with tears as she hugged her dad.

Someone had heard the screams and called the local authorities. The Farell family answered questions until midnight.

The next morning, the police force informed Beth that Nick's body had been found at the bottom of the ravine. It surprised Beth that she could feel the tension leave her body. The police asked a few more questions, then left.

A couple of hours later, Beth and her parents hired a driver to take them to The Shepherd's Little Flock. Beth didn't tell her mom how far away or how primitive it was there. She wouldn't have come.

When they pulled up, everyone was working on the new hut. As soon as the orphans saw Beth, they squealed, "E-liz-a-bet!" They trotted up to her with big smiles and generous hugs.

While still at a distance, the five-foot-eight, slender Brit, Pastor Andrew, greeted the visitors.

Glenn's face lit up as Beth raced into his arms. He scooped her off her feet and whirled around. She squealed with delight, and then their lips touched. He set her on her feet again and whispered, "I missed you."

"And I don't like being away from you." Beth grabbed his hand. "C'mon, it's time you meet my parents." She led him to where Ed and Carla stood. Glenn and Andrew were covered head to toe in bits of leaves and sweat.

"Mom, Dad, I'd like you to meet Glenn."

I am so proud of him, Beth thought.

Carla flicked her hand in front of her nose. Ed held a wide stance with hands on his hips and eyes narrowed.

"Nice to meet you." Bright-eyed, Glenn reached out his hand. "You have a remarkable daughter."

Dad shook Glenn's hand. "We think so. She deserves the best."

"She does." A warm smile formed on Glenn's face.

Glenn shook Mom's limp hand, but she did manage a forced smile.

Then Glenn introduced Andrew and the children. Kenta and Jekél greeted the Farells like they did Beth the first time.

How can Mom and Dad not love them?

Since the orphanage had no chairs, Carla sat on a barrel, bedecked with jewels, acting like offended royalty.

After bottled water and small talk, the three visitors told the traumatic tale of their battle with Nick and his demise.

Glenn's countenance grew troubled. "Thank God you're okay." He held Beth for a long moment. "I'm sorry I wasn't there for you." His voice lost its power. "I should have been there."

Beth went on with the story. By the time she finished, she was a little shaken.

With a kind expression, Glenn stroked her hair. "It must have been terrifying"—his tone soothing—"I'm proud of you, my little wildcat." He leaned in close to her ear. "If something had happened to you, I'd never get over it."

"You're stuck with me." Beth gave him a lopsided grin.

The children gave Ed and Carla a tour while the other three discussed wedding plans. Beth told them of her prayer while she soaked in the tub. "Hope that was okay to say a prayer where bathing. Oh, and I noticed that empty feeling is gone."

With watery eyes, Glenn embraced her.

The others joined them when the tour was over. Then Beth presented Andrew with a World Relief voucher for a new vehicle. She was rewarded with lots of hugs.

The Farell family had to leave after only a few hours. Dad opened the car door, hesitated, and instead of climbing in, turned to Glenn. He placed his hand on his future son's-in-law shoulder. "Thank you for taking care of our Beth."

Glenn smiled and nodded.

Beth raised her head toward heaven. *Thank you, Lord for changing Dad's heart. It's amazing how You work things out. I should trust You more.*

When the visitors drove off, the precious Malawians ran behind their vehicle, waving and cheerfully yelling something in their language.

The stress of the last several days sent everyone crashing into bed early that night. Rosie, Bob, and Beth had an early flight to Mozambique, anyway.

They arrived back in Blantyre near Chikwawa the next day, Friday. When the plane's wheels hit the tarmac, Beth's excitement in becoming Mrs. McKlain spread like wildfire within her. That gave her plenty of energy to finish the wedding preparations. She was surprised how fast that last day whizzed by.

While in her room late that afternoon, a *Seattle Times* reporter, Joel, called and explained why he was in Chikwawa. "Nick Thoren kidnapped you a few years ago. Then he just kidnapped your parents and hijacked the corporation's jet to Malawi. Would you give me an interview?"

Beth hesitated. "Goodness, I'm tired, and I am going to be too busy tomorrow for interviews."

"Busy? Yeah, you're going to be busy getting married. Just

give me fifteen minutes. After coming all this way, I won't go home without a story, even if it's half truths from someone else. Chikondi's Bar and Grill has American food. Will you meet me there?"

Stalling, she asked, "But why would you come all this way to interview me?"

"Your parents refused to talk to me, and the story is unusual enough."

He has no idea how unusual, Beth mused. She didn't care what the world thought of her anymore. How freeing that felt. She only cared what Glenn and Kathrin thought. *Our story is beautiful. For me to talk to a reporter—knowing the world will find out—my goodness, have I changed.*

"Well?" Joel sounded impatient.

Beth agreed to meet him.

Young Joel asked the typical questions. At first, he didn't recognize her finance's name. When he finally put it together, his countenance brightened. The questions came faster as he scribbled to keep up with her story.

"Thank you. This *is* an unusual story." Joel tucked his tablet in his pocket. The interview was over. An hour had passed. "May I take pictures of your wedding?"

"No, but my friend will send you some. Bye." Beth walked out of the building, feeling secure and loved by Jesus. She escaped to her room, dropped keys on a desk, and sighed.

Chamomile tea relaxed her to sleep.

Early the next morning the wedding party attended the rehearsal. Beth cherished every moment with Glenn and the orphans. Afterward, they went to brunch with family and friends—Kathrin, Paster Lewis, and Glenn's sister, Lauren.

Rosie glanced at Lauren and whispered to Beth, "Apparently, the gene for beautiful blue eyes is strong in the McKlain family."

"Yeah. I'm so glad Lauren could come." Beth was too excited to eat much. She wanted only to visit with everyone.

That afternoon just before the wedding, a violin and cello played softly. At the entrance of a rock wall behind the seated guests, Beth sat on a sidesaddle atop a white Arabian horse. Now and then, the impressive animal pawed the ground and tossed his head.

Beth's long, beaded, ivory-colored gown draped over the tail end of the horse. "This dress and this beautiful Arabian make me feel like a princess."

"You *are* a princess." Dad smiled and patted Beth's hand.

The music stopped. A hush fell over the crowd.

Another majestic white Arabian pranced in from a side garden. Mane flowing, the horse proudly arched his neck. The bridegroom sat lifted high on this great horse. The *clomp, clomp, clomp* of his hooves resounded against the curved, stone wall behind him.

Glenn wore a white tuxedo with light-blue accessories and his gray Stetson. *Glenn surpasses any handsome prince in fairytale books,* Beth mused.

In front of Andrew, Glenn dismounted, removed his hat, and stood facing Beth from across the gathering.

The music began again.

The adorable orphans dressed in ivory and light-blue ambled slowly two by two with Amie dropping flower petals along the path. The children moved into their pre-assigned positions as the wedding party. Beth's heart warmed as she watched the children.

It was Beth's turn to ride down the aisle with Dad leading her mount. Once they reached the front, Dad assisted her off the magnificent Arabian, and gave his daughter's hand to Glenn. The dress's train rustled as the wedding couple stepped up the stairs to where Andrew waited.

Now standing face to face, Glenn's incredible good looks and blue eyes took Beth's breath away. *The way he's looking at me—full of love and joy—makes him even more stunning. I can't believe my dream is coming true. It far transcends my imagination.*

The missionary prayed, then led them through the ceremony of wedding vows and rings.

Composed of violin, djembe drum, cello, and guitars, the band picked a few chords. Meanwhile, Andrew moved his microphone stand in front of Glenn.

I bet everyone's wondering if Glenn can carry a tune. Beth's face beamed.

Glenn's rich, smooth tones merged with the band. His broad hand gently touched the side of the Beth's blushing face.

"The first time ever I saw your face,

I thought the sun rose in your eyes."

His voice sailed up, fell, and crested again in a beautiful wave of music. Plainly, what he was feeling deep in his heart came pouring forth into his song.

"The first time ever I held you close,

I felt your heart so close to mine.

I knew our joy would fill the earth,

And last … 'til the end of time, my love."

Glenn sang with such tenderness that it melted Beth's heart. Enraptured tears welled up and traced down her cheeks. He gently wiped them. After the song was over, sniffles were heard across the group.

Andrew spoke, but Beth's mind kept returning to Glenn.

She heard familiar words, even though said with a British accent. "I now pronounce you husband and wife."

People clapped and cheered.

"You may kiss your bride."

Euphoria overtook Beth as her husband drew her to himself, enfolded her into his arms, and covered her mouth with his. They lingered there while people applauded and whistled. Soon it became quiet. Beaming, the couple drew back and gazed into each other's eyes. Then they turned to their guests.

"Ladies and gentlemen, let me introduce Mr. and Mrs. Glenn McKlain."

Beth treasured the beautiful sound of those words.

After another round of applause, the instruments began their lovely music. The orphans walked out with the youngest leading. Glenn replaced his Stetson, led Beth to her faithful steed, and with powerful arms lifted her onto the sidesaddle. Then he mounted the horse behind his bride. The animal braced himself against the tall man's weight.

Reminded of when Glenn did that the first time—when she was kidnapped and blindfolded—Beth marveled at how strange and unpredictable life can be.

She twisted around and in a hushed voice said, "Well, look at that. The ugly, old frog turned into my handsome prince after all." They chuckled.

Then with Glenn surrounding Beth, he gathered the reins and set horse and riders into motion. Her whole being relished her husband's closeness.

Friends and family stood to the side and threw rice. Everyone—even Mom—had a sunny expression.

Glenn rode beyond the crowd, and then clicked the gelding into a full gallop. With the wind blowing through her hair and feeling the warmth of her husband against her, Beth and Glenn rode off into the sunset … together.

Come see if your idea of Beth and Glenn is different than the photos on my website **www.theresawiseauthor.com**. You'll also find character bios, scene photos, and other fun stuff.

Made in the USA
Middletown, DE
08 February 2021